OPUS 200

OPUS
200

ISAAC ASIMOV

HOUGHTON MIFFLIN
COMPANY, BOSTON
1979

Library of Congress Cataloging in Publication Data
Asimov, Isaac, date
   Opus 200.

   Bibliography: p.
   I. Title.
PS3551.S5065   813'.5'4   78–27368
ISBN 0–395–27625–X

Printed in the United States of America

M 10 9 8 7 6 5 4 3 2 1

The author wishes to thank the following for permission to quote selections from
the works listed:
   Apocalypse: *Good Taste.* Copyright © 1976 by Isaac Asimov.
   Atomic Energy Commission: *Worlds Within Worlds.*
   Thomas Y. Crowell: *Earth: Our Crowded Spaceship.* Copyright © 1974 by
Isaac Asimov. A John Day book. Quoted by permission of Thomas Y. Crowell.
   Doubleday & Company, Inc.: *Asimov's Guide to Shakespeare.* Copyright ©
1970 by Isaac Asimov. *Asimov's Annotated Don Juan.* Copyright © 1972 by Isaac
Asimov. *The Gods Themselves.* Copyright © 1972 by Isaac Asimov. *The
Tragedy of the Moon.* Copyright © 1972 by Mercury Press, Inc. *Asimov's Anno-
tated Paradise Lost.* Copyright © 1974 by Isaac Asimov. *Before the Golden Age.*
Copyright © 1974 by Doubleday & Company, Inc. *Tales of the Black Widowers.*
Copyright © 1974 by Isaac Asimov. *By Jupiter and Other Stories.* Copyright ©
1973 by Saturday Evening Post Company. *Of Matters Great and Small.* Copy-
right © 1974 by Mercury Press, Inc. *The Bicentennial Man and Other Stories.*
Copyright © 1976 by Random House, Inc. *More Tales of the Black Widowers.*
Copyright © 1976 by Isaac Asimov. *Murder at the ABA.* Copyright © 1976 by
Isaac Asimov. *The Beginning and the End.* Copyright © 1974 by Triangle Publi-
cations, Inc. *Familiar Poems Annotated.* Copyright © 1977 by Isaac Asimov.
   Follett Publishing Company: *Comets and Meteors.* Text copyright © 1972 by
Isaac Asimov. *Light.* Text copyright © 1970 by Isaac Asimov. Used by permis-
sion of Follett Publishing Co., a division of Follett Corporation.

DEDICATION

To Janet

Who saw me through the second hundred

Contents

INTRODUCTION

IN OCTOBER 1969, Houghton Mifflin published my book *Opus 100*. It wasn't named at random. It was the hundredth book of mine to be published.

That hundredth book took its time coming, of course. It wasn't till I was eighteen, after all, that I became a professional writer. (To be specific, my first sale took place on October 21, 1938.) Then, for eleven years after that, my only sales were to the science fiction magazines, so that I became a well-known and successful writer (within the highly specialized and non-numerous ranks of the science fiction world, anyway) without having a single book to my name.*

Then, on January 19, 1950, just after I had turned thirty, I finally published my first book, *Pebble in the Sky*. It was a science fiction novel.

After that, first slowly (two books in 1950 and two more in 1951) and then more rapidly (eight books in 1960 and twelve books in 1966), I began to pile them up.

What with one thing and another, I finally managed to reach the hundredth book not quite twenty years after I had published the first one. That's an average of five books a year, which isn't bad, at least as far as quantity is concerned.

With regard to quality, it is perhaps harder to judge, but even if we disregard my own personal opinion that my books are great, it remains fair to assume that publishers are reasonably sane and would not have published so many of my books if they didn't think they were good.

Once a hundred books had come boiling out of my typewriter ribbons, I could have been forgiven if I had then retired. I might have considered a hundred books a reasonable life's work and spent the rest of my existence doing other things — having a good time, for instance.

---

* In later years, these early stories were included in various books, so they didn't go to waste forever, you may be sure.

There was a catch, though; two catches, in fact.

In the first place, when my hundredth book came out I was still ten weeks on the sunny side of fifty (which may not be much of a sunny side, but where age is concerned, I'll snatch at a hair's breadth), and I didn't feel old enough to retire.

In the second place, I was *already* having a good time and, if I retired, the only thing I would really want to do in retirement would be to write. So why retire only to do what I was already doing?

So I kept on working; and to such good effect — for one gets better (or at least faster) with practice — that in a surprisingly brief period of time I found I was reaching my two hundredth book.

The second hundred was completed by 1979, so that it had only taken me ten years to turn them out, which is an average of ten books a year.

Naturally, Houghton Mifflin (stifling who-knows-how-many sighs) feels honor-bound to publish *Opus 200* now, and I'm perfectly content to let them do so.

Let me emphasize now that, in publishing first *Opus 100* and then *Opus 200*, neither I nor Houghton Mifflin is in any way celebrating the matter of quantity. My two hundred books are far from being a record.

According to *The Guinness Book of World Records*, an Englishman named Charles Hamilton and an American named Charles Andrews each published about 100,000,000 words in their lifetimes, whereas my published output so far comes to perhaps 15,000,000 words. Even supposing I live out a reasonably long life and continue writing at a reasonably fast clip, I don't think I can possibly surpass 25,000,000 published words at most.

Furthermore, Charles Andrews, according to the *Book of Records,* wrote 100,000 words a week when at his peak, and I think I do well if I manage a measly 15,000 words of finished material in one week.

Then, too, the British novelist John Creasey and the Belgian novelist Georges Simenon each published over 500 books in the course of their careers, and I don't see that it is at all likely that even a long and continually busy life is going to lift me past the 400 mark.

Nevertheless, I do not labor under any sense of failure because of this. Those authors who surpass me in quantity have (as far as I know) an only limited range. Their domain is fiction, and usually but one or two kinds of fiction, so that they attain speed by rolling down well-oiled tracks.

I, on the other hand, write not only fiction but nonfiction. I write different kinds of nonfiction for different kinds of audiences, and that is the purpose of my *Opus* books — to celebrate that variety.

For *Opus 100* I took passages from my first hundred books and carefully divided them into categories. For *Opus 200* I've taken passages from my second hundred books and divided them into the same categories — plus several additional ones.

Nobody who reads my writings, after all, is very likely to have read all my books, or even most of them, and many people who do read and are, presumably, fond of some of my books are not aware of some of the other kinds of writing I do.

In these *Opus* books, then, the average reader will get a chance to sample the variety to a fuller extent than he would otherwise have a chance to do. If he already likes part of what I write, he may find he also likes, or is at least curious about, some other parts of what I write. It might give him additional pleasure to read those other parts *in toto*, and that would then certainly please me.

And if he doesn't already like part of what I write ... then he might not buy this book in the first place, which would be a shame, but there's no law against it.

PART 1

ASTRONOMY

TO ANYONE who got his start writing science fiction in the days before World War II, astronomy was the science. No one envisioned space travel outside science fiction (except for a very few people working on rockets, who were considered by all the "hardheaded" people around them to be but a half-step removed from science fiction writers). That meant that some facets of astronomy used to be the exclusive domain of those who wrote and read science fiction. For instance, where but in science fiction could one describe the surface of the Moon as seen from the surface of the Moon? Astronomy lost some of its exclusivity, where science fiction writers were concerned, by the time my second hundred books began to be written in the late 1960s. Astronauts strove to reach the Moon, and in 1969, the year in which Opus 100 was published, they succeeded. We know the surface of the Moon in great detail now and science fiction has had to come to terms with that.

But we have only reached the Moon; no one has yet actually lived on it. Therefore, the description of a working and viable settlement on the Moon still lies within the province of fiction.

For instance, in 1972 (by which time several spaceships had landed on the Moon and returned safely), my science fiction novel The Gods Themselves (Book 121) was published by Doubleday. It won both the Nebula (the award of the Science Fiction Writers of America) and the Hugo (the award of the fans gathered in a world convention).* The third part of the novel is set on the Moon, which is pictured as an elaborate human settlement. Here is a passage in which Selene, the young woman born and bred on the Moon, teaches Ben, who arrived from Earth but a month before, how to maneuver on the Moon's surface.

---

* I mention this for no reason other than that it gives me pleasure to do so.

from THE GODS THEMSELVES (*1972*)

Selene laughed, and the sound was metallic in Denison's earpiece. Her figure was lost in the spacesuit she wore.

She said, "Now come, Ben, there's no reason to be afraid. You're an old hand by now — you've been here a month."

"Twenty-eight days," mumbled Denison. He felt smothered in his own suit.

"A month," insisted Selene. "It was well past half-Earth when you came; it is well past half-Earth now." She pointed to the brilliant curve of the Earth in the southern sky.

"Well, but wait. I'm not as brave out here as I am underground. What if I fall?"

"What if you do? The gravity is weak by your standards, the slope is gentle, your suit is strong. If you fall, just let yourself slide and roll. It's almost as much fun that way, anyhow."

Denison looked about doubtfully. The Moon lay beautiful in the cold light of the Earth. It was black and white; a mild and delicate white as compared with the sunlit views he had seen when he had taken a trip a week before to inspect the solar batteries that stretched from horizon to horizon along the floor of Mare Imbrium. And the black was somehow softer, too, through lack of the blazing contrast of true day. The stars were supernally bright and the Earth — the Earth was infinitely inviting with its swirls of white on blue, and its peeping glimpse of tan.

"Well," he said, "do you mind if I hang on to you?"

"Of course not. And we won't go all the way up. It will be the beginners' slope for you. Just try to keep in time with me. I'll move slowly."

Her steps were long, slow, and swinging, and he tried to keep in synchronization. The up-sloping ground beneath them was dusty and with each step he kicked up a fine powder that settled quickly in the airlessness. He matched her stride for stride, but with an effort.

"Good," said Selene, her arm locked in his; steadying him. "You're very good for an Earthie — no, I ought to say Immie."

"Thank you."

"That's not much better, I suppose. Immie for Immigrant is as insulting as Earthie for Earthman. Shall I just say you're simply very good for a man your age?"

"*No!* That's much worse." Denison was gasping a little and he could feel his forehead moistening.

Selene said, "Each time you reach the point where you're about to put your foot down, give a little push with your other foot. That will lengthen your stride and make it all the easier. No, no — watch me."

Denison paused thankfully and watched Selene take off with low, effortless leaps. Somehow, despite the grotesquery of the suit, she appeared slim and graceful when she moved. She returned and knelt at his feet.

"Now you take a slow step, Ben, and I'll hit your foot when I want it to shove."

They tried several times, and Denison said, "That's worse than running on Earth. I better rest."

"All right. It's just that your muscles aren't used to the proper coordination. It's yourself you're fighting, you know, not gravity . . . Well, sit down and catch your breath. I won't take you up much farther."

Denison said, "Will I do any damage to the pack if I lie down on my back?"

"No, of course not, but it's not a good idea. Not on the bare ground. It's only at 120 degrees absolute — 150 degrees below zero, if you prefer — and the smaller the area of contact the better. I'd sit down."

"All right." Gingerly, Denison sat down with a grunt. Deliberately, he faced northward, away from the Earth. "Look at those stars!"

Selene sat perpendicular to him. He could see her face dimly through the faceplate now and then when the Earthlight caught it at the proper angle.

She said, "Don't you see the stars on Earth?"

"Not like this. Even when there are no clouds, the air on Earth absorbs some of the light. Temperature differences in the atmosphere make them twinkle, and city lights, even distant city lights, wash them out."

"Sounds disgusting."

"Do you like it out here, Selene? On the surface?"

"I'm not crazy about it really, but I don't mind it too much, now and then. It's part of my job to bring tourists out here, of course."

"And now you have to do it for me."

"Can't I convince you it's not the same thing at all, Ben? We've got a set route for the tourists. It's very tame, very uninteresting. You don't think we'd take them out here to the slide, do you? This is for Lunarites — and Immies. Mostly Immies, actually."

"It can't be very popular. There's no one here but ourselves."

"Oh, well, there are particular days for this sort of thing. You should see this place on race days. You wouldn't like it then, though."

"I'm not sure I like it *now*. Is gliding a sport for Immies in particular?"

"Rather. Lunarites don't like the surface generally."

"How about Dr. Neville?"

"You mean, how he feels about the surface?"

"Yes."

"Frankly, I don't think he's ever been up here. He's a real city boy. Why do you ask?"

"Well, when I asked permission to go along on the routine servicing of the solar batteries, he was perfectly willing to have me go, but he wouldn't go himself. I rather asked him to, I think, so I could have someone answer my questions, if there were any, but his refusal was rather strong."

"I hope there was someone else to answer your questions."

"Oh, yes. He was an Immie, too, come to think of it. Maybe that explains Dr. Neville's attitude toward the electron pump."

"What do you mean?"

"Well—" Denison leaned back and kicked his legs up alternately, watching them rise and fall slowly with a certain lazy pleasure. "Hey, that's not bad. Look, Selene, what I mean is that Neville is so intent on developing a pump station on the Moon when the solar batteries are perfectly adequate for the job. We couldn't use solar batteries on Earth, where the Sun is never as unfailing, as prolonged, as bright, as radiant in all wave lengths. There's not a single planetary body in the solar system, no body of any size, that is more suitable for the use of the batteries than the Moon is. Even Mercury is too hot. But the use does tie you to the surface, and if you don't like the surface —"

Selene rose to her feet suddenly and said, "All right, Ben, you've rested enough. Up! Up!"

He struggled to his feet and said, "A pump station, however, would mean that no Lunarite would ever have to come out on the surface if he didn't want to."

"Uphill we go, Ben. We'll go to that ridge up ahead. See it, where the Earthlight cuts off in a horizontal line?"

They made their way up the final stretch silently. Denison was aware of the smoother area at their side — a wide swath of slope from which most of the dust had been brushed.

"That's too smooth for a beginner to work up," Selene said, answering his thoughts. "Don't get too ambitious or you'll want me to teach you the kangaroo-hop next."

She made a kangaroo-hop as she spoke, turned about-face almost before landing, and said, "Right here. Sit down and I'll adjust —"

Denison did, facing downhill. He looked down the slope uncertainly. "Can you really glide on it?"

"Of course. The gravity is weaker on the Moon than on Earth, so you press against the ground much less strongly, and that means there is much less friction. Everything is more slippery on the Moon than on the Earth. That's why the floors in our corridors and apartments seemed unfinished to you. Would you like to hear me give my little lecture on the subject? The one I give the tourists?"

"No, Selene."

"Besides, we're going to use gliders, of course." She had a small cartridge in her hand. Clamps and a pair of thin tubes were attached to it.

"What is that?" asked Ben.

"Just a small liquid-gas reservoir. It will emit a jet of vapor just under your boots. The thin gas layer between boots and ground will reduce friction virtually to zero. You'll move as though you were in clear space."

Denison said uneasily, "I disapprove. Surely it's wasteful to use gas in this fashion on the Moon."

"Oh, now. What gas do you think we use in these gliders? Carbon dioxide? Oxygen? This is waste gas to begin with. It's argon. It comes out of the Moon's soil in ton lots, formed by billions of years of the breakdown of potassium-40 . . . That's part of my lecture, too, Ben . . . The argon has only a few specialized uses on the Moon. We could use it for gliding for a million years without exhausting the supply . . . All right. Your gliders are on. Now wait till I put mine on."

"How do they work?"

"It's quite automatic. You just start sliding and that will trip the contact and start the vapor. You've only got a few minutes' supply, but that's all you'll need."

She stood up and helped him to his feet. "Face downhill . . . Come on, Ben, this is a gentle slope. Look at it. It looks perfectly level."

"No, it doesn't," said Denison sulkily. "It looks like a cliff to me."

"Nonsense. Now listen to me and remember what I told you. Keep your feet about six inches apart and one just a few inches ahead of the other. It doesn't matter which one is ahead. Keep your knees bent. Don't lean into the wind because there isn't any. Don't try to look up or back, but you can look from side to side if you have to. Most of all, when you finally hit level, don't try to stop too soon; you'll be going faster than you think. Just let the glider expire and then friction will bring you to a slow halt."

"I'll never remember all that."

"Yes, you will. And I'll be right at your side to help. And if you do fall and I don't catch you, don't try to do anything. Just relax and let yourself tumble or slide. There are no boulders anywhere that you can collide with."

Denison swallowed and looked ahead. The southward slide was gleaming in Earthlight. Minute unevennesses caught more than their share of light, leaving tiny uphill patches in darkness so that there was a vague mottling of the surface. The bulging half-circle of Earth rode the black sky almost directly ahead.

"Ready?" said Selene. Her gauntleted hand was between his shoulders.

"Ready," said Denison faintly.

"Then off you go," she said. She pushed and Denison felt himself begin to move. He moved quite slowly at first. He turned toward her, wobbling, and she said, "Don't worry. I'm right at your side."

He could feel the ground beneath his feet — and then he couldn't. The glider had been activated.

For a moment he felt as though he were standing still. There was no push of air against his body, no feel of anything sliding past his feet. But when he turned toward Selene again, he noticed that the lights and shadows to one side were moving backward at a slowly increasing speed.

"Keep your eyes on the Earth," Selene's voice said in his ear, "till you build up speed. The faster you go, the more stable you'll be. Keep your knees bent . . . You're doing very well, Ben."

"For an Immie," gasped Denison.

"How does it feel?"

"Like flying," he said. The pattern of light and dark on either side was moving backward in a blur. He looked briefly to one side, then the other, trying to convert the sensation of a backward flight of the surroundings into one of a forward flight of his own. Then, as soon as he succeeded, he found he had to look forward hastily at the Earth to regain his sense of balance. "I suppose that's not a good comparison to use to you. You have no experience of flying on the Moon."

"Now I know, though. Flying must be like gliding — I know what *that* is."

She was keeping up with him easily.

Denison was going fast enough now so that he got the sensation of motion even when he looked ahead. The Moonscape ahead was opening before him and flowing past on either side. He said, "How fast do you get to go in a glide?"

"A good Moon-race," said Selene, "has been clocked at speeds in excess of a hundred miles an hour — on steeper slopes than this one, of course. You'll probably reach a top of thirty-five."

"It feels a lot faster than that somehow."

"Well, it isn't. We're leveling off now, Ben, and you haven't fallen. Now just hang on; the glider will die off and you'll feel friction. Don't do anything to help it. Just keep going."

Selene had barely completed her remarks when Denison felt the beginning of pressure under his boots. There was at once an overwhelming sensation of speed and he clenched his fists hard to keep from throwing his arms up in an almost reflex gesture against the collision that wasn't going to happen. He knew that if he threw up his arms, he would go over backward.

He narrowed his eyes, held his breath till he thought his lungs would explode, and then Selene said, "Perfect, Ben, perfect. I've never known an Immie to go through his first slide without a fall, so if you do fall, there'll be nothing wrong. No disgrace."

"I don't intend to fall," whispered Denison. He caught a large, ragged breath, and opened his eyes wide. The Earth was as serene as ever, as uncaring. He was moving more slowly now — more slowly — more slowly —

"Am I standing still now, Selene?" he asked. "I'm not sure."

"You're standing still. Now don't move. You've got to rest before we make the trip back to town ... Damn it, I left it somewhere around here when we came up."

Denison watched her with disbelief. She had climbed up with him, had glided down with him. Yet he was half-dead with weariness and tension, and she was in the air with long kangaroo-leaps. She seemed a hundred yards away when she said, "Here it is!" and her voice was as loud in his ears as when she was next to him.

She was back in a moment with a folded, paunchy sheet of plastic under her arm.

"Remember," she said cheerily, "when you asked on our way up what it was, and I said we'd be using it before we came down?" She unfolded it and spread it on the dusty surface of the Moon.

"A lunar lounge is its full name," she said, "but we just call it a lounge. We take the adjective for granted here on this world." She inserted a cartridge and tripped a lever.

It began to fill. Somehow Denison had expected a hissing noise, but of course there was no air to carry sound.

"Before you question our conservation policies again," said Selene, "this is argon also."

It blossomed into a mattress on six stubby legs. "It will hold you," she said. "It makes very little actual contact with the ground and the vacuum all around will conserve its heat."

"Don't tell me it's hot," said Denison, amazed.

"The argon is heated as it pours in, but only relatively. It ends up at 270 degrees absolute, almost warm enough to melt ice, and quite warm enough to keep your insulated suit from losing heat faster than you can manufacture it. Go ahead. Lie down."

Denison did so, with a sensation of enormous luxury.

"Great!" he said with a long sigh.

"Mamma Selene thinks of everything," she said.

She came from behind him now, gliding around him, her feet placed heel to heel as though she were on skates, and then let them fly out from under her, as she came down gracefully on hip and elbow on the ground just beside him.

Denison whistled. "How did you do that?"

"Lots of practice! And don't you try it. You'll break your elbow."

Some of the real findings on the Moon tended to destroy a few of the more interesting science fictional notions. For instance, to the best of our knowledge, there have always been not more than small traces of water on the Moon, and even these are vanishing. Our study of the Moon rocks has shown that. Yet, in the science fiction written before we reached the Moon, it was often assumed that there was some water on the Moon that might be frozen under the soil or chemically combined with the molecules of the crustal rock.

Even as late as 1972 I held on to the hope that this might be so despite the negative findings of the first astronauts on the Moon. Thus, here is another scene from The Gods Themselves. *This time Selene and Ben are inside the settlement.*

Denison tried to beat down his self-consciousness. Time and again, he made a groping motion as though to hitch upward the pants he wasn't wearing. He wore only sandals and the barest of briefs, which were uncomfortably tight. And, of course, he carried the blanket.

Selene, who was similarly accoutered, laughed. "Now, Ben, there's nothing wrong with your bare body, barring a certain flabbiness. It's perfectly in fashion here. In fact, take off your briefs if they're binding you."

"No!" muttered Denison. He shifted the blanket so that it draped over his abdomen and she snatched it from him.

She said, "Now give me that thing. What kind of a Lunarite will you make if you bring your Earth puritanism here? You *know* that prudery is only the other side of prurience. The words are even on the same page in the dictionary."

"I have to get used to it, Selene."

"You might start by looking at me once in a while without having your glance slide off me as though I were coated with oil. You look at other women quite efficiently, I notice."

"If I look at you —"

"Then you'll seem too interested and you'll be embarrassed. But if you look hard, you'll get used to it, and you'll stop noticing. Look, I'll stand still and you stare. I'll take off my briefs."

Denison groaned, "Selene, there are people all around and you're making intolerable fun of me. Please keep walking and let me get used to the situation."

"All right, but I hope you notice the people who pass us don't look at us."

"They don't look at *you*. They look at me all right. They've probably never seen so old-looking and ill-shaped a person."

"They probably haven't," agreed Selene cheerfully, "but they'll just have to get used to it."

Denison walked on in misery, conscious of every gray hair on his chest and of every quiver of his paunch. It was only when the passageway thinned out and the people passing them were fewer in number that he began to feel a certain relief.

He looked about him curiously now, not as aware of Selene's conical breasts as he had been, nor of her smooth thighs. The corridor seemed endless.

"How far have we come?" he asked.

"Are you tired?" Selene was contrite. "We could have taken a scooter. I forget you're from Earth."

"I should hope you do. Isn't that the ideal for an immigrant? I'm not the least bit tired. Hardly the least bit tired at any rate. What I am is a little cold."

"Purely your imagination, Ben," said Selene firmly. "You just think you ought to feel cold because so much of you is bare. Put it out of your head."

"Easy to say," he sighed. "I'm walking well, I hope."

"Very well. I'll have you kangarooing yet."

"And participating in glider races down the surface slopes. Remember, I'm moderately advanced in years. But really, how far have we come?"

"Two miles, I should judge."

"Good Lord! How many miles of corridors are there altogether?"

"I'm afraid I don't know. The residential corridors make up comparatively little of the total. There are the mining corridors, the geological ones, the industrial, the mycological . . . I'm sure there must be several hundred miles altogether."

"Do you have maps?"

"Of course there are maps. We can't work blind."

"I mean you, personally."

"Well, no, not with me, but I don't need maps for this area; it's quite familiar to me. I used to wander about here as a child. These are old corridors. Most of the new corridors — and we average two or three miles of new corridors a year, I think — are in the north. I couldn't work my way through them, without a map, for untold sums. Maybe not even with a map."

"Where are we heading?"

"I promised you an unusual sight — no, not me, so don't say it — and you'll have it. It's the Moon's most unusual mine and it's completely off the ordinary tourist trails."

"Don't tell me you've got diamonds on the Moon?"

"Better than that."

The corridor walls were unfinished here — gray rock, dimly but adequately lit by patches of electroluminescence. The temperature was comfortable and at a steady mildness, with ventilation so gently effective there was no sensation of wind. It was hard to tell here that a couple of hundred feet above was a surface subjected to alternate frying and freezing as the Sun came and went on its grand biweekly swing from horizon to horizon and then underneath and back.

"Is all this airtight?" asked Denison, suddenly uncomfortably aware that he was not far below the bottom of an ocean of vacuum that extended upward through infinity.

"Oh, yes. Those walls are impervious. They're all boobytrapped, too. If the air pressure drops as much as ten percent in any section of the corridors there is a hooting and howling from sirens such as you've never heard and a flashing of arrows and blazing of signs directing you to safety such as you've never seen."

"How often does this happen?"

"Not often. I don't think anyone has been killed through air-lack in at least five years." Then, with sudden defensiveness, "You have natural catastrophes on Earth. A big quake or a tidal wave can kill thousands."

"No argument, Selene." He threw up his hands. "I surrender."

"All right," she said. "I didn't mean to get excited . . . Do you hear that?"

She stopped in an attitude of listening.

Denison listened, too, and shook his head. Suddenly, he looked around. "It's so quiet. Where is everybody? Are you sure we're not lost?"

"This isn't a natural cavern with unknown passageways. You have those on Earth, haven't you? I've seen photographs."

"Yes, most of them are limestone caves formed by water. That certainly can't be the case on the Moon, can it?"

"So we can't be lost," said Selene, smiling. "If we're alone, put it down to superstition."

"To what?" Denison looked startled and his face creased in an expression of disbelief.

"Don't do that," she said. "You get all lined. That's right. Smooth out. You look much better than you did when you first arrived, you know. That's low gravity and exercise."

"And trying to keep up with nude young ladies who have an uncommon amount of time off and an uncommon lack of better things to do than to go on busmen's holidays."

"Now you're treating me like a tourist guide again, and I'm not nude," Selene retorted.

"At that, even nudity is less frightening than Intuitionism . . . But what's this about superstition?"

"Not really superstition, I suppose, but most of the people of the city tend to stay away from this part of the corridor complex."

"But why?"

"Because of what I'm going to show you." They were walking again. "Hear it now?"

She stopped and Denison listened anxiously. He said, "You mean that small tapping sound? *Tap — tap.* Is that what you mean?"

She loped ahead with the slow-motion movement of the Lunarite in unhurried flight. He followed her, attempting to ape the gait.

"Here — here —"

Denison's eye followed Selene's eagerly pointing finger. "Good Lord," he said. "Where's it coming from?"

There was a drip of what was clearly water; a slow dripping, with each drip striking a small ceramic trough that led into the rock wall.

"From the rocks. We do have water on the moon, you know. Most of it we can bake out of gypsum; enough for our purposes, since we conserve it pretty well."

"I know. I know. I've never yet been able to manage one complete shower. How you people manage to stay clean I don't know."

"I *told* you. First, wet yourself. Then turn off the water and smear just a little detergent on you. You rub it — Oh, Ben, I'm not going through it yet again. And there's nothing on the Moon to get you all that dirty anyway ... But that's not what we're talking about. In one or two places there are actually water deposits, usually in the form of ice near the surface in the shadow of a mountain. If we locate it, it drips out. This one has been dripping since the corridor was first driven through, and that was eight years ago."

"But why the superstition?"

"Well, obviously, water is the great material resource on which the Moon depends. We drink it, wash with it, grow our food with it, make our oxygen with it, keep everything going with it. Free water can't help but get a lot of respect. Once this drip was discovered, plans to extend the tunnels in this direction were abandoned till it stopped. The corridor walls were even left unfinished."

"That sounds like superstition right there."

"Well — a kind of awe, maybe. It wasn't expected to last for more than a few months; such drips never do. But after this one had passed its first anniversary, it began to seem eternal. In fact, that's what it's called: The Eternal. You'll even find it marked that way on the maps. Naturally people have come to attach importance to it, a feeling that if it stops it will mean some sort of bad fortune."

Denison laughed.

Selene said warmly, "No one *really* believes it, but everyone part-believes it. You see, it's not really eternal; it must stop sometime. As a matter of fact, the rate of drip is only about a third of what it was when it was first discovered, so that it is slowly drying. I imagine people feel that if it happened to stop when they were actually here, they would share in the bad fortune. At least, that's the rational way of explaining their reluctance to come here."

"I take it that you don't believe this."

"Whether I believe it or not isn't the point. You see, I'm quite certain that it won't stop sharply enough for anyone to be able to take the blame. It will just drip slower and slower and slower and no one will ever be able to pinpoint the exact time when it stopped. So why worry?"

"I agree with you."

At the start, my writing consisted almost entirely of science fiction. Of my first hundred books, nearly one third is science fiction. That fell off with time, however. Of my second hundred books, only thirteen can be considered science fiction under even the most liberal interpretation.

That did not end my concern with astronomy, however, for I continued to deal with it in my nonfiction and for every age level.

I wrote some picture books for Walker & Company, for instance, at the suggestion of Beth Walker. They were ABC books, actually, in which two words were defined for each letter of the alphabet. The idea was that an eight-year-old could read the definitions (or, at least, have an adult read it to him) and then be fascinated by the pictures.

The first and most successful of these was ABC's of Space (Book 101), which was published in 1969. Here, for instance, are the definitions of the two words under O:

from ABC's of Space (1969)

O is for *Ocean of Storms*

> a dark, smooth area on the Moon where the first unmanned spaceship landed in 1966. It is not really an ocean, because there is probably no water on the Moon. There are no storms either, but we still use the name.

o is for *orbit*

> the path a small world takes around a larger one. The Moon moves in an orbit around the Earth. The Earth moves in an orbit around the Sun. Both orbits are almost like circles. An orbit is also the path a spaceship takes around the Earth or Moon.

I was not particularly fond of the ABC books, of which three others were published by Walker by 1972. These were ABC's of the Ocean *(Book 107),* ABC's of the Earth *(Book 117), and* ABC's of Ecology *(Book 124). The ABC format didn't leave me enough scope.*

I did, however, start another series of books for Walker & Company with which I had a good deal more fun.

The title of each book in the series, which was originally suggested by my editor, Millicent Selsam, was to begin How Did We Find Out. *They were to deal with science history on a junior high school level.*

The first one of these was How Did We Find Out the Earth Is Round? *(Book 133), which Walker published in 1973. Writing the book was sheer pleasure, and I knew I had something I would continue. Indeed, of my second hundred books, no fewer than thirteen are members of the* How Did We Find Out *series.*

One of the things that made the series pleasurable for me was that the books varied widely in subject matter. Three of them dealt with astronomy, four with physics, two with biology, one with mathematics, one with chemistry, one with geology, and one with anthropology.

One of the "astronomicals" was How Did We Find Out About Comets? (*Book 162*), *which was published in 1975. Millie requested that topic during the hullabaloo concerning the then forthcoming comet Kohoutek. Though, alas, the comet fizzled, the book certainly remained valid. Here's how I handled the way in which cometary orbits were finally worked out.*

from HOW DID WE FIND OUT ABOUT COMETS (*1975*)

A German astronomer, Johannes Kepler, who had been one of Tycho's assistants, disagreed with part of Copernicus's theory. After studying the motions of the planets in the sky, Kepler said, in 1609, that the planets moved around the sun in orbits that were not circles. Each planet moved around the sun in an "ellipse."

An ellipse looks like a flattened circle. It can be so slightly flattened that you cannot tell it from a circle. It can be more flattened, so that you can see at a glance that it is not a circle. Or it can be very flattened, so that it looks long and thin, something like a cigar.

The orbit of the earth around the sun is an ellipse that is only very slightly flattened. It is almost circular. The moon's orbit around the earth is more flattened, and Mercury's orbit around the sun is still more flattened. Even Mercury's orbit, which is more flattened than that of any other planet known in Kepler's time, is not *very* flattened. Its orbit still looks like a circle.

The sun is not at the very center of the elliptical orbits of the planets around it. The flatter the ellipse, the closer one end of it is to the sun.

When the earth moves around the sun, it is only 91,500,000 miles from the sun at one end of its orbit, but 94,500,000 miles from the sun at the other end. The farther distance is less than 4 percent greater than the nearer distance.

Mercury's orbit around the sun is more elliptical, so there is a bigger difference. When Mercury is at the end of the ellipse nearer the sun, it is only 28,000,000 miles away. At the other end, it is 44,000,000 miles from the sun. The farther distance is about 50 percent greater than the nearer distance.

Kepler was able to work out elliptical orbits for all the planets, but what about the comets? If they were heavenly bodies, did that mean they had orbits, too?

Kepler carefully studied the reports he had about the changing positions of comets in the sky. Finally, he decided that comets must move in straight lines. He thought they came from far out in space, passed near the sun, then traveled onward far out in space in the other direction.

They could only be seen when they were close to the sun and reflected its light. Before they came close enough to the sun, they could not be seen. After they moved far enough from the sun, they again could not be seen. According to Kepler's view, comets were not part of the solar system. Each comet just passed through the solar system once and was never seen again.

An Italian astronomer, Giovanni Alfonso Borelli, carefully studied the positions of a comet that appeared in the sky in 1664. He found he had to disagree with Kepler.

The only way to make sense out of the path the comet took across the sky, Borelli said, was to suppose that it changed direction as it passed the sun. It came closer and closer to the sun, along a line that was nearly straight. Then it moved around the sun, and left along a line that was again nearly straight but had changed direction.

The way Borelli explained this was to point out that ellipses could be very flattened indeed. They could be so flattened that they would resemble a very long, thin cigar. In fact, if you imagined an ellipse that was more and more flattened, and longer and longer, you could eventually imagine one that was so flattened it just went on and on forever. Such an ellipse would be closed only at one end. In the other direction, it would never be closed, but would just go on and on. A one-ended ellipse that goes on and on forever is called a "parabola."

Borelli decided that a comet's orbit was a parabola, with the sun very near the closed end. The comet came in at one side of the parabola, went whizzing around the sun, and then moved outward along the other side of the parabola.

Borelli's view was like that of Kepler, except that the orbit he conceived was not a straight line. Like Kepler, Borelli thought a comet was originally so far away it could not be seen. As it came closer and closer to the sun, it grew bright enough to be seen, and then as it went farther and farther from the sun, it once more became too dim to be seen. In Borelli's view, as in Kepler's, the comets were not members of the solar system. Each comet just passed through the solar system once and never returned.

Kepler's notion of elliptical orbits worked very well for the planets, but there were lots of questions left. Why did the planets go around the sun in ellipses instead of circles (or some other curve)? Why did planets move faster when they were nearer the sun than when they were farther away?

These questions and many others were answered by the English scientist Isaac Newton. In 1687, he published a book in which he described his theory of universal gravitation. According to this theory, every body in the universe attracted every other body. The strength of the attraction between two particular bodies depended on the "mass" of each body (how much matter it contained) and on how far apart the two bodies were. The strength of the attraction could be calculated by a simple mathematical equation.

Newton showed how to use the equation to work out the exact orbit of the moon around the earth and of the planets around the sun.

The same equation explained why each planet moved quickly at some times and slowly at other times, and why some planets moved faster than others. It explained little changes in the motion of the planets that were produced by the tiny pulls of one planet on another even as all were caught in the gigantic pull of the much larger sun. It explained the tides on the earth and many other things, too.

But comets were the one set of heavenly bodies that remained puzzling. If comets traveled in orbits that were parabolas, Newton's theory could account for that fact. Suppose, though, the orbits were not quite parabolas. Suppose the orbits were just very long ellipses and were closed at the other end.

We can only observe the comet at the end of the orbit near the sun. The shape of that small part of the enormous orbit would be a narrow curve if the ellipse were very long. The shape would be slightly wider, if the ellipse were even longer, and still wider if the ellipse never closed at all and were a parabola.

The differences in the shapes of the small bit of orbit we could see, as predicted by Newton's theory, were so tiny that astronomers in Newton's time could not tell them apart. They couldn't really say whether the orbit of a comet was a very long ellipse or whether it was a parabola.

It made a difference. If a comet's orbit were a parabola, it would visit the solar system once and would never be seen again. If the orbit were a very, very long ellipse, then eventually the comet would come to the other end of the ellipse, turn around, and begin to approach the sun again. The comet would return.

In fact, if astronomers could calculate the exact length of the orbit, they could even predict *when* the comet would return. That would be a big victory for Newton's theory.

Newton had a young friend, Edmund Halley, who had helped Newton publish his book and who was interested in the comet problem.

In 1682, a comet appeared and Halley very carefully studied its positions and the way it moved across the sky. From the part of the orbit he could see, he couldn't tell whether it would ever return.

It seemed to him, though, that if a comet did return it should do so at regular periods — every so many years — and that it should always trace the same curve across the sky. He therefore began to collect all the reports on the positions of earlier comets that he could find. By 1705, he had collected good reports on two dozen comets of the past and began to compare them.

He noticed that the comet of 1682, which he had himself observed, followed the same curve across the sky that the comet of 1607 had. The same curve had also been followed by the comet of 1532 (which Fracastoro and Apian had studied) and the comet of 1456.

These comets had come at seventy-five- or seventy-six-year periods. Could it be that it was a single comet that returned every seventy-five years or so? Could it be that it was a "periodic comet"?

Halley worked out the orbit for a comet that returned every

seventy-five years and followed the same curve in the sky that the comet of 1682 had followed.

The results were quite amazing. Saturn, the planet farthest from the sun (as far as was known in Halley's time) was never farther from the sun than 930,000,000 miles. The comet of 1682, however, moved out as far as 3,200,000,000 miles from the sun before it reached the other end of its elliptical orbit and began moving inward again. The comet moved over three times as far away from the sun as Saturn ever moved.

On the other hand, when the comet passed along the end of the ellipse that was near the sun, it came as close as 54,000,000 miles from the sun. This was only about half of earth's distance from the sun.

After Halley had calculated the orbit, he announced that the comet of 1682 would return some time in 1758 and would follow a particular path across the sky.

Halley did not live long enough to see the comet's return. He was eighty-six years old when he died in 1742, but that was much too soon to see the return.

There were, however, others who were watching for it. A French astronomer, Alexis Claude Clairault, considered the orbit as outlined by Halley. He realized that the gravitational pull of the large planets, Jupiter and Saturn, would delay the comet a little bit. It would not pass around the sun till some time in 1759.

In 1758, astronomers eagerly watched that part of the sky in which Halley had said the comet should appear. They did not have to depend only on their eyes as Tycho and earlier astronomers had done. The telescope had been invented in 1609.

On December 25, 1758, Christmas Day, a German farmer named Johann Georg Palitzch, who was an amateur astronomer, spotted the comet. The comet of 1682 appeared in the sky where Halley had said it would and proceeded to move along the path Halley had predicted for it. It moved around the sun quite close to the time Clairault had predicted.

There was no question that it was the comet of 1682 and that it had returned. That meant that some of the mystery of comets was cleared up. They followed the same rules as the other bodies of the solar system except that their orbits were more elliptical.

Naturally, the comet of 1682 that returned and passed around the sun in 1759 came to be called "Halley's comet."

Halley's comet is the most famous comet there is. It happens to be the one that was in the sky in 1066 when William of Normandy was preparing to invade England. It was also in the sky in 11 B.C., about the time when Jesus may have been born. Some people think it may have been the Star of Bethlehem.

Halley's comet has returned twice since Palitzch saw it. It came back in 1835 and was glowing in the sky when Mark Twain was born. Then it came back in 1910 and Mark Twain died when it was glowing in the sky. It will come back yet again in 1986.

Writing for different age levels has its problems, of course, since the boundaries are not clear. I let myself be guided by instinct, and if I must err, I prefer to err on the side of difficulty. I like to think that the kind of youngster who is interested in my books would rather stretch a little and stand on his mental tiptoes than stoop to something he might consider babyish.

Thus, for Follett Publishing Company, I did a series of eight books on science that were intended for an age level higher than that of my ABC books and lower than that of my How Did We Find Out books.

The first four of the Follett series were published among my first hundred books, but the second four, including three on astronomy, were in my second hundred books. They are Comets and Meteors *(Book 134),* The Sun *(Book 135), and* The Solar System *(Book 160). Here is how I handled the matter of cometary orbits in* Comets and Meteors:

from COMETS AND METEORS (1973)

Comets go around the sun the way planets do, but with a difference. Planets move in paths, called "orbits," that are nearly circles. They stay almost the same distance from the sun all the time. Comets move in orbits that are long and narrow. Both comet orbits and planet orbits are "ellipses."

At one end of the orbit, comets pass near the sun, perhaps only a few million miles away. At the other end, they are much farther away, sometimes farther than any planet. At this point, they are billions of miles away from the sun.

A comet has no light of its own. To be seen, it must be near a large bright object, like the sun. Sunlight makes a comet shine.

Comets get very little sunlight at the far end of their orbits. They are small and dim then. They cannot be seen even with a telescope. As they move closer to the sun, they get more sunlight. They become bright enough to be seen.

People see comets only at the end of their orbits close to the sun. Then they are close to the earth, too.

Centuries ago, people believed that comets came from nowhere. They couldn't tell when another comet might come.

About three hundred years ago, an English astronomer, Edmund Halley, studied records of comets that had been seen. He found that every seventy-six years or so, a comet crossed a certain part of the sky. He decided it must be a single comet that came close to the sun every seventy-six years.

Halley said the comet would come back in 1758 and cross the same part of the sky. By then, Halley was dead. But the comet returned just as he said it would. It is known as Halley's comet for that reason.

This business of aiming high for each age group means that almost no effort is involved if I aim for the teenage market. I always assume that a teenager is as intelligent as an adult and has the vocabulary of one. What he lacks is merely the opportunity to have read as widely as an adult. (Naturally, I am talking of an intelligent, well-read adult.)

Consequently, in writing for teenagers, I take particular care to make no assumptions of previous knowledge and to explain everything that doesn't come within the range of common experience — but I make sure I use a full vocabulary to do so. Teenagers are sensitive (and rightly so) to any hint of condescension.

Included among my second hundred books are three on astronomy for teenagers, which I wrote at the suggestion of Chaucy Bennetts of Lothrop, Lee & Shepard Company. She is a very capable editor who, coincidentally, became my cousin by marriage after the series started. The three books are Jupiter, the Largest Planet (*Book 139*); Alpha Centauri, the Nearest Star (*Book 179*); *and* Mars, the Red Planet (*Book 188*). *Here are two excerpts from* Alpha Centauri:

from ALPHA CENTAURI, THE NEAREST STAR (*1976*)

In the case of the Alpha Centauri system, the average separation of the two stars Alpha Centauri A and Alpha Centauri B is greater than that of Uranus and the sun, and less than that of Neptune and the sun. If the Alpha Centauri system were superimposed on the solar system, however, with Alpha Centauri A in place of our sun, Alpha Centauri B would not take up a circular orbit between those of Uranus and Neptune. Things would be a little more complicated than that.

If the orbit of an object moving around a star were an exact circle, the star would remain at the precise center of the orbit and that would represent a very simple situation. Actually, the orbit is always an ellipse, a kind of flattened circle. An ellipse has a major axis (its longest diameter) and a minor axis (its shortest diameter). The center of the ellipse is at the point where the two axes cross.

There are two focus points, or foci, in the ellipse. They are located on the major axis, one on each side of the center and at an equal distance from it. The more flattened the ellipse, the farther the foci are from the center and the closer they are to the ends.

These foci are located in such a way that if a straight line is drawn from one focus to any point on the ellipse, and another straight line is drawn from that point to the other focus, the sum of the lengths of the two straight lines is always the same and always equal in size to the major axis.

As it happens, when an object moves about a star in an elliptical orbit, the star is always at one of the foci and is, therefore, nearer to one end of the orbit than to the other. If the ellipse is very flattened, the star is far to one end and the orbiting object is very close to the star at that end of the orbit and very far from it at the other end.

The point of closest approach is called the "periastron," from Greek words meaning "near the star." The farthest point is the "apastron," from Greek words meaning "away from the star."

In a binary system both stars, under the pull of gravity, move in orbits around a point between them called the "center of gravity." As they move, both stars always remain on opposite sides of the center of gravity, and the larger star is always closer to it. This means that although both stars have orbits that are ellipses of the same shape, the larger star always moves through the smaller orbit.

When one object in a binary system is very much larger than the other, it makes such a small ellipse about the center of gravity that it is practically stationary. This is true of the sun and Earth, for instance, where the sun scarcely moves at all while tiny Earth moves in a large ellipse.

It is always possible, however, to suppose that the larger of two objects in a binary system is standing still and to calculate the orbit of the smaller about it. This distorts the situation relative to observers in other planetary systems — relative to us, for instance. However, if we could imagine ourselves observing the binary system from the larger of the two stars, what we would observe would be the smaller star moving about a motionless larger one.

When astronomers observe a binary system, they are not at all likely to be viewing it from directly above, so to speak, so as to see the elliptical orbits marked out exactly as they are. They usually view the orbits from a tilted position, so that the ellipses they see are not the ellipses marked out by the orbiting stars. What they see are ellipses that are more flattened, sometimes very much more flattened. In these distorted ellipses, however, the larger star, which is supposed to be stationary, is not at the focus of the smaller star's orbit. If astronomers tilt the orbit, in imagination, until the star moves into the focus, they get the true ellipse.

The degree of flattening of an ellipse is measured as its "eccentricity" (from Greek words meaning "out of center"), since the greater the eccentricity, the farther the foci are from the center.

The eccentricity of a circle, which is not flattened at all, is 0. For an ellipse, the eccentricity is always between 0 and 1. If an ellipse has a low eccentricity, say, less than 0.1, it is so slightly flattened that to the eye it looks very much like a circle. The flatter an ellipse is, the more it approaches a value of 1. An orbit with an eccentricity of 0.9, then, looks quite cigar-shaped.

An example of a high degree of eccentricity in a binary system is Gamma Virginis, where the eccentricity is 0.88. This means that the distance from the center of the ellipse to the focus is 0.88 times the distance from the center of the ellipse to the end. With the larger star at one focus, the end of the orbit of the other star in the direction of that focus (the periastron) is only 0.12 times the distance from the center and only 0.06 times the entire width of the ellipse from end to end. The other end of the ellipse (the apastron) is distant from the larger star by an amount equal to 0.94 times the entire width of the ellipse.

In the case of Gamma Virginis, then, although the average distance separating the two stars of the binary is 6,800,000,000 kilometers (4,200,000,000 miles), at periastron the distance of separation is only 810,000,000 kilometers (500,000,000 miles) while at apastron it is 12,800,000,000 kilometers (7,900,000,000 miles).

In other words, the two stars of Gamma Virginis, as they circle each other, swoop together to a separating distance equal to that of Jupiter and the sun, and then move apart to a distance more than twice that between Pluto and the sun. (The system was at apastron in 1920 and the two stars have been moving closer ever since. They will be at periastron in 2006.)

In general, stars separated by quite a large average distance are likely to have large eccentricities. A binary like Capella with an average separation of only 84,000,000 kilometers (52,000,000 miles) has quite a low eccentricity, one of only 0.0086. This means that the distance between the two stars of the Capella system varies from 83,300,000 kilometers (51,600,000 miles) at periastron to 84,700,000 kilometers (52,400,000 miles) at apastron.

This is so small a change that from the standpoint of one of the stars of the Capella system, the other would scarcely seem to change in brightness during the 104-day period of revolution. In the case of Gamma Virginis, on the other hand, an observer near one of the stars would see the other as 250 times brighter at periastron than at apastron.

The eccentricities of the planetary orbits of the solar system, by the way, are much more like those of the Capella stars than those of the Gamma Virginis stars. The eccentricities of the orbits of Venus and Neptune are just about those of the Capella system, while that of Earth (0.017) is only a little higher. This is a good thing, too, for a highly eccentric orbit would introduce such changes in temperature in the course of the year that a planet with even a suitable average distance from its sun might prove uninhabitable.

Let us take, now, a group of binaries that have average separations of about 3.0 to 3.5 billion kilometers (1.9 to 2.2 billion miles), a group that includes the Alpha Centauri system. In the table below, the eccentricity and the distances at periastron and apastron are given for this group.

Eccentricities of Binary Systems

STAR SYSTEM	ECCEN-TRICITY	PERIASTRON		APASTRON	
		MILLIONS OF KILOMETERS	MILLIONS OF MILES	MILLIONS OF KILOMETERS	MILLIONS OF MILES
70 Ophiuchi	0.50	1750	1100	5250	3300
Zeta Sagittarii	0.2	2700	1700	4300	2700
Alpha Centauri	**0.521**	**1700**	**1000**	**5300**	**3400**
Eta Ophiuchi	0.90	320	200	6080	3800
Zeta Cancri	0.31	2200	1350	4100	2570
Sirius	0.575	1280	800	4720	3000
Xi Scorpii	0.74	780	500	5200	3300

As you see, the apastrons are not extraordinarily different, varying from 4100 to 6080 million kilometers (2570 to 3800 million miles), a difference of only about 50 percent. The periastrons differ, however, from 320 to 2700 million kilometers (200 to 1700 miles), a difference of 800 percent.

The Alpha Centauri system is rather intermediate with respect to eccentricity. The orbits of the two stars Alpha Centauri A and

B are more eccentric than those of the planets of our solar system, but less eccentric than those of some of the comets, asteroids, and satellites of our solar system.

If Alpha Centauri A were in the place of our sun, then Alpha Centauri B at its farthest would be 5,300,000,000 kilometers (3,400,000,000 miles) away, or just about at the average distance of Pluto from our sun. From Earth's position near Alpha Centauri A, Alpha Centauri B would seem a starlike point, but it would be far brighter than any star we see in our own sky. It would shine with a brilliance about 100 times greater than our full moon, though it would still be only 1/4500 as bright as Alpha Centauri A or our sun.

From its farthest point, however, Alpha Centauri B would slowly decrease its distance to Alpha Centauri A (and ourselves) as it moved along its orbit, until after forty years it would be at periastron and only 1,700,000,000 kilometers (1,000,000,000 miles) from Alpha Centauri A. At that point it would be a little farther from Alpha Centauri A than Saturn is from the sun. And when Earth would be on the side of its orbit toward Alpha Centauri B, the companion star would be only 1,550,000,000 kilometers (900,000,000 miles) from us.

At that distance, Alpha Centauri B would be a little over 14 times as bright as at apastron. It would be 1400 times as bright as the full moon, but still only 1/326 as bright as Alpha Centauri A.

Suppose Alpha Centauri B were in place of our sun, and that we calculated the orbit of Alpha Centauri A on the assumption that Alpha Centauri B was motionless. Alpha Centauri A would then seem to move in the same orbit that Alpha Centauri B had in the other case.*

Viewed from an Earth that was circling Alpha Centauri B instead of our own sun, Alpha Centauri A would go through the same period of brightening as it moved from apastron to periastron, and the same period of dimming as it moved back to

---

* Because Alpha Centauri B is the smaller of the two stars, it seems to move in the larger orbit of the two when viewed from *outside* the system. When viewed from inside the system, however, an observer on each star would see the other moving in the same orbit. Thus, on Earth, if we pretend that the Earth is motionless, the sun moves in an orbit about the Earth that is just like the orbit that the Earth (in reality) moves in as it circles the sun.

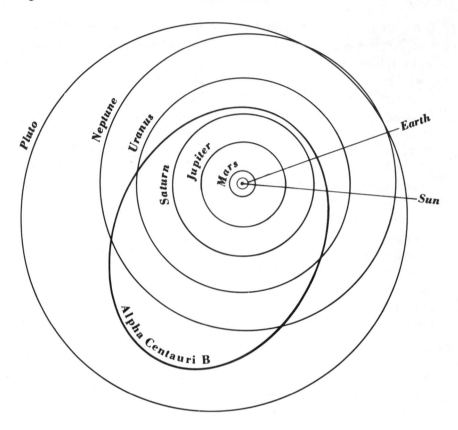

*The Orbit of Alpha Centauri B
superimposed on our solar system*

apastron. However, since Alpha Centauri A is 3¼ times as bright
as Alpha Centauri B, Alpha Centauri A would seem that much
brighter at every point in its orbit. At its brightest, it would be
5000 times brighter than our full moon now, and 1/100 as bright
as our sun appears to us. Since Alpha Centauri B would appear
dimmer than the sun, if we imagined the former in the latter's
place, Alpha Centauri A at its closest approach would appear 1/30
as bright as Alpha Centauri B.

If we were circling Alpha Centauri A instead of the sun, the
presence of Alpha Centauri B would cause us no trouble. Despite

the eccentricity of its orbit, which allows Alpha Centauri B to swoop in and pull out in forty-year alternations, it would remain so far away at all times that its gravitational pull would never be strong enough to affect Earth's orbit seriously. What's more, its addition to the light and heat delivered by Alpha Centauri A would never be more than a third of 1 percent. And think of what a marvelous spectacle it would make in the sky.

If we were circling Alpha Centauri B, the superior brightness of Alpha Centauri A would be more disturbing, but if we imagined Earth pulled in closer to Alpha Centauri B in order to receive as much heat and light from that smaller sun as we receive from our own sun, the interference of Alpha Centauri A would not be too disturbing.

And what about Alpha Centauri C — Proxima Centauri — which is the distant companion of the Alpha Centauri A/B binary? Even though it would be far nearer to us, if Earth were circling either Alpha Centauri A or Alpha Centauri B, than any star is to us in our own solar system, it would not be at all bright. It would be a fairly dim star of magnitude 3.7. What's more, its proper motion, as a result of its 1,300,000-year-long revolution around the center of gravity of the system, would be just about exactly 1 second of arc per year.

Neither its brightness nor its proper motion would attract much attention, and stargazers might look at the sky forever and not suspect this dim star of belonging to their own system. The only giveaway would come when astronomers decided to make a routine check of the parallaxes of the various visible stars in the sky. After a month or so, they would begin to get a hint of an extraordinarily large parallax and in the end they would measure one of 20 seconds of arc, which would be so much higher than that of any other star that they would at once suspect it of being a member of their own system.

Can there be a dim star somewhere out there that belongs to our own solar system? Can it be that we remain unaware of it because astronomers haven't happened to study it closely enough to detect an unusually high parallax? It isn't very likely — but it is conceivable.

◆ ◆ ◆

In general, the hotter a star is, the brighter it is. It's no surprise, therefore, that so many of the bright stars in the sky are hotter than the sun is, or that so many of the dim stars we see are cooler than the sun is.

What *is* surprising is that some stars are cool and yet are very bright. The two prime examples of this are Antares and Betelgeuse. Both are in spectral class M and are therefore possessed of a surface temperature of only 3000° C or so and, what's more, neither one is particularly close to us — and yet each is among the brightest stars in the sky.

In 1905 a Danish astronomer, Ejnar Hertzsprung, reasoned that a cool star must have a dim surface, but if it had a very large surface, the dimness of each bit would add up to a great *total* brightness. In other words, a bright star that was cool and red had to be a very large star indeed in order to be bright.

Hertzsprung published this idea in a journal of photography, and astronomers didn't notice it. Then, in 1914, the American astronomer Henry Norris Russell had the same idea independently, and this time the idea stuck. Both astronomers are usually given credit.

The Hertzsprung-Russell reasoning led to the concept of "red giants" among the stars. When attempts were made to calculate how large these red giants would have to be in order to be as bright as they were despite their low surface temperature, the results seemed almost unbelievable. In 1920, however, the German-American physicist Albert Abraham Michelson was able to check the matter directly.

To do this, he made use of an instrument he had invented twenty years earlier, an instrument he called an interferometer. It was capable of measuring, with great delicacy, the manner in which two trains of light waves, which were not quite parallel to each other, interfered with each other. When such trains of light waves were not quite parallel, the waves as they merged sometimes reinforced each other and sometimes canceled each other, setting up patterns of alternate light and dark. From the details of such an interference pattern, the exact angle at which the light waves met could be deduced.

Such an instrument can be applied to the stars. A star is so small, as seen from Earth, that it is virtually a dot of light. The light rays coming from the two opposite edges of so tiny a dot seem to come to us almost from the same direction, and are therefore almost parallel — almost, *but not quite.* The light rays come from very slightly different directions as they reach us from opposite sides of a star; they converge just a tiny bit, enough to produce an interference pattern if the interferometer is large enough.

Michelson made use of a twenty-foot interferometer, the largest he had constructed up to that time. He attached it to the new hundred-inch telescope that had just been put into use at Mount Wilson in California, and which was then the largest telescope in the world. He turned this instrument on the star Betelgeuse.

From the nature of the interference pattern, Michelson could determine the apparent diameter of Betelgeuse. It turnd out to be 0.045 seconds of arc. This is a very small width, for it would take 41,500 little dots of reddish light just like Betelgeuse, placed side by side, to stretch across the width of the moon.

Yet, Betelgeuse has the largest apparent diameter of any star. Any star that has a true size greater than Betelgeuse is so far away as to have a smaller apparent size. Then, too, any star that is closer than Betelgeuse is so much smaller in true size that its apparent size never comes up to the Betelgeuse mark.

To be even 0.045 seconds in diameter — tiny though that angle is — at the vast distance of Betelgeuse, the star must have an enormous real diameter. In fact, it turns out that the diameter of Betelgeuse is at least 800 times that of the sun.

The interferometer result showed that the reasoning of Hertzsprung and Russell was correct and there really were red giant stars, with Betelgeuse, large as it is, not the largest in actual size. In the table below, the diameters of some of the giant stars are given.

The large red giants would seem to be impressive objects indeed. Imagine Betelgeuse in place of our sun. We could not see it from Earth, because there would be no Earth. The place where Earth would be, if it existed, would be *within* Betelgeuse. The diameter of Betelgeuse is so large that, if substituted for the sun, it would include the orbits of Mercury, Venus, Earth, Mars, and Jupiter.

Epsilon Aurigae B would do better than that. It would swallow

Giant Stars

DIAMETER

STAR	MILLIONS OF KILOMETERS	MILLIONS OF MILES	SUN = 1
Epsilon Aurigae B	2800	1700	2000
VV Cephei A	1700	1200	1400
Betelgeuse	1100	700	800
Mira (Omicron Ceti)	550	350	400
Antares	550	350	400
Xi Aurigae A	420	260	300
Epsilon Aurigae A	280	170	200
Beta Pegasi	150	95	110
Aldebaran	61	38	44
Arcturus	37	23	27

up the orbit of Saturn as well, and its surface would be nearly at the orbit of Uranus. What's more, that supergiant Epsilon Aurigae B is part of a binary system, with the other star, Epsilon Aurigae A, considerably smaller but still large enough to swallow up the orbit of Mars. What a view those stars must be from not too nearby.

Another way of emphasizing the size of the red giants is to imagine a hollow sphere the size of Beta Pegasi, which is only a moderate-sized giant. It would still be large enough to hold 1,300,000 objects the size of our sun. A hollow sphere the size of Betelgeuse would hold nearly 43,000,000 objects the size of our sun, and one the size of Epsilon Aurigae B would hold 8,000,000,000 suns.

And yet, for all that, the red giants are perhaps not as impressive as they seem from their size alone. They are more massive than the sun, but not very much more massive. Betelgeuse might take up 43,000,000 times as much space as the sun does, but the red giant is only about 20 times as massive as the sun; it contains only 20 times as much matter.

If the mass of Betelgeuse (not so very great) is spread over the enormous volume taken up by Betelgeuse, that mass must be spread very, very thin.

The sun's average density is 1.41 grams per cubic centimeter, but Betelgeuse's average density is 1/10,000,000 of that. If the sun were only as dense, on the average, as Betelgeuse is, it would have a mass of not more than 1/30 that of the Earth, and only 2.7 times that of the moon.

Epsilon Aurigae B would be far less dense. The red giants are thin collections of gas that stretch out over enormous distances and glow red-hot, but on an earthly scale they are almost vacuums. The average density of Epsilon Aurigae B is only 1/1000 that of Earth's atmosphere, and in its outer regions the density is far less even than that. (Like all objects, red giants get denser as one approaches their centers, and in the core they can get very dense indeed. This must be true of all stars, since only in a very dense core can the nuclear conflagration that powers them be ignited.)

A situation the reverse of the red giants' arose in connection with Sirius B. That was known to be a very dim star with a magnitude of 10 and a luminosity only 1/130 that of our sun. It was taken for granted that it had to be both small and cool to deliver only 1/130 as much light as our sun.

In 1915, however, the American astronomer Walter Sydney Adams succeeded in taking the spectrum of Sirius B and found it to be just as hot as Sirius A and, therefore, considerably hotter than our sun.

Yet, if Sirius B were that hot, its surface should blaze with white light, and the only way of explaining its dimness was to suppose that it had very little surface.

Sirius B had to have so little surface as to be a dwarf star, far smaller than anyone then had believed a star could be. Because of its white-hot temperature, it was called a "white dwarf." To account for its dimness, its diameter had to be only 30,000 kilometers (19,000 miles) across, so that it was about as large as a medium-sized planet and took up only about 13 times as much volume as the Earth. Sirius B has only 1/100 the volume of the large planet Jupiter.

In the relatively small volume of Sirius B, however, is packed just as much mass as in the sun — as we can tell from the strength of its gravitational pull on Sirius A. If red giants have very low densities, white dwarfs have very high ones. The average density of Sirius B is about 90,000 times that of the sun, or 6000 times that of platinum.

This would have seemed ridiculous only a couple of decades earlier, but by 1915 it had been discovered that atoms were made up of still smaller "subatomic particles," with almost all the mass concentrated in a very tiny "atomic nucleus" at the center of the atom. In white dwarfs, then, matter didn't exist as ordinary atoms, but as a chaotic mixture of subatomic particles squeezed much more closely together than they are in atoms as we know them.

There are white dwarfs smaller and denser than Sirius B, and in recent years astronomers have discovered new types of stars that are much smaller than white dwarfs and correspondingly more dense. These are "neutron stars" in which the subatomic particles are practically in contact, and in which the mass of a star like our sun would be compacted into a tiny body only a dozen kilometers across.

Then, of course, there is writing for the general reader, or, if you choose, for "adults."

It does not seem to me that there is much difference between writing for adults and writing for teenagers. In my general books, I don't question the use of an unusual word or of an extra convolution in a sentence. I allow the syllables and clauses to lie as they fall. Then, too, if there are literary allusions to make, I make them and assume the general reader — or at least anyone likely to read my books — is literate enough to get them. And I suspect that the intelligent teenager has no trouble following my "adult" books.

Among my second hundred books is one on astronomy for the general reader. It is called The Collapsing Universe: The Story of Black Holes *(Book 182). Beth Walker of Walker & Company persistently urged me to write the book. She was almost a Cato the Elder about it. (See what I mean by literary allusions?) Whenever I visited Walker & Company, and whatever the topic of conversation, she would always end by saying "Think black holes, Isaac."*

I had no real objection. In the first place, I was interested in black holes and wanted to write about them. In the second, it would give me a chance to update an earlier book, The Universe, *which was among my first hundred books and which was also published by Walker. (My favorite method of updating a book is to write a new one centered upon a facet of the subject which flowered only after the earlier book was written.)*

It was just a matter of time, therefore, and finally I got to it. In early 1977, The Collapsing Universe *was finally published, and it proved, at once, to be the most popular astronomy book I had ever done. My delight was second only to that of the Walkers.*

Here I would like to include the final pages of The Collapsing Universe, *in which the wildest speculations are to be found. It is just possible that you can't get their true flavor without having read the rest of the book, but that's all right.* Opus 200 *is intended to give you a potpourri of this book and that, which you may then follow up at your leisure in whatever direction pleases you.*

from THE COLLAPSING UNIVERSE (1977)

In theory, up to 30 percent of the entire energy of a rotating black hole can be milked out of it by carefully sending objects through the stationary limit and collecting them on the way out, and this is another way in which some advanced civilizations might use black holes as an energy source.* Once all the rotational energy is gone, the black hole has only mass; the stationary limit coincides with the Schwarzschild radius. The black hole is then said to be "dead," since no further energy can be obtained from it directly (though some can be obtained from matter as it spirals into it).

Even stranger than the possibility of stripping rotational energy from the black hole is that the Kerr analysis offers a new kind of end for matter entering a black hole. This new kind of end was foreshadowed by Albert Einstein and a co-worker named Rosen some thirty years earlier.

---

* Not all astronomers agree with this concept of stripping the rotational energy of a black hole. In fact almost anything some astronomers suggest about a black hole is denied by other astronomers. We are here at the very edge of knowledge, and everything, one way or the other, is very uncertain and iffy.

The matter crowding into a rotating black hole (and it is very likely that there is no other kind) can, in theory, squeeze out again somewhere else, like toothpaste blasting out of a fine hole in a stiff tube that is brought under the slow pressure of a steamroller.*

The transfer of matter can apparently take place over enormous distances — millions or billions of light-years — in a trifling period of time. Such transfers cannot take place in the ordinary way, since in space as we know it the speed of light is the speed limit for any object with mass. To transfer mass for distances of millions or billions of light-years in the ordinary way takes millions or billions of years of time.

One must therefore assume that the transfer goes through tunnels or across bridges that do not, strictly speaking, have the time characteristics of our familiar universe. The passageway is sometimes called an "Einstein-Rosen bridge," or, more colorfully, a "wormhole."

If the mass passes through the wormhole and suddenly appears a billion light-years away in ordinary space once more, something must balance that great transfer in distance. Apparently this impossibly rapid passage through space is balanced by a compensating passage through time, so that it appears one billion years ago.

Once the matter emerges at the other end of the wormhole, it expands suddenly into ordinary matter again and, in doing so, blazes with radiated energy — the energy that had, so to speak, been trapped in the black hole. What we have emerging, then, is a "white hole," a concept first suggested in 1964.

If all this is really so, white holes, or at least some of them, might conceivably be detected.

That would depend, of course, upon the size of the white hole and upon its distance from us. Perhaps mini–black holes form mini–white holes at a vast distance, and we would surely never see them. Huge black holes would form huge white holes, however, and these we might see. Are there any signs of such white holes?

There may be —

◆ ◆ ◆

---

* This suggestion, too, is denied by some astronomers.

In the 1950s, sources of radio waves were detected that on closer inspection seemed to be very compact, emerging from mere pinpoint sections of the sky. Ordinarily, radio sources found in those early days of the science were from dust clouds or from galaxies and were therefore more or less spread out over a portion of the sky.

Among the compact radio sources were those known as 3C48, 3C147, 3C196, 3C273, and 3C286. (Many more have been discovered since.) The 3C is short for *Third Cambridge Catalog of Radio Stars,* a list compiled by the English astronomer Martin Ryle.

In 1960 the areas containing these compact radio sources were investigated by the American astronomer Allan Rex Sandage, and in each case something that looked like a dim star seemed to be the source. There was some indication that they might not be normal stars, however. Several of them seemed to have faint clouds of dust or gas about them, and one of them, 3C273, showed signs of a tiny jet of matter emerging from it. In fact there are two radio sources in connection with 3C273, one from the star and one from the jet.

There was some reluctance, therefore, to call these objects stars, and they were instead described as "quasi-stellar (starlike) radio sources." In 1964 Hong-Yee Chiu shortened that to "quasar," and that name has been kept ever since.

The spectra of these quasars were obtained in 1960, but they had a pattern of lines that were completely unrecognizable, as though they were made up of substances utterly alien to the universe. In 1963, however, the Dutch-American astronomer Maarten Schmidt solved that problem. The lines would have been perfectly normal if they had existed far in the ultraviolet range. Their appearance in the visible-light range meant they had been shifted a great distance toward the longer wavelengths.

The easiest explanation for this was that the quasars are very far away. Since the universe is expanding, galactic units are separating, and all seem to be receding from us. Therefore, all distant objects have their spectral lines shifted toward the longer waves because that is what is to be expected when a source of light is receding from us. Furthermore, since the universe is expanding, the farther an object, the faster it is receding from us and the greater the shift in spectral lines. From the spectral shift, then, the distance of an object can be calculated.

It turned out that the quasars were billions of light-years away. One of them, OQ172, is about 12 billion light-years away, and even the nearest, 3C273, is over a billion light-years away and farther than any nonquasar object we know about. There may be as many as 15 million quasars in the universe.

A quasar is a very dim object, as we see it, but, for it to be visible at all at those enormous distances, it must be exceedingly luminous. The quasar 3C273 is five times as luminous as our galaxy, and some quasars may be up to 100 times as luminous as the average galaxy.

Yet, this being so, if quasars were simply galaxies with up to a hundred times as many stars as an average galaxy and therefore that much brighter, they ought to have dimensions large enough to make them appear, even at their vast distances, as tiny patches of light and not as starlike points. Thus, despite their brightness, they must be more compact than ordinary galaxies.

As early as 1963 the quasars were found to be variable in the energy they emitted, both in the visible-light region and in the microwave region. Increases and decreases of as much as three magnitudes were recorded over the space of a few years.

For radiation to vary so markedly in so short a time, a body must be small. Such variations must involve the body as a whole, and, if that is so, some effect must be felt across the full width of the body within the time of variation. Since no effect can travel faster than light, it means that if a quasar varies markedly over a period of a few years, it cannot be more than a light-year or so in diameter and may be considerably smaller.

One quasar, 3C446, can double its brightness in a couple of days, and it must therefore be not more than 0.005 light-year (50 billion kilometers) in diameter, or less than five times the width of Pluto's orbit around the sun. Compare this with an ordinary galaxy, which may be 100,000 light-years across and in which even the dense central core may be 15,000 light-years across.

This combination of tiny dimensions and enormous luminosity makes the quasars seem like a class of objects entirely different from anything else we know. Their discovery made astronomers aware of the possibility of hitherto unknown large-scale phenomena in the universe and spurred them on, for the first time, to consider such phenomena, including the black hole.

And it is conceivable that there is a link between black holes and quasars. The Soviet astronomer Igor Novikov and the Israeli astronomer Yuval Ne'eman have suggested that quasars are giant white holes at the other end of a wormhole from a giant black hole in some other part of the universe.*

But let's take another look at quasars. Are they really unique, as they seem to be, or are they merely extreme examples of something more familiar?

In 1943 a graduate student in astronomy, Carl Seyfert, described a peculiar galaxy. It is one of a group now termed Seyfert galaxies. These may make up 1 percent of all known galaxies (meaning as many as a billion altogether), though actually only a dozen examples have been discovered.

In most respects Seyfert galaxies seem normal and are not unusually distant from us. The cores of the Seyfert galaxies, however, are very compact, very bright, and seem unusually hot and active — rather quasarlike, in fact. They show variations in radiation that imply the radio-emitting centers at their core are no larger than quasars are thought to be. One Seyfert galaxy, 3C120, has a core that makes up less than one-eighth the diameter of the galaxy as a whole but is three times as luminous as the rest of the galaxy combined.

The strongly active center would be visible at greater distances than the outer layers of the Seyfert galaxy would be, and if such a galaxy were far enough, all we would see by either optical or radio telescopes would be the core. We would then consider it a quasar, and the very distant quasars may simply be the intensely luminous nuclei of very large, very active Seyfert galaxies.

But then consider the core of a Seyfert galaxy — very compact, very hot and active. One Seyfert galaxy, NGC 4151, may have as many as ten billion stars in a nucleus only twelve light-years across.

These are precisely the conditions that would encourage the formation of black holes. Perhaps the mere fact that a certain

* This is purely speculative, of course. In fact, the remainder of the book is almost entirely speculation, some of it my own.

volume of space is subject to black hole formation may also make it subject to the blossoming out of a white hole.

We can imagine black holes forming here and there in the universe, each producing an enormous strain in the smooth fabric of space. Wormholes form between them, and matter may leak across at a rate slow in comparison with the total quantity in the black hole serving as source but large enough to produce enormous quantities of radiation in some cases. The rate of matter flow may vary for reasons we do not as yet understand, and this may bring about the variations in the brightness of quasars.

There may be many white holes of all sizes, each connected to its black hole (which itself may come in any size), and we may be aware only of the giant-sized ones. It may be that if all black holes/white holes were taken into account, it would be seen that the wormholes connecting them may crisscross the universe quite densely.

This thought has stimulated the imaginative faculties of astronomers such as Carl Sagan. It is impossible to think of any way of keeping any sizable piece of matter intact as it approaches a black hole, let alone having it pass intact through a wormhole and out the white hole, yet Sagan does not allow that to limit his speculations.

After all, we can do things that to our primitive forebears would seem inconceivable, and Sagan wonders if an advanced civilization might not devise ways of blocking off gravitational and tidal effects so that a ship may make use of wormholes to travel vast distances in a moment of time.

Suppose there were an advanced civilization in the universe right now that had developed a thorough map on which the wormholes were plotted with their black hole entrances and their white hole exits. The smaller wormholes would be more numerous, of course, and therefore more useful.

Imagine a cosmic empire threaded together through a network of such wormholes, with civilized centers located near the entrances and exits. It would be as important, after all, for a world to be located near a transportational crossing point of this sort as it is for an Earth city to be built near an ocean harbor or a river.

The planets nearest the tunnels might be a safe distance away, but nearer still would be enormous space stations built as bases for the ships moving through the tunnels and as power stations for the home planets.

And how does the wormhole theory affect the past and future of the universe? Even though the universe is expanding, is it possible that the expansion is balanced by matter being shifted into the past through the wormholes?

Certainly the dozens of quasars we have detected are all billions of light-years away from us, and we see them, therefore, as they were billions of years ago. Furthermore, they are heavily weighted toward the greater distances and more remote past. It is estimated that if quasars were evenly spaced throughout the universe, there would be several hundred of them nearer and brighter than 3C273, which is the nearest and brightest now.

Well, then, do we have an eternal universe after all, a kind of continuous creation in another sense?

Has the universe been expanding for countless eons, through all eternity in fact, without ever having expanded beyond the present level because the wormholes create a closed circuit, sending matter back into the more contracted past to begin expansion all over?

Has the universe never really been entirely contracted, and has there never really been a big bang? Do we think there was a big bang only because we are more aware of the expansion half of the cycle involving the galaxies and are not aware of matter sweeping back through wormholes?

But if there was no big bang, how do we account for the background radiation that is the echo of the big bang? Can this radiation be the product of the overall backward flow of matter into the far past? Can the white holes or quasars be numerous "little bangs" that add up to the big bang and produce the background radiation?

And if all this is so, where does the energy come from that keeps the universe endlessly recycling? If the universe runs down as it expands (this is referred to as an "increase of entropy" by physicists), does it wind up again ("decreasing entropy") as it moves back in time through the wormholes?

There are no answers to any of these questions at present. All is speculation, including the very existence of wormholes and white holes.

◆ ◆ ◆

It must be admitted that the notion that the universe is continually recycling is a rather tenuous speculation.

If we dismiss it, however, we are left with the big bang — either as a one-time affair if we are living in an open universe, or as an endlessly repeated phenomenon if the universe is closed and oscillating. Either way there is a problem. What is the nature of the cosmic egg?

When the cosmic egg was first suggested, it was viewed very much as we now view neutron stars. The trouble is that a cosmic egg with all the mass of the universe (equal to the mass of 100,000,000,000 galaxies, perhaps) is certainly too large to be a neutron star. If it is true that anything with more than 3.2 times the mass of our sun must form a black hole when it collapses, then the cosmic egg was the biggest of all black holes.

How, then, could it have exploded and yielded the big bang? Black holes do not explode.

Suppose we imagine a contracting universe, which would form black holes of varying sizes as it contracted. The individual black holes might bleed away some of their mass through wormholes, counteracting the overall contraction but not by enough to stop it altogether (or neither the expanding universe nor we would be here today).

As the universe compresses, the black holes grow at the expense of non–black hole matter and, more and more frequently, collide and coalesce. Eventually, of course, all the black holes coalesce into the cosmic egg. It loses matter through its wormhole at an enormous rate, producing the biggest conceivable white hole at the other end. It is the white hole of the cosmic egg, then, that was the big bang that created our expanding universe. This would hold good whether the universe is open or closed, whether the cosmic egg formed only once or repeatedly.

Of course, this solution will only work if wormholes and white holes truly exist, which is uncertain. And even if they do exist, it will only work if the cosmic egg is rotating. But is it?

There is certainly angular momentum in the universe, but it could have been created, despite the conservation law, where none had earlier existed.

That is because there are two kinds of angular momentum, in

opposite senses. An object can rotate either clockwise or counter-clockwise (positively or negatively, if you prefer). Two objects with equal angular momentum, one positive and one negative, will, if they collide and coalesce, end with zero angular momentum, the energy of the two rotatory motions being converted into heat. In reverse, an object with zero angular momentum can, with the addition of appropriate energy, split to form two sub-objects, one with positive angular momentum and the other with negative angular momentum.

The objects in the universe may all have angular momentum, but it is very likely that some of that angular momentum is positive and some negative. We have no way of knowing whether one kind is present in greater quantities than the other. If such lopsidedness does exist, then when all the matter of the universe collapses into a cosmic egg, that cosmic egg will end up with an amount of angular momentum equal to the excess of one kind over the other.

It may be, however, that the amount of angular momentum of one kind in the universe is equal to the amount of the other kind. In that case, the cosmic egg, when it forms, will have no angular momentum and will be dead. We can't rely on wormholes and white holes for the big bang, then.

What else?

Just as angular momentum of two opposite kinds exists, so matter of two opposite kinds exists.

An electron is balanced by an antielectron, or positron. When an electron and a positron combine, there is a mutual annihilation of the two particles. No mass at all is left. It is converted into energy in the form of gamma rays. In the same way, a proton and an antiproton will combine to lose mass and form energy; and so will a neutron and an antineutron.

We can have matter built up of protons, neutrons, and electrons; and antimatter built up of antiprotons, antineutrons, and antielectrons. In that case, any mass of matter combining with an equal mass of antimatter will undergo mutual annihilation to form gamma rays.

In reverse, mass can be formed from energy, but never as one kind of particle only. For every electron that is formed an antielectron must be formed, for every proton an antiproton, for every neutron an antineutron. In short, when energy is turned into matter, an equal quantity of antimatter must also be formed.

But if that is so, where is the antimatter that must have been formed at the same time that the matter of the universe was formed?

The Earth is certainly entirely matter (except for small traces of antimatter formed in the laboratory or found among cosmic rays). In fact the whole solar system is entirely matter, and, in all probability, so is the entire galactic unit of which we are part.

Where is the antimatter? Perhaps there are also galactic units that are entirely antimatter. There may be galactic units and antigalactic units, which because of the general expansion of the universe never come in contact and never engage in mutual annihilation. Just as matter forms black holes, antimatter will form anti–black holes. These two kinds of black holes are in all respects identical except for being made up of opposite substances.

If the universe was ever, in the past, contracting, black holes and anti–black holes formed even more easily; and as contraction continued, the chances of collision between two black holes of opposite nature, and a consequent enormous mutual annihilation, increased. In the final coalescence there was the greatest of all great mutual annihilations.

The total mass of the universe disappeared and with it the gravitational field that keeps the black hole, and the cosmic egg for that matter, in existence. In its place was incredibly energetic radiation, which expanded outward. That would be the big bang.

Some period after the big bang the energy, becoming less intense through expansion, would be tame enough to form matter and antimatter once more — the two forming separate galactic units by some mechanism that, it must be admitted, has not been worked out — and the expanding universe would take shape.

From this view of the big bang as the mutual annihilation of matter and antimatter, it doesn't matter whether the cosmic egg is rotating or not, or whether it is alive or dead.

Yet we have no evidence that there exist antigalactic units. Can it be that for some reason we do not as yet understand that the universe consists simply of matter?

We might argue that this is impossible; the universe cannot

consist simply of matter, as that would make the big bang impossible. Or we might think of a way of accounting for the big bang even in a universe of matter only, and even if, on contracting, that universe forms a cosmic egg that is not rotating and is therefore a dead black hole.

Well, according to the equations used to explain the formation of black holes, the size of the Schwarzschild radius is proportional to the mass of the black hole.

A black hole the mass of the sun has a Schwarzschild radius of 3 kilometers and is therefore 6 kilometers across. A black hole that is twice the mass of the sun is twice as large across — 12 kilometers. However, a sphere that is twice as large across as a smaller sphere has eight times as much volume as the smaller sphere. It follows that a black hole with twice the mass of the sun has that twice the mass spread over eight times the volume. The density of the larger black hole is only one-fourth the density of the smaller black hole.

In other words, the more massive a black hole is, the larger and the less dense it is.

Suppose our entire galaxy, which is about 100,000,000,000 times the mass of our sun, were squeezed into a black hole. Its diameter would be 600,000,000,000 kilometers, and its average density would be about 0.000001 gram per cubic centimeter. The galactic black hole would be more than fifty times as wide as Pluto's orbit and would be no more dense than a gas.

Suppose that all the galaxies of the universe, possibly 100,000,-000,000 of them, collapsed into a black hole. Such a black hole, containing all the matter of the universe, would be 10,000,000,000 light-years across, and its average density would be that of an exceedingly thin gas.

Yet no matter how thin this gas, the structure is a black hole.

Suppose the total mass of the universe is 2.5 times as large as it seems to astronomers to be. In that case the black hole formed by all the matter of the universe is 25,000,000,000 light-years across, and that happens to be about the diameter of the actual universe we live in (as far as we know).

It is quite possible, then, that the entire universe is itself a black hole (as has been suggested by the physicist Kip Thorne).

If it is, then very likely it has always been a black hole and will always be a black hole. If that is so, we live within a black hole, and if we want to know what conditions are like in a black hole (provided it is extremely massive), we have but to look around.

As the universe collapses, then, we might imagine the formation of any number of relatively small black holes (black holes within a black hole!) with very limited diameters. In the last few seconds of final catastrophic collapse, however, when all the black holes coalesce into one cosmic black hole, the Schwarzschild radius springs outward and outward to the extremity of the known universe.

And it may be that *within* the Schwarzschild radius there is the possibility of explosion. It may be that as the Schwarzschild radius recedes billions of light-years in a flash, the cosmic egg at the very instant of formation springs outward to follow, and *that* is the big bang.

If that is so, we might argue that the universe cannot be open whatever the present state of the evidence, since the universe cannot expand beyond its Schwarzschild radius. Somehow the expansion will have to cease at that point, and then it must inevitably begin to contract again and start the cycle over. (Some argue that with each big bang, a totally different expanding universe with different laws of nature gets under way.)

Can it be, then, that what we see all about us is the unimaginably slow breathing cycle (tens of billions years in and tens of billions of years out) of a universe-sized black hole?

And can it be that, separated from our universe in some fashion we cannot as yet grasp, there are many other black holes of various sizes, perhaps an infinite number of them, all expanding and contracting, each at its own rate?

And we are in one of them — and through the wonders of thought and reason it may be that, from our station on a less-than-dust speck lost deep within one of these universes, we have drawn ourselves a picture of the existence and behavior of them all.

PART 2

ROBOTS

IN THE YEARS in which science fiction was the major part of my production, robots were a favorite subject of mine. In the first twenty years of my writing career, I wrote seventeen short stories and three novels in which robots were a key element in the plots, plus a few other short stories that involved computers.

Since my hundredth book was published, however, my science fiction production has decreased a great deal — yet it has not dwindled to zero.

In 1976, for instance, Doubleday published The Bicentennial Man and Other Stories *(Book 176), a collection of eleven stories, three of which involved robots.*

The first of these was "Feminine Intuition," which first appeared in the October 1969 Fantasy and Science Fiction *(usually known as F & SF). In it, my favorite psychologist, Susan Calvin, appears. Susan first appeared in my story "Liar!" which was published in the May 1941 issue of* Astounding Science Fiction *(usually known as ASF). I fell in love with her. I didn't portray her in any very attractive way — she was frozen intellect, and only rarely and secretly seemed to allow a touch of human feeling to show — but I loved her anyway. Before "Feminine Intuition," she had appeared in nine of my robot stories, the last being "Galley Slave" in the December 1957 issue of* Galaxy. *Of these nine stories, five appear in* I, Robot *and four in* The Rest of the Robots, *both of which are among my first hundred books. I had not seriously considered bringing her back until the managing editor of* Galaxy, *Judy-Lynn Benjamin (who later married Lester Del Ray), casually suggested I write a story about a woman robot. It was that which led to "Feminine Intuition," in which I brought back Susan Calvin as an old woman but with her brain functioning as well as ever. It was the tenth story involving her, and it appeared twenty-eight years after the first.*

The second robot story in The Bicentennial Man and Other Stories *was "... That Thou Art Mindful of Him," which first ap-*

peared in the May 1974 issue of F & SF. *This arose because Ed Ferman of* F & SF *and Barry Malzberg, the science fiction writer, wanted to put out an anthology of stories, each of which would carry a particular category to its ultimate end. They asked me to do a robot story that would carry my three laws of robotics as far as possible — and I stretched them to the point where they subverted themselves out of their original purpose. In a way that brought the whole robot saga to a fitting, and ironic, conclusion — though, of course, it would not and did not prevent me from writing additional robot stories.*

Finally, there was "The Bicentennial Man," the title story of the book, which had its genesis in January 1975 when Naomi Gordon of Philadelphia visited and urged me to write a story with that title and with any plot I wished, as long as it was inspired by the title. It would then be included in an anthology (also with that title) to be published in the bicentennial year of 1976.

Alas, the anthology did not come to pass for various reasons, and "The Bicentennial Man" was left homeless. It was rescued by Judy-Lynn Del Rey and appeared in her anthology of original stories Stellar Science Fiction Stories, No. 2, *which was published in February 1976.*

And then, in 1977, "The Bicentennial Man" won both the Nebula and the Hugo awards as the best novelette to appear in 1976. It was the first time any of my stories shorter than a novel had won these awards, and I was delighted to be able to demonstrate that the old man still had it.

Each of the stories strongly appeals to me for one reason or the other, but I only wanted to include one of them in this book, and, after some hesitation, my vanity over the awards won out. Here, then, is "The Bicentennial Man" in full:

"The Bicentennial Man" (1976)

The Three Laws of Robotics:

1. A robot may not injure a human being or, through inaction, allow a human being to come to harm.
2. A robot must obey the orders given it by human beings except where such orders would conflict with the First Law.

3. A robot must protect its own existence
as long as such protection does not conflict with the First or Second Law.

Andrew Martin said, "Thank you," and took the seat offered him.
He didn't look driven to the last resort, but he had been.

He didn't, actually, look anything, for there was a smooth blankness to his face, except for the sadness one imagined one saw in
his eyes. His hair was smooth, light brown, rather fine, and there
was no facial hair. He looked freshly and cleanly shaved. His
clothes were distinctly old-fashioned, but neat and predominantly
a velvety red-purple in color.

Facing him from behind the desk was the surgeon, and the
nameplate on the desk included a fully identifying series of letters
and numbers, which Andrew didn't bother with. To call him Doctor would be quite enough.

"When can the operation be carried through, Doctor?" he
asked.

The surgeon said softly, with that certain inalienable note of
respect that a robot always used to a human being, "I am not
certain, sir, that I understand how or upon whom such an operation could be performed." There might have been a look of respectful intransigence on the surgeon's face — if a robot of his
sort, in lightly bronzed stainless steel, could have such an expression, or any expression.

Andrew Martin studied the robot's right hand, his cutting hand,
as it lay on the desk in utter tranquillity. The fingers were long
and shaped into artistically metallic looping curves so graceful
and appropriate that one could imagine a scalpel fitting them and
becoming, temporarily, one piece with them.

There would be no hesitation in his work, no stumbling, no
quivering, no mistakes. That came with specialization, of course,
a specialization so fiercely desired by humanity that few robots
were, any longer, independently brained. A surgeon, of course,
would have to be. And this one, though brained, was so limited
in his capacity that he did not recognize Andrew — had probably
never heard of him.

Andrew said, "Have you ever thought you would like to be a
man?"

The surgeon hesitated a moment as though the question fitted nowhere in his allotted positronic pathways. "But I am a robot, sir."

"Would it be better to be a man?"

"It would be better, sir, to be a better surgeon. I could not be so if I were a man, but only if I were a more advanced robot. I would be pleased to be a more advanced robot."

"It does not offend you that I can order you about? That I can make you stand up, sit down, move right or left, by merely telling you to do so?"

"It is my pleasure to please you, sir. If your orders were to interfere with my functioning with respect to you or to any other human being, I would not obey you. The First Law, concerning my duty to human safety, would take precedence over the Second Law relating to obedience. Otherwise, obedience is my pleasure . . . But upon whom am I to perform this operation?"

"Upon me," said Andrew.

"But that is impossible. It is patently a damaging operation."

"That does not matter," said Andrew calmly.

"I must not inflict damage," said the surgeon.

"On a human being, you must not," said Andrew, "but I, too, am a robot."

Andrew had appeared much more a robot when he had first been manufactured. He had then been as much a robot in appearance as any that had ever existed, smoothly designed and functional.

He had done well in the home to which he had been brought in those days when robots in households, or on the planet altogether, had been a rarity.

There had been four in the home: Sir and Ma'am and Miss and Little Miss. He knew their names, of course, but he never used them. Sir was Gerald Martin.

His own serial number was NDR—— He forgot the numbers. It had been a long time, of course, but if he had wanted to remember, he could not forget. He had not wanted to remember.

Little Miss had been the first to call him Andrew because she could not use the letters, and all the rest followed her in this.

Little Miss . . . She had lived ninety years and was long since dead. He had tried to call her Ma'am once, but she would not allow it. Little Miss she had been to her last day.

Andrew had been intended to perform the duties of a valet, a butler, a lady's maid. Those were the experimental days for him and, indeed, for all robots anywhere but in the industrial and exploratory factories and stations off Earth.

The Martins enjoyed him, and half the time he was prevented from doing his work because Miss and Little Miss would rather play with him.

It was Miss who understood first how this might be arranged. She said, "We order you to play with us and you must follow orders."

Andrew said, "I am sorry, Miss, but a prior order from Sir must surely take precedence."

But she said, "Daddy just said he hoped you would take care of the cleaning. That's not much of an order. I *order* you."

Sir did not mind. Sir was fond of Miss and of Little Miss, even more than Ma'am was, and Andrew was fond of them, too. At least, the effect they had upon his actions were those which in a human being would have been called the result of fondness. Andrew thought of it as fondness, for he did not know any other word for it.

It was for Little Miss that Andrew had carved a pendant out of wood. She had ordered him to. Miss, it seemed, had received an ivorite pendant with scrollwork for her birthday, and Little Miss was unhappy over it. She had only a piece of wood, which she gave Andrew together with a small kitchen knife.

He had done it quickly and Little Miss said, "That's *nice*, Andrew. I'll show it to Daddy."

Sir would not believe it. "Where did you really get this, Mandy?" Mandy was what he called Little Miss. When Little Miss assured him she was really telling the truth, he turned to Andrew. "Did you do this, Andrew?"

"Yes, Sir."

"The design, too?"

"Yes, Sir."

"From what did you copy the design?"

"It is a geometric representation, Sir, that fit the grain of the wood."

The next day, Sir brought him another piece of wood, a larger one, and an electric vibro-knife. He said, "Make something out of this, Andrew. Anything you want to."

Andrew did so and Sir watched, then looked at the product a long time. After that, Andrew no longer waited on tables. He was ordered to read books on furniture design instead, and he learned to make cabinets and desks.

Sir said, "These are amazing productions, Andrew."

Andrew said, "I enjoy doing them, Sir."

"Enjoy?"

"It makes the circuits of my brain somehow flow more easily. I have heard you use the word 'enjoy' and the way you use it fits the way I feel. I enjoy doing them, Sir."

Gerald Martin took Andrew to the regional offices of United States Robots and Mechanical Men, Inc. As a member of the Regional Legislature he had no trouble at all in gaining an interview with the chief robopsychologist. In fact, it was only as a member of the Regional Legislature that he qualified as a robot owner in the first place — in those early days when robots were rare.

Andrew did not understand any of this at the time, but in later years, with greater learning, he could re-view that early scene and understand it in its proper light.

The robopsychologist, Merton Mansky, listened with a gathering frown and more than once managed to stop his fingers at the point beyond which they would have irrepressibly drummed on the table. He had drawn features and a lined forehead and looked as though he might be younger than he looked.

He said, "Robotics is not an exact art, Mr. Martin. I cannot explain it to you in detail, but the mathematics governing the plotting of the positronic pathways is far too complicated to permit of any but approximate solutions. Naturally, since we build everything about the Three Laws, those are incontrovertible. We will, of course, replace your robot —"

"Not at all," said Sir. "There is no question of failure on his part. He performs his assigned duties perfectly. The point is, he also carves wood in exquisite fashion and never the same twice. He produces works of art."

Mansky looked confused. "Strange. Of course, we're attempting generalized pathways these days... Really creative, you think?"

"See for yourself." Sir handed over a little sphere of wood on which there was a playground scene in which the boys and girls were almost too small to make out, yet they were in perfect proportion and blended so naturally with the grain that that, too, seemed to have been carved.

Mansky said, "*He* did that?" He handed it back with a shake of his head. "The luck of the draw. Something in the pathways."

"Can you do it again?"

"Probably not. Nothing like this has ever been reported."

"Good! I don't in the least mind Andrew's being the only one."

Mansky said, "I suspect that the company would like to have your robot back for study."

Sir said with sudden grimness, "Not a chance. Forget it." He turned to Andrew. "Let's go home now."

"As you wish, Sir," said Andrew.

Miss was dating boys and wasn't about the house much. It was Little Miss, not as little as she once was, who filled Andrew's horizon now. She never forgot that the very first piece of wood carving he had done had been for her. She kept it on a silver chain about her neck.

It was she who first objected to Sir's habit of giving away the productions. She said, "Come on, Dad, if anyone wants one of them, let him pay for it. It's worth it."

Sir said, "It isn't like you to be greedy, Mandy."

"Not for us, Dad. For the artist."

Andrew had never heard the word before and when he had a moment to himself he looked it up in the dictionary. Then there was another trip, this time to Sir's lawyer.

Sir said to him, "What do you think of this, John?"

The lawyer was John Feingold. He had white hair and a pudgy belly, and the rims of his contact lenses were tinted a bright green. He looked at the small plaque Sir had given him. "This is beautiful... But I've heard the news. This is a carving made by your robot. The one you've brought with you."

"Yes, Andrew does them. Don't you, Andrew?"

"Yes, Sir," said Andrew.

"How much would you pay for that, John?" asked Sir.

"I can't say. I'm not a collector of such things."

"Would you believe I've been offered two hundred fifty dollars for that small thing? Andrew has made chairs that have sold for five hundred dollars. There's two hundred thousand dollars in the bank out of Andrew's products."

"Good heavens, he's making you rich, Gerald."

"Half rich," said Sir. "Half of it is in an account in the name of Andrew Martin."

"The robot?"

"That's right, and I want to know if it's legal."

"Legal?" Feingold's chair creaked as he leaned back in it. "There are no precedents, Gerald. How did your robot sign the necessary papers?"

"He can sign his name, and I brought in the signature. I didn't bring him in to the bank himself. Is there anything further that ought to be done?"

"Um." Feingold's eyes seemed to turn inward for a moment. Then he said, "Well, we can set up a trust to handle all finances in his name, and that will place a layer of insulation between him and the hostile world. Further than that, my advice is you do nothing. No one is stopping you so far. If anyone objects, let *him* bring suit."

"And will you take the case if suit is brought?"

"For a retainer, certainly."

"How much?"

"Something like that," and Feingold pointed to the wooden plaque.

"Fair enough," said Sir.

Feingold chuckled as he turned to the robot. "Andrew, are you pleased that you have money?"

"Yes, sir."

"What do you plan to do with it?"

"Pay for things, sir, which otherwise Sir would have to pay for. It would save him expense, sir."

The occasions came. Repairs were expensive, and revisions were even more so. Over the years, new models of robots were produced, and Sir saw to it that Andrew had the advantage of every new device, until he was a paragon of metallic excellence. It was all at Andrew's expense. Andrew insisted on that.

Only his positronic pathways were untouched. Sir insisted on that.

"The new ones aren't as good as you are, Andrew," he said. "The new robots are worthless. The company has learned to make the pathways more precise, more closely on the nose, more deeply on the track. The new robots don't shift. They do what they're designed for and never stray. I like you better."

"Thank you, Sir."

"And it's your doing, Andrew, don't you forget that. I am certain Mansky put an end to generalized pathways as soon as he had a good look at you. He didn't like the unpredictability . . . Do you know how many times he asked for you so he could place you under study? Nine times! I never let him have you, though, and now that he's retired, we may have some peace."

So Sir's hair thinned and grayed and his face grew pouchy, while Andrew looked rather better than he had when he first joined the family.

Ma'am had joined an art colony somewhere in Europe and Miss was a poet in New York. They wrote sometimes, but not often. Little Miss was married and lived not far away. She said she did not want to leave Andrew, and when her child, Little Sir, was born, she let Andrew hold the bottle and feed him.

With the birth of a grandson, Andrew felt that Sir had someone now to replace those who had gone. It would not be so unfair to come to him with the request.

Andrew said, "Sir, it is kind of you to have allowed me to spend my money as I wished."

"It was your money, Andrew."

"Only by your voluntary act, Sir. I do not believe the law would have stopped you from keeping it all."

"The law won't persuade me to do wrong, Andrew."

"Despite all expenses, and despite taxes, too, Sir, I have nearly six hundred thousand dollars."

"I know that, Andrew."

"I want to give it to you, Sir."

"I won't take it, Andrew."

"In exchange for something you can give me, Sir."

"Oh? What is that, Andrew?"

"My freedom, Sir."

"Your —"

"I wish to buy my freedom, Sir."

It wasn't that easy. Sir had flushed, had said, "For God's sake!" had turned on his heel, and stalked away.

It was Little Miss who brought him around, defiantly and harshly — and in front of Andrew. For thirty years, no one had hesitated to talk in front of Andrew, whether the matter involved Andrew or not. He was only a robot.

She said, "Dad, why are you taking it as a personal affront? He'll still be here. He'll still be loyal. He can't help that. It's built in. All he wants is a form of words. He wants to be called free. Is that so terrible? Hasn't he earned it? Heavens, he and I have been talking about it for years."

"Talking about it for years, have you?"

"Yes, and over and over again, he postponed it for fear he would hurt you. I *made* him put it up to you."

"He doesn't know what freedom is. He's a robot."

"Dad, you don't know him. He's read everything in the library. I don't know what he feels inside but I don't know what *you* feel inside. When you talk to him you'll find he reacts to the various abstractions as you and I do, and what else counts? If someone else's reactions are like your own, what more can you ask for?"

"The law won't take that attitude," Sir said angrily. "See here, you!" He turned to Andrew with a deliberate grate in his voice. "I can't free you except by doing it legally, and, if it gets into the courts, you not only won't get your freedom, but the law will take official cognizance of your money. They'll tell you that a robot has no right to earn money. Is this rigmarole worth losing your money?"

"Freedom is without price, Sir," said Andrew. "Even the chance of freedom is worth the money."

The court might also take the attitude that freedom was without price, and might decide that for no price, however great, could a robot buy its freedom.

The simple statement of the regional attorney who represented those who had brought a class action to oppose the freedom was this: The word "freedom" had no meaning when applied to a robot. Only a human being could be free.

He said it several times, when it seemed appropriate; slowly, with his hand coming down rhythmically on the desk before him to mark the words.

Little Miss asked permission to speak on behalf of Andrew. She was recognized by her full name, something Andrew had never heard pronounced before:

"Amanda Laura Martin Charney may approach the bench."

She said, "Thank you, your honor. I am not a lawyer and I don't know the proper way of phrasing things, but I hope you will listen to my meaning and ignore the words.

"Let's understand what it means to be free in Andrew's case. In some ways, he *is* free. I think it's at least twenty years since anyone in the Martin family gave him an order to do something that we felt he might not do of his own accord.

"But we can, if we wish, give him an order to do anything, couch it as harshly as we wish, because he is a machine that belongs to us. Why should we be in a position to do so, when he has served us so long, so faithfully, and earned so much money for us? He owes us nothing more. The debt is entirely on the other side.

"Even if we were legally forbidden to place Andrew in involuntary servitude, he would still serve us voluntarily. Making him free would be a trick of words only, but it would mean much to him. It would give him everything and cost us nothing."

For a moment the judge seemed to be suppressing a smile. "I see your point, Mrs. Charney. The fact is that there is no binding law in this respect and no precedent. There *is*, however, the unspoken assumption that only a human can enjoy freedom. I can make new law here, subject to reversal in a higher court, but I cannot lightly run counter to that assumption. Let me address the robot. Andrew!"

"Yes, your honor."

It was the first time Andrew had spoken in court and the judge seemed astonished for a moment at the human timbre of the voice. He said, "Why do you want to be free, Andrew? In what way will this matter to you?"

Andrew said, "Would you wish to be a slave, your honor?"

"But you are not a slave. You are a perfectly good robot, a genius of a robot I am given to understand, capable of an artistic expression that can be matched nowhere. What more could you do if you were free?"

"Perhaps no more than I do now, your honor, but with greater joy. It has been said in this courtroom that only a human being can be free. It seems to me that only someone who wishes for freedom can be free. I wish for freedom."

And it was that that cued the judge. The crucial sentence in his decision was: "There is no right to deny freedom to any object with a mind advanced enough to grasp the concept and desire the state."

It was eventually upheld by the World Court.

Sir remained displeased, and his harsh voice made Andrew feel almost as though he were being short-circuited.

Sir said, "I don't want your damned money, Andrew. I'll take it only because you won't feel free otherwise. From now on, you can select your own jobs and do them as you please. I will give you no orders, except this one — that you do as you please. But I am still responsible for you; that's part of the court order. I hope you understand that."

Little Miss interrupted. "Don't be irascible, Dad. The responsibility is no great chore. You know you won't have to do a thing. The Three Laws still hold."

"Then how is he free?"

Andrew said, "Are not human beings bound by their laws, Sir?"

Sir said, "I'm not going to argue." He left, and Andrew saw him only infrequently after that.

Little Miss came to see him frequently in the small house that had been built and made over for him. It had no kitchen, of course, nor bathroom facilities. It had just two rooms; one was a library and one was a combination storeroom and workroom. Andrew accepted many commissions and worked harder as a free robot than he ever had before, till the cost of the house was paid for and the structure legally transferred to him.

One day Little Sir came . . . No, George! Little Sir had insisted on that after the court decision. "A free robot doesn't call anyone

Little Sir," George had said. "I call you Andrew. You must call me George."

It was phrased as an order, so Andrew called him George — but Little Miss remained Little Miss.

The day George came alone, it was to say that Sir was dying. Little Miss was at the bedside but Sir wanted Andrew as well.

Sir's voice was quite strong, though he seemed unable to move much. He struggled to get his hand up. "Andrew," he said, "Andrew — Don't help me, George. I'm only dying; I'm not crippled . . . Andrew, I'm glad you're free. I just wanted to tell you that."

Andrew did not know what to say. He had never been at the side of someone dying before, but he knew it was the human way of ceasing to function. It was an involuntary and irreversible dismantling, and Andrew did not know what to say that might be appropriate. He could only remain standing, absolutely silent, absolutely motionless.

When it was over, Little Miss said to him, "He may not have seemed friendly to you toward the end, Andrew, but he was old, you know, and it hurt him that you should want to be free."

And then Andrew found the words to say. He said, "I would never have been free without him, Little Miss."

It was only after Sir's death that Andrew began to wear clothes. He began with an old pair of trousers at first, a pair that George had given him.

George was married now, and a lawyer. He had joined Feingold's firm. Old Feingold was long since dead, but his daughter had carried on and eventually the firm's name became Feingold and Martin. It remained so even when the daughter retired and no Feingold took her place. At the time Andrew put on clothes for the first time, the Martin name had just been added to the firm.

George had tried not to smile the first time Andrew put on the trousers, but to Andrew's eyes the smile was clearly there.

George showed Andrew how to manipulate the static charge so as to allow the trousers to open, wrap about his lower body, and move shut. George demonstrated on his own trousers, but Andrew was quite aware that it would take him awhile to duplicate that one flowing motion.

George said, "But why do you want trousers, Andrew? Your body is so beautifully functional it's a shame to cover it — especially when you needn't worry about either temperature control or modesty. And it doesn't cling properly, not on metal."

Andrew said, "Are not human bodies beautifully functional, George? Yet you cover yourselves."

"For warmth, for cleanliness, for protection, for decorativeness. None of that applies to you."

Andrew said, "I feel bare without clothes. I feel different, George."

"Different! Andrew, there are millions of robots on Earth now. In this region, according to the last census, there are almost as many robots as there are men."

"I know, George. There are robots doing every conceivable type of work."

"And none of them wears clothes."

"But none of them is free, George."

Little by little, Andrew added to the wardrobe. He was inhibited by George's smile and by the stares of the people who commissioned work.

He might be free, but there was built into him a carefully detailed program concerning his behavior toward people, and it was only by the tiniest steps that he dared advance. Open disapproval would set him back months.

Not everyone accepted Andrew as free. He was incapable of resenting that, and yet there was a difficulty about his thinking process when he thought of it.

Most of all, he tended to avoid putting on clothes — or too many of them — when he thought Little Miss might come to visit him. She was old now and was often away in some warmer climate, but when she returned the first thing she did was visit him.

On one of her returns, George said ruefully, "She's got me, Andrew. I'll be running for the Legislature next year. Like grandfather, she says, like grandson."

"Like grandfather —" Andrew stopped, uncertain.

"I mean that I, George, the grandson, will be like Sir, the grandfather, who was in the Legislature once."

Andrew said, "It would be pleasant, George, if Sir were still —"

He paused, for he did not want to say, "in working order." That seemed inappropriate.

"Alive," said George. "Yes, I think of the old monster now and then, too."

It was a conversation Andrew thought about. He had noticed his own incapacity in speech when talking with George. Somehow the language had changed since Andrew had come into being with an innate vocabulary. Then, too, George used a colloquial speech, as Sir and Little Miss had not. Why should he have called Sir a monster when surely that word was not appropriate?

Nor could Andrew turn to his own books for guidance. They were old and most dealt with woodworking, with art, with furniture design. There were none on language, none on the way of human beings.

It was at that moment that it seemed to him he must seek the proper books; and as a free robot, he felt he must not ask George. He would go to town and use the library. It was a triumphant decision, and he felt his electropotential grow distinctly higher until he had to throw in an impedance coil.

He put on a full costume, even including a shoulder chain of wood. He would have preferred the glitter plastic, but George had said that wood was much more appropriate and that polished cedar was considerably more valuable as well.

He had placed a hundred feet between himself and the house before gathering resistance brought him to a halt. He shifted the impedance coil out of circuit, and, when that did not seem to help enough, he returned to his home and on a piece of notepaper wrote neatly, "I have gone to the library," and placed it in clear view on his worktable.

Andrew never quite got to the library. He had studied the map. He knew the route but not the appearance of it. The actual landmarks did not resemble the symbols on the map and he would hesitate. Eventually he thought he must have somehow gone wrong, for everything looked strange.

He passed an occasional field robot, but at the time he decided he should ask his way, there was none in sight. A vehicle passed and did not stop. He stood irresolute, which meant calmly motionless, and then coming across the field toward him were two human beings.

He turned to face them, and they altered their course to meet him. A moment before, they had been talking loudly; he had heard their voices; but now they were silent. They had the look that Andrew associated with human uncertainty, and they were young, but not very young. Twenty perhaps? Andrew could never judge human age.

He said, "Would you describe to me the route to the town library, sirs?"

One of them, the taller of the two, whose tall hat lengthened him still farther, almost grotesquely, said, not to Andrew but to the other, "It's a robot."

The other had a bulbous nose and heavy eyelids. He said, not to Andrew but to the first, "It's wearing clothes."

The tall one snapped his fingers. "It's the free robot. They have a robot at the Martins who isn't owned by anybody. Why else would it be wearing clothes?"

"Ask it," said the one with the nose.

"Are you the Martin robot?" asked the tall one. ·

"I am Andrew Martin, sir," said Andrew.

"Good. Take off your clothes. Robots don't wear clothes." He said to the other, "That's disgusting. Look at him."

Andrew hesitated. He hadn't heard an order in that tone of voice in so long that his Second Law circuits had momentarily jammed.

The tall one said, "Take off your clothes. I order you."

Slowly, Andrew began to remove them.

"Just drop them," said the tall one.

The nose said, "If it doesn't belong to anyone, he could be ours as much as someone else's."

"Anyway," said the tall one, "who's to object to anything we do? We're not damaging property . . . Stand on your head." That was to Andrew.

"The head is not meant —" began Andrew.

"That's an order. If you don't know how, try anyway."

Andrew hesitated again, then bent to put his head on the ground. He tried to lift his legs and fell, heavily.

The tall one said, "Just lie there." He said to the other, "We can take him apart. Ever take a robot apart?"

"Will he let us?"

"How can he stop us?"

There was no way Andrew could stop them if they ordered him not to resist in a forceful enough manner. The Second Law of obedience took precedence over the Third Law of self-preservation. In any case, he could not defend himself without possibly hurting them and that would mean breaking the First Law. At that thought, every motile unit contracted slightly and he quivered as he lay there.

The tall one walked over and pushed at him with his foot. "He's heavy. I think we'll need tools to do the job."

The nose said, "We could order him to take himself apart. It would be fun to watch him try."

"Yes," said the tall one thoughtfully, "but let's get him off the road. If someone comes along —"

It was too late. Someone had indeed come along, and it was George. From where he lay, Andrew had seen him topping a small rise in the middle distance. He would have liked to signal him in some way, but the last order had been, "Just lie there!"

George was running now and he arrived somewhat winded. The two young men stepped back a little and then waited thoughtfully.

George said anxiously, "Andrew, has something gone wrong?"

Andrew said, "I am well, George."

"Then stand up . . . What happened to your clothes?"

The tall young man said, "That your robot, mac?"

George turned sharply. "He's no one's robot. What's been going on here?"

"We politely asked him to take his clothes off. What's that to you if you don't own him?"

George said, "What were they doing, Andrew?"

Andrew said, "It was their intention in some way to dismember me. They were about to move me to a quiet spot and order me to dismember myself."

George looked at the two and his chin trembled. The two young men retreated no further. They were smiling. The tall one said lightly, "What are you going to do, pudgy? Attack us?"

George said, "No. I don't have to. This robot has been with my family for over seventy years. He knows us and he values us more than he values anyone else. I am going to tell him that you two are threatening my life and that you plan to kill me. I will ask him to defend me. In choosing between me and you two, he will choose me. Do you know what will happen to you when he attacks you?"

The two were backing away slightly, looking uneasy.

George said sharply, "Andrew, I am in danger and about to come to harm from these young men. Move toward them!"

Andrew did so, and the two young men did not wait. They ran fleetly.

"All right, Andrew, relax," said George. He looked unstrung. He was far past the age where he could face the possibility of a dustup with one young man, let alone two.

Andrew said, "I couldn't have hurt them, George. I could see they were not attacking you."

"I didn't order you to attack them; I only told you to move toward them. Their own fears did the rest."

"How can they fear robots?"

"It's a disease of mankind, one of which it is not yet cured. But never mind that. What the devil are you doing here, Andrew? I was on the point of turning back and hiring a helicopter when I found you. How did you get it into your head to go to the library? I would have brought you any books you needed."

"I am a —" began Andrew.

"Free robot. Yes, yes. All right, what did you want in the library?"

"I want to know more about human beings, about the world, about everything. And about robots, George. I want to write a history about robots."

George said, "Well, let's walk home ... And pick up your clothes first. Andrew, there are a million books on robotics and all of them include histories of the science. The world is growing saturated not only with robots but with information about robots."

Andrew shook his head, a human gesture he had lately begun to make. "Not a history of robotics, George. A history of *robots,* by a robot. I want to explain how robots feel about what has happened since the first ones were allowed to work and live on Earth."

George's eyebrows lifted, but he said nothing in direct response.

Little Miss was just past her eighty-third birthday, but there was nothing about her that was lacking in either energy or determination. She gestured with her cane more often than she propped herself up with it.

She listened to the story in a fury of indignation. She said, "George, that's horrible. Who were those young ruffians?"

"I don't know. What difference does it make? In the end they did no damage."

"They might have. You're a lawyer, George, and if you're well off, it's entirely due to the talent of Andrew. It was the money *he* earned that is the foundation of everything we have. He provides the continuity for this family, and I will *not* have him treated as a wind-up toy."

"What would you have me do, Mother?" asked George.

"I said you're a lawyer. Don't you listen? You set up a test case somehow, and you force the regional courts to declare for robot rights and get the Legislature to pass the necessary bills, and carry the whole thing to the World Court, if you have to. I'll be watching, George, and I'll tolerate no shirking."

She was serious, and what began as a way of soothing the fearsome old lady became an involved matter with enough legal entanglement to make it interesting. As senior partner of Feingold and Martin, George plotted strategy but left the actual work to his junor partners, with much of it a matter for his son, Paul, who was also a member of the firm and who reported dutifully nearly every day to his grandmother. She, in turn, discussed it every day with Andrew.

Andrew was deeply involved. His work on his book on robots was delayed again as he pored over the legal arguments and even, at times, made very diffident suggestions.

He said, "George told me that day that human beings have always been afraid of robots. As long as they are, the courts and the legislatures are not likely to work hard on behalf of robots. Should there not be something done about public opinion?"

So while Paul stayed in court, George took to the public platform. It gave him the advantage of being informal, and he sometimes even went so far as to wear the new, loose style of clothing that he called drapery. Paul said, "Just don't trip over it onstage, Dad."

George said despondently, "I'll try not to."

He addressed the annual convention of holo-news editors on one occasion and said, in part:

"If, by virtue of the Second Law, we can demand of any robot unlimited obedience in all respects not involving harm to a human being, then any human being, *any* human being, has a fearsome power over any robot, *any* robot. In particular, since the Second Law supersedes the Third Law, *any* human being can use the law of obedience to overcome the law of self-protection. He can order any robot to damage itself or even destroy itself for any reason, or for no reason.

"Is this just? Would we treat an animal so? Even an inanimate object that has given us good service has a claim on our consideration. And a robot is not insensible; it is not an animal. It can think well enough to enable it to talk to us, reason with us, joke with us. Can we treat them as friends, can we work together with them, and not give them some of the fruit of that friendship, some of the benefit of co-working?

"If a man has the right to give a robot any order that does not involve harm to a human being, he should have the decency never to give a robot any order that involves harm to a robot, unless human safety absolutely requires it. With great power goes great responsibility, and if the robots have Three Laws to protect men, is it too much to ask that men have a law or two to protect robots?"

Andrew was right. It was the battle over public opinion that held the key to courts and Legislature and in the end a law passed which set up conditions under which robot-harming orders were forbidden. It was endlessly qualified and the punishments for violating the law were totally inadequate, but the principle was established. The final passage by the World Legislature came through on the day of Little Miss's death.

That was no coincidence. Little Miss held on to life desperately during the last debate and let go only when word of victory arrived. Her last smile was for Andrew. Her last words were: "You have been good to us, Andrew."

She died with her hand holding his, while her son and his wife and children remained at a respectful distance from both.

Andrew waited patiently while the receptionist disappeared into the inner office. It might have used the holographic chatterbox, but unquestionably it was unmanned (or perhaps unroboted) by having to deal with another robot rather than with a human being.

Andrew passed the time revolving the matter in his mind. Could "unroboted" be used as an analogue of "unmanned," or had "unmanned" become a metaphoric term sufficiently divorced from its original literal meaning to be applied to robots — or to women, for that matter?

Such problems came up frequently as he worked on his book on robots. The trick of thinking out sentences to express all complexities had undoubtedly increased his vocabulary.

Occasionally, someone came into the room to stare at him and he did not try to avoid the glance. He looked at each calmly, and each in turn looked away.

Paul Martin finally came out. He looked surprised, or he would have if Andrew could have made out his expression with certainty. Paul had taken to wearing the heavy makeup that fashion was dictating for both sexes, and though it made sharper and firmer the somewhat bland lines of his face, Andrew disapproved. He found that disapproving of human beings, as long as he did not express it verbally, did not make him very uneasy. He could even write the disapproval. He was sure it had not always been so.

Paul said, "Come in, Andrew. I'm sorry I made you wait but there was something I *had* to finish. Come in. You had said you wanted to talk to me, but I didn't know you meant here in town."

"If you are busy, Paul, I am prepared to continue to wait."

Paul glanced at the interplay of shifting shadows on the dial on the wall that served as timepiece and said, "I can make some time. Did you come alone?"

"I hired an automatobile."

"Any trouble?" Paul asked with more than a trace of anxiety.

"I wasn't expecting any. My rights are protected."

Paul looked the more anxious for that. "Andrew, I've explained that the law is unenforceable, at least under most conditions . . . And if you insist on wearing clothes, you'll run into trouble eventually — just like that first time."

"And only time, Paul. I'm sorry you are displeased."

"Well, look at it this way; you are virtually a living legend, Andrew, and you are too valuable in many different ways for you to have any right to take chances with yourself . . . How's the book coming?"

"I am approaching the end, Paul. The publisher is quite pleased."

"Good!"

"I don't know that he's necessarily pleased with the book as a book. I think he expects to sell many copies because it's written by a robot and it's that that pleases him."

"Only human, I'm afraid."

"I am not displeased. Let it sell for whatever reason since it will mean money and I can use some."

"Grandmother left you —"

"Little Miss was generous, and I'm sure I can count on the family to help me out further. But it is the royalties from the book on which I am counting to help me through the next step."

"What next step is that?"

"I wish to see the head of U. S. Robots and Mechanical Men, Inc. I have tried to make an appointment, but so far I have not been able to reach him. The corporation did not cooperate with me in the writing of the book, so I am not surprised, you understand."

Paul was clearly amused. "Cooperation is the last thing you can expect. They didn't cooperate with us in our great fight for robot rights. Quite the reverse, and you can see why. Give a robot rights and people may not want to buy them."

"Nevertheless," said Andrew, "if you call them, you may obtain an interview for me."

"I'm no more popular with them than you are, Andrew."

"But perhaps you can hint that by seeing me they may head off a campaign by Feingold and Martin to strengthen the rights of robots further."

"Wouldn't that be a lie, Andrew?"

"Yes, Paul, and I can't tell one. That is why you must call."

"Ah, you can't lie, but you can urge me to tell a lie, is that it? You're getting more human all the time, Andrew."

It was not easy to arrange, even with Paul's supposedly weighted name.

But it was finally carried through and, when it was, Harley Smythe-Robertson, who, on his mother's side, was descended from the original founder of the corporation and who had adopted the hyphenation to indicate it, looked remarkably unhappy. He was approaching retirement age and his entire tenure as president had been devoted to the matter of robot rights. His gray hair was plastered thinly over the top of his scalp, his face was not made up, and he eyed Andrew with brief hostility from time to time.

Andrew said, "Sir, nearly a century ago, I was told by a Merton Mansky of this corporation that the mathematics governing the plotting of the positronic pathways was far too complicated to permit of any but approximate solutions and that therefore my own capacities were not fully predictable."

"That was a century ago." Smythe-Robertson hesitated, then said icily, "*Sir*. It is true no longer. Our robots are made with precision now and are trained precisely to their jobs."

"Yes," said Paul, who had come along, as he said, to make sure that the corporation played fair, "with the result that my receptionist must be guided at every point once events depart from the conventional, however slightly."

Smythe-Robertson said, "You would be much more displeased if it were to improvise."

Andrew said, "Then you no longer manufacture robots like myself that are flexible and adaptable."

"No longer."

"The research I have done in connection with my book," said Andrew, "indicates that I am the oldest robot presently in active operation."

"The oldest presently," said Smythe-Robertson, "and the oldest ever. The oldest that will ever be. No robot is useful after the twenty-fifth year. They are called in and replaced with newer models."

"No robot *as presently manufactured* is useful after the twenty-fifth year," said Paul pleasantly. "Andrew is quite exceptional in this respect."

Andrew, adhering to the path he had marked out for himself, said, "As the oldest robot in the world and the most flexible, am I not unusual enough to merit special treatment from the company?"

"Not at all," said Smythe-Robertson freezingly. "Your unusualness is an embarrassment to the company. If you were on lease, instead of having been a sale outright through some mischance, you would long since have been replaced."

"But that is exactly the point," said Andrew. "I am a free robot and I own myself. Therefore I come to you and ask you to replace me. You cannot do this without the owner's consent. Nowadays, that consent is extorted as a condition of the lease, but in my time this did not happen."

Smythe-Robertson was looking both startled and puzzled, and for a moment there was silence. Andrew found himself staring at the holograph on the wall. It was a death mask of Susan Calvin, patron saint of all roboticists. She was dead nearly two centuries now, but as a result of writing his book Andrew knew her so well he could half persuade himself that he had met her in life.

Smythe-Robertson said, "How can I replace you for you? If I replace you as a robot, how can I donate the new robot to you as owner since in the very act of replacement you cease to exist?" He smiled grimly.

"Not at all difficult," interposed Paul. "The seat of Andrew's personality is his positronic brain, and it is the one part that cannot be replaced without creating a new robot. The positronic brain, therefore, is Andrew the owner. Every other part of the robotic body can be replaced without affecting the robot's personality, and those other parts are the brain's possessions. Andrew, I should say, wants to supply his brain with a new robotic body."

"That's right," said Andrew calmly. He turned to Smythe-Robertson. "You have manufactured androids, haven't you? Robots that have the outward appearance of humans complete to the texture of the skin?"

Smythe-Robertson said, "Yes, we have. They worked perfectly well, with their synthetic fibrous skins and tendons. There was virtually no metal anywhere except for the brain, yet they were nearly as tough as metal robots. They were tougher, weight for weight."

Paul looked interested. "I didn't know that. How many are on the market?"

"None," said Smythe-Robertson. "They were much more expensive than metal models and a market survey showed they would not be accepted. They looked too human."

Andrew said, "But the corporation retains its expertise, I assume. Since it does, I wish to request that I be replaced by an organic robot, an android."

Paul looked surprised. "Good Lord," he said.

Smythe-Robertson stiffened. "Quite impossible!"

"Why is it impossible?" asked Andrew. "I will pay any reasonable fee, of course."

Smythe-Robertson said, "We do not manufacture androids."

"You do not *choose* to manufacture androids," interposed Paul quickly. "That is not the same as being unable to manufacture them."

Smythe-Robertson said, "Nevertheless, the manufacture of androids is against public policy."

"There is no law against it," said Paul.

"Nevertheless, we do not manufacture them, and we will not."

Paul cleared his throat. "Mr. Smythe-Robertson," he said, "Andrew is a free robot who is under the purview of the law guaranteeing robots' rights. You are aware of this, I take it?"

"Only too well."

"This robot, as a free robot, chooses to wear clothes. This results in his being frequently humiliated by thoughtless human beings despite the law against the humiliation of robots. It is difficult to prosecute vague offenses that don't meet with the general disapproval of those who must decide on guilt and innocence."

"U. S. Robots understood that from the start. Your father's firm unfortunately did not."

"My father is dead now," said Paul, "but what I see is that we have here a clear offense with a clear target."

"What are you talking about?" said Smythe-Robertson.

"My client, Andrew Martin — he has just become my client — is a free robot who is entitled to ask U. S. Robots and Mechanical

Men, Inc., for the right of replacement, which the corporation supplies anyone who owns a robot for more than twenty-five years. In fact, the corporation insists on such replacement."

Paul was smiling and thoroughly at his ease. He went on, "The positronic brain of my client is the owner of the body of my client — which is certainly more than twenty-five years old. The positronic brain demands the replacement of the body and offers to pay any reasonable fee for an android body as that replacement. If you refuse the request, my client undergoes humiliation and we will sue.

"While public opinion would not ordinarily support the claim of a robot in such a case, may I remind you that U. S. Robots is not popular with the public generally. Even those who most use and profit from robots are suspicious of the corporation. This may be a hangover from the days when robots were widely feared. It may be resentment against the power and wealth of U. S. Robots, which has a worldwide monopoly. Whatever the cause may be, the resentment exists and I think you will find that you would prefer not to withstand a lawsuit, particularly since my client is wealthy and will live for many more centuries and will have no reason to refrain from fighting the battle forever."

Smythe-Robertson had slowly reddened. "You are trying to force me to —"

"I force you to do nothing," said Paul. "If you wish to refuse to accede to my client's reasonable request, you may by all means do so and we will leave without another word . . . But we will sue, as is certainly our right, and you will find that you will eventually lose."

Smythe-Robertson said, "Well —" and paused.

"I see that you are going to accede," said Paul. "You may hesitate but you will come to it in the end. Let me assure you, then, of one further point. If, in the process of transferring my client's positronic brain from his present body to an organic one, there is any damage, however slight, then I will never rest till I've nailed the corporation to the ground. I will, if necessary, take every possible step to mobilize public opinion against the corporation if one brain path of my client's platinum-iridium essence is scrambled." He turned to Andrew and said, "Do you agree to all this, Andrew?"

Andrew hesitated a full minute. It amounted to the approval of lying, of blackmail, of the badgering and humiliation of a human being. But not physical harm, he told himself, not physical harm.

He managed at last to come out with a rather faint "Yes."

It was like being constructed again. For days, then for weeks, finally for months, Andrew found himself not himself somehow, and the simplest actions kept giving rise to hesitation.

Paul was frantic. "They've damaged you, Andrew. We'll have to institute suit."

Andrew spoke very slowly. "You mustn't. You'll never be able to prove — something — m-m-m-m —"

"Malice?"

"Malice. Besides, I grow stronger, better. It's the tr-tr-tr —"

"Tremble?"

"Trauma. After all, there's never been such an op-op-operation before."

Andrew could feel his brain from the inside. No one else could. He knew he was well, and during the months that it took him to learn full coordination and full positronic interplay, he spent hours before the mirror.

Not quite human! The face was stiff — too stiff — and the motions were too deliberate. They lacked the careless free flow of the human being, but perhaps that might come with time. At least he could wear clothes without the ridiculous anomaly of a metal face going along with it.

Eventually he said, "I will be going back to work."

Paul laughed and said, "That means you are well. What will you be doing? Another book?"

"No," said Andrew seriously. "I live too long for any one career to seize me by the throat and never let me go. There was a time when I was primarily an artist and I can still turn to that. And there was a time when I was a historian and I can still turn to that. But now I wish to be a robobiologist."

"A robopsychologist, you mean."

"No. That would imply the study of positronic brains and at the moment I lack the desire to do that. A robobiologist, it seems to me, would be concerned with the working of the body attached to that brain."

"Wouldn't that be a roboticist?"

"A roboticist works with a metal body. I would be studying an organic humanoid body, of which I have the only one, as far as I know."

"You narrow your field," said Paul thoughtfully. "As an artist, all conception was yours; as a historian, you dealt chiefly with robots; as a robobiologist, you will deal with yourself."

Andrew nodded. "It would seem so."

Andrew had to start from the very beginning, for he knew nothing of ordinary biology, almost nothing of science. He became a familiar sight in the libraries, where he sat at the electronic indices for hours at a time, looking perfectly normal in clothes. Those few who knew he was a robot in no way interfered with him.

He built a laboratory in a room he had added to his house, and his library grew, too.

Years passed, and Paul came to him one day and said, "It's a pity you're no longer working on the history of robots. I understand U. S. Robots is adopting a radically new policy."

Paul had aged, and his deteriorating eyes had been replaced with photoptic cells. In that respect, he had drawn closer to Andrew. Andrew said, "What have they done?"

"They are manufacturing central computers, gigantic positronic brains, really, which communicate with anywhere from a dozen to a thousand robots by microwave. The robots themselves have no brains at all. They are the limbs of the gigantic brain, and the two are physically separate.

"Is that more efficient?"

"U. S. Robots claims it is. Smythe-Robertson established the new direction before he died, however, and it's my notion that it's a backlash at you. U. S. Robots is determined that they will make no robots that will give them the type of trouble you have, and for that reason they separate brain and body. The brain will have no body to wish changed; the body will have no brain to wish anything.

"It's amazing, Andrew," Paul went on, "the influence you have had on the history of robots. It was your artistry that encouraged U. S. Robots to make robots more precise and specialized; it was your freedom that resulted in the establishment of the principle of robotic rights; it was your insistence on an android body that made U. S. Robots switch to brain-body separation."

Andrew said, "I suppose in the end the corporation will produce one vast brain controlling several billion robotic bodies. All the eggs will be in one basket. Dangerous. Not proper at all."

"I think you're right," said Paul, "but I don't suspect it will come to pass for a century at least, and I won't live to see it. In fact, I may not live to see next year."

"Paul!" said Andrew in concern.

Paul shrugged. "We're mortal, Andrew. We're not like you. It doesn't matter too much, but it does make it important to assure you on one point. I'm the last of the human Martins. There are collaterals descended from my great-aunt, but they don't count. The money I control personally will be left to the trust in your name, and, as far as anyone can foresee the future, you will be economically secure."

"Unnecessary," said Andrew with difficulty. In all this time, he could not get used to the deaths of the Martins.

Paul said, "Let's not argue. That's the way it's going to be. What are you working on?"

"I am designing a system for allowing androids — myself — to gain energy from the combustion of hydrocarbons, rather than from atomic cells."

Paul raised his eyebrows. "So that they will breathe and eat?"

"Yes."

"How long have you been pushing in that direction?"

"For a long time now, but I think I have designed an adequate combustion chamber for catalyzed controlled breakdown."

"But why, Andrew? The atomic cell is surely infinitely better."

"In some ways, perhaps, but the atomic cell is inhuman."

It took time, but Andrew had time. In the first place, he did not wish to do anything till Paul had died in peace.

With the death of the great-grandson of Sir, Andrew felt more nearly exposed to a hostile world, and for that reason was the more determined to continue the path he had long ago chosen.

Yet he was not really alone. If a man had died, the firm of Feingold and Martin lived, for a corporation does not die any more than a robot does. The firm had its directions and it followed them soullessly. By way of the trust and through the law firm, Andrew continued to be wealthy. And in return for their own large annual retainer, Feingold and Martin involved themselves in the legal aspects of the new combustion chamber.

When the time came for Andrew to visit U. S. Robots and Mechanical Men, Inc., he did it alone. Once he had gone with Sir and once with Paul. This time, the third time, he was alone and manlike.

U. S. Robots had changed. The production plant had been shifted to a large space station, as was the case with more and more industries. With them had gone many robots. The Earth itself was becoming parklike, with its one-billion-person population stabilized and perhaps not more than 30 percent of its at least equally large robot population independently brained.

The director of research was Alvin Magdescu, dark of complexion and hair, with a little pointed beard and wearing nothing above the waist but the breastband that fashion dictated. Andrew himself was well covered in the older fashion of several decades back.

Magdescu said, "I know you, of course, and I'm rather pleased to see you. You're our most notorious product, and it's a pity old Smythe-Robertson was so set against you. We could have done a great deal with you."

"You still can," said Andrew.

"No, I don't think so. We're past the time. We've had robots on Earth for over a century, but that's changing. It will be back to space with them and those that stay here won't be brained."

"But there remains myself, and I stay on Earth."

"True, but there doesn't seem to be much of the robot about you. What new request have you?"

"To be still less a robot. Since I am so far organic, I wish an organic source of energy. I have here the plans —"

Magdescu did not hasten through them. He might have intended to at first, but he stiffened and grew intent. At one point he said, "This is remarkably ingenious. Who thought of all this?"

"I did," said Andrew.

Magdescu looked up at him sharply, then said, "It would amount to a major overhaul of your body, and an experimental one, since it has never been attempted before. I advise against it. Remain as you are."

Andrew's face had limited means of expression, but impatience showed plainly in his voice. "Dr. Magdescu, you miss the entire point. You have no choice but to accede to my request. If such devices can be built into my body, they can be built into human bodies as well. The tendency to lengthen human life by prosthetic devices has already been remarked on. There are no devices better than the ones I have designed and am designing.

"As it happens, I control the patents by way of the firm of Feingold and Martin. We are quite capable of going into business for ourselves and developing the kind of prosthetic devices that may end by producing human beings with many of the properties of robots. Your own business will then suffer.

"If, however, you operate on me now and agree to do so under similar circumstances in the future, you will receive permission to make use of the patents and control the technology of both robots and the prosthetization of human beings. The initial leasing will not be granted, of course, until after the first operation is completed successfully, and after enough time has passed to demonstrate that it is indeed successful." Andrew felt scarcely any First Law inhibition to the stern conditions he was setting a human being. He was learning to reason that what seemed like cruelty might, in the long run, be kindness.

Magdescu looked stunned. He said, "I'm not the one to decide something like this. That's a corporate decision that would take time."

"I can wait a reasonable time," said Andrew, "but only a reasonable time." And he thought with satisfaction that Paul himself could not have done it better.

It took only a reasonable time, and the operation was a success.

Magdescu said, "I was very much against the operation, Andrew, but not for the reasons you might think. I was not in the least against the experiment, if it had been on someone else. I hated risking *your* positronic brain. Now that you have the positronic pathways interacting with simulated nerve pathways, it might be difficult to rescue the brain intact if the body went bad."

"I had every faith in the skill of the staff at U. S. Robots," said Andrew. "And I can eat now."

"Well, you can sip olive oil. It will mean occasional cleanings of the combustion chamber, as we have explained to you. Rather an uncomfortable touch, I should think."

"Perhaps, if I did not expect to go further. Self-cleaning is not impossible. In fact, I am working on a device that will deal with solid food that may be expected to contain incombustible fractions — indigestible matter, so to speak, that will have to be discarded."

"You would then have to develop an anus."

"The equivalent."

"What else, Andrew?"

"Everything else." -

"Genitalia, too?"

"Insofar as they will fit my plans. My body is a canvas on which I intend to draw —"

Magdescu waited for the sentence to be completed, and when it seemed that it would not be, he completed it himself. "A man?"

"We shall see," said Andrew.

Magdescu said, "It's a puny ambition, Andrew. You're better than a man. You've gone downhill from the moment you opted for organicism."

"My brain has not suffered."

"No, it hasn't. I'll grant you that. But, Andrew, the whole new breakthrough in prosthetic devices made possible by your patents is being marketed under your name. You're recognized as the inventor and you're honored for it — as you are. Why play further games with your body?"

Andrew did not answer.

The honors came. He accepted membership in several learned societies, including one that was devoted to the new science he had established; the one he had called robobiology but which had come to be termed prosthetology.

On the one hundred fiftieth anniversary of his construction, there was a testimonial dinner given in his honor at U. S. Robots. If Andrew saw irony in this, he kept it to himself.

Alvin Magdescu came out of retirement to chair the dinner. He was himself ninety-four years old and was alive because he had prosthetized devices that, among other things, fulfilled the function of liver and kidneys. The dinner reached its climax when Magdescu, after a short and emotional talk, raised his glass to toast "the Sesquicentennial Robot."

Andrew had had the sinews of his face redesigned to the point where he could show a range of emotions, but he sat through all the ceremonies solemnly passive. He did not like to be a Sesquicentennial Robot.

It was prosthetology that finally took Andrew off the Earth. In the decades that followed the celebration of the Sesquicentennial, the Moon had come to be a world more Earthlike than Earth in every respect but its gravitational pull, and in its underground cities there was a fairly dense population.

Prosthetized devices there had to take the lesser gravity into account and Andrew spent five years on the Moon working with local prosthetologists to make the necessary adaptations. When not at his work, he wandered among the robot population, every one of which treated him with the robotic obsequiousness due a man.

He came back to an Earth that was humdrum and quiet by comparison and visited the offices of Feingold and Martin to announce his return.

The current head of the firm, Simon DeLong, was surprised. He said, "We had been told you were returning, Andrew" (he had almost said "Mr. Martin"), "but we were not expecting you till next week."

"I grew impatient," said Andrew brusquely. He was anxious to get to the point. "On the Moon, Simon, I was in charge of a research team of twenty human scientists. I gave orders that no one questioned. The Lunar robots deferred to me as they would to a human being. Why, then, am I not a human being?"

A wary look entered DeLong's eyes. He said, "My dear Andrew, as you have just explained, you are treated as a human being by both robots and human beings. You are therefore a human being *de facto*."

"To be a human being *de facto* is not enough. I want not only to be treated as one, but to be legally identified as one. I want to be a human being *de jure*."

"Now that is another matter," said DeLong. "There we would run into human prejudice and into the undoubted fact that however much you may be like a human being, you are *not* a human being."

"In what way not?" asked Andrew. "I have the shape of a human being and organs equivalent to those of a human being. My organs, in fact, are identical to some of those in a prosthetized human being. I have contributed artistically, literarily, and scientifically to human culture as much as any human being now alive. What more can one ask?"

"I myself would ask nothing more. The trouble is that it would take an act of the World Legislature to define you as a human being. Frankly, I wouldn't expect that to happen."

"To whom on the Legislature could I speak?"

"To the chairman of the Science and Technology Committee perhaps."

"Can you arrange a meeting?"

"But you scarcely need an intermediary. In your position, you can —"

"No. *You* arrange it." (It didn't even occur to Andrew that he was giving a flat order to a human being. He had grown accustomed to that on the Moon.) "I want him to know that the firm of Feingold and Martin is backing me in this to the hilt."

"Well, now —"

"To the hilt, Simon. In one hundred seventy-three years I have in one fashion or another contributed greatly to this firm. I have been under obligation to individual members of the firm in times past. I am not now. It is rather the other way around now and I am calling in my debts."

DeLong said, "I will do what I can."

The chairman of the Science and Technology Committee was of the East Asian region and she was a woman. Her name was Chee Li-Hsing and her transparent garments (obscuring what she wanted obscured only by their dazzle) made her look plastic-wrapped.

She said, "I sympathize with your wish for full human rights. There have been times in history when segments of the human population fought for full human rights. What rights, however, can you possibly want that you do not have?"

"As simple a thing as my right to life. A robot can be dismantled at any time."

"A human being can be executed at any time."

"Execution can only follow due process of law. There is no trial needed for my dismantling. Only the word of a human being in authority is needed to end me. Besides — besides —" Andrew tried desperately to allow no sign of pleading, but his carefully designed tricks of human expression and tone of voice betrayed him here. "The truth is, I want to be a man. I have wanted it through six generations of human beings."

Li-Hsing looked up at him out of darkly sympathetic eyes. "The Legislature can pass a law declaring you one — they could pass a law declaring a stone statue to be defined as a man. Whether they will actually do so is, however, as likely in the first case as the second. Congresspeople are as human as the rest of the population, and there is always that element of suspicion against robots."

"Even now?"

"Even now. We would all allow the fact that you have earned the prize of humanity, and yet there would remain the fear of setting an undesirable precedent."

"What precedent? I am the only free robot, the only one of my type, and there will never be another. You may consult U. S. Robots."

" 'Never' is a long time, Andrew — or, if you prefer, Mr. Martin — since I will gladly give you my personal accolade as man. You will find that most congresspeople will not be willing to set the precedent, no matter how meaningless such a precedent might be. Mr. Martin, you have my sympathy, but I cannot tell you to hope. Indeed —"

She sat back and her forehead wrinkled. "Indeed, if the issue grows too heated, there might well arise a certain sentiment, both inside the Legislature and outside, for the dismantling you mentioned. Doing away with you could turn out to be the easiest way of resolving the dilemma. Consider that before deciding to push matters."

Andrew said, "Will no one remember the technique of prosthet-ology, something that is almost entirely mine?"

"It may seem cruel, but they won't. Or if they do, it will be remembered against you. It will be said you did it only for your-self. It will be said it was part of a campaign to roboticize human beings, or to humanify robots; and in either case evil and vicious. You have never been part of a political hate campaign, Mr. Martin, and I tell you that you will be the object of vilification of a kind neither you nor I would credit, and there would be people who'll believe it all. Mr. Martin, let your life be." She rose and, next to Andrew's seated figure, she seemed small and almost child-like.

Andrew said, "If I decide to fight for my humanity, will you be on my side?"

She thought, then said, "I will be — insofar as I can be. If at any time such a stand would appear to threaten my political fu-ture, I may have to abandon you, since it is not an issue I feel to be at the very root of my beliefs. I am trying to be honest with you."

"Thank you, and I will ask no more. I intend to fight this through whatever the consequences, and I will ask you for your help only for as long as you can give it."

It was not a direct fight. Feingold and Martin counseled pa-tience and Andrew muttered grimly that he had an endless supply of that. Feingold and Martin then entered on a campaign to narrow and restrict the area of combat.

They instituted a lawsuit denying the obligation to pay debts to an individual with a prosthetic heart on the grounds that the possession of a robotic organ removed humanity, and with it the constitutional rights of human beings.

They fought the matter skillfully and tenaciously, losing at every step but always in such a way that the decision was forced to be as broad as possible, and then carrying it by way of appeals to the World Court.

It took years, and millions of dollars.

When the final decision was handed down, DeLong held what amounted to a victory celebration over the legal loss. Andrew was, of course, present in the company offices on the occasion.

"We've done two things, Andrew," said DeLong, "both of which are good. First of all, we have established the fact that no number of artifacts in the human body causes it to cease being a human body. Secondly, we have engaged public opinion in the question in such a way as to put it fiercely on the side of a broad interpretation of humanity since there is not a human being in existence who does not hope for prosthetics if that will keep him alive."

"And do you think the Legislature will now grant me my humanity?" asked Andrew.

DeLong looked faintly uncomfortable. "As to that, I cannot be optimistic. There remains the one organ that the World Court has used as the criterion of humanity. Human beings have an organic cellular brain and robots have a platinum-iridium positronic brain if they have one at all — and you certainly have a positronic brain . . . No, Andrew, don't get that look in your eye. We lack the knowledge to duplicate the work of a cellular brain in artificial structures close enough to the organic type to allow it to fall within the Court's decision. Not even you could do it."

"What should we do, then?"

"Make the attempt, of course. Congresswoman Li-Hsing will be on our side and a growing number of other congresspeople. The President will undoubtedly go along with a majority of the Legislature in this matter."

"Do we have a majority?"

"No, far from it. But we might get one if the public will allow its desire for a broad interpretation of humanity to extend to you. A small chance, I admit, but if you do not wish to give up, we must gamble for it."

"I do not wish to give up."

Congresswoman Li-Hsing was considerably older than she had been when Andrew had first met her. Her transparent garments were long gone. Her hair was now close-cropped and her coverings were tubular. Yet still Andrew clung, as closely as he could within the limits of reasonable taste, to the style of clothing that had prevailed when he had first adopted clothing over a century before.

She said, "We've gone as far as we can, Andrew. We'll try once more after recess, but, to be honest, defeat is certain and the whole thing will have to be given up. All my most recent efforts have only earned me a certain defeat in the coming congressional campaign."

"I know," said Andrew, "and it distresses me. You said once you would abandon me if it came to that. Why have you not done so?"

"One can change one's mind, you know. Somehow, abandoning you became a higher price than I cared to pay for just one more term. As it is, I've been in the Legislature for over a quarter of a century. It's enough."

"Is there no way we can change minds, Chee?"

"We've changed all that are amenable to reason. The rest — the majority — cannot be moved from their emotional antipathies."

"Emotional antipathy is not a valid reason for voting one way or the other."

"I know that, Andrew, but they don't advance emotional antipathy as their reason."

Andrew said cautiously, "It all comes down to the brain, then, but must we leave it at the level of cells versus positrons? Is there no way of forcing a functional definition? Must we say that a brain is made of this or that? May we not say that a brain is something — anything — capable of a certain level of thought?"

"Won't work," said Li-Hsing. "Your brain is manmade, the human brain is not. Your brain is constructed, theirs developed. To any human being who is intent on keeping up the barrier between himself and a robot, those differences are a steel wall a mile high and a mile thick."

"If we could get at the source of their antipathy — the very source of —"

"After all your years," said Li-Hsing sadly, "you are still trying to reason out the human being. Poor Andrew, don't be angry, but it's the robot in you that drives you in that direction."

"I don't know," said Andrew. "If I could bring myself —"

If he could bring himself —

He had known for a long time it might come to that, and in

the end he was at the surgeon's. He found one, skillful enough
for the job at hand, which meant a robot surgeon, for no human
surgeon could be trusted in this connection, either in ability or in
intention.

The surgeon could not have performed the operation on a human being, so Andrew, after putting off the moment of decision
with a sad line of questioning that reflected the turmoil within
himself, put the First Law to one side by saying, "I, too, am a
robot."

He then said, as firmly as he had learned to form the words
even at human beings over these past decades, "I *order* you to
carry through the operation on me."

In the absence of the First Law, an order so firmly given from
one who looked so much like a man activated the Second Law
sufficiently to carry the day.

Andrew's feeling of weakness was, he was sure, quite imaginary.
He had recovered from the operation. Nevertheless, he leaned, as
unobtrusively as he could manage, against the wall. It would be
entirely too revealing to sit.

Li-Hsing said, "The final vote will come this week, Andrew. I've
been able to delay it no longer, and we must lose . . . And that
will be it, Andrew."

Andrew said, "I am grateful for your skill at delay. It gave me
the time I needed, and I took the gamble I had to."

"What gamble is this?" asked Li-Hsing with open concern.

"I couldn't tell you, or the people at Feingold and Martin. I
was sure I would be stopped. See here, if it is the brain that is at
issue, isn't the greatest difference of all the matter of immortality?
Who really cares what a brain looks like or is built of or how it
was formed? What matters is that brain cells die; *must* die. Even
if every other organ in the body is maintained or replaced, the
brain cells, which cannot be replaced without changing and therefore killing the personality, must eventually die.

"My own positronic pathways have lasted nearly two centuries
without perceptible change and can last for centuries more. Isn't
that the fundamental barrier? Human beings can tolerate an immortal robot, for it doesn't matter how long a machine lasts. They

cannot tolerate an immortal human being, since their own mortality is endurable only so long as it is universal. And for that reason they won't make me a human being."

Li-Hsing said, "What is it you're leading up to, Andrew?"

"I have removed that problem. Decades ago, my positronic brain was connected to organic nerves. Now, one last operation has arranged that connection in such a way that slowly — quite slowly — the potential is being drained from my pathways."

Li-Hsing's finely wrinkled face showed no expression for a moment. Then her lips tightened. "Do you mean you've arranged to die, Andrew? You can't have. That violates the Third Law."

"No," said Andrew, "I have chosen between the death of my body and the death of my aspirations and desires. To have let my body live at the cost of the greater death is what would have violated the Third Law."

Li-Hsing seized his arm as though she were about to shake him. She stopped herself. "Andrew, it won't work. Change it back."

"It can't be. Too much damage was done. I have a year to live — more or less. I will last through the two hundredth anniversary of my construction. I was weak enough to arrange that."

"How can it be worth it? Andrew, you're a fool."

"If it brings me humanity, that will be worth it. If it doesn't, it will bring an end to striving, and that will be worth it, too."

And Li-Hsing did something that astonished herself. Quietly, she began to weep.

It was odd how that last deed caught at the imagination of the world. All that Andrew had done before had not swayed them. But he had finally accepted even death in order to be human, and the sacrifice was too great to be rejected.

The final ceremony was timed, quite deliberately, for the two hundredth anniversary. The World President was to sign the act and make it law, and the ceremony would be visible on a global network and would be beamed to the Lunar state and even to the Martian colony.

Andrew was in a wheelchair. He could still walk, but only shakily.

With mankind watching, the World President said, "Fifty years ago, you were declared a Sesquicentennial Robot, Andrew." After a pause, and in a more solemn tone, he said, "Today we declare you a Bicentennial Man, Mr. Martin."

And Andrew, smiling, held out his hand to shake that of the President.

Andrew's thoughts were slowly fading as he lay in bed.

Desperately he seized at them. Man! He was a man! He wanted that to be his last thought. He wanted to dissolve — die — with that.

He opened his eyes one more time and for one last time recognized Li-Hsing waiting solemnly. There were others, but those were only shadows, unrecognizable shadows. Only Li-Hsing stood out against the deepening gray. Slowly, inchingly, he held out his hand to her and very dimly and faintly felt her take it.

She was fading in his eyes, as the last of his thoughts trickled away.

But before she faded completely, one last fugitive thought came to him and rested for a moment on his mind before everything stopped.

"Little Miss," he whispered, too low to be heard.

PART 3

MATHEMATICS

IT TAKES A LOT of ingenuity for me to write about mathematics, since I know so little about it.

Why bother to write about it, then? Because I love it, that's why. What I must do (and here is where the ingenuity comes in) is find some portion of mathematics so incredibly simple that I can understand it. Once I've done that, all I have to do is write about it in such a way (more ingenuity) that no one detects my essential ignorance.

For children, I wrote How Did We Find Out About Numbers? *(Book 142), and in it I presented a section on Roman numerals, which I had learned how to use when I was seven or eight and which, fortunately, I had never forgotten. Here it is:*

from HOW DID WE FIND OUT ABOUT NUMBERS? (*1973*)

About two thousand years ago, large sections of Europe, Asia, and Africa were ruled from the city of Rome. The Roman Empire, as it was called, used a system of numerals based on five.

The Romans used symbols taken from their alphabet. Fortunately, the people of Europe and America use the Roman alphabet so the Roman symbols are familiar to us.

The Romans began by letting the number one be written as I. For two, three, and four they had II, III, and IIII. So far it looks like the Egyptian system, but the Romans only allowed four of any symbol to be used before inventing a new symbol. Instead of writing five as the Egyptian IIIII they wrote it as V.

Instead of writing six as IIIIII they wrote it VI. Nine was VIIII. If they wrote ten as VIIIII, that would mean five of the symbol I and they didn't allow that. They used a new symbol for ten, which was X.

The list of symbols up to one thousand is as follows:

I = one
V = five
X = ten
L = fifty
C = one hundred
D = five hundred
M = one thousand

By using special symbols for five, fifty, and five hundred, the Romans never had to use more than four of any of the symbols for one, ten, or one hundred.

To write twenty-two they wrote XXII. Seventy-three is LXXIII. Four hundred eighteen is CCCCXVIII. One thousand nine hundred ninety-nine is MDCCCCLXXXXVIIII.

If you try to write one thousand nine hundred ninety-nine by the Egyptian system, you would need one symbol for thousand, and nine symbols each for hundred, ten, and one. That would mean twenty-eight symbols all together. In Roman numerals only sixteen symbols are needed.

The Egyptian system uses only four different kinds of symbols, while the Roman system uses seven. In the Roman system you need less counting but more memorizing.

When these Roman numerals were first developed, it didn't matter in what order the symbols were placed. Whether you wrote XVI or XIV or IXV or VIX, it all came to sixteen. No matter in what order you add ten, five, and one, you end up with sixteen.

Of course, it is easier to add up a number if you arrange the symbols according to some convenient system. The usual way is to put all the symbols of the same sort together. The largest symbol is on the left and as you move to the right you write down smaller and smaller symbols. Thus seventy-eight would always be written LXXVIII, working down from L to X to V to I.

The later Romans thought of a way of still further decreasing the number of a particular symbol that had to be written down. As long as symbols were always written from left to right and from large to small, why not sometimes reverse the order?

When you put the smaller symbol after the larger one in the usual way you add the two. Therefore, VI is "five plus one," or six. If on the other hand you put the smaller symbol *before* the larger one, you *subtract* it from the larger. In this way IV is "five minus one," or four.

By writing four as IV instead of IIII you have to write and read only two symbols instead of four, but you have to notice the positions and remember to subtract instead of add.

In the same way, XL is forty while LX is sixty and XC is ninety while CX is one hundred ten and CM is nine hundred while MC is one thousand one hundred.

The year nineteen seventy-three can be written MCMLXXIII instead of MDCCCCLXXIII — eight symbols instead of twelve. One thousand nine hundred ninety-nine can be written MCMXCIX instead of MDCCCCLXXXXVIIII — seven symbols instead of sixteen.

Of course, once you start using the subtracting notion, you can't scramble the order of the symbols anymore. It becomes important to place each symbol exactly.

The western part of the Roman Empire broke up just about one thousand five hundred years ago. The people of western Europe kept on using Roman numerals for more than seven hundred years after the Roman Empire had come to an end.

If Roman numerals are easy to grasp and explain, Arabic numerals are even easier, especially since everyone in our culture over the age of six already knows about them (or is supposed to). That means I can understand them, too, and need only find some aspect of them that isn't entirely familiar.

Suppose we let the Arabic numerals represent larger and larger numbers. How can we represent such very large numbers and where do we stop?

To answer questions like that, I have my F & SF essays. My first F & SF essay appeared in the November 1958 issue, and since then I have continued them at monthly intervals, without missing an issue, for twenty years. Six collections of F & SF essays are included among my first hundred books, but I did not stop there.

Among my second hundred books are seven more collections (plus four additional collections that included older F & SF essays, rearranged and updated, from my first hundred books).

One of these new collections, Of Matters Great and Small *(Book 159), which Doubleday published in 1975, contains the following essay on very much larger numbers:*

"Skewered!" (1974)

I don't write many mathematical articles in this series, and for a very good reason. I don't have a mathematical mind and I am not one of those who, by mere thought, finds himself illuminated by a mathematical concept.

I have, however, a nephew, Daniel Asimov by name, who *does* have a mathematical mind. He is the other Ph.D. in the family and he is now an Assistant Professor of Mathematics at the University of Minnesota.

Some years ago, when he was yet a student at M.I.T., Danny had occasion to write to Martin Gardner and point out a small error in Gardner's excellent "Mathematical Recreations" column in *Scientific American.* Gardner acknowledged the error and wrote me to tell me about it and to ask a natural question. "Am I correct in assuming," said he, "that Daniel Asimov is your son?"

Well! As everyone who knows me knows, I am only a little past thirty right now and was only a little past thirty at the time, some years ago, when this was taking place. I therefore wrote a letter to Gardner and told him, with some stiffness: "I am not old enough, Martin, to have a son who is old enough to be going to M.I.T. Danny is the son of my younger brother."

Friends of mine who have heard me tell this story keep assuring me that my statement involves a logical contradiction, but, as I say, I do not have a mathematical mind, and I just don't see that.

And yet I must write another mathematical article now because over eleven years ago I wrote one in which I mentioned Skewes' number as the largest finite number that ever showed up in a mathematical proof.* Ever since then, people have been asking

* See "T-Formation," reprinted in *Adding a Dimension* (New York: Doubleday, 1964).

me to write an article on Skewes' number. The first request came on September 3, 1963, almost immediately after the article appeared. On that date, Mr. R. P. Boas of Evanston, Illinois, wrote me a long and fascinating letter on Skewes' number, with the clear intention of helping me write such an article.

I resisted that, along with repeated nudges from others in the years that followed, until March 3, 1974, when, at Boskone 11 (a Boston science fiction convention at which I was guest of honor), I was cornered by a fan and had Skewes' number requested of me. So I gave in. Eleven years of chivvying is enough.* I am Skewered.

First, what is Skewes' number? Not the numerical expression, but the significance. Here's the story as I got it from Mr. Boas (though I will paraphrase it, and if I get anything wrong, it's my fault, not his).

It involves prime numbers, which are those numbers that cannot be divided evenly by any number other than themselves and one. The numbers 7 and 13 are examples.

There are an infinite number of prime numbers, but as one goes up the list of numbers, the fraction of these numbers that are prime decreases. There is a formula that tells you the number of primes to be found in the list of numbers up to a given number, but like everything else about prime numbers, the formula is not neat and definite. It only tells you approximately how many primes there will be up to some limiting number.

Up to the highest limit that has actually been tested, it turns out that the actual number of primes that exist is somewhat *less* than is predicted by the formula.

In 1914, however, the British mathematician John Edensor Littlewood demonstrated that if one lengthened the string of numbers one investigated for primes, one would find that up to some limits there would indeed be less than the formula predicted, but that up to other limits there would be more than the formula predicted.

---

* I'll admit that I've been chivvied longer than that in some respects. For seventeen years I have been requested, with varying degrees of impatience, to write another Lije Baley novel; and for over twenty years to write another *Foundation* novel. So please don't anybody write letters that begin with "If eleven years of chivvying is enough, why don't you ———." Because I'm doing all I can, that's why.

In fact, if one continued up the line of numbers forever, the actual total number of primes would switch from less than the formula prediction to more than the formula prediction to less than the formula prediction, and so on — and make the switch an infinite number of times. If that were *not* so, Littlewood demonstrated, there would be a contradiction in the mathematical structure and that, of course, cannot be allowed.

The only trouble is that as far as we have actually gone in the list of numbers, not even one shift has taken place. The number of primes is always less than the formula would indicate. Of course, mathematicians might just go higher and higher up the list of numbers to see what happens, but that isn't so easy. The higher one goes, the longer it takes to test numbers for primehood.

However, it might be possible to do some theoretical work and determine some number below which the first switch from less than the prediction to more than the prediction *must* take place. That will at least set a limit to the work required.

Littlewood set S. Skewes (pronounced in two syllables, by the way, Skew'ease) the task of finding that number. Skewes found that number and it proved to be enormously large; larger than any other number that ever turned up in the course of a mathematical proof up to that time, and it is this number that is popularly known as "Skewes' number."

Mind you, the proof does not indicate that one must reach Skewes' number before the number of primes shifts from less than the prediction to more. The proof merely says that some time *before* that number is reached — perhaps long long before — the shift must have occurred.

A number as large as Skewes' number is difficult to write. Some shorthand device must be used and the device used is the excellent one of exponential notation.

Thus, 1000 = 10 × 10 × 10, so 1000 can be written as 10^3 (ten to the third power), where the little 3 is called an "exponent." The little 3 signifies that 1000 can be considered the product of three 10s, or that it can be written as 1 followed by three zeros. In general, 10^x (ten to the xth power) is the product of x 10s and can be written as a 1 followed by x zeros.

Since 10,000,000,000 is written as a 1 followed by 10 zeros, it can be written exponentially as 10^{10} (ten to the tenth power). In the same way, a 1 followed by ten billion zeros, something that would be impractical to write, can be expressed exponentially as $10^{10,000,000,000}$ (ten to the ten billionth power). But since ten billion is itself 10^{10}, $10^{10,000,000,000}$ can be written, even more briefly, as $10^{10^{10}}$.

Writing exponentials is always a strain when an article is being written for a nonspecialized outlet. This is especially so when one is forced to place exponents on exponents. To avoid driving the Noble Printer crazy and to make the notation look prettier, I have invented a notation of my own. I make the exponent a figure of normal size and it is as though it is being held up by a lever, and its added weight when its size grows bends the lever down. Thus, instead of writing ten to the third power as 10^3, I will write it as 10\3.

In the same way, ten to the ten billionth power can be written as 10\10,000,000,000, or as 10\10\10.

Using this "Asimovian exponential notation," Skewes' number becomes 10\10\10\34.

Now let's see what Skewes' number might be in ordinary non-exponential notation. To do that, we must consider the components of the exponential notation from right to left. Starting at the right, we know what 34 is, we move leftward and consider 10\34. This is ten to the thirty-fourth power and can be written as a 1 followed by 34 zeros thus: 10,000,000,000,000,000,000,000,-000,000,000,000, or, in words, ten decillion (American style). This means that Skewes' number can be written ten 10\10\10,000,000,000,000,000,000,000,000,000,000.

So far, so good, if a bit disconcertingly formidable. The next step is to move one place to the left and ask how we might write: 10\10,000,000,000,000,000,000,000,000,000,000,000. Easy. You just put down a 1 and then follow it by ten million billion billion billion (or ten decillion, if you prefer) zeros.

If you were to try to write such a number by beginning with a 1 and then writing ten decillion zeros, each the size of a hydrogen atom, you would require nearly exactly the entire surface of the Earth to write the number. Furthermore, if you wrote each zero in a trillionth of a second and kept it up at that rate without cessation, it would take a thousand trillion years to write the entire number.

Anyway, let's call this number the "Earth-number," because it takes the Earth as a blackboard to write it, and imagine that we can write it. Now we can write Skewes' number as 10\Earth-number, and this means we now know how to write Skewes' number in the usual fashion. We start with a one and then follow it with an Earth-number of zeros.

This is tremendously more than the ten decillion zeros it took merely to write the Earth-number. A number itself is much greater than the number of zeros it takes to write it. It takes only one zero to write 10, but the result is a number that is ten times greater than the number of zeros required to write it. In the same way it takes ten zeros to write 10,000,000,000, but the number written is ten billion, which is a billion times greater in size than the number of zeros used to write it.

Similarly it takes only ten decillion zeros to write the Earth-number, but the Earth-number itself is enormously greater than that number of zeros.

To write not ten decillion zeros, but an Earth-number of zeros, would require far more than the surfaces of all the objects in the known universe, even with each zero the size of a hydrogen atom. A trillion such universes as ours might suffice, and that is just to *write* the Earth-number in a one followed by zeros. Skewes' number itself, written by a one followed by an Earth-number of zeros, is *enormously*, ENORMOUSLY greater than the Earth-number that suffices to count those zeros.

So let's forget about counting zeros; that will get us nowhere. And if we abandon counting zeros, we don't need to have our exponents as integers. Every number can be expressed as a power of ten if we allow decimal exponents. For instance, by using a logarithm table, we can see that 34 = 10\1.53. So instead of writing Skewes' number as 10\10\10\34, we can write it as 10\10\10\10\1.53. (Such fractional exponents are almost always only approximate, however.)

There are some advantages to stretching out the large numbers into as many tens as is required to make the rightmost number fall below ten. Then we can speak of a "single-ten number," a "double-ten number," a "triple-ten number," and so on. Skewes' number is a "quadruple-ten number."

We can't count objects and reach Skewes' number in any visualizable way. Counting zeros is no help either. Let us instead try to count permutations and combinations.

Let me give you an example. In the ordinary deck of cards used to play bridge, there are fifty-two different cards. (The number 52 is itself a single-ten number, as are all the numbers between 10 and 10,000,000,000; $52 = 10 \backslash 1.716$.)

In the game of bridge, each of four people is dealt thirteen cards. A player can, with equal probability, get any combination of thirteen cards, and the order in which he gets them doesn't matter. He rearranges that order to suit himself. The total number of different hands he can get by receiving any thirteen cards out of the fifty-two (and I won't bother you with how it is calculated) is about 635,000,000,000. Since this number is higher than ten billion, we can be sure it is beyond the single-ten-number stage. Exponentially, it can be expressed as $6.35 \times 10 \backslash 11$. Logarithms can help us remove that multiplier and put its value into the exponent at the cost of making that exponent a decimal. Thus $6.35 \times 10 \backslash 11 = 10 \backslash 11.80$. Since 11.80 is over ten, we can express that, exponentially, as $11.80 = 10 \backslash 1.07$.

Consequently, we can say that the total number of different hands a single bridge player can hold is $10 \backslash 10 \backslash 1.07$. Using only thirteen cards, we have, in a perfectly understandable way, reached a double-ten number. We might almost feel that we were halfway to the quadruple-ten number that is Skewes'.

So let's take all fifty-two cards and let's arrange to have the order count as well as the nature of the cards. You begin with a deck in which the cards are in a certain order. You shuffle it and end with a different order. You shuffle it again and end with yet another order. How many different orders are there? Remember that any difference in order, however small, makes a different order. If two orders are identical except for the interchange of two adjacent cards, they are two different orders.

To answer that question, we figure that the first card can be any of the fifty-two, the second any of the remaining fifty-one, the third any of the remaining fifty, and so on. The total number of different orders is $52 \times 51 \times 50 \times \ldots 4 \times 3 \times 2 \times 1$. In other words, the number of different orders is equal to the product of the first fifty-two numbers. This is called "factorial fifty-two" and can be written "52!"

The value of 52! is, roughly, a one followed by sixty-eight zeros; in other words, a hundred decillion decillion. (You are welcome to work out the multiplication if you doubt this, but if you try, please be prepared for a long haul.) This is an absolutely terrific number to get out of one ordinary deck of cards that most of us use constantly without any feeling of being overwhelmed. The number of different orders into which that ordinary deck can be placed is about ten times as great as all the subatomic particles in our entire Milky Way galaxy.

It would certainly seem that if making use of thirteen cards with order indifferent lifted us high up, making use of all fifty-two and letting order count will do much better still — until we try our exponential notation. The number of orders into which fifty-two different cards can be placed is $10\backslash 68 = 10\backslash 10\backslash 1.83$.

That may strike you as strange. The number of orders of fifty-two cards is something like a trillion trillion decillion times higher than the number of bridge hands of thirteen cards; yet, while the latter is $10\backslash 10\backslash 1.07$, the former is only $10\backslash 10\backslash 1.83$. We're still in the "double-ten numbers" and we haven't even moved up much.

The trouble is that the more tens we add to such exponential numbers, the harder it is to move that rightmost component. For instance, a trillion is ten times as great as a hundred billion, and counting a trillion objects would be an enormously greater task than counting a hundred billion. Write them exponentially, however, and it is $10\backslash 12$ as compared with $10\backslash 11$, and the rightmost components are only a unit apart. Write the twelve and the eleven as powers of ten so that you can make use of double-ten numbers, and a trillion becomes $10\backslash 10\backslash 1.08$, while a hundred billion is $10\backslash 10\backslash 1.04$ and the difference is scarcely noticeable.

Or put it another way. The number $10\backslash 3$ (which is 1000) is ten times as high as $10\backslash 2$ (which is 100), but the degree to which $10\backslash 10\backslash 3$ is greater than $10\backslash 10\backslash 2$ would require a 1 followed by 900 zeros to be expressed. As for comparing $10\backslash 10\backslash 10\backslash 3$ and $10\backslash 10\backslash 10\backslash 2$, I leave that to you.

This is disheartening. Perhaps reaching the quadruple-ten numbers won't be that easy after all.

Let's try one more trick with fifty-two cards. Suppose each

of the cards can be any card at all. Suppose the deck can have two tens of diamonds or three aces of clubs, or, for that matter, fifty-two threes of hearts. The total number of orders of such a chameleonic deck could be calculated by imagining that the first card could be any one of fifty-two, and the second card could be any one of fifty-two, and so on for all fifty-two. To calculate the number of different orders, you would have to take the product of $52 \times 52 \times 52 \times \ldots 52 \times 52 \times 52$; fifty-two 52s. This product which could be written $52 \backslash 52$ I might call "superfactorial fifty-two," but if so, I would be using a term I have just made up, so don't blame the mathematicians.

Superfactorials are immensely larger than factorials. Factorial fifty-two can be expressed by a one followed by sixty-eight zeros; but superfactorial fifty-two is a one followed by ninety zeros — ten billion trillion times higher. Yet express it exponentially and superfactorial $52 = 10 \backslash 90 = 10 \backslash 10 \backslash 1.95$.

No good. We're still in the double-ten numbers.

We'll just have to forget playing cards. We must have more than fifty-two units to play with, and we had better go all the way up; *all* the way up.

A generation or so ago, the British astronomer Arthur S. Eddington calculated that the total number of electrons, protons, and neutrons in the universe was $10 \backslash 79$, or $10 \backslash 10 \backslash 1.90$. This number is arrived at if we suppose that the sun is an average star, that there are about a hundred billion stars in the average galaxy, and that there are a hundred billion galaxies in the universe.

In addition to electrons, protons, and neutrons, of course, there are numbers of unstable particles unknown to Eddington, but their numbers are comparatively few. There are, however, massless particles such as neutrons, photons, and gravitons, which do not generally behave like particles but which are very numerous in the universe.

If we wish, we can suppose that the number of massless particles speeding through space at any time is nine times the number of massed particles (probably a grievous overestimate) and make the total number of subatomic particles in the universe $10 \backslash 80$, or $10 \backslash 10 \backslash 1.903$.

Now, at least, we are starting with a double-ten number and

that ought to do it. Skewes' number, here we come. All we have to do is take the superfactorial of 10\80, something we can express as (10\80)\(10\80).

Working that out (and I hope I'm doing it correctly), we get 10\10\81.9, or 10\10\10\1.91.

And that lifts us into the "triple-ten numbers" for the first time. In fact, if we compare the superfactorial of the total number of subatomic particles in the universe (which is 10\10\10\1.91) with Skewes' number (which, as a triple-ten number, is 10\10\10\34), we might think we were almost there.

We need to begin with something more than the number of subatomic particles in the universe — how about the amount of space in the universe?

The smallest unit of space we can conveniently deal with is the volume of a neutron, a tiny globe that is about 10\−13 centimeters in diameter, or one ten-trillionth of a centimeter.

The observable universe has a radius of 12.5 billion light-years, or 1.25 × 10\10 light-years, and each light-year is equal to just under 10\13 kilometers. Hence, the observable universe has a radius of roughly 10\23 kilometers. Since 1 kilometer = 100,000, or 10\5, centimeters, the observable universe has a radius of roughly 10\28 centimeters. From this we can calculate the volume of the observable universe to be roughly equal to 4.2 × 10\84 cubic centimeters.

A neutron, with a diameter of 10\−13 centimeters, has a volume that is equal to roughly 5 × 10\−40 cubic centimeters. That means that the volume of the observable universe is roughly 2 × 10\124, or 10\124.3 times the volume of a single neutron.

Suppose we call the volume of space equal to that of a neutron a "vacuon." We can then say that there are 10\124.3 vacuons in the universe and call that the "vacuon-number."

The vacuon-number is nearly a billion billion billion billion billion times greater than the number of subatomic particles in the universe, so we can feel pretty confident about the superfactorial of the vacuon-number, which is (10\124.3)\(10\124.3), except that this comes out to 10\10\10\2.10.

Despite the vastly greater quantity of empty space than of matter in the universe, the rightmost component of the triple-ten number went up only from 1.91 to 2.10, with 34 as the goal. That's enough to depress us, but wait —

In considering the number of vacuons in the universe, we imagined it as existing at a moment in time. But time moves, and the universe changes. A subatomic particle that occupies one place at one moment may occupy another place at another moment. The most rapidly moving particles are, of course, the massless ones which move at the speed of light.

The speed of light is just about 3×10^{10} centimeters per second, and the smallest distance one can move with some significance is the diameter of a neutron, which is 10^{-13} centimeters. A photon will flash the width of a neutron, then, in about 3×10^{-24} seconds. We can consider this the smallest unit of time that has physical meaning and call it the "chronon." *

To imagine a long period of time, let's consider what we can call the "cosmic cycle," one period of expansion and contraction of the universe (assuming it is oscillating). Some have guessed the length of the cosmic cycle to be 80,000,000,000, or 8×10^{10}, years.

The number of chronons in one cosmic cycle, then, is roughly 10^{42}.

In every chronon of time, the universe is slightly different from what it was in the preceding chronon or what it will be in the next chronon, because, if nothing else, every free-moving photon, neutrino, and graviton has shifted its position by the width of one neutron in some direction or other with each chronon that passes.

Therefore we might consider the total number of vacuons not only in the present universe, but also in the one that existed in the last chronon, the one that will exist in the next chronon, and, in general, all the universes in all the chronons through a cosmic cycle. (To be sure, the expansion and contraction of the universe alters its vacuon content — these increasing in number with expansion and decreasing with contraction — but we can suppose that the present size of the universe is about average.)

* Stanley G. Weinbaum once imagined space and time quantized in this fashion in one of his science fiction stories and used the word "chronon" for his ultimate particle of time.

In that case, then, the total number of vacuons through every chronon of the cosmic cycle is just about $10\backslash166.3$. What this means is that if you wish to place a proton somewhere in the universe at some instant in time, you have (under the conditions I've described) a choice of $10\backslash166.3$ different positions.

But if you take the superfactorial of this enormous "total-vacuon number," you end up with $10\backslash10\backslash10\backslash2.27$.

We have hardly moved. I just can't seem to move those triple-ten numbers and make progress toward Skewes' number. I am Skewered.

In fact, it's worse than that. According to Mr. Boas, Skewes' determination of Skewes' number depended on the supposition that something called the "Riemann hypothesis" is true. It probably is, but no one has proved it to be so.

In 1955 Skewes published a paper in which he calculated the value of the number below which the number of primes *must* be higher at some point than the formula would predict, if the Riemann hypothesis were *not* true.

It turns out that the Riemann-hypothesis-*not*-true case yields a number that is far higher than Skewes' number. The new number, or what I suggest we call the Super-Skewes number, is $10\backslash$ $10\backslash10\backslash1000$, or $10\backslash10\backslash10\backslash10\backslash3$.

The Super-Skewes number and Skewes' number are both quadruple-ten numbers — $10\backslash10\backslash10\backslash10\backslash3$ and $10\backslash10\backslash10\backslash10\backslash$ 1.53 respectively — and the difference in the rightmost component seems to be small. However, you saw what difficulty there was in budging the triple-ten numbers upward. Well, moving the quadruple-ten numbers upward is far harder still, and Skewes' number is virtually zero in comparison to the Super-Skewes number.

If I had reached Skewes' number, I would still have had the Super-Skewes number ahead of me. I would have been Super-Skewered.

PART 4

PHYSICS

MY MAJOR WORK, as far as physics is concerned, is my three-volume Understanding Physics, *which is included among my first hundred books. Once that was done, there was little I could do in physics but forage about the edges of the subject and approach a different audience.*

Among the small books for eight-year-olds that I wrote for Follett, and mentioned earlier, there is one book on physics — Light *(Book 108). From that book, here is the description of the spectrum:*

from LIGHT *(1970)*

Light energy comes out of atoms in tiny amounts called "photons." Different kinds of atoms give off different kinds of photons; each kind carries a different amount of energy.

Photons of light are said to move up and down rapidly as they speed outward. Scientists think of them as speeding along in a wavy motion. Photons travel as "light waves."

The photons in light cause our eyes to see certain colors. Certain low-energy photons make us see the color red. Those with a little more energy make us see orange. With still a little more energy we see yellow ... then green ... then blue, and finally violet.

Sunlight is made up of different kinds of light waves. Each kind has its own length, its own kind of photons, and its own amount of energy. The light waves in a sunbeam can be spread out separately. A special piece of glass with three flat sides will do this. Such a piece of glass is called a "prism."

When separated light from a prism falls on a white wall, you can see a band of assorted colors. These are made by the sorted-out light waves. Those having the lowest energy cause you to see the red at one end of the band. Those having the highest energy cause you to see violet at the other end. You can also see other colors in between. A beautiful band is made when you separate the light waves in sunlight. It is called the "solar spectrum." Other kinds of light give different spectrum patterns.

A rainbow looks like a spectrum because it is a spectrum. After a rainstorm, the air is still filled with tiny droplets of water. Each droplet acts like a prism. When the sun comes out and shines through the droplets, the photons are sorted out. Then we see a rainbow, a spectrum in the sky.

Back in 1966, the editor of Science Digest *asked if I would do a small item for him. The magazine had a department called "Please Explain," in which readers' questions were answered. One question was a poser that dealt with how often body cells are replaced.*

Knowing the answer wasn't enough; it had to be given in five hundred words and made both thorough and clear. Being a cheerful idiot not much given to worry and introspection, I undertook to answer the question for a reasonably small sum and did so. My essay was published in the June 1966 issue of the magazine.

What followed was absolutely predictable — which doesn't mean to say that I predicted it, for I am often thoroughly astonished when the predictable comes to pass. In a couple of months, the magazine asked me to do another essay on another catchy question, then another, and another, and before the year was out, I found that what I was doing was, in effect, a monthly column.

I was just getting ready to ask the editor if that was what he really had in mind, when I received an issue of the magazine in which the department was no longer headed "Please Explain"; it had become "Isaac Asimov Explains." That made it clear to the meanest intelligence (meaning mine, for instance) that indeed it was a column I was writing.

The column continued for over nine years before I managed to get out of it. In 1974, there was a change of editor, and when the new editor told me he wanted to reorganize the magazine, I promptly asked him if he wanted to end the column. He did.

I didn't consider it a tragic event, because I had completed a goal I had set myself some years before. I had written a hundred of these essays, and it had been my intention to put the essays into book form once a hundred of them had been done.

Houghton Mifflin published the collection in 1973 as Please Explain *(Book 143). Here are three selections dealing with physics:*

from PLEASE EXPLAIN (1973)

What is the speed of gravitation?

A longer but perhaps clearer way of putting the question is this: Suppose the sun suddenly ceased to exist and vanished into nothingness. How long would it be before the earth would cease to be held by its gravitational field?

A similar question might be: How long after the sun disappears would the earth cease receiving its light?

We know the answer to the second question quite well. We know that the sun is just under 93 million miles from earth and we also know that light travels at 186,282 miles per second through a vacuum. The last bit of light leaving the sun, just before it disappeared, would take 8.3 minutes to reach the earth. In other words, we would see the sun disappear 8.3 minutes after it really disappeared.

The reason it is easy to answer the question about light is that there are a number of ways of actually measuring the speed at which light travels. These measurements are made practical by our ability to detect changes in the very faint light emitted by a distant heavenly body, and by our own ability to produce quite strong beams of light.

We don't have these advantages with gravitational fields. It is very difficult to study faint changes in weak gravitational fields, and we can't produce strong gravitational effects extending over long distances here on earth.

So we have to fall back on theory. There are four types of interactions known in the universe: (1) strong nuclear, (2) weak nuclear, (3) electromagnetic, and (4) gravitational. Of these, the first two are short-range, falling off very rapidly with distance. At distances greater than the width of an atomic nucleus, the nuclear interactions are so weak they can be ignored. The electromagnetic and gravitational interactions are long-range, however. They fall off only at the square of the distance. This means they can make themselves felt even over astronomical distances.

Physicists believe that every interaction between two bodies takes place through the exchange of subatomic particles. The more massive the exchange particle, the shorter-ranged the interaction. Thus, the strong nuclear interaction results from the exchange of pions, which are 270 times as massive as electrons. The weak nuclear interaction results from the exchange of even more massive W-particles (which haven't been detected yet, by the way).

If an exchange particle has no mass at all, then the interaction is as long-range as possible, and this is the case with the electromagnetic interaction. The exchange particle there is the massless photon. A stream of such massless photons makes up a beam of light or related radiations. The gravitational interaction, exactly as long-range as the electromagnetic one, must also involve a massless exchange particle — which is called a graviton.

But physicists have strong reason to suppose that massless particles can travel through a vacuum only at the speed of light; that is, at 186,282 miles per second, neither more nor less.

If this is so, then gravitons travel at exactly the speed of photons. This means that if the sun were to disappear, the last gravitons it emits would reach us at just the same time that the last photons would. At the instant we saw the sun disappear, we would also cease to be under its gravitational pull.

In other words, gravitation travels at the speed of light.

Why can't matter travel faster than the speed of light?

Energy added to a body can affect it in a number of ways. If a hammer strikes a nail in midair, the nail goes flying off, gaining kinetic energy — in other words, energy of motion. If a hammer strikes a nail embedded in hard wood, so that the nail can't move, the nail still gains energy — but in the form of heat.

Albert Einstein, in his theory of relativity, showed that mass could be viewed as a form of energy (and the invention of the atom bomb certainly proved him correct). If energy is added to a body, that energy may therefore appear in the form of mass, as well as in other forms.

Under ordinary conditions, the gain of energy in the form of mass is so incomprehensibly tiny that no one could ever measure it. It was only in the twentieth century, when subatomic particles were observed to move at speeds of tens of thousands of miles per second, that examples of mass increase were found that were large enough to be detectable. A body moving at 160,000 miles a second relative to ourselves would be measured by us as having twice as much mass as when it was at rest relative to ourselves.

If energy is added to any freely moving body, that energy can enter the body in one of two ways: (1) as velocity, so that its speed of motion increases, and (2) as mass, so that it becomes "heavier." The division between these two forms of energy-gain, as measured by ourselves, depends upon the speed of the body to begin with, again as measured by ourselves.

If the body is going at ordinary velocities, virtually all the added energy enters the body as velocity, and the body moves faster and faster with hardly any change in mass.

As the speed of the moving body increases (and as we imagine additional energy constantly being pumped into it), less and less of the energy enters as velocity and more and more as mass. We note that, though the body is still moving faster and faster, its rate of gaining speed is falling off. Instead, we note that it is becoming more massive at a slightly greater rate.

As its speed increases still further and gets fairly close to the 186,282 miles per second that is the speed of light in a vacuum, almost all the added energy enters as mass. In other words, the speed of motion of the body increases very slowly, but now it is the mass that is moving upward by leaps and bounds. By the time the speed of light is reached, all the added energy is appearing as additional mass.

The body *cannot* go faster than the speed of light because to make it do so one must impart additional energy to it and, at the speed of light, all that additional energy, however great, will merely be converted into additional mass, and the body will not increase its speed one iota.

Nor is this "just theory." Scientists have been carefully observing speeding subatomic particles for years. Cosmic ray particles exist with unimaginably high energy contents, yet though their mass climbs high indeed, their speeds never quite reach that of light in a vacuum. The mass and velocity of subatomic particles work out to just what the theory of relativity predicts, and the speed of light is a maximum speed as a matter of observed fact and is *not* merely speculation.

◆ ◆ ◆

In the atom bomb, matter is converted into energy. Is it possible to do the reverse and convert energy into matter?

It is certainly possible to change energy into matter, but to do so in large quantities is impractical. Let us see why.

According to Einstein's special theory of relativity, $e = mc^2$, where e represents energy, measured in ergs, m represents mass in grams, and c is the speed of light in centimeters per second.

Light travels through a vacuum with a speed of very nearly 30 billion (3×10^{10}) centimeters per second. The quantity c^2 represents the product of c $\times$ c; that is, $3 \times 10^{10} \times 3 \times 10^{10}$, or 9×10^{20}. This means that c^2 is equal to 900,000,000,000,000,000,000.

A mass of 1 gram (m $=$ 1) can therefore be converted, in theory, into 9×10^{20} ergs of energy. The average American is more familiar with the ounce (equal to 28.35 grams) as a unit of mass. One ounce of matter represents 2.55×10^{22} ergs of energy.

The erg is a very small unit of energy. The more familiar kilocalorie is equal to nearly 42 billion ergs. An ounce of matter turned into energy would yield 6.1×10^{11} (or 610 billion) kilocalories. You can keep alive very comfortably on 2500 kilocalories a day, obtained from the food you eat. If you had the energy available to you that is represented by a single ounce of matter, you would have a supply that would last you 670,000 years, which is a lot by anybody's standards.

To put it another way, if the energy represented by a single ounce of matter could be turned completely into electrical energy, it would keep a hundred-watt electric light bulb burning continuously for 800,000 years.

To put it still another way, the energy represented by a single ounce of matter is equivalent to that obtained by burning 200 million gallons of gasoline.

It is no wonder, then, that in nuclear bombs, where sizable quantities of matter are turned into energy, so much destruction is turned loose in the explosion of one bomb.

The change works both ways. If matter can be turned into energy, then energy can be turned into matter. This can be done anytime in the laboratory. A very energetic particle of energy — a gamma ray photon — can be converted into an electron and a positron without much trouble. The process is thereby reversed, and energy is, in this way, turned into matter.

The matter formed, however, consists of two very light particles, almost vanishingly small in mass. Can the same principle be used to form more matter — even enough matter to be seen?

Ah, but you can't beat the arithmetic. If an ounce of matter can be converted into as much energy as is produced by burning 200 million gallons of gasoline, then it will take all the energy produced by burning 200 million gallons of gasoline to manufacture a mere ounce of matter.

Even if someone were willing to make the demonstration and go to all the expense involved in collecting all that energy (and perhaps several times as much, allowing for inevitable wastage) just to form an ounce of matter, it still couldn't be done. All that energy simply could not be produced quickly enough and concentrated into a small enough volume to produce an ounce of matter all at once.

Thus, the conversion is possible in theory, but is completely impracticable. To be sure, the matter of the universe was once formed presumably from energy, but certainly not under any set of conditions we can possibly duplicate in the laboratory today.

The Science Digest *column wasn't the only thing my inability to say a literary no had gotten me into. Among my first hundred books is a small one I did for the Atomic Energy Commission called* The Genetic Effects of Radiation. *It earned me only a small flat sum, and there were no royalties since the book-*

let was distributed by the AEC, as a public service, to anyone who asked for it.

Naturally, I couldn't very well argue myself into the proposition that I must never do a public service, so I had agreed to do the book. And, naturally, the AEC, having tasted blood, asked for more. In the course of my second hundred books, I did two more booklets for the AEC. One is Electricity and Man (*Book 123*) *and the other is* Worlds Within Worlds (*Book 131*), *both on physics.*

Worlds Within Worlds *was to be on the history of the development of nuclear energy, and it was to be only ten thousand words long. It ran away with me, however, as books sometimes do, and by the time I screeched to a halt, panting and lightly perspiring, I had done thirty thousand. The AEC cheerfully put it out as three booklets, but I listed it in my records as a single book.*

From Worlds Within Worlds, *here is my discussion of the development of the first nuclear reactor:*

from Worlds Within Worlds (1972)

Earlier in this history, we discussed chain reactions involving chemical energy. A small bit of energy can ignite a chemical reaction that would produce more than enough energy to ignite a neighboring section of the system, which would in turn produce still more — and so on, and so on. In this way the flame of a single match could start a fire in a leaf that would burn down an entire forest, and the energy given off by the burning forest would be enormously higher than the initial energy of the match flame.

Might there not be such a thing as a nuclear chain reaction? Could one initiate a nuclear reaction that would produce something that would initiate more of the same that would produce something that would initiate still more of the same and so on?

In that case, a nuclear reaction, once started, would continue of its own accord, and in return for the trifling investment that would serve to start it — a single neutron, perhaps — a vast amount of breakdowns would result with the delivery of a vast amount of energy. Even if it were necessary to expend quite a bit of energy to produce the one neutron that would start the chain reaction, the end profit would be enormous.

What's more, since the nuclear reaction would spread from nucleus to nucleus with millionths-of-a-second intervals, there would be, in a very brief time, so many nuclei breaking down that there would be a vast explosion. The explosion would be millions of times as powerful as ordinary chemical explosions involving the same quantity of exploding material, since the latter use only the electromagnetic interaction, while the former use the much stronger nuclear interaction.

The first to think seriously of such a nuclear chain reaction was the Hungarian physicist Leo Szilard. He was working in Germany in 1933 when Adolf Hitler came to power and, since he was Jewish, he felt it would be wise to leave Germany. He went to Great Britain and there, in 1934, he considered new types of nuclear reactions that had been discovered.

In these, it sometimes happened that a fast neutron might strike a nucleus with sufficient energy to cause it to emit two neutrons. In that way the nucleus, absorbing one neutron and emitting two, would become a lighter isotope of the same element.

But what would happen if each of the two neutrons that emerged from the original target nucleus struck new nuclei and forced the emission of a pair of neutrons from each. There would now be a total of four neutrons flying about, and if each struck new nuclei there would next be eight neutrons, and so on. From the initial investment of a single neutron there might soon be countless billions initiating nuclear reactions.

Szilard, fearing the inevitability of war and fearing that the brutal leaders of Germany might seek and use such a nuclear chain reaction as a weapon in warfare, secretly applied for a patent on a device that could make use of such a nuclear chain reaction. He hoped to turn it over to the British government, which might then use its possession as a way of restraining the Nazis and keeping the peace.

However, it wouldn't have worked. It took the impact of a very energetic neutron to bring about the emission of two neutrons. The neutrons that then emerged from the nucleus simply didn't have enough energy to keep things going. (It was like trying to make wet wood catch fire.)

But what about uranium fission? Uranium fission was initiated by slow neutrons. What if uranium fission produced neutrons as well as being initiated by a neutron? Would not the neutrons produced serve to initiate new fissions that would produce new neutrons and so on endlessly?

It seemed very likely that fission produced neutrons, and, indeed, at the conference where fission was first discussed, Enrico Fermi suggested it at once. Massive nuclei possessed more neutrons per proton than less massive ones did. If a massive nucleus was broken up into two considerably less massive ones, there would be a surplus of neutrons. Suppose, for instance, uranium-238 broke down into barium-138 and krypton-86. Barium-138 contains 82 neutrons, and krypton-86, 50 neutrons, for a total of 132. The uranium-238 nucleus, however, contains 146 neutrons.

The uranium fission process was studied at once to see if neutrons were actually given off, and a number of different physicists, including Szilard, found that they were.

Now Szilard was faced with a nuclear chain reaction he was certain would work. Only slow neutrons were involved and the individual nuclear breakdowns were far more energetic than anything else that had yet been discovered. If a chain reaction could be started in a sizable piece of uranium, unimaginable quantities of energy would be produced. Just one gram of uranium, undergoing complete fission, would deliver the energy derived from the total burning of three tons of coal and would deliver that energy in a tiny fraction of a second.

Szilard, who had come to the United States in 1937, clearly visualized the tremendous explosive force of something that would have to be called a nuclear bomb. Szilard dreaded the possibility that Hitler might obtain the use of such a bomb through the agency of Germany's nuclear scientists.

Partly through Szilard's efforts, physicists in the United States and in other Western nations opposed to Hitler began a program of voluntary secrecy in 1940 to avoid passing along any hints to Germany. What's more, Szilard enlisted the services of two other Hungarian refugees, the physicists Eugene Paul Wigner and Edward Teller, and all approached Einstein, who had also fled Germany and come to America.

Einstein was the most prestigious scientist then living, and it was thought that a letter from him to the President of the United States would be most persuasive. Einstein signed such a letter, which explained the possibility of a nuclear bomb and urged the United States not to allow a potential enemy to come into possession of it first.

Largely as a result of this letter, a huge research team was put together in the United States, to which other Western nations also contributed. It had but one aim — to develop the nuclear bomb.

Although the theory of the nuclear bomb seemed clear and simple, a great many practical difficulties stood in the way. In the first place, if only uranium atoms underwent fission, a supply of uranium had at least to be obtained in pure form, for if the neutrons struck nuclei of elements other than uranium, they would simply be absorbed and removed from the system, ending the possibility of a chain reaction. This alone was a heavy task. There had been so little use for uranium in quantity that there was almost no supply in existence and no experience in how to purify it.

Secondly, the supply of uranium might have to be a large one, for neutrons didn't necessarily enter the first uranium atom they approached. They moved about here and there, making glancing collisions and traveling quite a distance, perhaps, before striking head-on and entering a nucleus. If in that time they had passed outside the lump of uranium, they were useless.

As the quantity of uranium within which the fission chain reaction was initiated grew larger, more and more of the neutrons produced found a mark, and the fission reaction died out more and more slowly. Finally, at some particular size — the "critical size" — the fission reaction did not die at all, but maintained itself, with enough of the neutrons produced finding their mark to keep the nuclear reaction proceeding at a steady rate. At any greater size the nuclear reaction would accelerate and there would be an explosion.

It wasn't even necessary to send neutrons into the uranium to start the process. In 1941 the Russian physicist Georgii Nikolaevich Flerov found that every once in a while a uranium atom would undergo fission without the introduction of a neutron. Occasionally the random quivering of a nucleus would bring about a shape that the nuclear interaction could not bring back to normal, and the nucleus would then break apart. In a gram of ordinary uranium, there is a nucleus undergoing such "spontaneous fission" every two minutes on the average. Therefore, enough uranium need only be brought together to surpass critical size and it will explode within seconds, for the first nucleus that undergoes spontaneous fission will start the chain reaction.

First estimates made it seem that the quantity of uranium needed to reach critical size was extraordinarily great. Fully 99.3 percent of the metal is uranium-238, however, and, as soon as fission was discovered, Bohr pointed out that there were theoretical reasons for supposing that it was the uranium-235 isotope (making up only 0.7 percent of the whole) that was the one undergoing fission. Investigation proved him right. Indeed, the uranium-238 nucleus tended to absorb slow neutrons without fission, and to go on to beta-particle production that formed isotopes of neptunium and plutonium. In this way uranium-238 actually interfered with the chain reaction.

In any quantity of uranium, the more uranium-235 present and the less uranium-238, the more easily the chain reaction would proceed and the less the critical size need be. Vast efforts were therefore made to separate the two isotopes and prepare uranium with a higher than normal concentration of uranium-235 ("enriched uranium").

Of course, there was no great desire for a fearful explosion to get out of hand while the chain reaction was being studied. Before any bomb could be constructed, the mechanism of the chain reaction would have to be studied. Could a chain reaction capable of producing energy (for useful purposes as well as for bombs) be established? To test this, a quantity of uranium was gathered in the hope that a *controlled* chain reaction of uranium fission could be established. For that purpose, control rods of a substance that would easily absorb neutrons and slow the chain reaction were used. The metal, cadmium, served admirably for this purpose.

Then, too, the neutrons released by fission were pretty energetic. They tended to travel too far too soon and get outside the lump of uranium too easily. To produce a chain reaction that could be studied with some safety, the presence of a moderator was needed. This was a supply of small nuclei that did not absorb neutrons readily, but absorbed some of the energy of collision and slowed down any neutron that struck it. Nuclei such as hydrogen-2, beryllium-9, or carbon-12 were useful moderators. When the neutrons produced by fission were slowed, they traveled a smaller distance before being absorbed in their turn, and the critical size would again be reduced.

Toward the end of 1942 the initial stage of the project reached a climax. Blocks of graphite containing uranium metal and uranium oxide were piled up in huge quantities (enriched uranium was not yet available) in order to approach critical size. This took place under the stands of a football stadium at the University of Chicago, with Enrico Fermi (who had come to the United States in 1938) in charge.

The large structure was called an "atomic pile" at first because of the blocks of graphite being piled up. The proper name for such a device, and the one that was eventually adopted, was, however, "nuclear reactor."

On December 2, 1942, calculations showed that the nuclear reactor was large enough to have reached critical size. The only thing preventing the chain reaction from sustaining itself was the cadmium rods that were inserted here and there in the pile and that were soaking up neutrons.

One by one the cadmium rods were pulled out. The number of uranium atoms undergoing fission each second rose and, finally, at 3:45 P.M., the uranium fission became self-sustaining. It kept going on its own (with the cadmium rods ready to be pushed in if it looked as though it were getting out of hand — something calculations showed was not likely).

News of this success was announced to Washington by a cautious telephone call from Arthur Holly Compton to James Bryant Conant. "The Italian navigator has landed in the New World," said Compton. Conant asked, "How were the natives?" and the answer was, "Very friendly."

This was the day and moment when the world entered the "nuclear age." For the first time, mankind had constructed a device in which the nuclear energy being given off was greater than the energy poured in. Mankind had tapped the reservoirs of nuclear energy and could put it to use.

PART 5

CHEMISTRY

ALTHOUGH CHEMISTRY is the field in which I obtained my degrees (including my Ph.D.) and although I am still an associate professor of biochemistry at Boston University School of Medicine (though I haven't worked at it these past few decades), I do not write as much in the field of chemistry as I do in physics or astronomy.

In my first hundred books are such titles as The Noble Gases, Photosynthesis, and Life and Energy, which were all strongly chemical in content, but in the second hundred books not a single full-sized nonfiction book is devoted to chemistry. This was not on purpose, I assure you.

However, things work out.

In 1975, I received a suggestion from Alan R. Bechtold of Topeka, Kansas, that I write a science fiction short story for him. He wanted to put out a series of booklets of about six thousand words apiece, each to consist of an original story from a well-known science fiction writer. The booklets would be put out in strictly limited editions and would be sold primarily at fan conventions. When the limited edition was sold out, the story would revert to the author.

Unexpectedly, the concept appealed to me. For one thing, I got an idea at once and that always helps. As it happened, the idea resulted in one of the few science fiction stories I wrote that centered on chemistry. I called it Good Taste, and it was published in 1976, entering my list as Book 174.

I wish I could report that the envisioned series was a success, but it wasn't. My book did well, but waiting for the next writer to meet his obligation was a long procedure and Bechtold ran out of money, I'm sorry to say.

Anyway, here is Good Taste in full:

GOOD TASTE (1976)

It was quite clear that it would not have happened — the family would not have been disgraced and the world of Gammer would not have been stunned and horrified — if Chawker Minor had not made the Grand Tour.

It wasn't exactly illegal to make the Grand Tour but, on Gammer at least, it was not really socially acceptable. Elder Chawker had been against it from the start, to do him justice, but then Lady Chawker took the side of her minor, and mothers are, at times, not to be withstood. Chawker was her second child (both of them sons, as it happened) and she would have no more, of course, so it was not surprising that she doted on him.

Her younger son had wanted to see the Other-Worlds of the Orbit and had promised to stay away no longer than a year. She had wept and worried and gone into a tragic decline and then, finally, had dried her eyes and spoken stiffly to Elder Chawker — and Chawker Minor had gone.

Now he was back, one year to the day (he was always one to keep his word, and, besides, Elder's support would have ceased the day after, never fear), and the family made holiday.

Elder wore a new, black glossy shirt but would not permit the prim lines of his face to relax, nor would he stoop to ask for details. He had no interest — no interest *whatever* — in the Other-Worlds with their strange ways and their primitive browsing (no better than the ways on Earth, of which Gammerpeople *never* spoke).

He said, "Your complexion is dirtied and spoiled, Chawker Minor." (The use of the full name showed his displeasure.)

Chawker laughed and the clear skin of his rather thin face crinkled. "I stayed out of the sun as much as I could, Elder-mine, but the Other-Worlders would not always have it so."

Lady Chawker would have none of Elder's criticism either. She said warmly, "It isn't dirtied at all, Elder. It breathes a warmth."

"Of the Sun," grumbled Elder, "and it would be next that he would be grubbing in the filth they have there."

"No farming for me, Elder. That's hard work. I visited the fungus vats at times, though."

Chawker Major, older than Minor by three years, wider of face, heavier of body, but otherwise of close resemblance, was torn between envy of his younger brother's having seen different worlds of the Orbit and revulsion at the thought of it. He said, "Did you eat their Prime, Minor?"

"I had to eat something," said Chawker Minor. "Of course, there were your packages, Lady-mine — lifesavers, sometimes."

"I suppose," said Elder Chawker with distaste, "the Prime was inedible there. Who can tell the filth that found its way into it."

"Come now, Elder-mine." Chawker paused, as though attempting to choose words, then shrugged. "Well, it held body and soul together. One got used to it. I won't say more than that . . . But, Elder-Lady-mine, I am so glad to be home. The lights are so warm and gentle."

"You've enough of the Sun, I take it," said Elder. "But you *would* go. Well, welcome back to the inner world with light and warmth under our control, locked away from the patch and blaze of sunshine. Welcome back to the womb of the people, as the saying goes."

"Yet I'm glad I went," said Chawker Minor. "Eight different worlds, you know. It gives you a view you don't have otherwise."

"And would be better off not having," said Elder.

"I'm not sure about that," said Chawker Minor, and his right eyelid trembled just slightly as he looked at Major. Chawker Major's lips compressed but he said nothing.

It was a feast. Anyone would have had to admit that, and in the end it was Chawker Minor himself, the greediest to begin with, who was the first to push away. He had no choice; else Lady would have kept on supplying him with samples out of what seemed to be a bottomless larder.

"Lady-mine," he said affectionately, "my tongue wearies. I can no longer taste anything."

"*You* not taste?" said Lady. "What kind of nithling story is that? You have the skill of the Grand-Elder himself. At the age of six, you were already a Gustator; we had endless proof of that. There was not an additive you could not detect even when you could not pronounce it right."

"Taste buds blunt when not used," said Elder Chawker darkly, "and jogging the Other-Worlds can utterly spoil a man."

"Yes? Well, let us see," said Lady. "Minor-mine, tell your doubting Elder what you have eaten."

"In order?" said Chawker Minor.

"Yes. Show him you remember."

Chawker Minor closed his eyes. "It's scarcely a fair test," he said. "I so relished the taste I did not pause to analyze it — and it's been so long."

"He has excuses. See, Lady?" said Elder.

"But I will try," Chawker Minor said hastily. "In the first place, the Prime base for all of them is from the fungus vats of the East Section and the thirteenth corridor within it, I believe, unless great changes have been made in my absence."

"No, you are right," said Lady with satisfaction.

"And it was expensive," said Elder.

"The prodigal returns," said Chawker Major just a bit acidly, "and we must have the fatted fungus, as the saying goes . . . Get the additives, Minor, if you can."

"Well," said Chawker Minor, "the first dab was strongly Spring Morning with added Leaves A-Freshened and a touch, not more than a touch, of Spara-Sprig."

"Perfectly right," said Lady, smiling happily.

Chawker Minor went on with the list, his eyes still closed, his taste memory rolling backward and forward luxuriously over the tang and consistency of the samplings. He skipped the eighth and came back to it.

"That one," he said, "puzzles me."

Chawker Major grinned. "Didn't you get any of it?"

"Of course I did. I got most of it. There was Frisking Lamb — not Leaping Lamb, either, Frisking, even though it leaned just a little toward Leaping."

"Come on, don't try to make it hard. That's easy," said Chawker Major. "What else?"

"Green Mint, with just a touch of Sour Mint — *both* — and a dusting of Sparkle-Blood . . . But there was something else I couldn't identify."

"Was it good?" asked Chawker Major.

"Good? This isn't the day to ask me that. Everything is good.

Everything is succulent. And what I can't identify seems very succulent. It's close to Hedge Bloom, but better."

"Better?" said Chawker Major delightedly. "It's mine!"

"What do you mean, yours?" said Chawker Minor.

Elder said with stiff approval, "My stay-at-home son has done well while you were gone. He devised a computer program that has designed and produced three new life-compatible flavor molecules of considerable promise. Grand-Elder Tomasz himself has given one of Major's constructions tongue-room — the very one you just tested, Fly-away Minor-mine — and has given it his approval."

Chawker Major said, "He didn't actually say anything, Elder-mine."

Lady said, "His expression needed no words."

"It *is* good," said Chawker Minor, rather dashed at having the play taken away from him. "Will you be entering for the Awards?"

"It has been in my mind," said Chawker Major, with an attempt at indifference. "Not with this one — I call it Purple Light, by the way — but I believe I will have something else, more worthy of the competition."

Chawker Minor frowned. "I had thought that —"

"Yes?"

"— that I am ready to stretch out and think of nothing. Come, half a dab more of Major's construction, Lady-mine, and let's see what I can deduce concerning the chemical structure of his Purple Light."

For a week, the holiday atmosphere in the Chawker household continued. Elder Chawker was well known in Gammer, and it seemed that half the inhabitants of the world must have passed through his section before all had had their curiosity sated and could see with their own eyes that Chawker Minor had returned unscathed. Most remarked on his complexion, and more than one young woman asked if she might touch his cheek, as though the light tan were a layer that could be felt.

Chawker Minor allowed the touch with lordly complacency, though Lady disapproved of these forward requests and said so.

Grand-Elder Tomasz himself came down from his aerie, as

plump as a Gammerman ever permits himself to be and with no sign that age or white hair had blunted his talents. He was a Master-Gustator such as Gammer might never have seen before, despite the tales of Grand-Elder Faron of half a century ago. There was nothing that Tomasz tongued that did not open itself in detail to him.

Chawker Minor, who had no great tendency to underrate his own talent, felt no shame in admitting that what he himself had, innately, could not yet come anywhere near the old man's weight of experience.

The Grand Elder, who, for nearly twenty years now, had governed the annual Awards festival by force of his skill, asked closely after the Other-Worlds, which, of course, he himself had never visited.

He was indulgent, though, and smiled at Lady Chawker. "No need to fret, Lady," he said. "Young people these days are curious. In my time we were content to attend to our own cylinder of worth, as the saying goes, but these are new times and many are making what they call the Grand Tour. Good, perhaps, to see the Other-Worlds — frivolous, sun-drenched, browsive, nongustational, without a taste bud to content themselves with — makes one appreciate the eldest brother, as the saying goes."

Grand-Elder Tomasz was the only Gammerman whom Chawker Minor had ever heard actually speak of Gammer as "the eldest brother," although you could find it often enough in the video cassettes. It had been the third colony to be founded in the Moon's orbit back in the pioneering years of the twenty-first century; but the first two, Alfer and Bayter, had never become ecologically viable. Gammer had.

Chawker Minor said with tactful caution, "The Other-World people never tired of telling me how much the experience of Gammer meant to all the worlds that were founded afterward. All had learned, they said, from Gammer."

Tomasz beamed. "Certainly. Certainly. Well said."

Chawker Minor said with even greater caution, "And yet such is self-love, you understand, Grand-Elder, that a few thought they had improved on Gammer."

Grand-Elder Tomasz puffed his breath out through his nose

("Never breathe through your mouth any more than you can help," he would say over and over again, "for that blunts the Gustator's tongue") and fixed Chawker with his deep blue eyes that looked the bluer for the snow-white eyebrows that curved above them.

"Improved in what way? Did they suggest a specific improvement?"

Chawker Minor, skating on thin ice and aware of Elder Chawker's awful frown, said softly, "In matters that they value, I gather. I am not a proper judge of such things, perhaps."

"In matters that *they* value. Did you find a world that knows more about food chemistry than we do?"

"No! Certainly not, Grand-Elder. None concern themselves with that as far as I could see. They all rely on our findings. They admit it openly."

Grand-Elder Tomasz grunted. "They can rely on us to know the effects and side effects of a hundred thousand molecules, and each year to study, define, and analyze the effects of a thousand more. They rely on us to work out the dietary needs of elements and vitamins to the last syllable. Most of all, they rely on us to work out the art of taste to the final, most subtly convoluted touch. They do so, do they not?"

"They admit all this, without hesitation."

"And where do you find computers more reliable and more complex than ours?"

"As far as our field is concerned, nowhere."

"And what Prime did they serve?" With heavy humor, he added, "Or did they expect a young Gammerman to browse."

"No, Grand-Elder, they had Prime. On all the worlds I visited they had Prime; and on all those I did not visit, I was told, there was also Prime. Even on the world where Prime was considered fit chiefly for the lower classes —"

Tomasz reddened. "Idiots!" he muttered.

"Different worlds, different ways," said Chawker Minor rather hurriedly. "But even then, Grand-Elder, Prime was popular when something was needed that was convenient, inexpensive, and nourishing. And they got their Prime from us. All of them had a fungal strain brought originally from Gammer."

"Which strain?"

"Strain A-5," said Chawker Minor apologetically. "It's the sturdiest, they said, and the most energy-sparing."

"And the coarsest," said Tomasz with satisfaction. "And what flavor additives?"

"Very few," said Chawker Minor. He thought a moment, then said, "There was, on Kapper, a place where they had an additive that was popular with the Kapperpeople and that had . . . possibilities. Those were not properly developed, however, and when I distributed tastes of what Lady-mine had sent me, they were forced to admit that it was to theirs as Gammer is to a space pebble."

"You had not told me that," said Lady Chawker, who, till then, had not ventured to interpose in a conversation that had the Grand-Elder as one of its participants. "The Other-Worlders liked my preparations, did they?"

"I didn't often hand it out," said Chawker Minor. "I was too selfish to do it. But when I did, they liked it a great deal, Lady-mine."

It was several days before the two brothers managed to find a way of being alone together.

Major said, "Weren't you on Kee at all?"

Chawker Minor lowered his voice. "I was. Just a couple of days. It was too expensive to stay long."

"I have no doubt Elder would not have liked even the two days."

"I don't intend telling him. Do you?"

"A witless remark. Tell me about it."

Chawker Minor did, in semi-embarrassed detail, and said, finally, "The point is, Major, it doesn't seem wrong to them. They don't think anything of it. It made me think that perhaps there is no real right and wrong. What you're used to, that's right. What you're not used to, that's wrong."

"Try telling that to Elder."

"What he thinks is right and what he is used to are precisely the same. You'll have to admit that."

"What difference does it make what *I* admit? Elder thinks that all rights and wrongs were written down by the makers of Gammer and that it's all in a book of which there is only one copy and we have it, so that all the Other-Worlds are wrong forever. I'm speaking metaphorically, of course."

"I believe that, too, Major — metaphorically. But it shook me up to see how calmly those Other-World people took it. I could — watch them browse."

A spasm of distaste crossed Major's face. "Animals, you mean?"

"It doesn't look like animals when they browse on it. That's the point."

"You watched them kill and dissect that — that —"

"No," he said hastily. "I just saw it when it was all finished. What they ate looked like some kinds of Prime and it smelled like some kinds of Prime. I imagine it tasted —"

Chawker Major twisted his expression into one of extreme revulsion, and Chawker Minor said defensively, "But browsing came first, you know. On Earth, I mean. And it could be that when Prime was first developed on Gammer it was designed to imitate the taste of browse food."

"I prefer not to believe that," said Chawker Major.

"What you prefer doesn't matter."

"Listen," said Chawker Major. "I don't care what they browse. If they ever got the chance to eat real Prime — not Strain A-5, but the fatted fungus, as the saying goes — and if they had the sophisticated additives and not whatever primitive trash they use, they would eat forever and never dream of browsing. If they could eat what *I* have constructed and will yet construct —"

Chawker Minor said wistfully, "Are you really going to try for the Award, Major?"

Chawker Major thought for a moment, then said, "I think I will, Minor. I really will. Even if I don't win, I eventually will. This program I've got is different." He grew excited. "It's not like any computer program I've ever seen or heard of — and it works. It's all in the —" But he pulled himself up sharply and said uneasily, "I hope, Minor, you don't mind if I *don't* tell you about it? I haven't told anyone."

Chawker Minor shrugged. "It would be foolish to tell anyone. If you really have a good program, you can make your fortune.

You know that. Look at Grand-Elder Tomasz. It must be thirty-five years since he developed Corridor Song and he still hasn't published his path."

Chawker Major said, "Yes, but there's a pretty good guess as to how he got to it. And it's not really, in my opinion —" He shook his head doubtfully, in preference to saying anything that might smack of lèse majesté.

Chawker Minor said, "The reason I asked if you were going to try for the Award —"

"Well?"

"Is that I was rather thinking of entering myself."

"You? You're scarcely old enough."

"I'm twenty-two. But would you mind?"

"You don't know enough, Minor. When have you ever handled a computer?"

"What's the difference? A computer isn't the answer."

"No? What is?"

"The taste buds."

"Hit and miss and taste buds all the way. We all know that sound, and I will jump through the zero axis in a bound, too, as the saying goes."

"But I'm serious, Major. A computer is only the starting point, isn't it? It all ends with the tongue no matter where you start."

"And, of course, a Master-Gustator like Minor-lad, here, can do it."

Chawker Minor was not too tanned to flush. "Maybe not a Master-Gustator, but a Gustator anyway, and you know it. The point is that being away from home for a year I've gotten to appreciate good Prime and what might be done with it. I've learned enough. Look, Major, my tongue is all I've got, and I'd like to make back the money that Elder and Lady spent on me. Do you object to my entering? Do you fear the competition?"

Chawker Major stiffened. He was taller and heavier than Chawker Minor and he didn't look friendly. "There is no competition to fear. If you want to enter, do so, Minor-child. But don't come whimpering to me when you're ashamed. And I tell you, Elder won't like your making a no-taste-batch of yourself, as the saying goes."

"Nobody has to win right away. Even if I don't win, I eventually will, as *your* saying goes." And Chawker Minor turned and left. He was feeling a little huffy himself.

Matters trailed off eventually. Everyone seemed to have had enough of the tales of the Other-Worlds. Chawker Minor had described the living animals he had seen for the fiftieth time and denied he had seen any of them killed for the hundredth. He had painted word-pictures of the grain fields and tried to explain what sunshine looked like when it glinted off men and women and buildings and fields, through air that turned a little blue and hazy in the distance. He explained for the two hundredth time that, no, it was not at all like the sunshine effect in the outer viewing rooms of Gammer (which hardly anyone visited anyway).

And now that it was all over, he rather missed not being stopped in the corridors. He disliked no longer being a celebrity. He felt a little at a loss as he spun the book film he had grown tired of viewing and tried not to be annoyed with Lady.

He said, "What's the matter, Lady-mine? You haven't smiled all day."

His mother looked up at him thoughtfully. "It's distressing to see dissension between major and minor."

"Oh, come." Chawker Minor rose irritably and walked over to the air vent. It was jasmine day and he loved the odor and, as always, automatically wondered how he could make it better. It was very faint, of course, since everyone knew that strong floral odors blunted the tongue.

"There's nothing wrong, Lady," he said, "with my trying for the Award. It's the free right of every Gammerperson over twenty-one."

"But it isn't in good taste to be competing with your brother."

"Good taste! Why not? I'm competing with everyone. So's he. It's just a detail that we're competing with each other. Why don't you take the attitude that he's competing with me?"

"He's three years older than you, Minor-mine."

"And perhaps he'll win, Lady-mine. He's got the computer. Has Major asked you to get me to drop out?"

"No, he did not. Don't think that of your brother." Lady spoke earnestly, but she avoided his eyes.

Chawker Minor said, "Well, then, he's gone moping after you and you've learned to tell what he wants without his having to say it. And all because I qualified in the opening round and he didn't think I would."

"Anyone can qualify," came Chawker Major's voice from the doorway.

Chawker Minor whirled. "Is that the way it is? Then why does it upset you? And why did a hundred people fail to qualify?"

Chawker Major said, "What some small-taste nitherlings decide means very little, Minor. Wait till it comes to the board."

"Since you qualified, too, Major, there's no need to tell me how little importance there is to some small-taste nitherlings —"

"Young-mine," said Lady rather sharply. "Stop it! Perhaps we can remember that it is very unusual for both major and minor of a single unit to qualify."

Neither ventured to break the silence in Lady's presence for a while thereafter — but their scowls remained eloquent.

As the days passed, Chawker Minor found himself more and more involved in preparing the ultimate sample of flavored Prime, which his own taste buds and olfactory area would tell him was to be nothing like anything that had ever rolled across a Gammer tongue before.

He took it upon himself to visit the Prime vats themselves, where the delectably bland fungi grew out of malodorous wastes and multiplied themselves at extraordinary speed, under ideal conditions, into three dozen basic strains, each with its varieties.

(The Master-Gustator, tasting unflavored Prime itself — the fungal unalterate, as the saying went — could be relied upon to pin its source down to the section and corridor. Grand-Elder Tomasz had more than once stated, publicly, that he could tell the very vat itself and, at times, the portion of the vat, though no one had ever quite put him to the full test.)

Chawker Minor did not pretend to the expertise of Tomasz, but he lipped and tongued and smacked and nipped till he had decided on the exact strain and variety he wanted, the one that would best blend with the ingredients he was mixing in his mind. A good Gustator, said Grand-Elder Tomasz, could combine ingredients mentally and taste the mixture in his imagination. With

Tomasz it might, for all one knew, be merely a statement, but Chawker Minor took it seriously and was sure he could do it.

He had rented out space in the kitchen — another expense for poor Elder, although Chawker Minor was making do with less than Major had demanded. Chawker Minor did not repine at having less, for, since he was eschewing computers, he didn't require much. Mincers, mixers, heaters, strainers, and the rest of the cookery tools took up little room. And at least he had an excellent hood for the masking and removal of all odors. (Everyone knew the horror tales of the Gustators who had been given away by a single sniff of odor and then found that some creative mixture was in the public domain before they could bring it before the board. To steal someone else's product might not be, as Lady would say, in good taste, but it was done and there was no legal recourse.)

The signal light flashed in a code sufficiently well known. It was Elder Chawker. Chawker Minor felt the thrill of guilt he had felt as a child when he had pilfered dabs of Prime reserved for guests.

"One moment, Elder-mine," he sang out, and, in a flurry of activity, set the hood on high, closed the partition, swept his ingredients off the tabletop and into the bins, then stepped out and closed the door quickly behind him.

"I'm sorry, Elder-mine," he said with an attempt at lightness, "but Gustatorship is paramount."

"I understand," said Elder stiffly, though his nostrils had flared momentarily as though he would have been glad to catch that fugitive whiff, "but you've scarcely been at home lately, scarcely more than when you were on your space folly, and I must come here to speak to you."

"No problem, Elder, we'll go to the lounge."

The lounge was not far away, and, fortunately, it was empty. Elder's sharp glances this way and that made the emptiness seem fortunate for him, and Chawker Minor sighed inaudibly. He would be lectured, he knew.

Elder said at last, "Minor, you are my son, and I will do my duty toward you. My duty does not consist, however, of more than paying your expenses and seeing to it that you have a fair start in life. There is also the matter of reproval in good time.

Who wishes fair Prime must not stint on foul waste, as the saying goes."

Chawker's eyes dropped. He, along with his brother, had been among the thirty who had now qualified for the final awarding to be held in a week, and the unofficial rumor had it that Chawker Minor had done so with a somewhat higher score than Chawker Major had.

"Elder," said Chawker Minor, "would you ask me to do less than my best for my brother's sake?"

Elder Chawker's eyes blinked in a moment of puzzlement and Chawker Minor clamped his mouth shut. He had clearly jumped in the wrong direction.

Elder said, "I do not ask you to do less than your best, but rather more than you are doing. Bethink you of the shaming you have inflicted on us in your little quarrel with Stens Major last week."

Chawker Minor had, for a moment, difficulty remembering what this could apply to. He had done nothing with Stens Major at all — a silly young woman with whom he was perfectly content to confine himself to mere talk, and not very much of that.

"Stens Major? Shaming? How?"

"Do not say you do not remember what you said to her. Stens Major repeated it to her elder and lady, good friends of our family, and it is now common talk in the section. What possessed you, Minor, to assault the traditions of Gammer?"

"I did not do such a thing. She asked me about my Grand Tour and I told her no more than I have told three hundred others."

"Didn't you tell her that women should be allowed to go on the Grand Tour?"

"Oh."

"Yes. Oh."

"But, Elder, what I said was that if she would take the Grand Tour herself there would be no need to ask questions, and when she pretended to be shocked at such a suggestion, I told her that, in my opinion, the more Gammerpeople saw of the Other-Worlds, the better it would be for all of us. We are too closed a society, in my opinion, and, Elder, I am not the first to say so."

"Yes, I have heard of radicals who have said so, but not in our section and certainly not in our family. We have endured longer than the Other-Worlds; we have a stabler and fitter society; we do not have their problems. Is there crime among us? Is there corruption among us?"

"But, Elder, it is at the price of immobility and living death. We're all so tied in, so enclosed."

"What can they teach us, these Other-Worlds? Were you not yourself glad to come back to the enclosed and comfortable sections of Gammer with their corridors lit in the gold light of our own energy?"

"Yes — but, you know, I'm spoiled, too. There are many things on the Other-Worlds that I would have very much liked to have made myself accustomed to."

"And just exactly what, Minor-madman-mine?"

Chawker Minor bit back the words. After a pause he said, "Why simply make assertions? When I can *prove* that a particular Other-World way is superior to Gammerfashion, I will produce the proof. Till then, what is the use of just talking?"

"You have already been talking idly without end, Minor, and it has done you so little good that we can call what it has done you harm outright. Minor, if you have any respect left for me after your Grand Tour — which Lady-yours wheedled out of me against my will, Gammer knows — or if you have any regard for the fact that I still deny you nothing that my credit can obtain for you, you will keep your mouth shut henceforward. Think not that I will halt at sending you away if you shame us. You may then continue on your Grand Tour for as long as the Orbit lasts — and be no son of mine thereafter."

Chawker Minor said in a low voice, "As you say, Elder. From this moment on, unless I have evidence, I will say nothing."

"Since you will never have evidence," said Elder grimly, "I will be satisfied if you keep your word."

The annual Finals was the greatest holiday occasion, the greatest social event, the greatest excitement of any sort in the course of the year. Each one of thirty dishes of elegantly flavored Prime had been prepared. Each one of the thirty judges would taste each dish at intervals long enough to restore the tongue. It would take all day.

In all honesty, Gammerpeople had to admit that the nearly one

hundred winners who had taken their prize and acclaim in Gammer history had not all turned out dishes that had entered the
Great Menu as classics. Some were forgotten and some were now
considered ordinary. On the other hand, at least two of Gammer's all-time favorites, combinations that had been best sellers
in restaurants and homes for two decades, had been also-rans in
the years in which they had entered the contest. Black Velvet,
whose odd combination of chocolate-warm and cherry blossom
had made it the standard sweet, did not even make it to the
Finals.

Chawker Minor had no doubt of the outcome. He was so confident that he found himself in continual danger of being bored.
He kept watching the faces of the individual judges as every once
in a while one of them would scoop up a trifle from one of the
dishes and place it on his tongue. There was a careful blankness
to the expression, a heavy-liddedness to the eye. No true judge
could possibly allow a look of surprise or a sigh of satisfaction to
escape him — certainly not a quiver of disdain. They merely
recorded their ratings on the little computer cards they carried.

Chawker Minor wondered if they could possibly restrain their
satisfaction when they tasted *his*. In the last week, his mixture
had grown perfect, had reached a pinnacle of taste glory that
could not be improved on, could *not* —

"Counting your winnings?" said Chawker Major in his ear.

Chawker Minor started, and turned quickly. Chawker Major
was dressed entirely in platon and gleamed beautifully.

Chawker Minor said, "Come, Major-mine, I wish you the best.
I really do. I want you to place as high as possible."

"Second place if you win, right?"

"Would you refuse second place if I win?"

"You can't win. I've checked somewhat. I know your strain of
Prime; I know your ingredients —"

"Have you spent any time on your own work, all this time
you've been playing detective?"

"Don't worry about me. It didn't take long to learn that there
is no way you can combine your ingredients into anything of
value."

"You checked that with the computer, I suppose?"

"I did."

"Then how did I get into the Finals, I wonder? Perhaps you don't know all there is to know about my ingredients. Look, Major, the number of effective combinations of even a few ingredients is astronomical if we can consider the various possible proportions and the possible treatments before and after mixing, and the order of mixing and the —"

"I don't need your lecture, Minor."

"Then you know that no computer in existence has been programmed for the complexity of a clever tongue. Listen, you can add some ingredients in amounts so small as to be indetectable even by tongue, and yet they add a cast of flavor that represents a marked change."

"They teach you that in the Other-Worlds, youngling?"

"I learned that for myself." And Chawker Minor walked away before he could be goaded into talking too much.

There was no question that Grand-Elder Tomasz this year, as in a large number of previous years, held the Judging Committee in the hollow of his tongue, as the saying went.

He looked up and down the long table at which all the judges had now taken their seats in order of preference, with Tomasz himself right in the middle. The computer had been fed; it had produced the result. There was complete silence in the room where the contestants, their friends, and their families sat waiting for glory or, failing that, for the consolation of being able to taste all the contesting samples.

The rest of Gammer, possibly without exceptions, watched by holo-video. There would, after all, be additional batches made up for a week of feasting, and the general opinion did not always match that of the judges either, though that did not affect the prize winning.

Tomasz said, "I do not recall an awarding in which there was so little doubt as to the computer decision, or such general agreement."

There was a nodding of heads, and smiles and looks of satisfaction.

Chawker Minor thought: They look sincere; not as if they're just going along with the Grand-Elder, so it must be mine.

Tomasz said, "It has been my privilege this year to taste a dish more subtle, more tempting, more ambrosial than anything I have ever, in all my time and experience, tasted. It is the best. I cannot imagine it being bettered."

He held up the computer cards. "The win is unanimous, and the computer was needed only to determine the order of the runners-up. The winner is —" just that pause for effect and then, to the utter surprise of everyone but the winner, "Chawker Minor, for his dish entitled Mountain Cap. Young man . . ."

Chawker Minor advanced for the ribbon, the plaque, the credits, the handshakes, the recording, the beaming, and the other contestants received their numbers in the list. Chawker Major was in fifth place.

Grand-Elder Tomasz sought out Chawker Minor after a while and tucked the young man's arm into his elbow.

"Well, Chawker Minor, it is a wonderful day for you and for all of us. I did not exaggerate. Your dish was the best I've ever tongued. And yet you leave me curious and wondering. I identified all the ingredients, but there was no way in which their combinations could produce what was produced. Would you be willing to impart your secret to me? I would not blame you if you refused, but in the case of an accomplishment so towering by one so young, to —"

"I don't mind telling you, Grand-Elder. I intend to tell everybody. I told my Elder that I would say nothing till I had proof. You supplied the proof!"

"What?" said Tomasz blankly. "What proof?"

"The idea for the dish occurred to me, actually, on the Other-World Kapper, which is why I called it Mountain Cap, in tribute. I used ordinary ingredients, Grand-Elder, carefully blended, all but one. I suppose you detected the Garden Tang?"

"Yes, I did, but there was a slight modification there, I think, that I did not follow. How did the Other-World you speak of affect matters?"

"Because it was not Garden Tang, Grand-Elder, not the chemical. I used a complicated mixture for the Garden Tang, a mixture whose nature I cannot be entirely certain of."

Tomasz frowned portentously. "You mean, then, you cannot reproduce this dish?"

"I *can* reproduce it; be certain of that, Grand-Elder. The ingredient to which I refer is garlic."

Tomasz said impatiently, "That is only the vulgar term for Mountain Tang."

"*Not* Mountain Tang. That is a known chemical mixture. I am speaking of the bulb of the plant."

Grand-Elder Tomasz's eyes opened wide and so did his mouth.

Chawker Minor continued enthusiastically, "No mixture can duplicate the complexity of a growing product, Grand-Elder, and on Kapper they have grown a particularly delicate variety which they use in their Prime. They use it incorrectly, without any appreciation of its potentiality. I saw at once that a true Gammer-person could do infinitely better, so I brought back with me a number of the bulbs and used them to good advantage. You said it was the best dish of Prime you had ever rolled tongue over, and if there is any better evidence than that for the value of opening our society, then —"

But he dwindled to a stop at last and stared at Tomasz with surprise and alarm. Tomasz was backing away rapidly. He said in a gargling voice, "A growth — from the dirt — I've eaten —"

The Grand-Elder had often boasted that such was the steadiness of his stomach that he had never vomited, not even in infancy. And certainly no one had ever vomited in the great Hall of Judgment. The Grand-Elder now set a precedent in both respects.

Chawker Minor had not recovered. He would never recover. If it were exile that Elder Chawker had pronounced, so be it. He would never return.

Elder had not come to see him off. Neither had Major, of course. It didn't matter. Chawker Minor swore inwardly that he would make out, somehow, without their help, even if it meant serving on Kapper as a cook.

Lady *was* there, however — the only one in all the field to see him off; the only one to dare accept the nonperson he had become. She shivered and looked mournful and Chawker Minor was filled with the desperate desire to justify himself.

"Lady-mine," he said in a fury of self-pity, "it's *unfair!* It was the best dish ever made on Gammer. The Grand-Elder said so *himself*. The *best*. If it had grated bulb in it, that didn't mean the dish was bad; it meant the bulb was good. Don't *you* see it? Look, I must board the ship. Tell me you see it. Don't you understand it means we must become an open society, learn from others as well as teach others or we'll wither?"

The platform was about to take him up to the ship's entrance. She was watching him sadly, as though she knew she would never see him again.

He began the final rise, leaned over the rail. "What did I do *wrong*, Lady-mine?"

And she said in a low, distraught voice, "Can't you see, Minor-mine, that what you did was not in —"

The clang of the ship's port opening drowned her last two words, and Chawker Minor moved in and put the sight of Gammer behind him forever.

PART 6

BIOLOGY

BIOLOGY SUFFERED in my second hundred books, as chemistry had. Whereas my first books include such works as The Human Body *and* The Human Brain, *nothing of the sort appears later.*

On the other hand, there is my How Did We Find Out *series for Walker. One of them,* How Did We Find Out About Vitamins? (*Book 158*), *published in 1974, is on the borderline between biology and chemistry. Another item in the series,* How Did We Find Out About Dinosaurs? (*Book 145*), *published in 1973, is on the borderline between biology and geology. A third,* How Did We Find Out About Germs? (*Book 153*), *published in 1974, is clearly about biology. Here is a passage from that book on the first medical victory over infectious disease.*

from HOW DID WE FIND OUT ABOUT GERMS? (*1974*)

Disease is a subject that concerns everyone. No one can ever be sure that he or she might not suddenly fall sick. A person can at any time begin to feel bad, develop a fever, or break out in a rash. Eventually, he or she might even die of a disease.

When one person falls sick, others might also. A disease can suddenly spread over a whole town or a whole region, and some diseases can be very deadly.

In the 1300s, for instance, a disease called the Black Death spread all over Europe, Asia, and Africa and killed millions of people. It was the greatest disaster in human history. One-third of all the people in Europe died.

At this time nobody in the world knew what caused disease. Some people thought demons or evil spirits took over the body. Some people thought it was bad air of some sort or another. Some people thought it was a punishment from Heaven for evil deeds.

Whatever it was, though, no one imagined the diseases could be stopped and no one knew when another Black Death might strike.

One hopeful thing about disease was that some diseases only hit a person once. If someone got measles or mumps or chicken pox and got well, that person would never get that particular disease again. He or she was "immune." His or her body had fought off the disease and had developed some kind of defense that would continue to work for many years.

One particularly dreadful disease that only struck once was smallpox. The trouble was that very often once was quite enough. Many people who got smallpox died. Many others recovered, but their faces and bodies were covered with scars left over from the terrible blisters they had had. Every once in a while, though, someone had only a light case that did not scar him or her much. When that happened, the person was just as immune afterward as if he or she had had a terrible case.

Naturally, it was much better to have a light case of smallpox than to have none at all. With a light case, you were safe for life; with none at all, you could never be sure you might not get it at any moment.

People knew that if you were near a person with smallpox you might catch it. Would it not be a good idea, then, to hang around a person with a light case? You might catch the light case and then be safe. To make sure, you might scratch your skin with a needle that had been dipped into some of the fluid in the smallpox blisters of the sick man. This was called "inoculation."

The trouble was, though, that a person might have a light case of smallpox, yet another person catching it might get a severe case. Inoculation just was not safe.

In the 1770s, an English doctor, Edward Jenner, grew interested in a disease called cowpox. It was called that because it was found in cows and in other farm animals. The disease was something like a very mild smallpox. If a person caught cowpox from a cow, he or she would get a blister or two and that was it. People would hardly ever know they were sick.

The country people where Jenner lived thought it was good luck to get cowpox because then you never got smallpox. Most doctors thought this was just a superstition, but Jenner wondered.

He did notice that people who worked with farm animals a good deal hardly ever got smallpox.

After twenty years of study, Jenner decided to try a very dangerous experiment. On May 14, 1796, he found a milkmaid who had just developed cowpox. He dipped a needle into the fluid inside a blister on her hand and scratched the skin of a boy who had never had either cowpox or smallpox. The boy got cowpox and developed a blister in the place where he had been scratched.

Jenner then waited for two months to make sure the boy was completely recovered. He was now immune to cowpox, but was he also immune to smallpox? Taking an enormous chance, Jenner deliberately scratched the boy with a needle that had been dipped in the fluid of a real smallpox blister. The boy did *not* catch smallpox.

Jenner tried the whole thing again two years later when he found another girl with cowpox. He again found he could make someone immune to smallpox by giving them fluid from a cowpox blister.

The medical name for cowpox is "vaccinia," from a Latin word for "cow." Jenner's system for giving people cowpox to save them from smallpox was therefore called "vaccination." When Jenner announced his findings, vaccination was quickly adopted all over the world. Smallpox disappeared from places where vaccination was used.

Of course, a book need not be entirely about biology in order to deal with biology. In 1975, a book of mine appeared entitled The Ends of the Earth *(Book 168), published by Weybright and Talley. It was about the polar regions, and I tried to cover every aspect of the subject, including the biological part.*

from THE ENDS OF THE EARTH (1975)

The smallest living organisms of the ocean float passively in the surface layers. The German physiologist Viktor Hensen, in 1889, called this floating life of the ocean "plankton," from a Greek word meaning "wandering," and this expression has been used ever since. Most of the plankton are microscopic in size, but the name is used also for such large plant organisms as seaweed and such large animal organisms as giant jellyfish.

The microscopic plant cells of the plankton ("phytoplankton," the prefix from a Greek word meaning "plant") are the basic food of all ocean animal life. All sea animals either eat phytoplankton or eat other animals that have eaten phytoplankton, or other animals that have eaten other animals that have eaten other animals — and so on, until we come to an animal that has eaten phytoplankton. This "food chain" can be of varying lengths.

The small animals of the surface ("zooplankton," the prefix from a Greek word meaning "animal") feed on the phytoplankton. The most common of the zooplankton are small crustacea called "copepods." There are six thousand species of copepods, with lengths varying from 0.5 millimeter (barely visible to the naked eye) to 1 centimeter. They make up about 70 percent of all the zooplankton and can sometimes turn the ocean pink with their numbers. A somewhat larger variety of shellfish is the small, shrimplike "krill," which is up to 5 centimeters in length.

Larger animals, such as young fish, feed on the zooplankton, and themselves serve as food for larger organisms.

Food is not converted into the tissues of the eater with perfect efficiency. There is roughly a 90 percent loss, so that, in general, the total mass of a species can only be about 10 percent that of the species it feeds upon.

Since plant life in general is the food of animal life in general, the mass of plant life on earth must be ten times that of animal life, and the total mass of the phytoplankton in the ocean must be roughly ten times that of all the animal life there. (Animal life in the ocean exists at all levels, but plant life is confined to the euphotic zone.)

Because each step upward in the food chain means a decrease in total mass of the organism by a factor of ten, the actual number of larger animals decreases drastically.

Thus, the white shark, which is the largest sea vertebrate with gills (12 meters long) that lives on other large organisms, is a relatively rare creature. The sea cannot support white sharks in the myriads that it can support herring, for instance, which live on plankton.

Large animals can be supported in large numbers if they cut

through the food chain by living on plankton directly. The whale shark and basking shark are even larger than the white shark (up to 15 meters long) but can be supported in surprising numbers because they live on plankton.

There are land animals that live primarily on sea life, and the distribution of these animals differs from that of land animals that live primarily on land life. Land plants grow stunted and sparse as one approaches the poles, and consequently land animals that live on them grow fewer, too. The sparseness of land life on the tundra and the virtual absence of land life in Antarctica have already been mentioned.

Sea life is, however, richer in the polar regions than in the tropics, thanks to the greater supply of oxygen and nutrients in cold water than in warm water. As a result, the polar regions are rich in land animal life that finds its food in the ocean.

Land life that depends on the sea for its food must be adapted to ocean feeding, and this takes place to a greater or lesser extent. In some cases, the adaptation is so extreme that the land animals are no longer really land animals, having adapted themselves to continuous life in the oceans, even to the point of developing the streamlined fish shape for more rapid motion.

The best known of the extremely adapted organisms are the whales and their smaller relatives the dolphins, which breathe by means of lungs, bring forth living young, and are, by every criterion, as fully mammalian as we ourselves, but which spend all their lives in the water.

The smallest dolphins are about 1.2 meters long and weigh about 45 kilograms. The largest dolphin is the killer whale, with males as long as 10 meters. The killer whale is an example of an organism that is at the top of the food chain. There are no other large organisms for whom the killer whale is a regular article of diet. A killer whale will die of disease, accident, or old age, not by ordinary predation.

The one exception to this in the case of the killer whale and of all other organisms that exist at the top of the food chain rests in the activity of man. In his natural physical state, man is no match for the larger animals, but armed with the products of the technology produced by his restless mind, he can destroy them all and is, indeed, in the process of doing so.

Another large dolphin, the narwhal, up to 5 meters long, is an Arctic animal. It inhabits the sea among the loose ice of the Arctic beyond 65° N, migrating farther northward as the pack ice melts and recedes in the polar summer. The most unusual characteristic of the narwhal is that one tooth on the left side of its jaw forms a straight, spiral tusk up to 2.5 meters long. Its appearance is exactly that of the fabled horn of the unicorn, which was supposed to have miraculous medical properties — and no wonder, since sailors brought home pieces of narwhal tooth and, claiming it to be unicorn horn, sold them for large sums.

The largest truly carnivorous whale is the sperm whale. The male sperm whale can be as long as 20 meters and may weigh as much as 60 tons. It lives largely on giant squid. It, too, is at the top of the food chain and is threatened only by man.

Still larger whales, like the largest sharks, must cut through the food chain if they are to be supported in any numbers. The largest of all whales (and, indeed, the largest animal that has ever lived) is the blue whale, which can be 30 meters long and weigh 135 tons. It feeds largely on krill, eating 3 tons per day. Whales that feed on plankton have fringes of horny plates, up to 3 meters long, extending down from the roof of the mouth and frayed and brushlike at the end. These, called "baleen" or "whalebone," trap and strain out the plankton.

Whales are worldwide in their distribution, but naturally they are most common where the food supply is richest, and this means the polar regions; and the Antarctic far more than the Arctic.

Whalers, hunting the whale for meat, oil, and whalebone, ventured into Arctic and Antarctic waters, and a great deal of the early exploration of the polar regions was performed by whalers and by those who hunted other sea mammals.

The search for whales was ruthless, however, and without any thought for preserving the species. In the eighteenth century, the large baleen whales of the Arctic were reduced to such small numbers that it was simply not worthwhile hunting them anymore.

With the passing of the baleen whales of the north, attention turned to the sperm whale when it was discovered that quantities of sperm oil could be obtained from the head of that organism and that such oil was particularly useful in oil lamps. The sperm whale was a more difficult and savage target (Moby Dick in Herman Melville's great novel was a sperm whale), but they would have been wiped out also if the electric light and the growing use of petroleum had not eased the need for sperm oil.

Whaling is now almost entirely confined to the Antarctic, where the food supply of the oceans is the richest in the world thanks to the Antarctic Convergence. Some 70 percent of the whales killed are hunted down in the Antarctic and, of these, 70 percent are the fin whale. Even now 35,000 whales are being killed each year, and these great animals will be wiped out if mankind does not manage to control the whalers.

Stepping down a notch in the extent of adaptation to the sea, we come to the seals. They, too, are typically polar in distribution because of the richness of the cold regions of the ocean.

Like the whales, the seals have been hunted down and slaughtered. Where the whales are bare skinned and depend on retaining warmth against the cold water of the polar oceans by thick layers of fat ("blubber") under the skin, seals have, in many cases, developed thick coats of hair. The coats of these "hair seals" have been coveted and have very nearly proved the doom of those animals.

The ones that yield the best "sealskins" are the Alaska fur seals. These gathered in huge hordes on the Pribilof Islands (discovered by the Russian navigator Gerasim Pribilof in 1786) in the Bering Sea. At the time of the discovery, some 5,000,000 seals formed the herd. They began to wither under the attack of the sealers until the Russian government exerted protection.

The Pribilof Islands, along with all of Alaska, passed to the United States in 1867, and at once the sealers began to make destructive inroads until only 125,000 seals remained in 1911. There seemed no way of making men forgo short-term profits in favor of a careful conservation that would, in the long run, yield greater returns.

Finally, when the United States and other nations imposed rigorous controls on sealing activities, the seal herds began to be restored. By now the herds are back up to 3,000,000 despite the fact that since 1911, under carefully rationed culling of the herds, 1,500,000 seals have been taken for their fur.

The most northerly of the seals is the ringed seal, which lives almost exclusively on and under the ice of the Arctic Ocean.

The largest of the seals is the elephant seal, so called more because of its trunklike nasal protuberance than its size. Species are found in both the Arctic and the Antarctic, with the latter somewhat the larger. The Antarctic males reach a length of 6.5 meters and a weight of nearly 4 tons.

The next largest seal is the walrus, which can reach a length of 3.5 meters and a weight of 1.4 tons. It differs from the other members of the seal family by possessing a pair of downward pointing tusks (the two upper canine teeth), which can be as long as 40 centimeters. The walruses are to be found only in the Arctic. Once 500,000 were to be found on the Arctic ice floes, but hunting has reduced their numbers to less than 50,000.

Of the forty-seven species of seals, five are native to the Antarctic. The largest of these (and third only to the elephant seal and the walrus) is the leopard seal. It is well named, for it is the most ferocious carnivore of the family. It needs to fear no other animal but the killer whale — and, of course, man.

The crab-eater seal, despite its name, lives on krill. It is the most common of the Antarctic seals and numbers 5,000,000 to 8,000,000.

The most thoroughly Antarctic of the seals, however, is the Weddell seal. It sticks close to the shores of Antarctica, while the other seals range well out to sea. The Weddell seal finds safety beneath the coastal ice, breaking holes in it to breathe through. It can dive to a depth of 600 meters and can remain submerged for nearly an hour. Ordinarily, however, it comes up for air every ten to thirty minutes. (The female spends considerable time on top of the ice, for only there can she feed her young.)

Another notch downward in adaptation to the sea, we come to what would seem so completely a land animal as the bear. Two species of bears are characteristic of the Arctic regions and they are the two largest: the Kodiak brown bear and the polar bear.

The more northerly of the two is the polar bear. Creamy white in fur, it is not noticeable against the snow and ice it lives among. It can be 2 meters or more in length and may weigh over 700 kilograms. The polar bear lives on fish and seals and is capable of swimming miles out to sea. It can also roam the Arctic ice all the way to the North Pole — followed by the Arctic fox, which scavenges the polar bear kills. (The polar bear's liver is so rich in vitamin A as to be actually poisonous to man.)

And while we're talking of land mammals adapted to seeking food by sea, we should mention man, too. The Eskimos, at least, live very well in the apparently bleak Arctic world by learning to turn to the rich sea for their food.

There are important sea birds in the polar regions. In the Arctic, the most typical examples are the members of the auk family. These are not strong fliers but are very well adapted to diving into water for the fish they eat. They are capable of swimming underwater by making the same wing movements they make in flight. One of the better-known auks is the puffin, which has a large head and a multicolored parrotlike beak.

The most tragic member of the family was the great auk, which stood about a meter high and was the most completely adapted to water life of any species of the family. It could swim underwater expertly, but its wings were paddles only, and it could not fly with them.

What with its nonflight, its habit of congregating in great numbers on the islands in the Atlantic section of the Arctic, its single egg laid on bare ground without protection, and its inability to recognize the presence of danger, the great auk was an easy prey. They were killed wantonly in huge numbers and the last members of the species were killed on June 4, 1844.

Not all polar sea birds are poor fliers. The gull-like Arctic tern is, in some way, a flying champion. It nests in the Arctic (as far north as 82°5N) but evades the winter by flying 17,500 kilometers to the Antarctic; then evades the Antarctic winter by flying back to the Arctic. It spends seven months of the year traveling, and at each end of its journey experiences some two and a half months of continuous sunlight.

Another Arctic bird, the golden plover, also undergoes a long migratory flight, much of it being over the ocean and therefore nonstop, since the plovers don't swim well. A three-month-old golden plover can make it successfully from its birthplace in Alaska down to Hawaii (some 3500 kilometers) in two days of flying.

Although the Antarctic region has no mammals except for

whales and seals, which remain in the waters off the shores of Antarctica, there are birds that make their way across portions of the continent itself. Considering that the birds usually possess the ability to fly, this is perhaps not so unusual.

Of the fifteen species of flying birds that are found in the Antarctic region, the most southerly is a predatory gull-like bird called the skua. It seems very likely that skuas have ranged over all Antarctica and that they are the only species of living creature that has reached the South Pole independently of man.

There are two Antarctic petrels, and one of these, the giant petrel, is the largest of the Antarctic flying birds — with a wingspread of 2 meters and a weight of over 4 kilograms.

The most characteristic birds of Antarctica, however, are species incapable of flight, birds that actually walk extensively over the barren ice of that frozen continent. They are penguins, which adapted to the same kind of life and have developed a similar form to the great auk of the Arctic.

Penguins are as closely adapted to sea life as the great auk was, maybe more so. Their wings are paddles that are useless for flying but that give them an almost unmatched speed (almost 50 kilometers an hour) and turning ability underwater. Such is the force of their swimming that they can leap out of the water to twice their own height. On land, however, the best they can do is waddle in ungainly fashion. (Their upright posture, their humorous waddle, and their black and white coloration, as though they were wearing suits, have endeared them to men and spared them carnage.)

There are seventeen species of penguins altogether, all of them native to the Southern Hemisphere. Of these, two species actually live on Antarctica. The smaller of the Antarctic penguins is the Adélie penguin, so called because it is found in Adélie Land. The Adélie penguins congregate in crowded nesting sites inland ("rookeries"). They are about 45 centimeters tall and weigh 6 to 7 kilograms.

The skua is always waiting to eat the eggs and the penguin chicks, while in the ocean the leopard seal waits for the adults. As long as man does not interfere, however, enough survive to keep the species going.

More astonishing is the emperor penguin, the largest of all

living penguins, standing over a meter high (twice the height of the Adélie) and weighing as much as 35 kilograms. (There are fossils of penguins, now extinct, that stood 1.6 meters high and weighed as much as 110 kilograms.)

Unlike the Adélie penguins, the emperors did not seem to possess rookeries. Edward Wilson, one of those fated to die later with Scott in the tragic attempt to reach the South Pole and return, was particularly interested in finding the eggs of the emperor penguin. He believed the emperor penguin to be the most primitive of all birds, and the species most closely related to the reptiles. (He was wrong in this.) He thought that a study of the embryos of these birds might clarify their position in the animal kingdom.

In 1902, he was the first to discover an emperor penguin rookery. (There are fourteen known rookeries now, sheltering perhaps 160,000 emperor penguins altogether.) For the first time, Wilson saw emperor chicks on the feet of adults. From their size, he realized the hatching of those chicks must have taken place quite awhile before, during what was then winter.

In fact, it was discovered that the female emperor penguin laid her single egg in the middle of the Antarctic winter, so that the egg had to be incubated under worse conditions, by far, than those experienced by any other bird in the world. The emperor penguin is the only bird that does not nest on bare land. It nests on ice, and the emperor penguin may, indeed, never feel bare land but find itself always on or in water in solid or liquid form. (The Adélie penguin nests on exposed land along the rim of the continent and lays its eggs at the beginning of summer.)

The emperor penguin rookeries are located inland, some 80 to 130 kilometers from the coast. (Emperor penguins are occasionally found as far as 400 kilometers from the nearest coast, stubbornly trudging along — the farthest south any nonflying vertebrate has ever reached independently of man.)

It takes a month for the emperor penguins to travel from the shores of Antarctica, where food can be obtained, to the inland rookeries where no food exists (but where, except for man and skua, isolation and security are absolute). The emperor penguins fast during this trek.

There, in the interior, in winter, the female lays her single egg.

There is no nest and no nesting territory, something that only the emperor penguin, of all birds, lacks. The single egg is taken by the male and placed on his feet, immediately under a bare and unfeathered patch of the abdomen. A flap of skin covers the egg, which is then incubated against the father's body and on his feet, so that the nesting territory is, so to speak, the ground on which the bird stands.

The male emperor penguins can waddle about clumsily without losing the eggs, and most of them huddle together for warmth, which they need, for the icy Antarctic midwinter temperatures go as low as $-60°$ C, and the gales whistle past the birds at speeds of up to 150 kilometers per hour.

Once the egg is transferred, the female takes off for food and the sea again — another month's journey. The male, however, stands his ground for sixty days, still fasting. Prior to the trek to the rookery, the male emperor penguin has eaten enough to lay by a sizable quantity of fat — attaining a weight of 35 kilograms — but this begins to melt away during the long fast.

Finally, when the chicks are near to hatching, the females return and take over. At last the males can head for the sea, which they finally reach after a four-month fast during which they lose 25 to 40 percent of their weight.

When the chick hatches, the mother feeds it with food she has stored in her crop, but this won't last. The father must return, and for a while the parents take turns walking to the sea, eating their fill, and returning to feed the chick. Fully one quarter of the chicks don't survive the rigors of that first winter — but by the time the Antarctic summer arrives and the coastal ice begins breaking up, those that have survived can make it to the sea and go out to feed on their own.

PART 7

WORDS

WORDS *are of natural interest to writers, and certainly to me. It is a source of delight to me that English is my first language, for no other language consists of so many words, so many madly spelled and madly pronounced words, so many lawless words. In no other language, I firmly believe, can you have such fun with words.*

What one-syllable word becomes two syllables if you subtract two letters?

What word changes pronunciation when it is capitalized?

What word has a spelling pattern xyzxyzx?

There are four common English words ending with "dous." Three of them are "tremendous," "stupendous," and "horrendous." What is the fourth?

What common words contain the following letters in order somewhere in their spelling: pefr, wsp, ckc, ufl, ufa?

I'll give you the answers at the end of this section. Meanwhile, you can have fun with them.

My chief pleasure has always been the origin and etymology of words. My first hundred books include no less than six (all published by Houghton Mifflin) that deal exclusively with etymology. These are Words of Science, Words from the Myths, Words in Genesis, Words from the Exodus, Words on the Map, Words from History.

These cover the subject rather thoroughly and there are no such easy pickings in the second hundred. I did manage one more with Houghton Mifflin, however. That was More Words of Science *(Book 122), published in 1972. Here are three essays from that book: one on a chemical word, one on a biological word, and one on a physical word.*

from MORE WORDS OF SCIENCE (1972)

HALLUCINOGENS

The brain, like every other part of the body, performs its functions through certain chemical reactions. These are produced by stimuli brought to the brain through the senses. It is possible to change the brain chemistry by taking substances that interfere with these chemical reactions. In that case, the body will respond to stimuli that don't relate to the outside world. Objects that are not really there seem to be sensed, while objects that are really there may be ignored. The results are "hallucinations," from a Latin word meaning "to wander in the mind."

Certain plants contain chemicals that can produce hallucinations. The peyote cactus and a mushroom called *Amanita muscaria* contain such chemicals. Sometimes these plants are eaten in primitive religious celebrations because the hallucinations are thought to be glimpses of another world (or an escape from this one). Another substance that produces hallucinations is hashish, one form of which is marijuana.

In 1943, a Swiss chemist, Albert Hofmann, was studying an organic compound called "lysergic acid diethylamide" and accidentally got a few tiny crystals of it on his fingers. He happened to touch his fingers to his lips and was soon overcome by odd hallucinations. It took him a full day to regain normality. He began careful studies and found that very small doses of the chemical could always produce hallucinations. The name was soon reduced to an abbreviation of the three words. Since the German word for "acid" is *Säure*, and Hofmann spoke German, the abbreviation is LSD.

Since many young people foolishly began to play games with their minds by taking LSD and other such substances, hallucination-producing drugs became important to study. They are now lumped together under the general name "hallucinogens" (producers of hallucinations).

PHEROMONE

Human beings can communicate by talking. Through sounds, gestures, and written symbols, abstract ideas can be transmitted from one person to another. Human beings are unique in this respect.

Yet other creatures must be able to communicate in some fashion, if only so that there can be cooperation between two individuals of a species in order that they might reproduce. Within a body, the different parts are made to behave in some cooperative fashion by means of chemical messengers called "hormones." Is it possible that chemical messages can be carried on, not only within an organism, but from one organism to another?

Such hormonal effects, carried through water or air from one member of a species to another, are called "pheromones," the prefix coming from a Greek word meaning "to carry." They are hormones carried over a distance.

Insect pheromones are the most dramatic. A female moth can liberate a compound that will act as a powerful sexual attractant on a male moth of the same species a mile away. Each species must have its own pheromone, for there is no point in affecting a male of another species. Each species must have receiving devices of tremendous delicacy because they must be able to react to just a few molecules in the air.

Pheromones are also used in interspecies conflict. Certain ants raid the nests of other ant species to kidnap the young, which they rear as slaves. The raiders use trails of pheromones which not only aid them to keep together and coordinate their attacks, but also act to alarm and scatter the ant species they are attacking.

Biologists are laboring to use insect pheromones to lure members of troublesome species to destruction. In this way, they can be absolutely specific, doing no direct harm to any other species.

SYNCHROTRON

In the 1930s, physicists developed methods for accelerating subatomic particles in order to give them high energies and send them smashing into atomic nuclei. The most successful of these was invented by the American physicist Ernest O. Lawrence in 1931. It whirled particles around and around, thanks to the driving force of a magnetic field, and it was therefore called a "cyclotron."

By making larger and larger magnets, one could whirl the particles to greater and greater energies. The device only works well, however, if the mass of the particles doesn't change. As the particles go faster, their mass increases considerably (as Albert Einstein predicted they would in his special theory of relativity). This lowers the efficiency of the cyclotron and limits the energies it can produce.

In 1945, the Soviet physicist Vladimir I. Veksler and the American physicist Edwin M. McMillan independently worked out a way to alter the strength of a magnetic field so as to match the increase in mass. The two effects were "synchronized" (from Greek words meaning "same time") and the efficiency remained high. Such a modified cyclotron was called a "synchrocyclotron."

In cyclotrons, the whirling particles spiral outward and eventually pass beyond the limits of the magnet. If the particles could be held in a tight circle, they could be whirled many more times before being released and still higher energies would be attained.

The English physicist Marcus L. E. Oliphant worked out a design for such a device in 1947, and in 1952 the first of the kind was built in Brookhaven National Laboratory on Long Island. It still made use of a synchronized increase in the strength of the field, but the spiraling of the particles, as in a cyclotron, was gone. The new device was therefore called simply a "synchrotron."

As for the puzzles I set you at the beginning of the section —
1. *The one-syllable word "plague" loses the first two letters and becomes the two-syllable "ague."*
2. *Capitalize the word "polish" and it becomes "Polish."*
3. *The most common word with the pattern xyzxyzx is "alfalfa." Second is "entente," but that is more French than English. There was once a breath freshener with the name "Sen-Sens."*
4. *The fourth common English word ending in "dous" is "hazardous."*
5. *The letter combinations and the words containing them are:*
   pefr — *grapefruit*
   wsp — *newspaper (Less good, because less common, is "bowsprit.")*
   ckc — *sackcloth or cockcrow*
   ufl — *genuflect*
   ufa — *manufacture (Oddly enough, this is the* only *common word with that combination.)*

PART 8

HISTORY

IN THE COURSE of my first hundred books, I wrote a history book for Houghton Mifflin entitled The Greeks. *I enjoyed doing that so much that I embarked on a whole series of histories, and by the time I had reached my hundredth book, Houghton Mifflin had published seven of them, all on ancient and medieval history.*

In the course of my second hundred books I did seven more histories for Houghton Mifflin. One of them, The Land of Canaan *(Book 116), was on ancient history. In this book, published in 1971, I told the tale of the Maccabean revolt.*

from THE LAND OF CANAAN (1971)

The high priests of the old line of Zadok, which dated back to Solomon's Temple, still held their state in Jerusalem. In 219 B.C., during the last years of Ptolemaic dominion, Onias II died and Simon II became high priest. He is known to later generations as Simon the Just and received an eloquent tribute in the fiftieth chapter of the apocryphal biblical book Ecclesiasticus. In 196 B.C., at about the time Judea passed under Seleucid dominion, Simon's son Onias III became high priest. He, too, is pictured as having been pious and devout.

Judea itself was confined to a small inland region bordering on the northwestern shores of the Dead Sea, with Jerusalem as its only city of note and with a total area of only about 750 square miles. To its north, where once Israel had been, was Samaria, and with the Samaritans the Jews maintained a deadly hostility, each group considering the other to be pernicious heretics. To the south of Judea lived the descendants of the Edomites, who had moved northward into land that had once been southern Judah and which was now Idumea. Between Jews and Idumeans there was also a deadly enmity.

To be sure, the Jews were not confined to Judea. Many of them colonized Galilee, the region north of Samaria. It had once made up northern Israel but in these days was so full of non-Jews that it was called Galilee of the Gentiles by the conservative and disapproving Jews of Judea itself. Then, of course, there were the Jews of the Diaspora (Greek for "dispersion"); that is, those who dwelt outside the borders of the land that had once been promised to Abraham. There were the Jews of the Tigris-Euphrates, of Alexandria, of the Greek cities in Asia Minor and elsewhere.

To all Jews, however, wherever located, Jerusalem and its Temple remained at the center of their national consciousness. At the time of the great festivals, Jerusalem was crowded with Jews from all over the Near East, coming to sacrifice. The development of Judaism was by this time almost complete. Virtually all the books of the Old Testament had by now been written.

Yet Judaism faced a new danger. The old Canaanite idolatries were long gone, but a new and even more attractive idolatry existed. Since the time of Alexander, Greeks had penetrated all the Mediterranean world and wherever they went they carried Greek culture with them. They were a city people, too, and wherever they went they founded cities. In Judea and surrounding lands, the penetration by the Greeks had been slow under the Ptolemys, but when the Greek-loving Seleucid kings took over, the trend accelerated.

And those who were not Greeks by race (or Hellenes, as the Greeks called themselves) nevertheless hastened to adopt Greek culture. They became Hellenized and the process of Hellenization became a dominating force in all the Mediterranean. Even the rough Romans of the west felt the force of Hellenization; and Scipio himself, the conqueror of Hannibal, was a leader of those who would adopt Greek ways.

The Jews were not immune. Many Jews, not only in Greek cities far from Jerusalem but even in Judea itself, adopted Greek ways of life while paying lip service to the older and less sophisticated notions of Judaism. Other Jews, however, particularly in Judea itself, clung entirely to the old ways and abhorred Greek notions.

The stage was set for a quarrel between these two kinds of Judaism, but anyone looking at the world in 183 B.C. could not possibly have foreseen that such a struggle could have any importance or that it could have any possible effect outside Judea. The thought that the struggle would have world-shaking effects and that it would dictate the nature of the religions that would dominate the world in centuries to come would have seemed utterly unbelievable.

Yet it happened; but so slowly that for centuries no one could possibly have noticed that anything important was taking place.

It began with the failure of Antiochus III. The large indemnity he had agreed to pay the Romans following his defeat was more than he had in his treasury. To get the money, he had to squeeze the rich temples of his land. It was while he was trying to carry the gold out of one of the temples in a far province that the rioting peasantry killed him in 187 B.C.

He was succeeded by his son Seleucus IV, who found the Seleucid realm weakened by defeat and plunder and the far-eastern provinces, so painstakingly retaken by Antiochus III, falling away again, this time permanently.*

Seleucus IV attempted to maintain a quiet and unadventurous reign, since the land needed time for recovery. He still needed money, however, as his father had, and one of the obvious sources was the Temple in Jerusalem. Seleucus sent an official named Heliodorus to see what could be done in that direction.

The tale of what follows is told in the apocryphal book of Second Maccabees in a garbled fashion. What may very likely have happened was that Onias III, the high priest, managed to make a deal with Heliodorus. He bribed Heliodorus generously, giving the underling a part in order to avoid having to give the master the whole. Heliodorus knew that he risked his neck if what he had done was discovered, so he arranged to have Seleucus IV assassinated in 175 B.C.

But Seleucus IV had a younger brother Antiochus, who had been born in Athens and who, after his father's defeat, had been sent as a hostage to Rome. The younger Antiochus was treated kindly there and conceived an admiration for Rome. He was also (perhaps because of his pride in his Athenian birth) an enthusiast of Greek culture. On hearing of his older brother's assassination, Antiochus left Rome and made his way to Antioch. Once

* For the subsequent history of these eastern provinces, see my book *The Near East* (Houghton Mifflin, 1968).

there, he had no trouble seizing control and beginning his reign as Antiochus IV.

Antiochus IV was a capable man who dreamed of restoring the Seleucid Empire to the power from which the defeat by the Romans had toppled it. To do this — the old story — he needed money. Among the sources of funds was still the Temple at Jerusalem. Onias III, who represented the more conservative factions of Judaism, was still high priest and Antiochus IV viewed him with disfavor. This might have been simply the result of the old man's stubborn refusal to part with Temple money, or perhaps Antiochus had heard rumors of the deal with Heliodorus. Then, too, Antiochus may well have thought his kingdom would be stronger if all its people were united in Hellenic culture, and the stubborn adherence of Onias III to conservative Judaism may have bothered him.

In any case, when Onias' brother Joshua approached Antiochus with suggestions of a deal, Antiochus listened. The suggestion was that Antiochus appoint Joshua as high priest in place of his brother. Joshua would then allow Antiochus a generous supply of the Temple funds. (In return, Joshua would have the prestige and power of the high priesthood and — as both men knew — a chance to enrich himself, as any high priest could do if he were a little unscrupulous.) To tempt Antiochus further, Joshua played up to his known pro-Greek proclivities by offering to encourage the Hellenization of the Jews. As a demonstration of his sincerity in this direction, he had changed his name from the Hebrew "Joshua" to the Greek "Jason."

Antiochus agreed to the deal. Onias III was taken off to house arrest in Antioch, and Joshua-Jason became high priest. Joshua-Jason promptly began to live up to his part of the bargain. Antiochus got his money and Joshua-Jason established a gymnasium in Jerusalem. At the gymnasium young men could exercise, Greek fashion, in the nude, and the more modish of the young Jews flocked to it. (And Joshua-Jason, who controlled the gymnasium financially, reaped generous profits.)

The conservative Jews were horrified by the arrest of Onias III and by the rifling of the treasury, but the gymnasium shocked them most of all. Not only was public nudity considered an abomination, but young Jews who wished to exercise often wore false foreskins to avoid advertising the fact that they were circumcised — thus denying the very mark of Judaism.

But Joshua-Jason had merely taught others to take the same route as himself. A cousin of his named Onias, who took the Greek name of Menelaus, offered Antiochus a still higher bribe if he were made high priest in his turn. Antiochus obliged in 172 B.C. and in succeeding years the Temple and the people were looted indeed.

When the depredation of Onias-Menelaus became plain, old Onias III, who was looked upon by all conservative Jews as the only legitimate high priest, had the courage to denounce the matter publicly, and then took sanctuary in a Greek temple in a suburb of Antioch. Onias-Menelaus, however, seems to have persuaded the Seleucid commander in the district (with bribes, perhaps) to induce Onias III to leave the sanctuary by giving an oath for his safety. Once Onias III was out of the temple, he was promptly murdered. This was in 170 B.C.

There was chaos in Judea among those factions supporting this high priest or that, but this was of little moment to Antiochus IV. The Hellenization of the land seemed to be progressing favorably and he had the money he needed from the Temple at Jerusalem and from other sources. He could now buy arms, pay soldiers, and begin the Seleucid comeback. He intended to begin the comeback by taking over Egypt, which was now under the rule of Ptolemy VI, an amiable person but a complete incompetent.

Antiochus IV had no trouble at all. He was a good general and he had a good army. Brushing aside feeble Ptolemaic resistance, he marched to Memphis, the ancient capital of the Egyptians, and in 170 B.C. had himself declared king of Egypt. He then took his army to the Ptolemaic capital of Alexandria and, in 169 B.C., placed it under siege.

While the siege was under way, however, news reached Antiochus that in his absence Joshua-Jason had attempted to take the high priesthood from Onias-Menelaus by force. Jerusalem was in a state of civil war and the Seleucid army, almost 350 miles west of its own borders, could not afford to have its line of communications threatened.

Furious, Antiochus IV hastened back to Judea and punished the troublesome Jews by occupying the city, entering the Temple himself at the head of an armed contingent, and dragging off all the valuables he could find. For the moment, Jerusalem was stricken and quiet.

In 168 B.C., then, Antiochus IV returned to Egypt, where he had as little trouble as before and where he once again resumed the siege of Alexandria. By now, however, the Ptolemys had squealed for help to Rome, which promptly answered the call. Outside the walls of Alexandria a Roman ambassador approached Antiochus IV. Antiochus recognized him as an old friend and approached gladly to greet him; but the old friend was an official emissary from Rome now and he had only one thing to say: Antiochus was either to leave Egypt or to accept war with Rome. Thunderstruck, Antiochus IV asked for time to consider. The Roman drew a circle in the ground around the king and said, "Decide before you leave the circle."

Antiochus dared not face Rome. Though his entire army was around him and though it had marched victoriously through Egypt, and though it was sure to take Alexandria, he and all his men had to back down in the face of a single unarmed Roman. There are few humiliations in history as dramatic as this one.

We can imagine Antiochus' angry frustration as he retreated, his need to get back at something or someone. Perhaps the news reached him that the Jews were jubilant over the state of his affairs, as well they might be in view of the troubles he had visited on them by his manipulation of the high priesthood and by his looting of the Temple.

In any case, Antiochus IV determined that, though the Romans might humiliate him, the Jews would not. On his return to Antioch in 167 B.C. he resolved to put an end to Judaism altogether. Let the Jews become Greeks and loyal subjects! It did not seem to him (probably) to be much of a task. Men such as Joshua-Jason and Onias-Menelaus seemed only too eager to be Greek, and they commanded sizable factions among the Jews.

Consequently, Antiochus ordered that the Temple in Jerusalem be made Greek and that within it there be erected a statue representing Zeus (with whom Yahweh was to be identified) and that on its altar there be sacrifices offered in Greek fashion. What's more, copies of the Jewish Scriptures were to be destroyed, Jewish dietary regulations ended, the Sabbath abolished, and the practice of circumcision forbidden. Those Jews who accepted Hellenization were to be left in peace as loyal subjects of Antiochus. For the first time in history a persecution began that was religious, not national, in character.

Words cannot describe the horror felt by the conservative Jews. Nebuchadnezzar, four centuries before, had merely destroyed the Temple, but Antiochus had desecrated it with idols and swine's flesh. Nebuchadnezzar had merely taken away the Jewish land, but Antiochus was taking away their ideal. The conservative Jews prepared to resist and to retain their way of life, even to death by torture.

Such deaths took place, according to the tales told later in Second Maccabees. Grisly tales of martyrdom, of Jews dying under torture rather than agreeing to taste swine's flesh, are recorded there. These were the first martyr tales in the Judeo-Christian tradition and they formed a precedent.

It was during this period of trial that the books of Daniel and of Esther were written with their (fictional) tales of the dangers and sufferings undergone by Jews under previous oppressors and of how these were overcome by faith and courage. The apocryphal books of Tobit and Judith were written in similar fashion. These were intended to serve, not as sober history (though they were taken as such by the pious of later ages), but as devices for stimulating and encouraging resistance. And eventually, the resistance ceased being that of passive acceptance of torture and death and became the active return of violence for violence.

This new turn of events began with an aged priest, Mattathias. He and his five sons left Jerusalem and retired to the comparative safety of a small town named Modin, seventeen miles to the northwest, outside Judea proper. According to Josephus, the great-great-grandfather of Mattathias was named Hashmon, so that Mattathias and his descendants are sometimes called the Hasmoneans. On the other hand, the third of his five sons, who was to turn out to be the most famous of them, was Judah Makkabi, or, in Greek form, Judas Maccabeus. The surname may mean the Hammerer, from his later victories. In any case, the family has come to be better known as the Maccabees, and the apocryphal books written about the events of this time, whether sober history in the case of First Maccabees, dramatized history in the case of Second Maccabees, or fiction in the case of Third Maccabees, all received this name.

The spark that initiated the Jewish rebellion against the Seleucids was set off by an officer of Antiochus who came to Modin to enforce the new laws. He asked Mattathias, as a prominent Jewish leader, to set a good example and to carry through a sacrifice to Zeus in the manner required. Mattathias refused. When another Jew offered to fulfill the royal command, Mattathias, in a rage, killed the Jew and the Seleucid officer.

There was then nothing to do but to leave Modin hastily. Mattathias and his sons made for the Gophna hills, some dozen miles northeast of Modin. Other Jews who resented the new laws came to join him there, and in no time a guerrilla band had been formed. Mattathias died very soon after the flight to the hills and the band came under the command of Judas Maccabeus.

Joining the Maccabee standard were bands of Hassidim (or, in the Greek version of the name, Hasideans), a term which means "the pious ones." Their sole concern lay in religion and they were uninterested in politics. It was only when the practice of Judaism was outlawed that they were willing to resort to violence, but under those conditions they were fanatical fighters indeed.

The Gophna hills lay in Samaritan territory, and the Seleucid governor of the region, Apollonius, moved quickly to nip the revolt before it got very far. Apollonius was, in all likelihood, overconfident. He must have been convinced he could easily handle a few rebels and he marched forward carelessly. Judas' men lay in ambush and swarmed down at the proper time. Apollonius' men were scattered, Apollonius himself was killed, and Judas took Apollonius' sword for use in later battles.

This victory encouraged the conservative Jews in Jerusalem and placed the pro-Hellenizers there in difficulties. Matters grew still worse for the latter. A larger Seleucid force was sent out in 166 B.C. to occupy Jerusalem and end the annoying revolt. Again Judas Maccabeus and his men lay in ambush, this time at Bethhoron, twelve miles northwest of Jerusalem. The second Seleucid force was also trapped and destroyed.

By now the Jewish guerrillas had made a first-class nuisance of themselves, but Antiochus IV could not turn his full attention to them. He needed money, money, money, and he had to get that somewhere in the east, where the provinces had declared themselves independent and where tax collections had dried up. Off he marched eastward, leaving the small Jewish war band to the attention of his minister, Lysias.

In 165 B.C. Lysias assembled a strong army at Emmaus, fifteen miles west of Jerusalem and eleven miles west of the Maccabean stronghold at Mizpeh. Judas held his ground and remained on the defensive. With only three thousand men he had to.

But the Seleucid army could not wait. If the rebels would not come out to fight, they would have to be flushed out. Its commander made a mistake, however; he divided his forces and sent only part to Mizpeh. That was what Judas was hoping for. With the enemy divided, Judas raced his men to Emmaus, where he attacked and defeated the part of the Seleucid army that had remained there. With that done, Judas whirled on the contingent that was returning fruitlessly from Mizpeh. For the third time, the Seleucids were defeated.

Later in the year Lysias tried once more, sending a troop around Judea into the friendly land of Idumea and then attacking toward Jerusalem from the south. The watchful Judas stopped him at Beth-zur, sixteen miles southwest of Jerusalem, and defeated him again.

By now, successive victories had brought enough of the Jews to the side of the Maccabees to make it possible for the guerrillas to enter Jerusalem. Seleucid forces and their Hellenized Jewish sympathizers still controlled the fortified portions of the city, but the Maccabees were able to seize the Temple.

Judas Maccabeus proceeded to rededicate the Temple, purifying it from its Seleucid profanation. He chose priests who had never compromised with the Seleucid authorities, tore down the altar on which swine had been sacrificed to Zeus, and buried the stones. A new altar was built, new vessels supplied, and proper sacrifices performed. The anniversary of the dedication of the Temple in 165 B.C. is celebrated to this day by the Jews as the eight-day feast of Hanukkah ("dedication").

Judas Maccabeus by no means considered this a final victory. It was merely an item. He had as his ambition the liberation of all Jews everywhere in the land that had once been Canaan. He led his army across the Jordan and northward, while his brother Simon, with another troop, took the route northward along the coast. Both defeated Seleucid contingents, enrolled fighters from among the Jewish population, and established strongpoints. By 163 B.C. the Seleucid power south of Damascus had been reduced to tatters, and far off, in what is now central Iran, Antiochus IV died, possibly from tuberculosis. Despite his very real ability, his reign had been a disaster.

The death of Antiochus IV did not end Seleucid attempts to repress the Maccabean revolt. Antiochus' nine-year-old son reigned as Antiochus V, with Lysias as his minister. In 162 B.C. yet another Seleucid army advanced to the attack. It was the strongest yet, and once again it attacked from the south, moving through Beth-zur. It had at least one elephant moving with it.

In a battle at Beth-zechariah, five miles north of Beth-zur, the Maccabeans were forced back. Eleazar, one of the brothers of Judas, fought his way to the elephant, thinking that it carried the king in person. He stabbed it in the abdomen and killed it, but the dying elephant fell on Eleazar and crushed him — and it did not, after all, carry the young king.

Eleazar's feat did not turn the tide of battle, and for the first time, in the face of overwhelming strength, Judas was defeated. He brought what he could save of his forces back to the Gophna hills, where he and his family had first sought refuge five years before, and the Seleucid forces reoccupied Jerusalem. This time, however, they were careful to make no attempt to interfere with the Temple services. Lysias' moderation was the result of trouble at home. Other generals were trying to seize control of the kingdom from Lysias, while Demetrius, a nephew of Antiochus IV, was grabbing at the throne itself.

Lysias therefore, in an effort to end the Judean revolt which was sapping his strength, offered a compromise. He would grant the Jews complete religious freedom if they would accept Seleucid political sovereignty. The Hassidim, who were interested only in Judaism as a religion, accepted this and retired from the battle. This meant that Lysias had gained his point, for, without the Hassidim, Judas' remaining forces were too weak to offer resistance and he could only maintain himself in the Gophna hills and await events.

In the Seleucid wars that followed, both Antiochus V and Lysias were killed, and Demetrius I ruled in their place. With Judea quiet, he attempted to restore the situation as it had once been, with the appointment of a high priest who would control Judaism in the Seleucid interest — at least to a reasonable degree. He appointed Eliakim as high priest; Eliakim, a Hellenizer, preferred to be known by the Greek name of Alcimus. Since Eliakim-Alcimus was of the old Zadokite line of priests, the Hassidim accepted him.

Now there was left only the small band of irreconcilables in the Gophna hills. Demetrius might have ignored them, but apparently Judas was attempting to interest Rome in the Jewish plight, and the Seleucid king decided to clean them out before it occurred to Rome to interfere. Demetrius therefore sent his general Bacchides with a strong force from Jerusalem toward the Gophna hills.

Battle was joined eight miles north of Jerusalem in 161 B.C. Judas, whose forces now were less than a thousand strong, was overwhelmed. He himself died on the battlefield and the few survivors scattered. Two of his brothers, Jonathan and Simon, who were among those survivors, managed to take Judas' body away from the battlefield and bury him in the family tomb at Modin. Thus died the most remarkable Jewish fighter since the time of David eight centuries before.

The Maccabean revolt appeared over. A few men lurked in the southern desert with Jonathan, the younger brother of Judas Maccabeus, but they were powerless and could be ignored. The moderate policy of Lysias and Demetrius I had worked where the stern force of Antiochus IV had failed.

The revolt had nevertheless accomplished one purpose: the Temple was Jewish again and the Seleucids made no attempt ever again to interfere with the ritual. This meant that Judaism had been saved and that — alone — meant that Judas' stand, though it had ended in defeat and death, was nevertheless of crucial importance to world history.

On the other hand, the danger was not entirely over. Judaism might have been saved only to die more slowly. The high priest, Alcimus, did all he could to Hellenize the religion. He died in

159 B.C. — the last high priest who was in any way Zadokite — but Hellenization continued after him. And it might have succeeded had the Seleucid kingdom remained a stable and effective governing force. What prevented the withering of Judaism was not so much what the surviving Maccabees could do, but the continuing dynastic struggle among the Seleucids. Demetrius I was constantly fighting rivals for the throne, and, when he was forced to pull soldiers out of Judea, Jonathan and his small band automatically began to increase in numbers and expanded to fill the vacuum.

Demetrius made the best of it. In 157 B.C. he appointed Jonathan to the post of royal governor and allowed him to enter Jerusalem and rule Judea, provided he acknowledged Seleucid sovereignty. Jonathan agreed to that, accepting the reality of power and letting the appearance go.

In 152 B.C. an imposter, Alexander Balas, who claimed to be a son of Antiochus IV, obtained the backing of Ptolemaic Egypt and launched a civil war against Demetrius I. Jonathan remained shrewdly uncommitted for a while, allowing both sides to bid for his services. Demetrius offered Jonathan rule over wider areas, and Balas offered to appoint him high priest. Jonathan accepted both offers.

In that year of 152 B.C., then, Jonathan donned the robes of the high priesthood, and for the first time in nine centuries an individual who was not descended from Solomon's high priest, Zadok, officiated in the Temple.

Finally, when Jonathan had to choose, he came down on the side of Balas. The choice seemed a good one, for in 150 B.C., in a final battle between the two claimants, Balas was victorious and Demetrius I was killed.

In 147 B.C., however, the son of Demetrius arrived in Syria and attacked Balas. The son was Demetrius II and he, of course, was hostile to the Maccabeans, who had supported — and were, perforce, continuing to support — Balas. An army loyal to Demetrius encamped in what was once the land of the Philistines and challenged Jonathan to battle. Jonathan, in that same year, accepted the challenge, and the battle was fought in Azotus, the Biblical Ashdod.

For the first time the Maccabean army was large enough to

fight as something more than a guerrilla force — to fight an organized battle rather than instituting a surprise attack from ambush — and it won. The Maccabees under Jonathan now controlled land on both sides of the Jordan over an area of some 800 square miles.

In 145 B.C. Demetrius II finally defeated Balas in battle and drove him to flight and eventual death, but by then the Seleucid monarchy was a worthless toy. The civil wars that had been nearly continuous since the death of Antiochus IV, eighteen years before, had seen a steady shrinkage of the dominions of Antioch. All the east, including the Tigris-Euphrates valley, was now part of the independent kingdom of Parthia (ruled by a people akin to the Persians). Only Syria remained to the Seleucids.

Demetrius II found his power so limited that he could no longer mount a real offensive against the Maccabean forces. In fact, he needed help against his own enemies. Jonathan offered such help, suggesting he would send a band of seasoned Jewish mercenaries to serve Demetrius if the king would hand over the fortified posts surrounding Jerusalem. Demetrius agreed, accepted the forces, used them to establish his power firmly in Antioch, and then refused to give up the fortified posts.

The angry Jonathan waited for the inevitable — more dynastic troubles. In 143 B.C. a general named Tryphon, making use of a young boy who was hailed as the son of Balas and given the title Antiochus VI, rebelled against Demetrius II. Jonathan threw his support to the new claimant at once.

But Tryphon wearied of the indirection of having to act under cover of a boy and planned to kill Antiochus VI. To do so, however, might have risked the good will of Jonathan, who was, at the moment, his strongest supporter. Tryphon therefore planned to plunge the Maccabean power into confusion in the most direct possible way first. He invited Jonathan to a conference in the royal city of Ptolemais, eighty-five miles north of Jerusalem. Jonathan, apparently flattered to be treated with considerable respect by the Seleucid power, allowed himself to be lured into the city with a very small band of men. He was captured and killed in 142 B.C.

But one Maccabean brother remained — Simon. He reclaimed Jonathan's body and buried it in the family tomb, then once more approached Demetrius II, who still maintained a force against Tryphon. Simon offered him an alliance against Tryphon in exchange for recognition of complete Judean independence. The deal was made, and 142 B.C. marked the moment when, for the first time since Nebuchadnezzar's destruction of Jerusalem, 445 years before, there was an independent Jewish state. Simon ruled both as king (though he did not use the title) and high priest.

Almost at once Simon began to strengthen himself. In 141 B.C. he took over the fortified posts in Jerusalem so that at least the capital city was entirely free of the foreign soldiery. He also took the coastal city of Joppa to give the newly independent kingdom a foothold at sea.

From a material standpoint my history books do not do particularly well. For instance, they have never moved into paperback editions. That doesn't matter to me, however, since I enjoy writing them, and my income is high enough to let me please myself in this respect.

Houghton Mifflin might object, to be sure, but they don't. Perhaps that is because they don't want to hurt my feelings and see a look of troubled sadness come into my eyes . . . So, among the second hundred, they loyally published two books of mine on medieval history: Constantinople *(Book 106) in 1970, and* The Shaping of France *(Book 126) in 1972.*

From the latter book, here is a passage in which France, having suffered disastrous defeats at the hands of the smaller nation of England, meets with an even worse enemy.

from THE SHAPING OF FRANCE (1972)

But once disasters begin to come, they come in battalions. France had suffered a disaster at sea at the Battle of Sluys, and a far worse disaster on land at the Battle of Crécy. Now there came a disaster worse than either, worse than both together, worse than anything mere medieval armies could do; something that placed not only France but England, too, and all Europe under a terror beyond that which mere armies could create.

It was the plague.

The plague is essentially a disease of rodents and is spread from rodent to rodent by fleas. Every once in a while, however, when the fleas spread the disease to rodents such as house rats, which live in close conjunction with human beings, the disease spreads also to men. Sometimes it affects the lymph nodes, particularly in the groin and the armpits, causing them to swell into painful "buboes" — hence "bubonic plague." Sometimes the lungs are affected ("pneumonic plague") and that is even worse, for then contagion proceeds from man to man via the air and there is no need for the intervention of rats and fleas.

Sometime in the 1330s, a new strain of plague bacillus made its appearance somewhere in central Asia; a strain to which human beings were particularly susceptible. Men began to die, and even while Edward and Philip fought their trivial battle over who was to rule France, the grinning specter of death was striding closer to Europe. By the time Calais fell, the plague had reached the Black Sea.

In the Crimea, the peninsula jutting into the north-central Black Sea, there was a seaport called Kaffa where the Genoese had established a trading post. In October 1347, a fleet of twelve Genoese ships just managed to make it back to Genoa from Kaffa. The few men on board who were not already dead were dying — and thus the plague entered western Europe. In early 1348 it was in France and in mid-1348 it had reached England.

Sometimes one caught a mild version of the disease, but very often it struck virulently. In the latter case, the patient was almost always dead within one to three days after the first symptoms. Because the extreme stages were marked by hemorrhagic spots that turned dusky, the disease was called the Black Death.

In a world innocent of hygiene, the Black Death spread unchecked. It is thought to have killed some 25 million people in Europe before it died down (more because all the most susceptible people were dead than because anyone did anything) and many more than that in Africa and Asia. About a third of the population of Europe died, perhaps more, and it took a century and a half before natural multiplication restored European population to what it had been at the time of the Battle of Crécy.

It was the greatest natural disaster to strike mankind in recorded history.

Its short-term effects were marked by the abject terror it inspired among the populace. It seemed as though the world were coming to an end, and everyone walked in fear. A sudden attack of shivering or giddiness, a mere headache, might mean that death had marked you for its own and had given you a couple dozen hours to live.

Whole towns were depopulated, with the first to die lying unburied while the initial survivors fled — only to spread the disease to wherever it was they fled to. Farms lay untended; domestic animals (who also died by the millions) wandered about uncared for. Whole nations (Aragon, for instance) were afflicted so badly that they never truly recovered.

Distilled liquors (alcoholic drinks produced by distilling wine, thus producing a stronger solution of alcohol than could be formed by natural fermentation) had first been developed in Italy about 1100. Now, two centuries later, they grew popular. The theory was that strong drink acted as a preventive against contagion. It didn't, but it made the drinker less concerned, which was something. The plague of drunkenness settled down over Europe to match the plague of disease and remained behind after the disease was gone.

Everyone suffered, with those who lived in crowded quarters the worst, of course. Towns suffered more than the countryside, and indeed the gradual urbanization of the west received a setback from which it did not recover for a century. Monastic communities were also particularly hard hit, and the quality of monastic life in some ways never recovered.

Even the highest were vulnerable. In 1348 and 1349, three archbishops of Canterbury died of the plague. In the papal capital of Avignon, five cardinals and a hundred bishops died. A daughter of Edward III, Joan, was on her way to Castile to marry the son of King Alfonso XI. She died of plague in Bordeaux on her way there. And in Castile, so did King Alfonso. In France, Philip's queen, Joan of Burgundy, died.

The terrified populace had to take action. Knowing nothing of the germ theory or of the danger of fleas, unable to keep clean in a culture which was rather suspicious of cleanliness and considered it unholy, they could do nothing useful. They could, however, find a scapegoat, and for that there were always Jews available.

The theory arose that the Jews had deliberately poisoned wells in order to destroy Christians. The fact that Jews were dying of the plague on equal terms with Christians was not allowed to interfere with the theory, and the Jews were slaughtered without mercy. Of course this did nothing at all to diminish the scourge.

Viewed from a longer range, the Black Death (which kept recurring at intervals — though never again as bad — after the first attack had died out in 1351) destroyed the medieval optimism of the thirteenth century. It placed a kind of gloom on the world and bred a growth of fatalistic mysticism that took a long time to dispel.

It also helped destroy the economic structure of feudalism. There had never been a surplus of labor in the fields and the towns, but with the devastation of the plague (which fell more violently upon the low-born than upon the aristocracy) there was a sudden extreme shortage. Savage laws were promulgated by governments in order to keep serfs and artisans from taking advantage of the suddenly increased value of their muscles and skills, but no laws could counter the economic facts of life.

Serfs who recognized the great need for their services dickered for better treatment and greater privileges and often got them. Artisans charged higher prices. Prices and wages rose, and to the difficulties produced by war and plague were added those of economic dislocation and inflation.

Under the double blow of the Battle of Crécy and the Black Death, the very basis of feudalism, both military and economic, was destroyed. In western Europe, it had to die. It took its time, but there was never a question of its surviving after the mid–fourteenth century; only of how long it would take before human beings realized that it was dead.

Then, half a century later, after the French had suffered civil war and additional defeats and the ever-victorious English were laying siege to Orléans with final victory at hand, here is what happened:

from THE SHAPING OF FRANCE (1972)

On February 12, 1429, when the siege was completing its fourth month, a column of French tried to intercept a wagon train being sent to the English from Paris. This included many barrels of dried herrings, for it was the Lenten season and fish was in high demand. The supply train was under the command of Sir John Fastolfe, who had fought well at Agincourt and in Normandy.

As soon as Fastolfe was aware of the oncoming French, he took vigorous measures for the defense. He drew his wagons into a line that served as an impromptu fortification. From behind the shelter of those wagons, he placed his English longbowmen at one flank, and Parisian crossbowmen (the Parisians were still hotly pro-Burgundy and anti-Armagnac) on the other.

The French fought well, but there was little they could do against the wagon-protected bowmen, and the English won again. Burst barrels strewed herring all over the field, so the action is known as the Battle of the Herrings.

The French relieving forces were particularly disheartened at this repulse because it seemed one more in an endless string of victories won in the field by the English. There seemed no use in fighting at all, so what was left of those forces marched hastily away. No other forces were sent with any intention of battle. Orléans was left to its fate, and, after two more months had passed, it seemed that Orléans must fall and that the Bastard, whatever his resolution and ability, would simply have to surrender.

And then a very strange thing happened, one of the strangest in history, and something that would have been derided as incredible if it had appeared in a work of fiction.

A peasant girl appeared on the scene.

Her name was Jeanne Darc and she was born about 1412 at the village of Domrémy, at the eastern borders of France, 160 miles east of Paris. After the Treaty of Troyes, Domrémy lay in that part of France which had been handed over to the overlordship of the English king.

Jeanne Darc, or Joan Darc in English, is never known by that name. Her last name has been misspelled as d'Arc, as though she were of the nobility, so that in English she is invariably known as Joan of Arc, although there is no place called Arc from which she came or over which she had some claim.

In her teens she was experiencing visions, hearing voices and imagining herself called on to save France. In 1429, these visions and voices finally drove her to action. Charles VII had still not been crowned at Reims, though six full years had passed since the death of his father. What's more, the siege of Orléans might end in another English victory, and that might defeat him forever. It seemed to Joan that her mission had to start at once, that she had to relieve the siege and crown Charles.

In January 1429, Joan left for Vaucouleurs, twelve miles north of Domrémy, where there was a fortified outpost that still held out for Charles VII. Its captain was sufficiently impressed by her (or perhaps sufficiently eager to get rid of her) to send her on to Charles VII with an escort of six men. Charles VII was then at Chinon, 90 miles southwest of Orléans and 270 miles from Domrémy. Joan had to cross English-controlled territory to reach Chinon, and so she dressed in a man's costume to avoid the kind of trouble a young girl might have if encountered by soldiers. She arrived at Chinon on February 24, 1429, two weeks after the Battle of the Herrings had ended French attempts to do anything active about the siege of Orléans.

It was a superstitious age. When a girl announced herself as a miraculous maid sent by God, she might be taken for exactly that — or as a dangerous witch sent by the Devil for the ensnarement of men. It was not easy to tell which. Charles VII actually received Joan, and she was then questioned by learned theologians for three weeks in order to determine whether she was of divine or diabolical inspiration.

It may well be that some of the worldly men around Charles were not really concerned with which she was, and perhaps didn't believe she could be either. They might have been trying to decide whether she would be accepted by the soldiers as a miracle maid or not. If the French and (even more) the English could be made to believe that God was fighting on the side of the French, that could have an important effect on morale on either side.

The decision arrived at was (theologically) that Joan was sent by God and (practically/politically) that this attitude would carry conviction. She was therefore sent to Orléans with an escort of about three thousand soldiers under John, Duke of Alençon, who had led the French forces at the lost Battle of Verneuil and had been in captivity for a while as a result. On April 29, 1429, Joan and her escort slipped into the city.

It is important to understand that by now the defending force within the city was quite substantial and, indeed, they outnumbered the thin line of besieging English. What kept the French from emerging to do battle was not the lack of means, but the lack of will. The French were simply unable to believe they could win. What's more, the English had suffered considerably in the course of a half-year siege, and all that kept them to their task was that they were simply unable to believe they could lose.

It was only a matter of morale that kept the situation going, against the military sense of it all. Once the news arrived that a miraculous maid was coming to the aid of the French, the situation with respect to morale changed suddenly and dramatically and what followed was almost inevitable. While few events in history have seemed so miraculous as what Joan of Arc accomplished, it is not really as miraculous as it seemed.

Very likely, the Bastard of Orléans counted on Joan's effect on the morale on both sides, and, within a week of her arrival, he launched an attack, on May 4, on the fortified posts set up by the English at the eastern approaches of the city. He did not even bother telling her about it. On learning of the fighting, however, Joan hastened to the eastern walls. The French soldiers, heartened at her appearance, fought the more savagely, and the English fell back.

The first sign of French victory set in motion a vicious cycle for the English. If the French advanced more than was their wont, it was a sign that Joan was heaven-sent or hell-sent but, in either case, of miraculous help to the French and not something mere men could fight against. The English were all the readier to retreat further, and to accept that further retreat as further evidence.

When Joan was struck by an arrow, the English cheered, but

it was a superficial wound and, when she appeared on the battlements again, it was easy to believe that she was invulnerable. And the English fell back still more readily.

By May 8, the English had abandoned the siege, leaving their strongpoints, their artillery, their dead and wounded. They made all haste to get out of the reach of Joan's influence.

Orléans was the Stalingrad of the Hundred Years' War. The siege of Orléans had been the high point of the English advance into France. The myth of English invincibility was broken, the hot glare of Agincourt dimmed; and from here on in, there could be only recession for the English forces.

Then, having written about ancient and medieval history, on and off, for about ten years, I grew eager to tackle modern history. Since by now the bicentennial year of 1976 was approaching, why not a history of the United States?

It seemed a shrewd idea to me, but I forgot to count words in my eagerness to write. Houghton Mifflin had provided that the histories run no more than 75,000 to 80,000 words each, since they were primarily aimed at a teenage audience (though adults, I am firmly convinced, can also profit from reading my histories).

I began my history of the United States with the Indians and with the discovery and settling of North America by Europeans, and when the allotted wordage was done, I was dismayed to find I was only up to 1763. I stopped, called the book The Shaping of North America *(Book 137), and it was published in 1973.*

I continued, then, with a second book but found I could only squeeze some fifty years into that . . . and another fifty years into a third . . . and another fifty years into a fourth. The Birth of the United States *(Book 149), published in 1974, took the history from 1763 to 1816;* Our Federal Union *(Book 161), published in 1975, took it from 1816 to 1865; and* The Golden Door *(Book 189), published in 1977, took it from 1865 to 1918. I had passed the bicentennial year and I had at least one more volume to do.*

From the last of these books, here is my description of the Spanish-American War, perhaps the least important war we fought:

from THE GOLDEN DOOR (1977)

The Americans had fewer ships than the Spanish, but those ships were new and beautifully designed. For once, the United States was ready for war, at least on the seas.

This was partly because of the work of the American naval officer Alfred Thayer Mahan (born in West Point, New York, on September 27, 1840). The son of a professor at West Point, he himself went to the Naval Academy at Annapolis. He served on blockade duty during the Civil War and remained in the Navy till his retirement as a rear admiral in 1896.

He was a great military theoretician, writing *The Influence of Sea Power upon History, 1660–1783* in 1890, *The Influence of Sea Power upon the French Revolution and Empire, 1793–1812* in 1892, and *The Interest of America in Sea Power, Present and Future* in 1897.

The thesis was this: The ocean is continuous and worldwide; the land, discontinuous and consisting of isolated portions. A landlocked military power can occupy regions adjacent to the home base, but must stop at the coast if it lacks a navy. A naval power, if separated from the military power by the ocean, can isolate itself and, by means of its navy, attack the enemy at every coastal point, safeguard its trade, and blockade its enemy. A sea power would have the world as its supply source and would, in the end, defeat a continental power. It was in this way, Mahan pointed out, that Great Britain had finally defeated all her enemies, including Napoleon, and had gained her world empire.

No nation could grow strong any longer without a navy, Mahan said. As for the United States, which had no powerful nations sharing land boundaries with it and which had two wide oceans on either side, it could be particularly strong, even invulnerable, if it had an effective navy. Mahan pointed out the necessity of a base in Hawaii and coaling stations on smaller islands since the Pacific Ocean was so much wider than the Atlantic. He also advocated the building of a canal across the isthmus of Panama, so that the United States could, in need, quickly concentrate its navy in either ocean.

Following Mahan, the Americans worked hard at developing an

efficient navy, and though at the time the war with Spain came, there was no canal across the isthmus, there were American ships in each ocean.

The Pacific Fleet was particularly well placed through a historical accident. The secretary of the navy, John Davis Long (born in Buckfield, Maine, October 27, 1838) was away from his desk, and his assistant secretary served briefly in his place as acting secretary. That assistant secretary was Theodore Roosevelt, who was a great admirer of Mahan's* and very keen on using the navy properly. He ordered six warships in the Pacific to proceed to Hong Kong in order to be ready to act against the Philippines the moment war was declared. Secretary Long, when he returned, was furious, but he did not countermand the order.

If the United States had a serviceable navy, it had virtually no army at all. Spain had 155,000 soldiers in Cuba at the time, while the United States had a total of 28,000 soldiers altogether, and these had fought no one but Indians for a generation.

Volunteers were called up, but the new, enlarged army units were not stiffened by scattering veterans throughout them. Instead, the veterans were kept intact and the rookies were left to themselves. Furthermore, the supply organization of both food and medical care was abysmally poor — the last war in which the United States permitted itself this disgrace.†

As soon as news of the declaration of war was received in Hong Kong, the American squadron, under Commodore George Dewey (born in Montpelier, Vermont, on December 26, 1837), a veteran of the Civil War, had to leave, as otherwise Hong Kong's status as a neutral port would be in question. That suited Dewey. His orders were to go to Manila, 1050 kilometers to the southeast.

Dewey had six ships under his command — four cruisers and

* Another admirer of Mahan's was Kaiser Wilhelm II of Germany. A month before the Spanish-American War started, Germany, aware of Mahan's theories, began the building of a modern navy designed eventually to surpass that of Great Britain. Great Britain was already suspicious of German ambitions, and this hit at the very heart of its strength. Great Britain and Germany became deadly enemies and sixteen years later they were on the opposite sides of a great war.

† It was also the last major war fought with gunpowder, which had been the mainstay of battle for five centuries and had fouled the guns, choked the gunners, and hidden the battlefield with its endless smoke. In 1891, the British chemists James Dewar and Frederick Augustus Abel had invented cordite, the first of the smokeless powders and a substance more powerful and shattering than gunpowder. Future wars would be fought with such smokeless powders.

two gunboats — and on April 27, 1898, after having put all his ships in complete battle readiness, he sailed for Manila. Waiting for him were ten Spanish ships together with Spanish shore batteries. The Europeans in Hong Kong, imagining the Spaniards to be what they once had been, were certain that Dewey was steaming to his destruction; but there was really no chance of that. Dewey's ships were of the latest design and in tiptop shape. The Spanish ships were little more than hulks, and the Spanish admiral was expecting defeat.

The Spanish admiral lined up seven of his ships just off Manila in order to protect the city, but there was nothing to protect the ships. Dewey reached Manila Bay, saw nothing to prevent his entering, did so, and reached the neighborhood of Manila itself on the night of April 30.

When daybreak of May 1, 1898, revealed the two opposing fleets to each other, the Spaniards fired high and did no damage. At 5:40 A.M. Dewey said quietly to Captain Charles Vernon Gridley (born in Logansport, Indiana, on November 24, 1844), captain of the flagship, *Olympia,* "You may fire when ready, Gridley."

The American ships paraded back and forth before the Spanish fleet, firing steadily. They pulled off briefly at 7:30 so that the men could have a quiet breakfast, then returned to work. By 11:00 A.M. the Spanish fleet was destroyed. Every ship had been sunk or beached and 381 Spaniards had been killed. In the process, Dewey lost not a man. Eight sailors had received minor wounds, that was all. And when the American ships moved in to bombard Manila itself, the Spaniards agreed to silence the shore batteries.

Despite the total victory at sea, Dewey could not take Manila. For that he needed a land force, and he had none. On May 19, he brought in Aguinaldo from Hong Kong so that he might lead his Filipino insurgents against the Spaniards on land and keep them occupied and incapable of taking any aggressive action against the ships. Even that didn't give Dewey the wherewithal to take the city, and he had to wait for the arrival of American soldiers.

The wait wasn't particularly comfortable. He was isolated and far from any friendly port, and, by June 12, British, French, and German ships had arrived. They were there, ostensibly, to guard the lives and properties of *their* nationals but were clearly hoping to pick up some pieces if the fall of Spanish power in the Philippines created a vacuum there. The Germans were especially aggressive in their provocations, and at one point the desperate Dewey was forced to tell a German officer, "Tell your admiral if he wants war I am ready."

But the Germans didn't actually want war; they just wanted whatever they could get without war. With Dewey ready (and the worth of his ships having been dramatically exhibited), and with the United States finally making it clear that, whatever happened to the Philippines, no other nations would be allowed a look-in, the German ships sailed off. Dewey settled down to maintain his blockade and wait for his soldiers.

Meanwhile, in the Atlantic, Spain's fleet had reached the West Indies, and by that time they were completely out of fuel. They could not possibly fight before getting into some Cuban port in order to load coal. The American Navy knew this, and it was only a matter of finding the fleet while it was in port and keeping it there. (From their Florida base, the American ships had to go only a few hundred kilometers to reach any part of the Cuban coast, so they had no fuel problem.)

On May 19, the Spanish fleet reached Santiago, on Cuba's southeastern coast, and entered. On May 29, the American fleet, under Rear Admiral William Thomas Sampson (born in Palmyra, New York, on February 9, 1840) — who had been head of the board of inquiry in connection with the sinking of the *Maine* — located the Spanish fleet there and instantly blockaded the harbor.

If the American fleet could have entered the harbor, as Dewey had entered Manila Bay, they would surely have destroyed the Spanish ships. However, the channel entrance was narrow and was littered with mines, and the United States did not wish to lose any of its modern and expensive ships if that could be avoided. Yet something had to be done, for as long as the Spanish ships were intact, there was always the possibility that they might do some damage.

It was decided to leave the American fleet outside the harbor and to invade Cuba with a land force that could attack Santiago from the rear. On June 10, marines landed in Guantánamo Bay, sixty-five kilometers east of Santiago, to establish a foothold.

(During some preliminary skirmishes, one American commander — a Confederate veteran — forgot who the enemy was and shouted, "Come on, boys, we've got the damn Yankees on the run.")

More than that was needed though, and the main American army, gathering in Tampa, Florida, had been ordered to Cuba on May 30. It was under General William Rufus Shafter (born in Galesburg, Michigan, on October 16, 1835). He was a veteran of the Civil War and had fought bravely and well, but he now weighed 310 pounds and did not know how to organize a large command.

It took eleven days before embarkation could get started and four days to complete the embarkation — everything done in complete chaos, with Shafter doing virtually nothing. By June 20, the transports reached the vicinity of Santiago. Shafter decided not to attempt a direct attack on the city but to land at a point thirty kilometers east of Santiago. In this, he followed the advice of General Calixto Garcia,* who commanded the Cuban rebels in this area.

The disembarkation was even more ragged and disorganized that the embarkation had been, and had the Americans faced an efficient and well-commanded enemy, most of them would probably have met their end. As it was, the Spanish command was bad enough to make even Shafter look good, and the Americans were placed on Cuban soil without opposition and without casualties resulting from enemy action.

By June 30, the Americans were ready to march on Santiago. On July 1, two battles were fought — one at El Coney, 8 kilometers northeast of Santiago, and the other at San Juan Hill, about 1.5 kilometers east of Santiago. Both were American victories, and it was in the latter that Theodore Roosevelt distinguished himself.

---

* In the course of the war, an American officer, Lieutenant Andrew Summers Rowan, had made contact with Garcia in order to coordinate action. In 1899, the American journalist Elbert Green Hubbard wrote a moralistic essay entitled "A Message to Garcia," exalting this action and using it as a lesson to "get things done" through what seems suspiciously like mindless obedience. The essay gained tremendous popularity and was read and memorized by uncounted hordes of schoolchildren — including the author of this book, who, even as a child, disagreed with its simplistic philosophy, but thought it the better part of valor not to say so.

At the outbreak of the war Roosevelt resigned and joined the First Volunteer Cavalry unit, as a lieutenant colonel. He wasn't its commander, but he was always spectacularly visible, and in the popular mind the unit was Roosevelt's Rough Riders. At San Juan Hill, the Americans were pinned by fire from Spaniards holding the heights and the Rough Riders weren't riding, roughly or otherwise, for they were dismounted. Fighting on foot, they led the charge under enemy fire, though it wasn't actually much of a charge since they moved up the heights slowly and with difficulty. But they moved, and drove the Spaniards off.

It was Roosevelt's only chance at the military glory he longed for. (As he said, "It wasn't much of a war, but it was all we had.") And it was better than nothing, for he made the most of it in later years. The American satirist Finley Peter Dunne (born in Chicago on July 10, 1867) had his famous Irish-dialect hero, Mr. Dooley, remark that when Roosevelt wrote up his Spanish-American experiences he should have entitled it "Alone in Cuba."

Once on the heights, the Americans were in a position to bombard the city of Santiago and the Spanish fleet from land. The Spanish admiral, whose orders forbade surrender, had no choice but to try to break out of the harbor. On July 3, he made the attempt and the American ships pounced at once. In four hours, every Spanish ship was destroyed, 474 Spaniards were killed or wounded, and 1750 were taken prisoner. The American loss was 1 killed and 1 wounded.

"Straight" history is not the only history there is, of course, and one of my interests has long been the history of science. In my first hundred books, the most important example of that is Asimov's Biographical Encyclopedia of Science and Technology (published by Doubleday), which covered all of science from the time of ancient Egypt to the present in a thousand biographical entries.

In the course of writing my second hundred books, I revised and enlarged that book to the point where I considered the result, published in 1972, the equivalent of a new book and listed it as Book 118.

I also did a history of the telescope for Houghton Mifflin —

Eyes on the Universe (Book 165). Here is the tale of the invention of the telescope from it:

from EYES ON THE UNIVERSE (1975)

You might even imagine a piece of glass that was symmetrical, a convex surface on both sides meeting in a line all around the edge. You can imagine it best, perhaps, as two plano-convex pieces of glass placed together flat side to flat side. The result is a "biconvex" piece of glass.

The biconvex piece of glass has the shape of a lentil seed, and it came to be called by the Latin version of that name. It was a "lens." Strictly speaking, only the biconvex piece of glass has a right to the name, but its use has spread to all kinds of transparent objects with smoothly curved surfaces. You can speak of a "plano-convex lens," for instance, even though there are no lentil seeds with a plano-convex shape.

Crude lenses have been unearthed in Crete and in Asia Minor, and some may date as far back as 2000 B.C. Alhazen's writing on light and refraction mentioned lenses and his books began to be translated into Latin about 1170. They served to stimulate thought and experiment in a Europe that was beginning to grow interested in science.

The first systematic studies of lenses in Europe were made by the English scholar Robert Grosseteste (1175–1253) and his pupil Roger Bacon (1220–1292). Neither knew what was happening to light, but they could observe the magnification. Bacon used lenses to magnify letters on a page and to aid himself in reading. He suggested the wearing of lenses to aid vision, and about 1300 spectacles came into use in Italy.

The first spectacles were made of biconvex lenses, which enlarged objects and which were particularly useful to old people, who are often far-sighted.

It is also possible to have a "biconcave" lens — one in which the glass is thick at the edge of the lens all around and in which the curve on each side bellies inward, so that the glass is thinner as one moves inward from the edge and is thinnest at the center. With such a lens, light is bent away from the center and the effect is just the opposite of that of a biconvex lens. Objects viewed through it seem smaller.

It may seem that such a lens is useless. What is the good in seeing things smaller? The fact is, however, that biconcave lenses are useful in correcting near-sightedness, and spectacles for that purpose began to be used about 1450.

The making of spectacles became an important industry in early modern times, particularly in the Netherlands, where men grew skilled in the manufacture of lenses.

Thus, rather than making lenses either biconvex or biconcave, men could make them convex on one side and concave on the other, so that the resulting "concavo-convex lens" is thinner and more delicate than either the biconcave or the biconvex lenses. If the curves are so chosen that the center of the concavo-convex lens is thinner than the edges, such a lens will correct near-sightedness; if the center is thicker than the edges it will correct far-sightedness.

The shop of a Dutch spectacles-maker, with lenses of every variety lying about, is an invitation to play games, for no one has ever had lenses available to him without at once beginning to peer through them at various objects. A magnification effect is most interesting, and it is only natural to attempt to make the magnification as great as possible.

Two English mathematicians, Leonard Digges (1510?–1571?) and John Dee (1527–1608), even experimented with combinations of lenses in an attempt to increase the magnifying effect, but reported no successes.

When the discovery came, according to the most often repeated version of the story, it came by accident.

Hans Lippershey (1570?–1619?) was a spectacles-maker in the city of Middelburg, in the Dutch province of Zeeland, about eighty miles southwest of Amsterdam. What is supposed to have happened is that an apprentice of his, idling away his time in the absence of his master, amused himself by looking at the world through the lenses that had been left in his care. Eventually, he took two lenses and held them both before his eyes, one nearby and one far off, and found, to his astonishment, that a distant weathervane appeared to be much larger and closer.

With considerable excitement, he showed this to Lippershey

when he returned to the shop. It may be that the apprentice was
not beaten for wasting time, for Lippershey seems to have caught
the significance of the finding at once.

Lippershey realized that one could not expect to stand about
holding two lenses in appropriate positions, one in each hand. He
therefore devised a metal tube into which the two lenses could
be fitted in the proper place, and he had what he called (in
Dutch) a "looker," something one could look through.

It came to be called, more pretentiously, an "optic tube" or
"optic glass" or "perspective glass." In the first book of *Paradise
Lost*, published in 1667, John Milton still refers to such a device
as an optic glass. In 1612, however, a Greek mathematician,
Ioannes Dimisiani, who was secretary to an Italian cardinal, suggested the word "telescope," from Greek words meaning "to see at
a distance." By about 1650 this word began to gain ground and
eventually drove out all others. We can say, then, that Lippershey had invented the first telescope.

But did he? Once the instrument became famous, other Dutch-
men lay claim to having been first in the field. This is very possible, for given a supply of lenses, anyone could invent it by
accident. One with a particularly good case is another optician
of Middelburg, a neighbor of Lippershey's named Zacharias
Janssen (1580–1638?). He claimed to have constructed a telescope in 1604, and he may have; Lippershey may have borrowed
the idea and made up the story of his apprentice to cover the
theft.

Nevertheless, Lippershey deserves credit whether he originated
the telescope in the strict sense of the word or not. All his com-
petitors for the honor did nothing with their telescopes, as far as
we know, except indulge in viewing for their own amusement.
Lippershey made the world conscious of the instrument by offering it to the Dutch government as a war weapon.

At that time, the Netherlands had been fighting a bitter war of
independence against Spain for forty years, and all that was
keeping the small nation alive against the superior military power
of Spain was the Dutch navy. An instrument that would allow
ships of the Dutch fleet to see the approach of an enemy long before that enemy could be aware of the Dutch would place the
Netherlands in a strong position.

Maurice of Nassau, the capable man who was then stadholder of the Dutch republic, was interested in science and saw the importance of the device at once. He paid Lippershey 900 florins and ordered him to produce for the government telescopes of a binocular variety, ones that could be looked through with both eyes at once.

Maurice tried to keep the telescope a secret, but that was impossible; the device was too simple. The mere rumor that such a thing existed meant that any ingenious man could duplicate it at once. Telescopes were offered to Henry IV of France before 1608 was over, but King Henry, while amused, was not interested.

The secret war weapon, then, was no secret — but the Dutch did not lose too much. In 1609, a truce with Spain was worked out and the Dutch were never in real danger (from Spain, at least) thereafter. The telescope could go its way, then, with not even the sketchiest attempt to keep it secret— and it did.

By all odds, though, the most unusual bit of history included in my second hundred books is fictional. In 1973, the Saturday Evening Post, *aware of the coming bicentennial, suggested that I write a fantasy about Benjamin Franklin, one in which I would talk to him, perhaps, and get the advice of the wise old sage with respect to our contemporary problems.*

I thought it was a fascinating idea, and I felt I could handle it since I had already written The Shaping of North America *and* The Birth of the United States *in addition to* The Kite That Won the Revolution, *a book specifically on Franklin, which was included in my first hundred.*

I therefore wrote a story called "The Dream" and it was published in the January–February 1974 Saturday Evening Post.

As so often happens, though, the publishers' appetite was only whetted and they came after me again. They wanted more dream conversations with Franklin, and I wrote three more before mounting one of my all-too-rare rebellions against such things and refusing to do any more.

I called the additional stories simply "Second Dream," "Third Dream," and "Fourth Dream," but the Saturday Evening Post *called them "Benjamin's Dream," "Party by Satellite," and "Benjamin's Bicentennial Blast."*

Then, in January 1976, the printers' union of New York held its annual banquet on Franklin's birthday (he being the patron saint of American printers). It was their custom to put out a small booklet of Frankliniana, and on this occasion, with my permission they put out a collection of three of the Dreams. (For some reason, they left out the third.)

It was a privately printed book, beautifully done, and longer than some of my children's books. What's more, it contained stories of mine that were not otherwise collected in book form, so I placed it on my list as Book 170 (with the most inconvenient name of all the books in my entire two hundred). From it, here is "The Dream," the first in the series, in its entirety:

"The Dream" (1974)

"I'm dreaming," I said. It seemed to me that I had said it aloud. I know that I was in bed. I was aware of the bedclothes. I was aware of the scattered city lights peeping through the slats of the Venetian blinds.

Yet he was there. As alive — as living — as real —

I could reach out and touch him, but I dared not move.

I recognized him. I've seen enough pictures of him, and so has everyone. He did not look quite like his pictures, for he was old, very old. White hair fringed his head. I recognized him. I simply knew who he was.

He said, "I'm dreaming."

We stared at each other and all the world faded away — the bed and the bedclothes and the room. I said, "You're Benjamin Franklin."

He smiled slowly and said, "It may be that this is not a dream only. I stand close to death and perhaps the dying may have their wishes answered, if the wish be sufficiently earnest. Of what year are you?"

I felt panic rise. It might be a dream, but it might be madness. "I am dreaming!" I insisted wildly.

"Of course, you are, after a fashion, dreaming," said Franklin —

what else could I call him? "And I as well. How is it conceivable that you and I could speak but by something outside reality? And how does man transcend reality but in dreams? Of what year are you, my good sir?"

I was silent. He waited patiently and then shook his head.

"Then I will speak first," he said. "I am old enough to have naught to fear. It is New Year's Eve of the Year of our Lord 1790, in the fourteenth year of the Independence of the United States, and in the first year of the presidency of George Washington. And in the last year of poor Benjamin Franklin, too. I will not last the new year. I know that.

"I do not die prematurely. In a fortnight and a few days I will mark my eighty-fourth birthday. A good old age, for it has made my life long enough to see my native land become a new nation among the nations of the earth, and I have had something to do with that. We have a Constitution that was hammered out, not without pain, and will perhaps serve. And General Washington is spared to lead us.

"Yet will our nation last? The great monarchies of Europe remain hostile and there are dissensions among ourselves. British forces still hold our frontier posts; Spain threatens in the south; our trade languishes; the party spirit grows. Will our nation last?"

I managed to nod my head.

He chuckled almost noiselessly. "Is that all you can say? A nod? I asked for two hundred years. With this new year coming in, my last year, I asked what the United States might be like on its two hundredth birthday. Are these, then, the only tidings I am vouchsafed?"

"Almost," I managed to say. "Almost. It is almost the bicentennial."

Franklin nodded. "You two centuries is a long time. It is two centuries since the first Englishmen stepped ashore on Roanoke Island; two centuries since Spain's invincible Armada was smashed. I fear the many inevitable changes two more centuries will bring."

He paused and then his voice seemed stronger, as though he were preparing to face whatever might be. "You speak of the bicentennial as though you accept the idea casually. The United States, then, still exists in your time?"

"Yes!"

"In what condition? Still independent? Still with the princely domain we won from Great Britain?"

"Still independent," I said, and I felt myself grow warm with the pleasure of bringing great news. "And far larger. It is a land as large as all of Europe, with a population of more than two hundred million drawn from every nation. Fifty states stretch from the Atlantic to the Pacific, with the fiftieth leaping the sea to the Hawaiian Islands of the mid-Pacific."

His eyes lightened with joy. "And Canada?"

"Not Canada. That remains under the British crown."

"Great Britain is still a monarchy then?"

"Yes. Queen Elizabeth II is on the throne, but Great Britain is our friend and has been for a long time."

"Let the Creator be praised for that. Does the nation prosper?"

"The richest on earth. The strongest."

Now Franklin paused. Then: "You say that because you think to please me, perhaps. Richer than Great Britain? Stronger than France?"

"If you asked to have the future revealed to you, would it be lies you would hear? The time has not been all bliss. If we are a mighty union of states now, under our thirty-seventh President in unbroken succession from George Washington, it is because we have survived a long and bloody war between the states. In this present century, we have fought war after war overseas. We have had periods of economic disaster and periods of political corruption. It has not been the best of all possible worlds, but we have survived, and, as we approach the bicentennial, we are the richest and strongest nation on earth."

The old man seemed restless. He stirred in his bed and said, "I feel that I would like to walk about. I am not yet so old as to be bedridden. Yet I fear it will break the vision. It grows stronger, do you not feel that?"

"Yes," I said. It was as though we two alone, separated by two centuries, were all that existed in a universe closed tightly about us.

Franklin said, "I feel your thoughts without asking. I begin to grow in you, or you in me. I sense your world — the world that is to come."

There was a tickling in my skull — not a tickling, either — a sensation I could not describe and still cannot. It was another mind which, even in great old age, was more powerful than my own and had gently inserted itself into the interstices of my own.

Franklin said, with infinite satisfaction, "Yours is an age in which natural philosophy, then, is highly advanced, I see."

"We call it science now," I said, "and you are right. We fly through the air and can circle the globe in less time than it took you to go from Boston to Philadelphia. Our words streak at the speed of light and reach any corner of the globe in a fraction of a second. Our carriages move without horses and our buildings tower a quarter of a mile into the air."

He was silent and for a time seemed to be attempting to absorb what might have seemed like wild fantasy.

I said, "Much of it stems from you. You were the first to penetrate the nature of electricity, and it is electricity that now powers our society. You invented the lightning rod, the first device, based on the findings of pure science, to defeat a natural calamity. It was with the lightning rod that men first turned to science for help against the universe."

He said, "You make it unnecessary for an old man to praise himself. I am too old to play at the game of modesty. I look back at my life and my eyes are not so blind as to fail to show me something of my true worth. Do you think, then, the lightning rod is my greatest invention?"

"One of them, certainly," I said.

"Not at all," said Franklin seriously, "for my greatest invention is the United States, which I see is fated to increase so mightily in strength and wealth. But you think I exaggerate?"

"Well," I said, "you were a member of the committee that wrote the Declaration of Independence —"

"Tom Jefferson did the writing," interrupted Franklin, "though I suggested a passage or two."

"And you were a member of the Constitutional Convention —"

"Where I devoted myself to quieting tempers. None of that. I invented the United States over a score of years before it was born. Have you forgotten that in your time?"

"I am not certain —"

"The French!" he said, impatiently. "Have the Americans of

the future forgotten the day when France controlled Canada
and Louisiana and reached out to take the Ohio Valley, too. The
day when they would have penned us between the mountains
and the sea, to take us at their leisure later?"

"We remember," I said. "We remember Wolfe and the capture
of Quebec."

"But that was victory, in 1759. Cast your mind back to 1754.
The French were at Fort Duquesne, only two hundred fifty miles
from Philadelphia. Young George Washington's mission to the
French — and he was Young George then, a lad of twenty-one —
had failed. Yet the colonies would not take action against the
menace. The Pennsylvania proprietary government was torpid.
The British were concerned with Europe, not with us. And
even the Iroquois, our old Indian allies, were threatening to
transfer their friendship to the French. Do you remember all
that?"

"Only dimly, sir."

"So Governor De Lancey of New York called a congress of the
colonies to meet and confer about the common danger. On June
19, 1754, twenty-five delegates from seven colonies — the four
of New England, plus New York, Pennsylvania, and Maryland —
met at Albany. We comforted the Iroquois and held them firm,
and then, on June 24, I presented my plan of union to the Albany
congress."

He paused dramatically, then said, "I suggested the colonies
be governed by a governor-general, appointed and paid by the
British crown. Partner with him was to be a grand council in
which delegates from the various colonies, in number proportional to population, would sit. The grand council would deal
with American affairs, and the governor-general would see to it
that the interests of the empire were preserved. The congress
accepted it — on July 4. It might have saved the colonies for
Great Britain."

I nodded. "It might have. Canada finally came to much the
same arrangement and is still under the British crown, though
it rules itself."

"Ah! But the colonies ignored my plan because it gave too
much power to the crown, and Parliament ignored it because it

gave too much power to the colonies. But the idea of union, which was *mine*, did not die, you see. And what I suggested, molded into modified form by time, came to pass, so that my intention became the United States of America. And," he added with deep satisfaction, "I lived to see it and to play my small — no, my *large* part."

I nodded again.

"And now," he said, "you live in a great world that has grown curiously small, a world far smaller than my thirteen colonies of 1754. Around the world in a day, you say? Words at the speed of light? The astronomer royal, Mr. Bradley, had worked that out to be some 180,000 miles per second."

"That is right; 186,282 miles per second."

"Even to the exact mile? And yet your world is as divided as our American states once were."

"More divided, I fear."

"I catch a dim view of devices that make war deadly," he said.

"We have bombs that can destroy —"

But old Franklin waved his hand. "Do not tell me. I see enough. And yet with the chance of universal destruction, there remains no certainty of peace?"

"The nations are armed and hostile."

"The United States arms also?"

"Certainly. It is the strongest nuclear power."

"Then man does not advance in wisdom as he does in power?"

I shrugged. What could I say?

Franklin said, "Are there no enemies against which the nations can unite? We tried to unite against France, but relied too greatly on Great Britain to feel the absolute need. We did unite against Great Britain, at last, when we stood alone."

I said, "There is no power against whom the nations of the world feel the need to unite. There is no enemy from beyond the earth to threaten us with universal defeat and slavery."

"Are there no enemies other than those who are living beings?" asked Franklin angrily. "Is there not ignorance? Is there not misery? Is there not hunger and disease, and hatred and bigotry, and disorder and crime? Has your world changed so much that these things do not exist?"

"No. We have them. Not all of man's material advance has ended the threat of those things you mention. We multiply still in great number — nearly four billion the world over — and that multiplies our problems and may even destroy us all."

"And mankind will not combine against this immaterial foe?"

I said, "No more than the colonies combined against France or even against Great Britain until bloodshed in New England brought them a clear and present danger."

Franklin said, "Can you wait for a clear and present danger? What you call a nuclear war would make it too late at once. If matters advanced to the point where your complex society broke down, then even in the absence of war you could not prevent catastrophe."

"You are correct, sir."

"Is there no way, then, to dramatize the —" His head bent in thought. He said, "You spoke of a war between the states. Are the states still at enmity? Is the nation still divided?"

"No, the wounds are healed."

"How? In what manner?"

"That is not easy to explain. For one thing, in the years after that war, the nation was engaged in building the West. In this great colonizing venture, all the states, north and south, combined. In that common task, and in the further task of strengthening the nation, smaller enmities were forgotten."

"I see," said Franklin. "And is there no great venture in which the world is engaged in your time. Is there nothing so grand that in it all the nations may find a common goal and, as you say, forget the smaller enmities?"

I thought for a moment. "Space, perhaps."

"Space?"

"Both ourselves and the Soviet Union — which used to be the Russian Empire — have sent out exploring vessels as far as the planets Mars and Jupiter."

For a moment Franklin seemed speechless. Then he said, "With men on board?"

"No, unmanned. But six vessels, carrying three men each, have traveled to the moon. Twelve Americans have walked on the moon. A seventh vessel miscarried but brought its crew safely back to earth."

Franklin said, "And with so majestic a feat at the disposal of mankind, the nations of the world can yet quarrel?"

"I am sorry, but it is so."

"Is the venture, perhaps, merely a useless show?"

"No. Not at all. Vessels bearing instruments circle earth. They help in our planetary communications. They serve as navigational aids. They report on our cloud cover and help us predict the weather. They investigate the properties of space and help us understand our universe. Through their observations we can plot earth's resources, pinpoint earth's physical problems of pollution, understand the planet as a whole in ways we never could before. We can add to our knowledge in an as yet unsuspected fashion that will help us in —"

"And *still* the nations quarrel?"

"Yes."

Franklin's eyes began to blaze at this. One arm reached out tremblingly toward me. "Then there must be further dramatization. Tell me, is it an American venture only — those vessels to the moon — or are other nations involved?"

"It is strictly American."

"Ah. And the bicentennial approaches. Then cannot the United States establish a birthday party that will be the greatest birthday party of all time by making it a celebration for mankind?"

"In what way, sir?"

"Launch one of your vessels on the bicentennial," he said energetically. "Or, if there is not time for that, announce one to be launched by the united aid of all the nations of the world. Let there be a celebration of the Fourth, not as the bicentennial of a single nation, but as a glorification of the principle of the union of political entities against a common foe and for a common purpose.

"Let there be the largest birthday cake in the world, if you will; the decoration of whole cities; the saluting of a thousand guns; the playing of ten thousand bands — but let it be for mankind. Let the leaders of all nations assemble to praise the union of mankind. Let them all plan their own part in the launching of vessels into space under the auspices of a united planet. Let the conquest of space be the source of pride for nothing smaller than mankind. Let it be that in which all men can find a common glory, and in which all men can forget small enmities."

I said, "But the problems of mankind will remain. They will not disappear."

Franklin's figure seemed to waver, grow less substantial. "Do you want everything at once? The American union did not solve all problems for Americans. But it made it possible for solutions to be sought, and sometimes found."

He grew dimmer still, wraithlike, and then vanished in a fading smoke. And I woke up.

If it were a dream, it was Franklin's dream, too. And a greater dream still — of a union beyond our Union.

But what could I do? I do not make policy.

Yet I am a writer. With help, I might make myself heard. With help!

So I picked up the telephone and called a certain editor, for, in addition to the lightning rod and the United States, hadn't Benjamin Franklin also invented the *Saturday Evening Post?*

PART 9

THE BIBLE

AMONG MY FIRST HUNDRED BOOKS is the two-volume Asimov's Guide to the Bible. *What could I do for an encore?*

One thing I could do was to write articles on biblical subjects for people who were impressed with the Guide. *Reader's Digest Books asked me to contribute essays to an elaborate book they were compiling about men and women in the Bible. I wrote articles for them on Jacob, Ruth, and so on.*

Although I was well paid, I didn't particularly enjoy the task since the editors had their ideas and they were not mine. Eventually, when the book came out, I found that everyone who had had anything to do with the book was carefully acknowledged — the editors, photographers, paper cutters, office boys, garbage collectors — everyone but the writers. The written words, it could only be assumed, had been carved on Sinai by direct revelation.

I was furious. Although I had contributed a substantial portion of the book, I refused to include it in my list — not if my authorship were in no way acknowledged. In fact, I didn't even keep the book.

It was not, however, an effort that had been entirely wasted. My biography on Ruth got me to thinking about the subject, and for Doubleday I wrote a book for young people called The Story of Ruth (*Book 127*). *It was published in 1972.*

I repeated the thesis of this book in an F & SF *essay, "Lost in Non-Translation," which appeared in March 1972 and was then included in my essay collection* The Tragedy of the Moon (*Book 144*), *published by Doubleday in 1973. The essay is included here in full.*

"Lost in Non-Translation" (1972)

At the Noreascon (the Twenty-ninth World Science Fiction Convention), which was held in Boston on the Labor Day weekend

of 1971, I sat on the dais, of course, since, as the Bob Hope of
science fiction, it is my perennial duty to hand out the Hugos. On
my left was my daughter, Robyn — sixteen, blond, blue-eyed,
shapely, and beautiful. (No, that last adjective is not a father's
proud partiality. Ask anyone.)

My old friend Clifford D. Simak was guest of honor, and he began his talk by introducing, with thoroughly justified pride, his
two children, who were in the audience. A look of alarm instantly
crossed Robyn's face.

"Daddy," she whispered urgently, knowing full well my capacity for inflicting embarrassment, "are you planning to introduce
me?"

"Would that bother you, Robyn?" I asked.

"Yes, it would."

"Then I won't," I said, and patted her hand reassuringly.

She thought awhile. Then she said, "Of course, Daddy, if you
have the urge to refer, in a casual sort of way, to your beautiful
daughter, that would be all right."

So you can bet I did just that, while she allowed her eyes to
drop in a charmingly modest way.

But I couldn't help but think of the blond, blue-eyed stereotype
of Nordic beauty that has filled Western literature ever since the
blond, blue-eyed Germanic tribes took over the western portions
of the Roman Empire, fifteen centuries ago, and set themselves up
as an aristocracy.

. . . And of the manner in which that stereotype has been used
to subvert one of the clearest and most important lessons in the
Bible — a subversion that contributes its little bit to the serious
crisis that today faces the world, and the United States in particular.

In line with my penchant for beginning at the beginning, come
back with me to the sixth century B.C. A party of Jews had returned from Babylonian exile to rebuild the Temple at Jerusalem,
which Nebuchadnezzar had destroyed seventy years before.

During the exile, under the guidance of the prophet Ezekiel,
the Jews had firmly held to their national identity by modifying,

complicating, and idealizing their worship of Yahweh into a form that was directly ancestral to the Judaism of today. (In fact Ezekiel is sometimes called "the father of Judaism.")

This meant that when the exiles returned to Jerusalem, they faced a religious problem. There were people who, all through the period of the exile, had been living in what had once been Judah, and who worshiped Yahweh in what they considered the correct, time-honored ritual. Because their chief city (with Jerusalem destroyed) was Samaria, the returning Jews called them Samaritans.

The Samaritans rejected the newfangled modifications of the returning Jews, and the Jews abhorred the old-fashioned beliefs of the Samaritans. Between them arose an undying hostility, the kind that is exacerbated because the differences in belief are comparatively small.

In addition there were, also living in the land, those who worshiped other gods altogether — Ammonites, Edomites, Philistines, and so on.

The pressures on the returning band of Jews were not primarily military, for the entire area was under the more or less beneficent rule of the Persian Empire; they were social pressures, and perhaps even stronger for that. To maintain a strict ritual in the face of overwhelming numbers of nonbelievers is difficult, and the tendency to relax that ritual was almost irresistible. Then, too, young male returnees were attracted to the women at hand and there were intermarriages. Naturally, to humor the wife, ritual was further relaxed.

But then, possibly as late as about 400 B.C., a full century after the second Temple had been built, Ezra arrived in Jerusalem. He was a scholar of the Mosaic law, which had been edited and put into final form in the course of the exile. He was horrified at the backsliding and put through a tub-thumping revival. He called the people together, led them in chanting the law and expounding on it, raised their religious fervor, and called for confession of sins and renewal of faith.

One thing he demanded most rigorously was the abandonment of all non-Jewish wives and their children. Only so could the holiness of strict Judaism be maintained, in his view. To quote the

Bible (and I will use the recent New English Bible for the purpose):

"Ezra the priest stood up and said, 'You have committed an offense in marrying foreign wives and have added to Israel's guilt. Make your confession now to the Lord the God of your fathers and do his will, and separate yourselves from the foreign population and from your foreign wives.' Then all the assembled people shouted in reply, 'Yes; we must do what you say . . .'" (Ezra 10:10–12).

From that time on, the Jews as a whole began to practice an exclusivism, a voluntary separation from others, a multiplication of peculiar customs that further emphasized their separateness; and all of this helped them maintain their identity through all the miseries and catastrophes that were to come, through all the crises, and through exiles and persecutions that fragmented them over the face of the earth.

The exclusivism, to be sure, also served to make them socially indigestible and imparted to them a high social visibility that helped give rise to conditions that made exiles and persecutions more likely.

Not everyone among the Jews adhered to this policy of exclusivism. There were some who believed that all men were equal in the sight of God and that no one should be excluded from the community on the basis of group identity alone.

One who believed this (but who is forever nameless) attempted to present this case in the form of a short piece of historical fiction. In this fourth-century-B.C. tale the heroine was Ruth, a Moabite woman. (The tale was presented as having taken place in the time of the judges, so the traditional view was that it was written by the prophet Samuel in the eleventh century B.C. No modern student of the Bible believes this.)

Why a Moabite woman, by the way?

It seems that the Jews, returning from exile, had traditions concerning their initial arrival at the borders of Canaan under Moses and then Joshua, nearly a thousand years before. At that time, the small nation of Moab, which lay east of the lower course of the Jordan and of the Dead Sea, was understandably alarmed at the incursion of tough desert raiders and took steps to oppose them. Not only did they prevent the Israelites from passing through their territory, but, tradition had it, they called in a seer, Balaam, and asked him to use his magical abilities to bring misfortune and destruction upon the invaders.

That failed, and Balaam, on departing, was supposed to have advised the king of Moab to let the Moabite girls lure the desert raiders into liaisons, which might subvert their stern dedication to their task. The Bible records the following:

"When the Israelites were in Shittim, the people began to have intercourse with Moabite women, who invited them to the sacrifices offered to their gods; and they ate the sacrificial food and prostrated themselves before the gods of Moab. The Israelites joined in the worship of the Baal of Peor, and the Lord was angry with them" (Numbers 25:1–3).

As a result of this, "Moabite women" became the quintessence of the type of outside influence that by sexual attraction tried to subvert pious Jews. Indeed, Moab and the neighboring kingdom to the north, Ammon, were singled out in the Mosaic code:

"No Ammonite or Moabite, even down to the tenth generation, shall become a member of the assembly of the Lord ... because they did not meet you with food and water on your way out of Egypt, and because they hired Balaam ... to revile you ... You shall never seek their welfare or their good all your life long" (Deuteronomy 23:3–4, 6).

And yet there were times in later history when there was friendship between Moab and at least some men of Israel, possibly because they were brought together by some common enemy.

For instance, shortly before 1000 B.C., Israel was ruled by Saul. He had held off the Philistines, conquered the Amalekites, and brought Israel to its greatest pitch of power to that point. Moab naturally feared his expansionist policies and so befriended anyone rebelling against Saul. Such a rebel was the Judean warrior David of Bethlehem. When David was pressed hard by Saul and had retired to a fortified stronghold, he used Moab as a refuge for his family.

"David ... said to the king of Moab, 'Let my father and mother come and take shelter with you until I know what God will do for me.' So he left them at the court of the king of Moab, and they stayed there as long as David was in his stronghold" (1 Samuel 22:3–4).

As it happened, David eventually won out, became king first of Judah, then of all Israel, and established an empire that took in the entire east coast of the Mediterranean, from Egypt to the Euphrates, with the Phoenician cities independent but in alliance with him. Later, Jews always looked back to the time of David and of his son Solomon as a golden age, and David's position in Jewish legend and thought was unassailable. David founded a dynasty that ruled over Judah for four centuries, and the Jews never stopped believing that some descendant of David would yet return to rule over them again in some idealized future time.

Yet, on the basis of the verses describing David's use of Moab as a refuge for his family, there may have arisen a tale to the effect that there was a Moabite strain in David's ancestry. Apparently, the author of the Book of Ruth determined to make use of this tale to point up the doctrine of nonexclusivism by using the supremely hated Moabite woman as his heroine.

The Book of Ruth tells of a Judean family of Bethlehem — a man, his wife, and two sons — who are driven by famine to Moab. There the two sons marry Moabite girls, but after a space of time all three men die, leaving the three women — Naomi, the mother-in-law, and Ruth and Orpah, the two daughters-in-law — as survivors.

Those were times when women were chattels, and unmarried women, without a man to own them and care for them, could subsist only on charity. (Hence the frequent biblical injunction to care for widows and orphans.)

Naomi determined to return to Bethlehem, where kinsmen might possibly care for her, but urged Ruth and Orpah to remain in Moab. She does not say, but we might plausibly suppose she is thinking, that Moabite girls would have a rough time of it in Moab-hating Judah.

Orpah remains in Moab, but Ruth refuses to leave Naomi, saying, "Do not urge me to go back and desert you . . . Where you go, I will go, and where you stay, I will stay. Your people shall be my people, and your God my God. Where you die I will die, and there I will be buried. I swear a solemn oath before the Lord your God: nothing but death shall divide us" (Ruth 1:16–17).

Once in Bethlehem, the two were faced with the direst poverty, and Ruth volunteered to support herself and her mother-in-law by gleaning in the fields. It was harvest time, and it was customary to allow any stalks of grain that fell to the ground in the process of gathering to remain there to be collected by the poor. This gleaning was a kind of welfare program for those in need. It was, however, backbreaking work, and any young woman, particularly a Moabite, who engaged in it underwent certain obvious risks at the hands of the lusty young reapers. Ruth's offer was simply heroic.

As it happened, Ruth gleaned in the lands of a rich Judean farmer named Boaz, who, coming to oversee the work, noticed her working tirelessly. He asked after her, and his reapers answered, "She is a Moabite girl . . . who has just come back with Naomi from the Moabite country" (Ruth 2:6).

Boaz spoke kindly to her and Ruth said, "Why are you so kind as to take notice of me when I am only a foreigner?" (Ruth 2:10). Boaz explained that he had heard how she had forsaken her own land for love of Naomi and how hard she worked to take care of her.

As it turned out, Boaz was a relative of Naomi's dead husband, which must be one reason why he was touched by Ruth's love and fidelity. Naomi, on hearing the story, had an idea. In those days, if a widow was left childless, she had the right to expect her dead husband's brother to marry her and offer her his protection. If the dead husband had no brother, some other relative would fulfill the task.

Naomi was past the age of childbearing, so she could not qualify for marriage, which in those days centered about children; but what about Ruth? To be sure, Ruth was a Moabite woman and it might well be that no Judean would marry her, but Boaz had proven kind. Naomi therefore instructed Ruth how to approach Boaz at night and, without crudely seductive intent, appeal for his protection.

Boaz, touched by Ruth's modesty and helplessness, promised to do his duty, but pointed out that there was a kinsman closer than he and that, by right, this other kinsman had to have his chance first.

The very next day, Boaz approached the other kinsman and suggested that he buy some property in Naomi's charge and, along with it, take over another responsibility. Boaz said, "On the day when you acquire the field from Naomi, you also acquire Ruth the Moabitess, the dead man's wife . . ." (Ruth 4:5).

Perhaps Boaz carefully stressed the adjectival phrase "the Moabitess," for the other kinsman drew back at once. Boaz therefore married Ruth, who in time bore him a son. The proud and happy Naomi held the child in her bosom and her women friends said to her, "The child will give you new life and cherish you in your old age; for your daughter-in-law who loves you, who has proved better to you than seven sons, has borne him" (Ruth 4:15).

In a society that valued sons infinitely more than daughters, this verdict of Judean women on Ruth, a woman of the hated land of Moab, is the author's moral — that there is nobility and virtue in all groups and that none must be excluded from consideration in advance simply because of their group identification.

And then, to clinch the argument for any Judean so nationalistic as to be impervious to mere idealism, the story concludes: "Her neighbors gave him a name: 'Naomi has a son,' they said; 'we will call him Obed.' He was the father of Jesse, the father of David" (Ruth 4:17).

Where would Israel have been, then, if there had been an Ezra present to forbid the marriage of Boaz with a "foreign wife"?

Where does that leave us? That the Book of Ruth is a pleasant story, no one will deny. It is almost always referred to as a "delightful idyll," or words to that effect. That Ruth is a most successful characterization of a sweet and virtuous woman is beyond dispute.

In fact everyone is so in love with the story and with Ruth that the whole point is lost. It is, by right, a tale of tolerance for the despised, of love for the hated, of the reward that comes of brotherhood. By mixing the genes of mankind, by forming the hybrid, great men will come.

The Jews included the Book of Ruth in the canon partly because it is so wonderfully told a tale but mostly (I suspect) because it gives the lineage of the great David, a lineage that is *not* given beyond David's father, Jesse, in the soberly historic books of the Bible that anteceded Ruth. But the Jews remained, by and large, exclusivistic and did not learn the lesson of universalism preached by the Book of Ruth.

Nor have people taken its lesson to heart since. Why should they, since every effort is made to wipe out that lesson? The story of Ruth has been retold any number of ways, from children's tales to serious novels. Even movies have been made of it. Ruth herself must have been pictured in hundreds of illustrations. And in every illustration I have ever seen, she is presented as blond, blue-eyed, shapely, and beautiful — the perfect Nordic stereotype I referred to at the beginning of the article.

For goodness' sake, why shouldn't Boaz have fallen in love with her? What great credit was there in marrying her? If a girl like that had fallen at your feet and asked you humbly to do your duty and kindly marry her, you would probably have done it like a shot.

Of course she was a Moabite woman, but so what? What does the word "Moabite" mean to you? Does it arouse any violent reaction? Are there many Moabites among your acquaintances? Have your children been chased by a bunch of lousy Moabites lately? Have they been reducing property values in your neighborhood? When was the last time you heard someone say, "Got to get those rotten Moabites out of here. They just fill up the welfare rolls"?

In fact, judging by the way Ruth is drawn, Moabites are English aristocrats and their presence would raise property values.

The trouble is that the one word that is *not translated* in the Book of Ruth is the key word "Moabite," and as long as it is not translated, the point is lost; it is lost in non-translation.

The word "Moabite" really means "someone of a group that receives from us and deserves from us nothing but hatred and contempt." How should this word be translated into a single word that means the same thing to, say, many modern Greeks? . . . Why, "Turk." And to many modern Turks? . . . Why, "Greek." And to many modern white Americans? . . . Why, "black."

To get the proper flavor of the Book of Ruth, suppose we think of Ruth not as a Moabite woman but as a black woman.

Reread the story of Ruth and translate "Moabite" to "black"

every time you see it. Naomi (imagine) is coming back to the
United States with her two black daughters-in-law. No wonder
she urges them not to come with her. It *is* a marvel that Ruth
so loved her mother-in-law that she was willing to face a society
that hated her unreasoningly and to take the risk of gleaning in
the face of leering reapers who could not possibly suppose they
need treat her with any consideration whatever.

And when Boaz asked who she was, don't read the answer as,
"She is a Moabite girl," but as, "She is a black girl." More likely,
in fact, the reapers might have said to Boaz something that was
the equivalent of (if you'll excuse the language), "She is a nigger
girl."

Think of it that way and you find the whole point is found in
translation and only in translation. Boaz' action in being willing
to marry Ruth because she was virtuous (and not because she was
a Nordic beauty) takes on a kind of nobility. The neighbors'
decision that she was better to Naomi than seven sons becomes
something that could have been forced out of them only by overwhelming evidence to that effect. And the final stroke that out
of this miscegenation was born none other than the great David
is rather breathtaking.

We get something similar in the New Testament. On one occasion a student of the law asks Jesus what must be done to gain
eternal life, and he answers his own question by saying, "Love
the Lord your God with all your heart, with all your soul, with all
your strength, and with all your mind; and your neighbor as
yourself" (Luke 10:27).

These admonitions are taken from the Old Testament, of course.
That last bit about your neighbor comes from a verse that says,
"You shall not seek revenge, or cherish anger towards your kinsfolk; you shall love your neighbor as a man like yourself" (Leviticus 19:18).

(The New English Bible translation sounds better to me here
than the King James's: "Thou shalt love thy neighbor as thyself."
Where is the saint who can truly feel another's pain or ecstasy
precisely as he feels his own? We must not ask too much. But

if we simply grant that someone else is "a man like yourself," then he can be treated with decency at least. It is when we refuse to grant even this, and talk of another as our inferior, that contempt and cruelty come to seem natural, and even laudable.)

Jesus approves the lawyer's saying, and the lawyer promptly asks, "And who is my neighbor?" (Luke 10:29). After all, the verse in Leviticus first speaks of refraining from revenge and anger toward *kinsfolk*; might not, then, the concept of "neighbor" be restricted to kinsfolk, to one's own kind, only?

In response, Jesus replies with perhaps the greatest of the parables — of a traveler who fell in with robbers, who was mugged and robbed and left half dead by the road. Jesus goes on, "It so happened that a priest was going down by the same road; but when he saw him, he went past on the other side. So too a Levite came to the place, and when he saw him went past on the other side. But a Samaritan who was making the journey came upon him, and, when he saw him, was moved to pity. He went up and bandaged his wounds, bathing them with oil and wine. Then he lifted him onto his own beast, brought him to an inn, and looked after him there" (Luke 10:31–34).

Then Jesus asks who the traveler's neighbor was, and the lawyer is forced to say, "The one who showed him kindness" (Luke 10:37).

This is known as the Parable of the Good Samaritan, even though nowhere in the parable is the rescuer called a *good* Samaritan, merely a Samaritan.

The force of the parable is entirely vitiated by the common phrase "good" Samaritan, for that has cast a false light on who the Samaritans were. In a free-association test, say "Samaritan" and probably every person being tested will answer, "Good." It has become so imprinted in all our brains that Samaritans are good that we take it for granted that a Samaritan would act like that and wonder why Jesus is making a point of it.

We forget who the Samaritans were, in the time of Jesus!

To the Jews, they were *not* good. They were hated, despised, contemptible heretics with whom no good Jew would have anything to do. Again, the whole point is lost through non-translation.

Suppose, instead, that it is a white traveler in Mississippi who has been mugged and left half dead. And suppose it was a minister and a deacon who passed by and refused to "become involved." And suppose it was a black sharecropper who stopped and took care of the man.

Now ask yourself: Who was the neighbor whom you must love as though he were a man like yourself if you are to be saved?

The Parable of the Good Samaritan clearly teaches that there is nothing parochial in the concept "neighbor," that you cannot confine your decency to your own group and your own kind. All mankind, right down to those you most despise, are your neighbors.

Well, then, we have in the Bible two examples — in the Book of Ruth and in the Parable of the Good Samaritan — of teachings that are lost in non-translation, yet are terribly applicable to us today.

The whole world over, there are confrontations between sections of mankind defined by a difference of race, nationality, economic philosophy, religion, or language, so that one is not "neighbor" to the other.

These more or less arbitrary differences among peoples who are members of a single biological species are terribly dangerous, and nowhere more so than here in the United States, where the most perilous confrontation (I need not tell you) is between white and black.

Next to the population problem generally, mankind faces no danger greater than this confrontation, particularly in the United States.

It seems to me that more and more, each year, both whites and blacks are turning, in anger and hatred, to violence. I see no reasonable end to the steady escalation but an actual civil war.

In such a civil war, the whites, with a preponderance of numbers and an even greater preponderance of organized power, would in all likelihood "win." They would do so, however, at an enormous material cost and, I suspect, at a fatal spiritual one.

And why? Is it so hard to recognize that we are all neighbors, after all? Can we, on both sides — on *both* sides — find no way of accepting the biblical lesson?

Or if quoting the Bible sounds too mealy-mouthed, and if repeating the words of Jesus seems too pietistic, let's put it another way, a practical way:

Is the privilege of feeling hatred so luxurious that it is worth the material and spiritual hell of a white-black civil war?

If the answer is really yes, then one can only despair.

PART 10

SHORT-SHORTS

I'VE ALWAYS LIKED short-short stories.

First, since they are brief and can be read quickly, you can get the value of one even if you only have five minutes to spare — while waiting for a telephone call or while drinking a cup of coffee. It can fill in a disregarded corner of the day.

Second, there can be no frills. You've got to have the story distilled down to 1500 words or less, and ideally that leaves room only for the point; and that point, when the story is well done, can jab itself into your mind and never be forgotten.

Third, writing one is a challenge, and I enjoy challenges.

In May 1973, the Saturday Evening Post *asked me to write a short-short science fiction story for them and I did. I meant to write a lighthearted robot story and even called it "Light Verse," intending a pun. Alas, the story squirmed in my hands (even short-shorts can do that) and became rather more tragic than I had intended.*

I included it eventually in my short-story collection Buy Jupiter and Other Stories *(Book 164), which Doubleday published in 1975. Here it is in full:*

"Light Verse" (1973)

The very last person anyone would expect to be a murderer was Mrs. Avis Lardner. Widow of the great astronaut-martyr, she was a philanthropist, an art collector, a hostess *extraordinaire*, and, everyone agreed, an artistic genius. But above all, she was the gentlest and kindest human being one could imagine.

Her husband, William J. Lardner, died, as we all know, of the effects of radiation from a solar flare, after he had deliberately remained in space so that a passenger vessel might make it safely to Space Station 5.

Mrs. Lardner had received a generous pension for that, and she had then invested wisely and well. By late middle age she was very wealthy.

Her house was a showplace, a veritable museum, containing a small but extremely select collection of extraordinarily beautiful jeweled objects. From a dozen different cultures she had obtained relics of almost every conceivable artifact that could be embedded with jewels and made to serve the aristocracy of that culture. She had one of the first jeweled wristwatches manufactured in America, a jeweled dagger from Cambodia, a jeweled pair of spectacles from Italy, and so on almost endlessly.

All was open for inspection. The artifacts were not insured, and there were no ordinary security provisions. There was no need for anything conventional, for Mrs. Lardner maintained a large staff of robot servants, all of whom could be relied on to guard every item with imperturbable concentration, irreproachable honesty, and irrevocable efficiency.

Everyone knew of the existence of those robots, and there is no record of any attempt at theft, ever.

And then, of course, there was her light-sculpture. How Mrs. Lardner discovered her own genius at the art, no guest at her many lavish entertainments could guess. On each occasion, however, when her house was thrown open to guests, a new symphony of light shone throughout the rooms; three-dimensional curves and solids in melting color, some pure and some fusing in startling, crystalline effects that bathed every guest in wonder and somehow always adjusted itself so as to make Mrs. Lardner's blue-white hair and soft, unlined face gently beautiful.

It was for the light-sculpture more than anything else that the guests came. It was never the same twice and never failed to explore new experimental avenues of art. Many people who could afford light-consoles prepared light-sculptures for amusement, but no one could approach Mrs. Lardner's expertise. Not even those who considered themselves professional artists.

She herself was charmingly modest about it. "No, no," she would protest when someone waxed lyrical. "I wouldn't call it 'poetry in light.' That's far too kind. At most, I would say it was mere 'light verse.'" And everyone smiled at her gentle wit.

Though she was often asked, she would never create light-sculpture for any occasion but her own parties. "That would be commercialization," she said.

She had no objection, however, to the preparation of elaborate holograms of her sculptures so that they might be made permanent and reproduced in museums of art all over the world. Nor was there ever a charge for any use that might be made of her light-sculptures.

"I couldn't ask a penny," she said, spreading her arms wide. "It's free to all. After all, I have no further use for it myself." It was true! She never used the same light-sculpture twice.

When the holograms were taken, she was cooperation itself. Watching benignly at every step, she was always ready to order her robot servants to help. "Please, Courtney," she would say, "would you be so kind as to adjust the stepladder?"

It was her fashion. She always addressed her robots with the most formal courtesy.

Once, years before, she had been almost scolded by a government functionary from the Bureau of Robots and Mechanical Men. "You can't do that," he said severely. "It interferes with their efficiency. They are constructed to follow orders, and the more clearly you give those orders, the more efficiently they follow them. When you ask with elaborate politeness, it is difficult for them to understand that an order is being given. They react more slowly."

Mrs. Lardner lifted her aristocratic head. "I do not ask for speed and efficiency," she said. "I ask goodwill. My robots love me."

The government functionary might have explained that robots cannot love, but he withered under her hurt but gentle glance.

It was notorious that Mrs. Lardner never even returned a robot to the factory for adjustment. Their positronic brains are enormously complex, and once in ten times or so the adjustment is not perfect as it leaves the factory. Sometimes the error does not show up for a period of time, but whenever it does, U.S. Robots and Mechanical Men, Inc., always makes the adjustment free of charge.

Mrs. Lardner shook her head. "Once a robot is in my house," she said, "and has performed his duties, any minor eccentricities must be borne. I will not have him manhandled."

It was the worst thing possible to try to explain that a robot was but a machine. She would say very stiffly, "Nothing that is as intelligent as a robot can ever be *but* a machine. I treat them like people."

And that was that!

She kept even Max, although he was almost helpless. He could scarcely understand what was expected of him. Mrs. Lardner denied that strenuously, however. "Not at all," she would say firmly. "He can take hats and coats and store them very well, indeed. He can hold objects for me. He can do many things."

"But why not have him adjusted?" asked a friend once.

"Oh, I couldn't. He's himself. He's very lovable, you know. After all, a positronic brain is so complex that no one can ever tell in just what way it's off. If he were made perfectly normal there would be no way to adjust him back to the lovability he now has. I won't give that up."

"But if he's maladjusted," said the friend, looking at Max nervously, "might he not be dangerous?"

"Never," laughed Mrs. Lardner. "I've had him for years. He's completely harmless and quite a dear."

Actually he looked like all the other robots — smooth, metallic, vaguely human, but expressionless.

To the gentle Mrs. Lardner, however, they were all individual, all sweet, all lovable. It was the kind of woman she was.

How could she commit murder?

The very last person anyone would expect to be murdered would be John Semper Travis. Introverted and gentle, he was *in* the world but not *of* it. He had that peculiar mathematical turn of mind that made it possible for him to work out in his head the complicated tapestry of the myriad positronic brain-paths in a robot's mind.

He was chief engineer of U.S. Robots and Mechanical Men, Inc.

But he was also an enthusiastic amateur in light-sculpture. He had written a book on the subject, trying to show that the type of mathematics he used in working out positronic brain-paths might be modified into a guide to the production of aesthetic light-sculpture.

His attempt at putting theory into practice was a dismal failure, however. The sculptures he himself produced, following his mathematical principles, were stodgy, mechanical, and uninteresting.

It was the only reason for unhappiness in his quiet, constrained, and secure life, and yet it was reason enough for him to be very unhappy indeed. He *knew* his theories were right, yet he could not make them work. If he could but produce *one* great piece of light-sculpture —

Naturally, he knew of Mrs. Lardner's light-sculpture. She was universally hailed as a genius, yet Travis knew she could not understand even the simplest aspect of robotic mathematics. He had corresponded with her, but she consistently refused to explain her methods, and he wondered if she had any at all. Might it not be mere intuition? But even intuition might be reduced to mathematics. Finally he managed to receive an invitation to one of her parties. He simply had to see her.

Mr. Travis arrived rather late. He had made one last attempt at a piece of light-sculpture and had failed miserably.

He greeted Mrs. Lardner with a kind of puzzled respect and said, "That was a peculiar robot who took my hat and coat."

"That is Max," said Mrs. Lardner.

"He is quite maladjusted, and he's a fairly old model. How is it you did not return it to the factory?"

"Oh, no," said Mrs. Lardner. "It would be too much trouble."

"None at all, Mrs. Lardner," said Travis. "You would be surprised how simple a task it was. Since I am with U.S. Robots, I took the liberty of adjusting him myself. It took no time and you'll find he is now in perfect working order."

A queer change came over Mrs. Lardner's face. Fury found a place on it for the first time in her gentle life, and it was as though the lines did not know how to form.

"You adjusted him?" she shrieked. "But it was *he* who created my light-sculptures. It was the maladjustment, the *maladjustment*, which you can never restore, that — that —"

It was really unfortunate that she had been showing her collection at the time and that the jeweled dagger from Cambodia was on the marble tabletop before her.

Travis's face was also distorted. "You mean if I had studied his uniquely maladjusted positronic brain-paths I might have learned —"

She lunged with the knife too quickly for anyone to stop her and he did not try to dodge. Some said he came to meet it — as though he *wanted* to die.

Short-shorts need not be fiction. On occasion I am asked to do short nonfiction articles for one outlet or another, and I particularly enjoy doing them for TV Guide, *since there the opportunity exists for immersing myself in any of a wide variety of subjects.*

There was a television special on various reputed monsters, for instance, such as the abominable snowman, Bigfoot, the Loch Ness monster, and so on. I view reports of such objects with the deepest skepticism, and when TV Guide *asked for a "backgrounder" on the program, I produced an article entitled "The Monsters We Have Lived With," which brought me angry letters from some readers who didn't want their monsters taken away from them just because they didn't exist.*

As it happens, Doubleday occasionally publishes collections of miscellaneous essays of mine that have appeared in places other than F & SF. *My second hundred books contain three of these collections, of which the latest is* The Beginning and the End *(Book 187), published in 1977. It includes my monster backgrounder, which is here reproduced in full.*

"The Monsters We Have Lived With" (1974)

Mankind has always lived with monsters. That fact dates back, no doubt, to the time when the early ancestors of man moved about in constant fear of the large predators around them. Fearful as the mammoths, saber-toothed tigers, and cave bears may have been, it is the essence of the human mind that still worse could be imagined.

The dread forces of nature were visualized as superanimals. The Scandinavians imagined the sun and the moon to be pursued forever by gigantic wolves, for instance. It was when these caught up with their prey that eclipses took place.

Relatively harmless animals could be magnified into terrors. The octopuses and squids, with their writhing tentacles, were elaborated into the deadly Hydra, the many-headed snake destroyed by Hercules; into Medusa with her snaky hair and her glance that turned living things to stone; into Scylla with her six heads, whom Ulysses encountered.

Perhaps the most feared animal was the snake. Slithering unseen through the underbrush, it came upon its victim unawares. Its lidless eyes, its cold and malignant stare, its sudden strike, all served to terrorize human beings. Is it any wonder that the snake is so often used as the very principle of evil — as, for instance, in the tale of the Garden of Eden.

But imagination can improve even on the snake. Snakes can be imagined who kill not by a bite, but merely by a look, and this is the "basilisk" (from the Greek word meaning "little king").

Or else make the snake much larger, into what the Greeks called Python, and it can represent the original chaos which had to be destroyed by a god before the orderly universe could be created. It was Apollo who killed the Python in the early days of the earth, according to the Greek myths, and who then established the oracle of Delphi on the spot.

Another Greek word for a large snake was "drakon," which has become our "dragon." To the snaky length of the dragon were added the thicker body and stubby legs of that other dread reptile, the crocodile. Now we have the monster Tiamat, which the Babylonian god Marduk had to destroy in order to organize the universe.

Symbolize the burning bite of the venomous snake and you have the dragon breathing fire. Dramatize the swift and deadly strike of the snake and you have the dragon flying through the air.

Some monsters are, of course, animals that have been misunderstood into beauty rather than horror. The one-horned rhinoceros may have contributed to the myth of the unicorn, the beautiful one-horned horse. And the horn of the mythical unicorn is exactly like the tooth of the real-life narwhal.

The ugly sea cow with its flippered tail, rising half out of the sea and holding a newborn young to its breast in the human position, may have dazzled shortsighted sailors into telling tales of beautiful mermaids.

Throughout history, of course, man's greatest enemy was man, so it is not surprising that man himself served as the basis for some of the most fearful monsters — the giants and cannibalistic ogres of all sorts.

It may well be that the origin of such stories lies in the fact that various groups of human beings made technological advances in different directions and at different times. A tribe of warriors armed with stone axes, meeting an army of soldiers in bronze armor and carrying bronze-tipped spears, will be sent flying in short order with many casualties. The Stone Age survivors may well have the feeling that they have met an army of man-eating giants.

Thus, the primitive Israelite tribes, on first approaching Canaan and encountering walled cities and well-armed soldiers, felt the Canaanites to be a race of giants. Traces of that belief remain in the Bible.

Then, too, a high civilization may fall and those who follow forget the civilization and attribute its works to giants of one kind or another. The primitive Greeks, coming across the huge, thick walls that encircled the cities of the earlier, highly civilized Mycenaeans, imagined those walls to have been built by giant Cyclopes.

Such Cyclopes were later placed in Sicily (where Ulysses encountered them in the tales told in the *Odyssey*) and were supposed to have but one eye. They may have been sky gods, and the single eye may represent the sun in heaven. It may also have arisen from the fact that elephants roamed Sicily in prehuman times. The skull of such an elephant, occasionally found, would show large nasal openings in front which might be interpreted as the single eye of a giant.

There can be giants in ways other than physical. Thus medieval Englishmen had no notion of how or why the huge monoliths of Stonehenge had been erected. They blamed it on Merlin's magic. He caused the stones to fly through the air and land in place. (The Greeks also had tales of musicians who played so beautifully that, captivated by the sweet strains, rocks moved into place and built a wall of their own accord.)

But as man's knowledge of the world expanded, the room available for the dread or beautiful monsters he had invented shrank, and belief in them faded. Large animals were discovered — giant whales, moose, Komodo lizards, okapis, giant squids, and so on. These were, however, merely animals and lacked the super-terror our minds had created.

What is left then?

The giant snakes and dragons that once fought with the gods and terrorized mankind have shrunk to a possible sea serpent reported to be cowering at the bottom of Loch Ness.

The giants, the ogres, the monstrous one-eyed cannibals that towered over our puny race of mortals, have diminished to mysterious creatures that leave footprints among the snows of the upper reaches of Mount Everest or show their misty shapes fugitively in the depths of our shriveling forests.

Even if these exist (which is doubtful), what a puny remnant they represent of the glorious hordes man's mind and imagination have created.

PART 11

HUMOR

I DISCUSSED in Opus 100 *my struggles to achieve a bit of humor in my writing. I may have succeeded there, for reviewers often mentioned my sense of humor (as revealed in my writing) and seemed to do so with approval.*

That may be, but it was not till my second hundred books that I produced volumes that dealt with humor per se or that were specifically humorous books rather than other kinds of books that just happened to have a bit of humor as seasoning.

The first book of this sort that I wrote was Isaac Asimov's Treasury of Humor (*Book 114*), *a large compendium of jokes and comments on humor and joke-telling. Houghton Mifflin published it in 1971.*

How I came to write it is described in the introduction to that book, and this is given here:

from Isaac Asimov's Treasury of Humor (1971)

For nearly all my life I have been swapping jokes. At almost every friendly gathering that I have attended, there have been two or three people present with a large repertoire of funny stories and the ability to tell them with finesse, and so joke-swapping was almost inevitable. Modesty compels me to refrain from saying that of all those present I generally had the largest repertoire of jokes and could tell them with the most finesse, but if I weren't modest I would say so.

This has led to my having been asked, on occasion, why someone like myself, with pretensions to intellect, should content himself with endless joke-telling while shunning the ardent discussions of politics, philosophy, and literature that might be proceeding in another corner of the room.

To this my answer is threefold, in order of increasing importance:

1) I spend most of my day being intellectual at my typewriter, and telling jokes on an evening now and then helps balance the situation.

2) Jokes of the proper kind, properly told, can do more to enlighten questions of politics, philosophy, and literature than any number of dull arguments.

3) I like to.

Then, too, as it happens, this whole business of joke-telling saved my life not too long ago —

In June 1969, my wife and I, along with another couple, Howard and Muriel Hirt, were off on a motor trip that was to end in a vacation. As it happens, vacations send me into deep melancholy and I had been achingly apprehensive of this one for weeks. It was only to last for a weekend but it was to be at an elaborate hotel of a type that I detested beyond measure.

With doom hastening closer at every turn of the whirling wheels, I tried to fight off my gathering misery by telling jokes in feverish succession.

Muriel was kind enough to laugh quite a bit, and then she said, "Listen, Isaac, why don't you write a jokebook?"

That made it my turn to laugh.

"Who would publish it?" I asked.

She said, "I thought you said you could get someone or other to publish anything you wrote."

I do say things like that when I am feeling more than ordinarily megalomaniac, but that was not what suddenly began to circle wildly through the tortuous meshes of my mind.

A new thought arose —

Suppose that while I was ostensibly vacationing, and while everyone around me was going through the horrifying ritual of lying in the sun and volleyballing and hiking and doing whatever other forms of refined torture are supposed to be fun, I was secretly writing down jokes and, in that way, working on a book.

I would then be having no vacation at all! (Oh, magic words!)

As soon as we had registered and unpacked, therefore, I approached the desk and said, "I would like to check out a typewriter for the weekend."

This hotel, you must understand, is marvelously equipped. I do not remember the exact figures, but the impression I have is that the hotel possesses three swimming pools, four golf links, seventeen tennis courts, twenty-eight miles of hiking trails, and seventy-five thousand reclining beach chairs in serried ranks and files, each one laden with a vacationer slowly frying in his own juice. It also has an enormous nightclub, fourteen buildings, and sixty miles of corridors.

With a hotel that has everything, I had no hesitation in asking for a typewriter.

I was quickly disabused. The desk clerk said, "You want to check out a *what?*"

"A typewriter!" I said.

He looked blank, and I could see he was wondering if a typewriter might be anything like a set of golf clubs.

I said, "Well, then, do you have writing paper?"

He handed me a sheet of writing paper in which the monogram of the hotel took up half the area, leaving just enough room to write a message to a friend that might go: "Here I am at the X Hotel, dying."

I said, "Give me about fifty."

He handed them over, and for the next two and a half days, wherever we were — tramping the corridors, lying in the sun, sitting in the shade, waiting for food at the table, enduring the unbelievable, dinning mayhem at the nightclub — I quietly scribbled jokes on paper while carefully maintaining a fixed smile on my face to indicate how much I was enjoying the vacation.

Occasionally, I would overhear someone at a neighboring table say, "Watch out, Sadie, and be careful what you say. That fellow there is writing down every word he hears."

It was undoubtedly all that kept me alive.

I finished the vacation with a sheaf of handwritten jokes, which I converted into typescript and brought to Houghton Mifflin as a sample.

And eventually the book was completed and published, and here it is!

It would scarcely be suitable to let it go at that. The book contains 640 jokes (almost all of them quite clean), and I include several of them here.

from ISAAC ASIMOV'S TREASURY OF HUMOR (*1971*)

Moskowitz had bought a parrot and one morning found the bird at the eastern side of the cage, with a small prayer shawl over its head, rocking to and fro and mumbling. Bending low to listen, Moskowitz was thunderstruck to discover the parrot was intoning prayers in the finest Hebrew.

"You're Jewish?" asked Moskowitz.

"Not only Jewish," said the parrot, "but Orthodox. So will you take me to the synagogue on Rosh Hashanah?"

Rosh Hashanah, the Jewish New Year, was indeed only two days off, and it would as always usher in the high-holiday season which would end with Yom Kippur, the Day of Atonement, ten days later.

Moskowitz said, "Of course, I'll take you, but can I tell my friends about you? It isn't a secret, I hope?"

"No secret at all. Tell anyone you want to." And the parrot returned to his praying.

Moskowitz went to all his friends, full of the story of his Jewish parrot. Of course no one believed him, and in no time at all Moskowitz was taking bets. By Rosh Hashanah, he had a hundred dollars, all told, riding on the parrot.

Grinning, Moskowitz brought the parrot to the synagogue in its cage. He put him in a prominent place and everyone turned to watch, even as they mumbled their prayers. Even the rabbi watched, for he had seven dollars that said the parrot could not pray.

Moskowitz waited. Everyone waited. And the parrot did nothing. Moskowitz carefully arranged the prayer shawl over the bird's head, but the parrot ducked and the shawl fell off.

After the services, Moskowitz's friends, with much mockery, collected their money. Even the rabbi snickered as he took his profit of seven dollars.

Utterly humiliated, Moskowitz returned home, turned viciously on the parrot, and said, "Prepare to die, you little monster, for I'm going to wring your neck. If you can pray, now's the time."

Whereupon the parrot's voice rang out clearly: "Hold it, you dumb jerk. In ten days it's Yom Kippur, when all Jews will sing the tragic, haunting Kol Nidre. Well, bet everybody that I can sing the Kol Nidre."

"Why? You didn't do anything today."

"Exactly! So for Yom Kippur, just think of the odds you'll get!"

◆ ◆ ◆

A young man is reported to have approached the renowned composer Wolfgang Amadeus Mozart (one of the great musical prodigies of all time) and asked, "Herr Mozart, I have the ambition to write symphonies, and perhaps you can advise me how to get started."

Mozart said, "The best advice I can give you is to wait until you are older and more experienced, and try your hand at less ambitious pieces to begin with."

The young man looked astonished. "But, Herr Mozart, you yourself wrote symphonies when you were considerably younger than I."

"Ah," said Mozart, "but I did so without asking advice."

◆ ◆ ◆

Young Leah, in the old days of eastern Europe, was the sole support of her mother, and had been fortunate enough to marry a substantial young man, despite the miserable state of her dowry. Leah was happy and her mother was ecstatic.

Imagine her mother's shock then, when, on the morning after the wedding, Leah returned in misery and announced she would not return to her husband. "I love him madly," she said, "but I had to leave him."

Stubbornly, she refused to give the reason, but, from what she said, it was apparent that the young man had made some rather sophisticated sexual demands on her.

As the days passed, both mother and daughter grew more and more miserable, the former out of frustrated finances, the latter out of frustrated love. Finally, the mother suggested that they visit the town rabbi, the beloved Rabbi Joshua of Khaslavich. After all, in such matters one needed guidance.

They were granted an audience, and when the rabbi demanded the details and Leah hung back, Rabbi Joshua said kindly, "Whisper it into my ear, my daughter. No one will know but we ourselves and God."

She did so, and as she whispered, the rabbi's kindly brow furrowed, and lightning flashed from his mild eyes.

"My daughter," he thundered, "it is not fitting for a Jewish girl to submit to such vile indignities. It would be a deadly sin, and because of it a curse would be laid on our whole town."

Back went mother and daughter, disconsolate, and after a week of continued privation, the mother said, "You know, our rabbi is a wonderful man, but it is sometimes wise to get a second opinion. Why not consult Rabbi Samuel of Krichev? He is very highly spoken of as a man of learning."

Why not, indeed? They got into the wagon and bumped their way to the next town. As Leah whispered the tale into Rabbi Samuel's ear, the old man's earlocks uncurled and turned distinctly grayer. He said in strangled tones, "My daughter, it was for sins such as this that the Holy One, blessed be He, sent down upon the earth a flood in days of yore. You must not agree to his demands."

Again mother and daughter returned, and now, for a long time, the dreary round of day-to-day living continued, until the mother said, "Let us make one final attempt to obtain guidance. Let us go to the Grand Rabbi of Vilna. There is no one in the whole world as wise as he and as learned. And whatever he says we may accept as the final word."

They bought their railway tickets, which seriously depleted their meager savings, and rode to Vilna. For the third time, Leah whispered her story into a rabbinical ear. The Grand Rabbi listened with equanimity and then said, "My daughter, be guided by your husband. He is a young and vigorous man, and it is fitting that you both enjoy yourselves. Have no qualms concerning this thing."

Leah was thunderstruck. She said, "But, Grand Rabbi, how can you say this? Rabbi Joshua of Khaslavich said it would bring a curse upon our town. Rabbi Samuel of Krichev said such sins caused the flood."

But the Grand Rabbi merely stroked his white beard and smiled. "My daughter," he said, "what do those small-town rabbis know about big-city sex?"

◆ ◆ ◆

Among the Germans, Berlin is considered the very epitome of Prussian brusqueness and efficiency, while Vienna is the essence of Austrian charm and slipshoddery.

The tale is told of a Berliner visiting Vienna who was lost and in need of directions. What would such a Berliner do? He grabbed at the lapel of the first passing Viennese and barked out, "The post office? Where is it?"

The startled Viennese carefully detached the other's fist, smoothed his lapel, and said in a gentle manner, "Sir, would it not have been more delicate of you to have approached me politely and to have said, 'Sir, if you have a moment and happen to know, could you please direct me to the post office?' "

The Berliner stared in astonishment for a moment, then growled, "I'd rather be lost!" and stamped away.

That very same Viennese was visiting Berlin later that year, and it turned out that now it was he who had to search for the post office. Approaching a Berliner, he said politely, "Sir, if you have a moment and happen to know, could you please direct me to the post office?"

With machinelike rapidity, the Berliner replied, "About face, two blocks forward, sharp turn right, one block forward, cross street, half-right under arch, sharp left over railroad tracks, past newsstand, into post office lobby."

The Viennese, more bewildered than enlightened, nevertheless murmured, "A thousand thanks, kind sir —"

Whereupon the Berliner snatched furiously at the other's lapel and shouted, "Never mind the thanks! *Repeat the instructions!*"

◆ ◆ ◆

Pierre was celebrating his silver wedding, and while all were unrestrainedly merry over the ample liquor provided by the host,

Pierre himself remained in the corner, nursing a drink and following one of the guests with baleful eyes.

A friend noticed this strange action, all the more strange on so happy an occasion, and said, "At whom are you glaring, Pierre my friend?"

"At my lawyer, may his soul rot."

"But why are you so angry with him?"

"It is a sad tale. After I had been married ten years, I decided I had had enough and that the cleanest solution would be to kill my wife. Painlessly, of course, for I am no monster. Being a methodical man, I approached my lawyer — that one there — and asked him of the possible consequences. He told me that whereas killing a husband is, here in France, a mere misdemeanor, killing a wife is a felony, and that even with a most skillful defense I would have to count on fifteen years in jail. He urged me not to do it and I let myself be guided by his advice."

"Well, then, why are you angry?"

"Because," said Pierre, "if I had not listened to his idiotic advice, on this very day I would have been a free man at last."

Although Isaac Asimov's Treasury of Humor *was the first humorous book I wrote, it was not the first I published.*

On March 12, 1971, I had lunch with Beth Walker and Millicent Selsam of Walker and Company to discuss my ABC's of the Earth. *When that was done, the two editors talked shop and the conversation veered to* The Sensuous Woman *and* The Sensuous Man, *two sleazy books that were making money out of prurience.*

Beth turned to me and said, "Why don't you write a dirty book, Isaac?"

I thought of my own propensities and said dryly, "What do you want me to write? The Sensuous Dirty Old Man?"

That turned out to be a dreadful thing to say, for Beth fell in love with the title and hounded me into doing the book. She then raced it into print and it appeared less than ninety days after my original mocking suggestion, appearing as Book 112.

In no way, of course, was The Sensuous Dirty Old Man *merely sex. I should hope that I don't have to stoop to try to write and*

*sell a book on the basis of salacity alone. It was satire and was
intended, at all points, to be more humorous than salacious.*

*Don't get me wrong. I don't eschew the salacious. I merely in-
sist that humor be primary. Thus:*

from THE SENSUOUS DIRTY OLD MAN (1971)

Sometime during the 1930s, women, having stripped off enough
layers of frontal textile, discovered that insufficient material was
left to protect the delicate tissues of the bosom. To protect these,
modern engineering devised a structure that served to compress
the bosom into firm cone-shaped objects which, far from requir-
ing protection, could allow unlimited maneuver without danger.
Unavoidably it caught the masculine eye — or some other part of
the male anatomy if he weren't careful, leaving a nasty bruise.

The service performed to womankind by this new garment can
not easily be exaggerated. It was first designed by an organization of bioengineers who, although individually anonymous, have
become world famous by the corporate title of Bosom Rehabilita-
tion Associates. The garment they engineered possessing the
small initials BRA on the strap quickly became known, in consequence, as the "bra."

The gentlemen of B.R.A. carefully labored to give each woman
that firmly jutting profile one would naturally associate with
strength of will and character, and it worked. Many a woman
who in her natural unprotected state would have slunk into a
room, abashed and uncertain, could, with her bra firmly in place,
walk in, shoulders back and chest thrown out, proudly aware that
every man in the place would at once note and admire her
strength of character.

Every woman felt uplifted by the experience, so the industry
began to speak of the "uplift bra."

And yet the uplift bra had its troubles. For one thing, the
designers had unaccountably placed its hooks in the back. In addition, the straps cut the shoulders, and in hot weather there were
such matters as heat, perspiration, and skin rashes.

Little by little the thought came that it might be possible to
eliminate the bra and allow the contents to find their natural

level; or, as President Nixon so succinctly put it in discussing this very problem, the time had come for America to adopt a lower profile.

Certain of the more excitable women determined not merely to eliminate the bra but to burn it as a gesture of contempt. The slogan arose: LET'S IGNITE BRAS. This was abbreviated to L.I.B. and in no time at all Women's Lib was a power in the land.

The result was, in the light of hindsight, inevitable. The ladies found themselves back where they had been in the 1930s and, indeed, worse off than ever. The sturdier fabrics of a much earlier day, the taffeta dress and corduroy blouse, had given way to sheer synthetics. What had earlier been hidden and protected by the bra was hidden and protected no longer by virtually anything. Indeed, the tender caress of the soft synthetic irritated the delicate bosom surface till every unevenness was accentuated and softly revealed.

At a time when President Nixon was making one point very, very clear, the average young girl on the streets of New York was doing exactly twice as well.

And dirty old men, on those same streets, found that they had a new target — and new hazards. Without the constriction of the bra, the average young lady, moving forward in a healthy free-swinging stride, presents what can only be described as a moving target.

It is therefore difficult for the dirty old man to get to the point; for the point shifts. It moves wildly at the slightest bodily motion. It jiggles, wobbles, and dangles; heaves, yaws, and rolls; vibrates, oscillates, and undulates.

The dirty old man may find himself trying to follow every movement by use of eye muscles, head muscles, or both. This is not advisable. Aside from the fact that in the attempt to concentrate too entirely on the target he may walk into a wall, the constant movement of eyes or head or both will induce dizziness, headache, nausea, and even that dread affliction of the inveterate leerer, watering eyes. The whole complex of symptoms makes up the syndrome of "mammamobilism."

Mammamobilism is known to the medical profession by the euphemistic phrase "nipple shock," but in this book I have no use for euphemisms and do not intend to employ them. The general public, the taxi driver, the construction worker, everyone, says "mammamobilism," and that's what I shall say, too.

The Italians, far wiser than we in their attitude toward sex, have no compunctions about using the phrase. You will recall that in the great opera *Rigoletto* the Duke, when Gilda runs past him jiggling, claps his hand to his brow and begins the brilliant tenor aria: "Oh, mammamobile —"

Although you can see that the disease played so important a part in the opera written by Joe Green* a century and a quarter ago, thanks to the extraordinary equipment of the pasta-consuming coloratura soprano of his day, it did not strike the American public till just a few short years ago. Mammamobilism is not amenable to penicillin or to any of the other antibiotics. Prevention, then, is the key. Do *not* try to follow the moving target. Fix the eye rather upon some key portion of the dress pattern and allow the sense of sight to be titillated sporadically.

Oddly enough, a new career (if you want to call it that) started for me quite unexpectedly in 1974.

I was returning by ship (I don't fly) from a visit to Great Britain, and things were a little dull. At the table at luncheon, as conversation flagged and as I looked aimlessly at the ocean outside the window from my seat in the Queen's Grill of the Queen Elizabeth II, *a limerick occurred to me.*

I had made up an occasional limerick in my life but had never paid much attention to them. This time, though, the limerick flowed into my mind so easily that I found myself unable to resist quoting it. I began, without warning, by saying, "There was a young girl from Decatur."

What conversation there was stopped, and everyone at the table turned to look at me.

"Who went out to sea on a freighter," I said, and now attention was focused on me with an almost painful intensity.

"She was screwed by the Master — an utter disaster," said I,

---

* Green, having emigrated to Italy, adopted the Italian version of his name, Giuseppe Verdi. For reasons known only to opera buffs, the Italian name is actually better known today than the name he was born with in Poughkeepsie, New York.

and paused a little to let the suspense gather, and then I added, "But the crew all made up for it later."

There was an explosion of laughter.

I was very pleased and, for the first time, took the trouble to write down one of my own limericks.

That was fatal, for from that moment on, every time I made up a limerick I wrote it down. What's more, I began to concentrate on constructing them. By the time I had sixteen, I brought them to Walker and Company with the glad tidings that when I had a hundred I would make a book out of them, which Walker might then publish. Sam Walker winced at that but, like a good sport, agreed.

I then got to work seriously, using the same criterion I had used for The Sensuous Dirty Old Man. *A limerick could be as salacious as necessary, provided it was more funny than salacious. And I added another rule: it could never be physically repulsive.*

Before I was through, I had not only a hundred limericks and a published book (complete with lengthy introduction and commentary on each limerick) but four hundred and forty-four limericks and four published books.

These were: Lecherous Limericks *(Book 166), in 1975;* More Lecherous Limericks *(Book 177), in 1976;* Still More Lecherous Limericks *(Book 185), in 1977; and* Limericks: Too Gross *(Book 196), in 1978. The limericks were numbered consecutively through the three volumes, from 1 to 300, and the happy tale of the young girl from Decatur was, very appropriately, given pride of place as number 1.*

Here are two limericks from each of the first three books:

from LECHEROUS LIMERICKS (1975)

Well, Hardly Ever

There was an old maid of Peru
Who swore that she never would screw
    Except under stress
    Of forceful duress
Like, "I'm ready, dear, how about you?"

Impatience

There was a young couple from Florida
Whose passion grew steadily torrider.
    They were planning to sin
    In a room in an inn.
Who can wait? So they screwed in the corridor.

from MORE LECHEROUS LIMERICKS (1976)

Shutting the Barn Door

There was an effete lazy fop
Who preferred all his women on top.
    He said, "I'm no jerk,
    Let *them* do the work,
But if I get pregnant, I'll stop."

You Mean

A young fellow, divinely endowed,
Once said, very haughty and proud,
    When a girl, much too free,
    Placed her hand on his knee,
"That isn't my knee, Miss McCloud."

from STILL MORE LECHEROUS LIMERICKS (1977)

Reasons Enough

The virginal nature of Donna
Had for many long years been a goner.
    When asked why she screwed,
    She replied, "Gratitude,
Politeness — and just 'cause I wanna."

Emily Post

There was a young man of Connecticut
Who tore off a young woman's petticoat.
    Said she, with a grin,
    "You will have to get in.
For to do nothing more isn't etiquette."

PART 12

SOCIAL SCIENCES

UNTIL NOW I have carefully followed the order of the sections as originally given in Opus 100: *from Part 1, Astronomy, to Part 11, Humor.*

I would hate, though, to have you think that, having established a certain diversity in my writings in my first hundred books, I would allow that diversity to stand, that I would seek out no new fields for my second hundred. That is not so. There are no less than four additional sections in this present book.

First, the social sciences. This, I must admit, is not my forte, and consequently I have done very little writing in this field. It is important, after all, for any versatile writer to have a keen perception of his limitations. Otherwise, the ease with which he may hop from subject to subject, and his vanity over being able to do so, may lure him to write on something he knows nothing about with disastrous consequences.

To be sure, some of my F & SF essays deal with one aspect or another of the social sciences — the essays that I refer to as "controversials" in my correspondence with my editor, Edward L. Ferman. There, however, I am writing informally to an audience of friends and giving only my opinions, making no pretense of speaking authoritatively.

In one instance during my second hundred books, however, I allowed myself to be talked into doing a book that edges rather far into the social.

Frances Schwartz of Abelard-Schuman phoned me in 1973 and asked me to do a book on population aimed at an audience of young people. It is a subject near to my heart, for I firmly believe that if the world does not master the population problem, civilization is very likely going to collapse within half a century.

I agreed to do the book therefore, and it appeared in 1974 under the imprint of the John Day Company, which by then was a sister house of Abelard-Schuman. The title is Earth: Our Crowded Spaceship *and it is Book 156. Here is an excerpt:*

from EARTH: OUR CROWDED SPACESHIP (1974)

There are many people who are educated and who know about the world population and the way it is growing but think there is no danger. They tell themselves that people who talk of the danger are foolish and wrong.

People who don't believe there is a crisis can point to the Netherlands, for instance. They say that the Netherlands is prosperous and yet is much more densely populated than the world average. They say that it would do no harm to let the whole world become that densely populated. They don't seem to realize that the Netherlands is prosperous because it has fertile soil and much water; that it makes use of a great deal of industrial products like fertilizer and insecticides; that it imports a great deal of oil and that it has no forests to speak of.

There just isn't enough fertile soil and enough water to make the entire world into one gigantic Netherlands. There isn't enough fertilizer and insecticides and oil, and we don't really want to cut down all the forests. Besides, it won't take very long for the earth to be as densely populated all over as the Netherlands is now, and if it could be done, how would we stop the population increase at that point?

Some people think that science will solve all problems. They say that more people will just mean more scientists working on those problems. They don't realize that the problems get worse and worse, faster and faster, and that sooner or later — probably sooner — science just won't be able to keep up the pace.

Some people even think that population means strength. They think that large nations with many people can conquer neighboring nations with fewer people. They think that many people means a large, powerful army. They think that if their own nation does not increase its population, a neighboring nation which *does* increase its population will conquer them. For this reason, some nations think that they must have more and more babies, more and more people, if they are to remain strong and free.

Even if war is not involved, some people think a nation with a large population can keep its own customs, languages, and attitudes better than a nation with a small population. If a neighboring nation grows faster, they think, that neighboring nation might impose *its* customs, language, and attitudes on the smaller one, just by outnumbering them.

Actually, this is not so. Very often in history, small nations have conquered large ones. It's not so much the size of the army as its organization and the technical level of its weapons. Thus, Greece took over Persia in the 300s B.C., Mongolia took over China in the 1200s, and Great Britain took over India in the 1700s, even though Persia, China, and India were far more populous than Greece, Mongolia, and Great Britain.

Then, too, the Greek language and culture in ancient times and the English language and culture in modern times spread over the world even though those languages were spoken by few people to begin with.

If a nation wishes to avoid being dominated by its neighbors, its best chance is to raise its standard of living and its level of technology. This can be done best by not allowing its population to grow to such a point that it is sunk in misery and poverty. In fact, the worst way in which a nation can try to avoid being dominated by its neighbor is to increase its population to the point of misery and poverty.

If every nation tries to compete with its neighbors by raising its population, then the whole world will be sunk in misery and poverty. The nations will all decline in a catastrophe that will leave nothing behind that is worth dominating. No one will have gained anything. Everyone will have lost everything.

Once all this is understood, and people generally agree that population growth must not be allowed to continue, they must also come to understand how that growth can be stopped. Population grows because more people are being born than are dying. There are two ways, then, in which the growth can be stopped. You can increase the number of people who die until it matches the number of people who are being born. Or else you can decrease the number of people who are born until it matches the number of people who are dying.

The first method — increasing the death rate — is the usual way in which population is controlled in all species of living things other than ourselves. It is the method by which human populations have been controlled in the past. It is the "natural" method. If there are too many people, some starve or die of disease or by violence. If we don't do anything now, it will be the way population will be controlled in the future. Billions will die.

Must we let that happen because it is the "natural" way?

Through all the history of mankind, the human brain has been bending nature to its will. If we had really decided that the "natural" way was the right way, we would never have begun to make tools or build fires or develop agriculture or study science. It is because mankind has bent nature to its will that there are now many, many people who live more comfortably and better than people ever have before. We must continue to work out ways to be more comfortable by using the intelligent way, and not just the "natural" way.

The "natural" way to control population is by raising the death rate, but we don't want that, for catastrophe lies that way. The intelligent way is to reduce the birth rate. If, say, 40,000,000 people die each year, then not more than 40,000,000 people should be born each year. In fact, we may want to *reduce* the world population to some reasonable value, in which case, if 40,000,000 people die each year, we may want only 30,000,000 people to be born, or only 20,000,000, till the desired population level is reached.

But how can the birth rate be reduced?

One way is for people to stop mating. This, however, is not very practical, since people enjoy it too much to stop. A better way is to let mating continue but to use methods that keep it from resulting in babies.

There are a number of different ways in which the birth rate can be made to drop without interfering with people's pleasure. In the last twenty years, the birth rate in the United States and in some other countries has dropped because more and more women are using pills to keep from having babies they don't want.

To make sure that mating doesn't result in babies is called "birth control." It is by adopting methods of birth control that population growth can be stopped with the least damage.

There are many difficulties here. Certain religious organizations are against birth control. Many groups of people have ways of life that would not fit in easily with birth control.

Then, too, even if birth control were desired, there are many places in the world where people are so poor they can't afford to buy the materials that make it possible.

So you see, it comes down to education again. People not only have to be taught that a problem exists, they have to be taught exactly how to solve it by birth control and why it is right to do so. And they must be given the necessary materials without charge.

PART 13

LITERATURE

PERHAPS THE MOST OUTRAGEOUS books among my second hundred are my annotations of literary classics.

In the first place, it does take a certain amount of overweening self-assurance for a person whose intellectual expertise is in the sciences to decide to do large and complicated books on a subject that may easily be mistaken for literary criticism. Literary critics (who are bound to be asked to review the books) are sure to be annoyed at this invasion of their home turf.

Secondly, the books tend to be elaborate and expensive and Doubleday (whom I stuck with the publication thereof) was sure to be forced to risk considerable sums on them that they might not earn back. (Doubleday has never uttered a word of complaint in the matter, but that doesn't stop me from worrying about it.)

After my two-volume Asimov's Guide to the Bible, *it was inevitable that I would plan* Asimov's Guide to Shakespeare.

What I did, in the latter case, was to take up each of Shakespeare's plays in turn, go through it carefully, describing as much of the plot as was necessary for my purposes, and quoting those passages that contained historical, mythological, biographical, or geographical allusions. Since these might not be plain to the reader and might get in the way of a proper understanding of the text, I explained each one.

I did not in the least attempt to discuss the plays as dramatic vehicles or indulge in true literary criticism.

Asimov's Guide to Shakespeare *appeared in two volumes in 1970 as Books 104 and 105, and here is my treatment of the opening soliloquy from* Richard III, *in volume 2:*

from ASIMOV'S GUIDE TO SHAKESPEARE (1970)

Richard III deals with events that immediately follow *Henry VI, Part 3*, and it is very likely that Shakespeare began work on it as soon as he was through with the *Henry VI* trilogy. It was probably completed by 1593 at the latest.

At that time Shakespeare was still at the beginning of his career. He had written two narrative poems, a number of sonnets, a couple of light comedies, and the *Henry VI* trilogy, all popular and successful, but none, as yet, a blockbuster. With *Richard III* Shakespeare finally made it big.

It is a play after the manner of Seneca, like *Titus Andronicus*, which Shakespeare was also working on at the time, but infinitely more successful.

Indeed, *Richard III* was so full of harrowing and dramatic episodes, and Richard III himself was so successful a character, so wonderful a villain, with so much bravery and dry humor mingled with his monstrous behavior, that the play pleased all and made it quite plain that Shakespeare was a new star of brilliant magnitude on the literary scene. Indeed, despite the fact that the play is quite raw compared to the polished mastery of Shakespeare's later plays, it is still one of his most popular and successful plays today.

The play opens with Richard of Gloucester, youngest brother of King Edward IV, alone on the stage. He sets the time of the scene by saying:

> *Now is the winter of our discontent*
> *Made glorious summer by this sun of York;*
> (Act 1, scene 1, lines 1–2)

This ties in well with the final speech in *Henry VI*, Part 3, in which Edward IV says happily that the troubles are all over and that only joy is left.

It was in 1471 that the last serious Lancastrian threat was smashed at Tewkesbury. Old King Henry VI and his son, Prince Edward, were dead immediately after that battle, and no one was left to dispute the right of King Edward to the throne.

The "sun of York" (and a sun was one of the symbols of the Yorkist house) was indeed shining.

The sun of York does not satisfy Richard, however. In a speech that resembles one he had made in the earlier play, he explains that he is so physically deformed that the joys of peace, such as dancing and lovemaking, are beyond him. He will therefore confine himself to the joys of ambition, and labor to make himself a king. After all, in *Henry VI*, Part 3, he waxed lyrical over the joys of being a king, and it is not to be wondered at that he should want those joys.

In order to become a king, he must get out of the way those who have a prior right to the throne. Among them, of course, is his older brother George of Clarence. Richard explains in his soliloquy:

> *Plots have I laid, inductions* [beginnings] *dangerous,*
> *By drunken prophecies, libels, and dreams,*
> *To set my brother Clarence and the king*
> *In deadly hate the one against the other;*
> *And if King Edward be as true and just*
> *As I am subtle, false, and treacherous,*
> *This day should Clarence closely be mewed up*
> *About a prophecy which says that G*
> *Of Edward's heirs the murderer shall be.*
>
> (Act 1, scene 1, lines 32–40)

Shakespeare is here condensing time, for George of Clarence's final break with his royal brother came in 1477, six years after the climactic Battle of Tewkesbury, despite the appearance in the first two lines of the soliloquy that it is the very morrow of the battle that is in question.

Why did the break between the brothers come? Well, it required no plot on the part of Richard, really, for George of Clarence had some of the characteristics in reality that Richard was later slanderously described as having.

It was George who was ambitious and faithless. He had deserted Edward and sided with Warwick in 1469, and had come back to his allegiance to York, we may be sure, only out of a feeling that Warwick was going to lose and that he himself would gain more by a second double-cross.

Edward had forgiven the twice faithless George, but that did not prevent George from continuing to scheme for his own aggrandizement in such a way that the king was bound, eventually, to suspect his brother of aiming at the throne.

George did his best, for instance, to keep his hands on the

whole enormous Warwick estate. This may have been out of mere avarice, but it may also have been out of a realization of how useful wealth would be in planning a revolt. He had married Warwick's elder daughter, Isabella, in the days when he and Warwick had been friends and allies. The younger daughter, Anne, had been married to Edward, prince of Wales, the son of old King Henry. Prince Edward was now dead and Anne was a widow; and George was determined to keep her a widow, lest some new husband insist on a half share in the Warwick estate. While Anne remained a widow, George controlled it all, and he kept the poor lady a virtual prisoner to see to it that the situation would continue.

This intentness on wealth at all costs would naturally disturb Edward.

Then there arose a new matter. Charles the Bold of Burgundy died in battle in 1477, leaving behind a twenty-year-old daughter, Mary, as his only heir. (Charles's wife had been Margaret of York, the sister of George of Clarence, but Mary was his daughter by a previous wife.)

Burgundy had, for over half a century, been the wealthiest nation in Europe, and under Charles it had reached its political peak, for Charles had almost defeated France and made an independent kingdom of his land. Now, with only a young woman to rule Burgundy, its days seemed numbered under the pressure of France to the west and the Holy Roman Empire to the east. Unless, that is, some strong independent prince quickly married Mary and carried on where Charles the Bold had left off. George of Clarence was now a widower and he saw himself as husband of Mary and as the new duke of Burgundy.

King Edward thoroughly disapproved of this scheme. It seemed to him that if his ambitious, faithless brother became duke of Burgundy, with all the resources of Burgundy at his call, he would be a source of endless trouble. He would have the money to finance plots against Edward and scheme at a double throne.

Edward therefore forbade the marriage and the two brothers became open enemies. It did not take much more for Edward to begin to suspect George of plotting his death. Two of George's henchmen were accused of trying to bring about that death by sorcery, and when George insisted they were innocent, Edward angrily had his brother arrested and thrown in the Tower of London.

Whether George was actually plotting Edward's death we cannot say, but certainly his past and his character gave cause for suspicion, and in those troubled times that was enough.

And what had been Richard's record through all this? Well, for one thing, he had remained utterly faithful to Edward in the hard times when Warwick had temporarily hurled him from the throne. He had fought with bravery and distinction at the battles of Barnet and Tewkesbury. He had done Edward's dirty work (probably) in arranging the death of old King Henry VI in the Tower. In all respects, Richard was as much the loyal brother as George was the faithless one.

This helps explain the frustrating manner in which the characters in *Richard III* fall prey to villainous Richard, though his villainy is made to appear patent to all. In actual history, you see, he *wasn't* a villain.

Thus, consider the prophecy that helped set the king against his brother: that someone with the initial G would be a traitor to him. (Undoubtedly, there were prophecies extant of this sort, and of every other too, for there are astrologers and prophets everywhere and at all times, even in our own country now, and only those prophecies that come true or seem to come true are later remembered.) The king felt this applied to George of Clarence; but why not to Richard of Gloucester? The king suspected George because George deserved it; he did not suspect Gloucester because the real Gloucester's unshakable loyalty left no room for suspicion.

We can also ask ourselves whether Richard really had a hand in raising Edward's suspicions against George. There is no evidence of that at all until the later anti-Richard polemicists got to work. They say that he spoke openly in favor of his brother to the king in order to hide his secret maneuverings. The "maneuverings," however, are a later invention presented even by the polemicists as only a matter of suspicion, whereas the one *fact* they admit is that Richard defended his brother Clarence openly — which took courage.

By the time Asimov's Guide to Shakespeare *had come out, my marriage had broken up and I found myself in New York in a two-room hotel suite and rather at a loss.*

For the first time in my life I needed to consult no one's taste but my own, so I went to lower Fourth Avenue to poke around the secondhand bookstores, something I had always wanted to do.

I came across a Modern Library edition of Lord Byron's great comic epic Don Juan, *which I had read (or had, at least, begun to read) in my college days. I brought it home in triumph, feeling that I could now have something to read at night when I couldn't sleep (and I wasn't sleeping very well in my lonely hotel apartment).*

The first night, I had hardly managed to read the seventeen-stanza dedication and the very beginning of the first canto before all was lost. I put the book aside and spent the rest of the night in restless waiting for the morning so that I could begin to annotate it.

I did annotate *it, and, unlike my treatment of the Bible and Shakespeare, I quoted the entire epic along with the annotations. I managed to persuade Doubleday to publish it (which they eventually did — their own idea — in a very beautiful and expensive edition).*

Asimov's Annotated "Don Juan" (Book 130) was published in 1972, and I have rarely had such fun writing a book. Here is the first verse of the first canto just to give you a notion of what I was doing:

from ASIMOV'S ANNOTATED "DON JUAN" (1972)

I want a hero: an uncommon want,
    When every year and month sends forth a new one,
Till, after cloying the gazettes with cant,[1]
    The age discovers he is not the true one:
Of such as these I should not care to vaunt,
    I'll therefore take our ancient friend Don Juan[2] —
We all have seen him, in the pantomime,
Sent to the devil somewhat ere his time.[3]

Canto 1 was written between September 6 and November 1, 1818, in Venice, Italy.

1. The gazettes were not then, as now in the American sense of the word, simply newspapers. They were official weekly journals, publishing statistics of governmental interest: movements of the royal family, lists of honors granted, those killed in battle, and so on. Byron refers to the gazettes now and then in *Don Juan*, chiefly in order to bestow a sardonic glance at their role as a military obituary list.

2. Don Juan is an "ancient friend" because he was a well-known figure out of Spanish folklore. He first received recognized literary presentation in the drama *El Burlador de Sevilla*, written in 1630 by the Spanish dramatist Gabriel Téllez (who wrote under the pseudonym Tirso de Molina).

In the original folk tale, Don Juan was the epitome of the licentious man, who aspired (usually successfully) to make love to every woman he met, and who did so with utter disregard for any law. The climax of his story is his liaison with a noblewoman and its consequences. He kills the woman's father in a duel. The father is buried and an effigy of him is placed over the tomb. Don Juan, seeing that effigy, mockingly invites it to dinner. The stone figure duly arrives at the meal and drags the rake and blasphemer to Hell.

Various versions of this legend had already appeared in Spain and elsewhere by Byron's time. Molière had written a play on the theme and Mozart, an opera. Byron, with no compunction whatever, utterly altered the plot in his own version. In fact, all that Byron left of the traditional Don Juan is his name and birthplace; *nothing more!* Don Juan's character is utterly changed. From a heartless blasphemer, seducer, and libertine (as the world viewed Byron), he becomes an innocent, far more sinned against than sinning (as Byron viewed himself). Even the hero's name was tampered with, for Byron abandoned the universal "Don Wahn" and called him, with sturdy English disregard for the eccentric pronunciations of foreigners, "Don Joo'un," as we can tell by the fact that he rhymed Juan with "new one" and "true one."

3. Don Juan was also a favorite in pantomimes and puppet shows, particularly one adapted from the play *The Libertine* by Thomas Shadwell. The climax of such shows invariably came at

the point where Don Juan, defiant to the last, is dragged down
to Hell by the devil to the screaming enthusiasm of the audience.

Nor did working on Don Juan *in the least sate me. While it was
in press, I did the same for Milton's great tragic epic* Paradise
Lost, *throwing in* Paradise Regained *for good measure. In this
case, too, I quoted the entire work along with the annotations.*

Doubleday did Asimov's Annotated "Paradise Lost" *also, and
without a murmur. It was published in 1974 as Book 154.*

I had thought, when I first began to work on Paradise Lost,
*that it would be hard work since I was under the firm impression
that I didn't like Milton's style. I changed my mind, however.
Once I immersed myself in it, I found I loved the long and rolling
sonority of those magnificent Latinate sentences of his. Here's
the very first sentence in the epic, one that rumbles on for sixteen
lines of iambic pentameter — together with my annotations, of
course.*

from ASIMOV'S ANNOTATED "PARADISE LOST" (1974)

> Of Man's First disobedience,[1] and the Fruit
> Of that Forbidden Tree,[2] whose mortal taste
> Brought Death into the World, and all our woe,
> With loss of Eden,[3] till one greater Man[4]
> Restore us, and regain the blissful Seat,
> Sing, Heav'nly Muse,[5] that on the secret top
> Of Oreb, or of Sinai,[6] didst inspire
> That Shepherd, who first taught the chosen Seed,[7]
> In the Beginning how the Heav'ns and Earth[8]
> Rose out of Chaos:[9] Or if Sion Hill[10]
> Delight thee more, and Siloa's Brook that flow'd
> Fast by the Oracle of God;[11] I thence
> Invoke thy aid to my advent'rous song,
> That with no middle flight intends to soar
> Above th' Aonian Mount,[12] while it pursues
> Things unattempted yet in Prose or Rhyme.

1. The epic poem *Paradise Lost* begins immediately with a statement of purpose. Its story is that told in the second and third chapters of the biblical book of Genesis: that of Eve's, then Adam's, disobedience to God and their violation of the one negative command given them after their creation. Since Adam and Eve were the first (and, till then, the only) human beings to exist, according to the biblical account, and since this was their first disobedience, it was the first disobedience of mankind generally.

2. It was this tree that was involved in the one negative command given to Adam: "And the Lord God commanded the man, saying, 'Of every tree of the garden thou mayest freely eat: But of the tree of the knowledge of good and evil, thou shalt not eat of it; for in the day that thou eatest thereof thou shalt surely die' " (Genesis 2:16–17).

The quotation I have just given is from the Authorized Version of the Bible (generally known as the King James Bible), which was first published in 1611, fifty-six years before the publication of *Paradise Lost*. It has been the traditional Bible of English-speaking Protestants, both in Milton's time and now, so I will use it for quotations throughout these notes.

3. It was the land of Eden in which Adam and Eve existed before their disobedience and from which they were evicted afterward, as the poem will describe in great detail. Specifically it was in a garden in that region in which they dwelt: "And the Lord God planted a garden eastward in Eden; and there he put the man whom he had formed" (Genesis 2:8).

It is common, but not correct, to refer to the garden itself as Eden, as Milton does here. This is not to say that Milton did not know better, of course. In the constricting bounds of poetry, the necessities of rhyme, rhythm, or imagery may require a certain departure from strict accuracy. This is tolerated as "poetic license."

4. The "greater Man" is Jesus. The New Testament worked out the doctrine that there was a symmetry in the story of man. By the sin of one man, Adam, all mankind was condemned, and by the virtue of one man, Jesus, all mankind was saved again: "For as by one man's disobedience many were made sinners, so by the obedience of one shall many be made righteous" (Romans 5:19).

5. Milton draws his sources not only from the Bible but from

Greek and Latin literature, primarily the great epic poems: Homer's *Iliad* and *Odyssey* and Vergil's *Aeneid*. *Paradise Lost* is quite obviously and undeniably an imitation of all of these, particularly the last. Indeed, so densely packed with classical allusions is Milton's epic, so reverent is its treatment of classical myths, and so slavish (almost) is its picture of angels as Homeric heroes, that we are bound to consider *Paradise Lost* a pagan translation (and a gloriously majestic one) of the biblical creation tale.

It was customary for the pagan epic poets to invoke the Muse at the start of their poem, the Muse being the spirit of poetic inspiration. Homer and Vergil both did so and Milton does so as well.

6. There is a limit, of course, to how pagan the rigidly Puritan Milton can allow himself to be. The Muse must therefore be identified with the revealing and inspiring Spirit of God.

One place where the divine Spirit revealed itself was at "the secret top of Oreb" (Mount Horeb). Thus the Bible tells us that Moses, while still in exile in Midian, "led the flock to the backside of the desert, and came to the mountain of God, even to Horeb. And the angel of the Lord appeared unto him in a flame of fire out of the midst of a bush" (Exodus 3:1–2).

After Moses went to Egypt, at the behest of God, and then led the Israelites out of Egypt, he brought them to Mount Sinai: "And the Lord came down upon Mount Sinai, on the top of the mount: and the Lord called Moses up to the top of the mount; and Moses went up" (Exodus 19:20).

Many biblical commentators decided that Horeb and Sinai are alternate names for the same mountain, and that is how Milton treats them here.

7. It is Moses who is "that Shepherd" who received the message of God on Mount Horeb, or Sinai. Though raised in the palace of Egypt's pharaoh, he had killed an Egyptian and been forced to flee the land. He reached Midian and married the daughter of an important man of the region, one with large herds of sheep. "Now Moses kept the flock of Jethro his father in law, the priest of Midian" (Exodus 3:1).

The teachings of Moses were addressed to the Israelites, who believed themselves divinely chosen to keep God's commandments and to worship him in the correct manner. Thus: "O ye seed of Israel his servant, ye children of Jacob, his chosen ones" (1 Chronicles 16:13). Hence the reference to "the chosen Seed."

8. It was Moses, according to a Jewish tradition adopted by the Christians, who wrote the first five books of the Bible, under the inspiration of God. In particular, he was supposed to have written the first verse, which opens with the phrase used here by Milton: "In the beginning God created the heavens and the earth" (Genesis 1:1).

9. In the Hebrew tradition, it is stated in the very first biblical verse that heaven and earth were created. The implication was that, before the creation, *nothing* existed.

In the Greek tradition, however, chaos existed to begin with, and even antedated the gods. Chaos was viewed as matter in formless disorder, so the creation of the universe in the Greek view consisted of imposing form on formlessness and extracting order out of disorder.

Milton accepts the pagan view when he speaks of "how the Heav'ns and Earth/Rose out of Chaos." He is not, however, entirely without biblical authority, for the Bible goes on to say after the initial verse, "And the earth was without form, and void" (Genesis 1:2). In other words, even though heaven and earth were created out of nothing, they appeared as chaos to begin with, and it was out of that that God, in six days, extracted form and order.

10. "Sion hill" is Mount Zion, which was the height about which the city of Jerusalem was built. It was the fortified center of the city, the site of the ruler's palace, the place of last defense. It was David's capture of Mount Zion that placed Jerusalem in Israelite hands: "Nevertheless David took the strong hold of Zion" (2 Samuel 5:7). It was on Mount Zion that David's son, Solomon, built the Temple. Zion therefore became the religious center of the kingdom as well. It was on Mount Zion, with its Temple, that the Spirit of God might be thought to be resting.

11. Siloa ("Siloam," in the Greek form) is a tunnel in Mount Zion through which water was conducted. The water formed a pool at the base of the mountain and served as a water supply. Its connection with divine inspiration comes in a tale of the manner in which Jesus cured a blind man by placing saliva-caked

soil on his eyes, "And said unto him, 'Go, wash in the pool of Siloam' " (John 9:7). Since the pool was at the base of the mount on which the Temple stood, it "flow'd Fast by the Oracle of God."

12. Milton never stays long with biblical allusions, but always finds himself irresistibly drawn back to the classical. He moves now from biblical to pagan sources of inspiration. Aonia is an alternate name for the Greek district known as Boeotia. The "Aonian Mount" is Helicon, a mountain in Boeotia sacred to the Muses and therefore symbolizing a source of poetic inspiration.

In 1975, I had lunch with James Fixx of Horizon *over the possibility of my doing a piece for it. Fixx was astonished at the variety of my writing, and since I don't suffer from overdeveloped humility, I cheerfully described some of the books I had done and rather emphasized my annotations — of which I am inordinately proud.*

He hadn't heard of them and asked if I could annotate a poem for Horizon. *I agreed readily, even jubilantly, and decided to do Rudyard Kipling's "Recessional."*

Alas Horizon *rejected it with, I suspect, something akin to horror. Fixx had gotten the idea, I think, that my annotations were satirical or humorous and, of course, they are completely serious.*

I shrugged off the rejection, and since I am strongly averse to letting anything I have written go to waste, I annotated three dozen other poems and persuaded Doubleday to publish Familiar Poems Annotated *in 1977 (Book 181). From that book, here is my originally rejected annotation of "Recessional":*

from FAMILIAR POEMS ANNOTATED (1977)

Recessional [1]
by RUDYARD KIPLING[2]

God of our fathers, known of old,[3]
Lord of our far-flung battle line,[4]
Beneath whose awful hand we hold

Dominion over palm and pine —[5]
Lord God of Hosts,[6] be with us yet,
Lest we forget — lest we forget! [7]

The tumult and the shouting dies,
    The captains and the kings depart:[8]
Still stands Thine ancient sacrifice,
    An humble and a contrite heart.[9]
Lord God of Hosts, be with us yet,
Lest we forget — lest we forget!

Far-called, our navies melt away;[10]
    On dune and headland sinks the fire:[11]
Lo, all our pomp of yesterday
    Is one with Nineveh[12] and Tyre! [13]
Judge of the Nations,[14] spare us yet,
Lest we forget — lest we forget!

If, drunk with sight of power, we loose
    Wild tongues that have not Thee in awe,
Such boastings as the Gentiles[15] use,
    Or lesser breeds without the Law —[16]
Lord God of Hosts, be with us yet,
Lest we forget — lest we forget!

For heathen heart[17] that puts her trust
    In reeking tube and iron shard,[18]
All valiant dust[19] that builds on dust,[20]
    And, guarding, calls not Thee to guard —
For frantic boast and foolish word,
Thy Mercy on Thy People, Lord![21]

1. By 1897, the year "Recessional" was written, Great Britain was at the peak of its power. Victoria had been queen for sixty years — sixty years that had seen the nation advancing steadily in population, prosperity, prestige, and power. Now the nation was celebrating the Diamond Jubilee, the sixtieth anniversary of Victoria's accession to the throne.

Great Britain ruled over an empire that had been expanding throughout the nineteenth century and was still expanding. To symbolize British glory and success, Victoria had been promoted to a higher title and had been made empress of India in 1876. Small though Great Britain might be in area, she ruled nearly a quarter of the world directly, and dominated virtually all the rest financially.

And yet the most famous literary work to emerge from this ecstatic celebration turned out to be this somber poem. Its very name indicates the manner in which its mood went precisely contrary to that of the happy nation.

A recession is an act of retiring or withdrawing, and a recessional is a piece of music played at the end of some performance or ceremony, as the audience is leaving. The poem, therefore, deals with the possible decline of the empire; its departure, so to speak, from the stage of history.

2. Joseph Rudyard Kipling was born in Bombay, India, on December 30, 1865, and India was the very epitome of imperial success. It was India that was the most populous, the most historic, the most exotic, and the most impressive of all British possessions. It was of India that the British monarch became empress. In the years Kipling spent in India, he grew interested in Indian life and culture but always from the viewpoint of a member of a master race.

Kipling came to be viewed as the outstanding literary spokesman for imperialism — that is, for the view that men of European descent (and of British descent in particular) had a kind of natural right to rule over non-Europeans, and that it was even their duty to do so. Yet in the midst of the frantic Jubilee celebration, a chill foretaste of the nemesis of imperialism seemed to come over him.

He died in London on January 18, 1936.

3. The poem is biblical in tone and flavor. The British, in Kipling's view, were God's chosen people, destined for world rule, and it was impossible for him not to hark back to that other chosen people, the Israelites. Throughout the poem, the British are made into the contemporary equivalent of biblical Israel.

Thus, when Moses came to the Israelite slaves in Egypt with the news that God would rescue them, he had to assure them that it was no invention of his own that he was bringing, no unknown deity, but an ancestral God of proven work, one that was known of old. God's instructions to Moses were: "Thus shalt thou say unto the Children of Israel, the Lord God of your fathers, the God of Abraham, the God of Isaac, and the God of Jacob, hath sent me unto you" (Exodus 3:15).

And so Kipling, in addressing God, stresses the same historic continuity, the same ancestral respectability, to lend a more somber note to the prayer.

4. "Far-flung" indeed! The empires of the past had been limited in size. The largest had been that of the Mongols, who from 1240 to 1340 had ruled over most of Asia and half of Europe. Even that empire had been contiguous, however, with all parts land-connected; it was not truly intercontinental; not truly a world empire.

It was only after the opening of the age of exploration that world empires became possible. In the course of the sixteenth century, Portugal and Spain each established trading posts on every continent and took over large land areas in the Americas. Indeed, from 1580 to 1640 Spain took over Portugal and combined both empires. These Iberian empires could only be held together feebly, however, in the days of sailing ships, especially since the home nations were in the grip of a depressed and declining economy.

It was with the coming of industrialization that a real gap opened between those nations that could impose colonialization and those that must suffer it. Great Britain, which was the first to industrialize, forged on to outstrip the earlier world empires in extent, far outstrip them in population, and far, far outstrip them in power.

Of the previous world empires, it had been said that the sun never set upon them. At every moment during earth's rotation some region forming part of the empire was on the day-lit portion of the globe. The earlier examples were forgotten, however, in the greater example of the newer empire. Throughout the nineteenth century, it was common to say that "the sun never set upon the British Empire." And it was easy to begin to believe this in the figurative sense, too — that the sun of history and power would never set and that the British Empire would remain basking in an eternal noon.

5. Again a reference to the wide extent of the British Empire. The palm is a characteristic tree of the tropics, and the pine the

characteristic tree of the northernmost forests. The palm trees of India and the pine forests of Canada were both under the rule of the government in London. (Canada had dominion status and considerable self-rule, to be sure.)

6. The ancient peoples all had war gods, lords of the hosts (armies), and why not? When did a people need their god more than when they were meeting their enemies in battle (and when, presumably, the enemies were busily calling upon *their* gods for help). Kipling specifically recognizes the role of God as generalissimo when he refers to him earlier as "Lord of our far-flung battle line."

In the Bible, the Creator is sometimes spoken of as "God of hosts" or "Lord of hosts" when the divine role on the battlefield, or as an agent of destruction, is to be emphasized. Thus, when the Bible describes the manner in which God will inflict military defeat upon the Egyptians, it says, "And the Egyptians will I give over into the hand of a cruel lord; and a fierce king shall rule over them, saith the Lord, the Lord of hosts" (Isaiah 19:4).

Again, in a plea to reverse the civil war that is giving the enemy an opportunity to destroy Israel, we have, "Turn us again, O Lord God of hosts, cause thy face to shine; and we shall be saved" (Psalms 80:19).

7. To the biblical writers, the military defeat and physical destruction of a land are the direct result of forgetting what is due to God, since God's people cannot suffer defeat except as punishment by an angry and forgotten God. Thus, the Bible quotes God as saying: "For Israel hath forgotten his Maker, and buildeth temples; and Judah hath multiplied fenced cities, but I will send a fire upon his cities, and it shall devour the palaces thereof" (Hosea 8:14).

8. Tumult and shouting evoke a picture of the clamor of battle, and "captains" and "kings" are the leaders of armies. There is a biblical passage describing the war horse that is reminiscent of these lines: "He saith among the trumpets, Ha, ha; and he smelleth the battle afar off, the thunder of the captains and the shouting" (Job 39:25).

But the noise dies and the warriors depart. Military glory *alone* is insufficient, for the wars end and there must be something to maintain the nation afterward.

These two lines also evoke the "tumult and the shouting" of the Jubilee, the gathering of royalty and of military notables from every European nation. The noise of the Jubilee has to die, too, and the celebrants must depart, and what then?

9. It is a common biblical notion that it is not the proud, the powerful, and the arrogant who are cared for by God, but the humble, the repentant, and the unassuming. The former are too apt to be tempted into feeling they have no need of God and are therefore likely to forget Him. The latter cannot forget Him because they have nowhere else to turn.

Thus: "The Lord is nigh unto them that are of a broken heart; and saveth such as be of contrite spirit" (Psalms 34:18). Again: "The sacrifices of God are a broken spirit: a broken and a contrite heart, O God, thou wilt not despise" (Psalms 51:17).

10. Great Britain's prime defense was its navy. It was through its navy's defeat of the Spanish Armada in 1588 that England became an important power on the stage of the modern world. It was because its navy patrolled and controlled the waters about itself that Great Britain was held inviolate from the armies of Philip II of Spain and of Louis XIV and Napoleon of France — armies that would have destroyed the nation, could they have but set foot on it.

What's more, it was British control of the sea beyond its own waters that controlled the trade of the world, poured wealth into the unblockaded island, and, in the end, wore out and frustrated all the Continental conquerors and left their land victories useless.

But what if Great Britain, foolishly vainglorious, attempted tasks too great for her, or entered into tasks without careful forethought and planning? The navy, "far-called" (that is, spread thin over the waters of a worldwide empire, too thin) would melt away. The links binding the empire would be broken, and the homeland itself would be left defenseless before the attack of armies that could not be prevented from landing.

11. Dunes are sandy ridges common along seashores. Headlands are spits and capes, bits of land jutting out into the sea. Lighthouses on such places guide incoming ships at night or in fogs. They are necessary for a maritime nation, whose ships are its life line. They are unnecessary once a navy no longer exists, since trade can no longer be protected once the life line is cut.

And with the life line cut, the sinking of the fire in the lighthouses becomes a symbolic way of representing the dying of the nation.

12. Nineveh was the capital of the Assyrian Empire in the seventh century B.C. during the days of its greatest glory. Under Ashurbanipal, it became not only the military center of western Asia, but the cultural center as well. It might have seemed to the proud warrior caste of Assyria that their power and rule were eternal, yet Ashurbanipal died in 627 B.C. with his empire essentially intact, and within twenty-five years it was all gone, forever.

Nineveh fell to Chaldean rebels from within the empire and to Median horsemen from without in 612 B.C. It was never rebuilt, and two centuries later, when a Greek army passed that way, they had to ask what the mounds were.

13. Tyre is a particularly close approximation to Great Britain. It, too, was a naval power, with a citadel on an island that could not be forced while its ships controlled the seas about it. Tyre, too, built up a vast network of trading posts and flung its merchantmen and warships far out, from end to end of the Mediterranean and even into the Atlantic.

Tyre's prosperity declined slowly as it adjusted to the realities of the mighty Asian empires of Assyria and its successors. Finally, in 323 B.C., Tyre was besieged by Alexander the Great, who filled in the sea between the island and the coast. He took the city after nine months and destroyed it. It exists to this day as a small coastal city in Lebanon, but no shadow of its former glory remains.

14. This title, given to God, harks back to the biblical passage in which Abraham attempts to dissuade God from destroying Sodom with indiscriminate anger against its inhabitants. After all, there may be some people of Sodom who are righteous. Abraham said, "That be far from thee to do after this manner, to slay the righteous with the wicked; and that the righteous should be as the wicked, that be far from thee: Shall not the Judge of all the earth do right?" (Genesis 18:25).

15. It is the wild overweening pride, the "hubris" of the Jubilee, that makes Kipling uneasy. The behavior is not British in his opinion, but is more suited to other and inferior people (a viewpoint which is itself an example of hubris, of course).

"Gentiles" are, strictly speaking, related members of a tribe or clan (from the Latin word "gens," meaning tribe or clan). Any group that considers itself in a special relationship to God, or as having a special significance in history, is likely to lump all other people as Gentiles, as members of the (other) tribes. Thus, to Jews, all non-Jews are Gentiles; and to Mormons, all non-Mormons are Gentiles.

To Kipling, with his attitude that the British are the modern Israelites and the new-chosen of God, all non-British are Gentiles, and therefore inferior beings who know no better than to indulge in vainglorious boasting. That the British should do that as well would be shameful.

16. The agreement, or covenant, by which the Israelites became the chosen of God, required that, in exchange, they obey the Law as delivered to Moses on Mount Sinai. Thus, God says, "Now, therefore, if ye will obey my voice indeed, and keep my covenant, then ye shall be a peculiar treasure unto me above all people" (Exodus 19:5).

To be "without the Law," then, is not to be of the elect. Again, there is the flavor of inferiority about those not chosen. They are not British (Israelite), and therefore they are "lesser breeds."

17. The word "heathen" is used in the English translation of the Bible for those who did not worship the God of Israel: "Why do the heathen rage —" (Psalms 2:1). The word means those of the heath, or backwoods, who are unsophisticated and cling to primitive traditions and worship.

18. The "reeking tube" is the gun barrel generally, of all sizes, and the "iron shard" is the bullet or other object fired from it. The trust in force exclusively, without regard to moral justification, is exemplified in a jingle that became current in Great Britain after the invention of a new and improved machine gun by the American inventor Hiram Stevens Maxim in 1884:

> Whatever happens, we have got
> The Maxim-gun, and they have not.

Ironically enough, even as Kipling wrote, the word "reeking" became obsolete.

For six hundred years the chemical explosive used on the battlefield to propel bullets and balls had been gunpowder. That had produced smoke, soot, and reeking odors that fouled the guns, choked the gunners, and obscured the battlefield. In the last decades of the nineteenth century, however, smokeless powders were developed. In the wars of the twentieth century, various smokeless powders were used, and though the "tube" grew steadily more deadly, it was no longer "reeking."

19. From the biblical view, man was a creature compounded of dust: "And the Lord God formed man of the dust of the ground, and breathed into his nostrils the breath of life" (Genesis 2:7). In battle, man might display valor, but that did not dignify his origins; he was merely "valiant dust," a phrase William Shakespeare uses in *Much Ado About Nothing*.

20. This is a reference to the biblical parable of the "foolish man, who built his house upon the sand: And the rain descended, and the floods came, and the winds blew, and beat upon that house; and it fell" (Matthew 7:26–27).

21. The last plea is, of course, biblical: "Be merciful, O Lord, unto thy people Israel —" (Deuteronomy 21:8), and Kipling here directly equates the British with Israel.

Yet God chose *not* to have mercy, for immediately after 1897, the year of the Diamond Jubilee, the British Empire began its decline.

Even while the Jubilee was being celebrated, British imperialism was pressing hard on the independent Boer territories north of British dominions in South Africa. In 1899 this turned into open war, which, to British surprise and humiliation, lasted nearly three years. The British won in the end after they had sufficiently reinforced their armies, but world sympathy was with the Boers.

The British, surprised at being cast in the role of villains, and cast down at finding they had not a friend in the world, lost the euphoria of 1897, and it was never, quite, to return.

One more bit of literature remains to be mentioned, something rather widely removed from the great literary classics I have referred to.

Somehow, almost accidentally, I found myself involved with the Baker Street Irregulars, a group of lovable eccentrics who find no pleasure greater than reading, rereading, analyzing, and dis-

cussing the sixty stories and novels that involve Sherlock Holmes plus all the simple and arcane side-issues thereof.

Drawn in, I found myself producing items of Sherlockian interest.

Otto Penzler, a book collector and the proprietor of Mysterious Press, a small house given over to items of specialized interest to mystery fans, suggested in July 1977 that I write sixty limericks, one for each of the items in the Sherlock Holmes canon. Since I was about to make a small trip on the Queen Elizabeth II *and wanted desperately to keep myself busy while doing so (I have an aversion to pure vacationing), I agreed.*

The sixty limericks that resulted, all written on the QE II, *were put together as Asimov's Sherlockian Limericks (Book 191), which was published on January 6, 1978, Sherlock Holmes's one hundred twenty-fourth birthday (by BSI reckoning) and the day of that year's meeting of the Baker Street Irregulars.*

Here is the last of my Sherlockian limericks:

from ASIMOV'S SHERLOCKIAN LIMERICKS (1978)

Farewell, Sherlock! Farewell, Watson, too.
First to last, you've been loyal and true.
    Of the human totality
    Who've lived in reality
There've been none quite as real as you.

PART 14

MYSTERIES

ALTHOUGH THE LIST of my second hundred books is disturbingly short on science fiction, things aren't altogether bad. At least, I have begun to write mystery fiction in addition.

This is not to say I was a complete stranger to the mystery story in my first hundred books. A number of my science fiction stories were mysteries, including my two novels The Caves of Steel *and* The Naked Sun.

I wrote only one "straight" mystery among my first hundred books, The Death Dealers, *but that involved scientists and science all the way through. Even the gimmick was a chemical one. The small number of straight mystery short stories I wrote were similarly saturated with science and scientists.*

From 1971 onward, however, I have written no less than thirty straight mystery short stories that had nothing to do with science — rather old-fashioned mysteries in the ratiocinative tradition of Agatha Christie and John Dickson Carr. The first twelve of them were collected in Tales of the Black Widowers *(Book 155), which Doubleday published in 1974, and the next twelve in* More Tales of the Black Widowers *(Book 178), which they published in 1976. The remaining six, along with six more yet to be written, will someday (I hope) be included in a third book.*

How I came to write these mysteries I explain in the introduction to Tales of the Black Widowers.

from THE TALES OF THE BLACK WIDOWERS (1976)

But then, back in 1971, I received a letter from that gorgeous blond young lady Eleanor Sullivan, who is managing editor of *Ellery Queen's Mystery Magazine* (or *EQMM,* for short), asking if I would consider writing a short story for the magazine. Of

course, I jubilantly agreed, because I thought that if they *asked*
for one, they couldn't possibly have the cruelty to reject it once
written, and that meant I could safely write my own kind of story
— very cerebral.

I began revolving plot possibilities in my head rather anxiously,
for I wanted something with a reasonable twist to it and Agatha
Christie, all by herself, had already used virtually all possible
twists.

While the wheels were slowly turning in the recesses of my
mind, I happened to be visiting the actor David Ford (who was
in both the Broadway and Hollywood versions of *1776*). His
apartment is filled with all kinds of interesting oddities, and he
told me that he was convinced once that someone had taken
something from his apartment, but he could never be sure because he couldn't tell whether anything was missing.

I laughed and all the wheels in my head, heaving a collective
sigh of relief, stopped turning. I had my twist.

I then needed a background against which to display the twist,
and here we have something else.

Back in the early 1940s, legend has it, a man married a lady
who found his friends unacceptable, and vice versa. In order to
avoid breaking off a valued relationship, those friends organized
a club, without officers or bylaws, for the sole purpose of having
a dinner once a month. It would be a stag organization so that
the husband in question could be invited to join and his wife
legitimately requested not to attend. (Nowadays, with women's
lib so powerful, this might not have worked.)

The organization was named the Trap-Door Spiders (or TDS,
for short) probably because the members felt themselves to be
hiding.

Thirty years have passed since the TDS was organized, but it
still exists. It is still stag, though the member whose marriage inspired the organization is long since divorced. (As a concession
to male nonchauvinism, a cocktail party was given on February
3, 1973, at which the TDS wives could meet one another — but
this did not become an annual custom.)

Once a month the TDS meets, always on a Friday night, almost
always in Manhattan, sometimes in a restaurant, sometimes in a

member's apartment. Each meeting is co-hosted by two volunteers who bear all the expenses for the occasion and who may each bring a guest. The average attendance is twelve. There are drinks and conversation from 6:30 to 7:30 P.M.; food and conversation from 7:30 to 8:30 P.M.; and just conversation thereafter.

After the meal each guest is grilled on his interests, his profession, his hobbies, his views, and the results are almost always interesting, often fascinating.

The chief among the general eccentricities of the TDS are these: (1) Every member is addressed as "Doctor" by the others, the title going along with the membership, and (2) each member is supposed to try to arrange for a mention of the TDS in his obituary.

I had been a guest myself on two different occasions, and when I moved to New York in 1970, I was elected to membership.

Well, then, thought I, why not tell my mystery story against the background of the meeting of an organization something like the TDS? My club would be called the Black Widowers and I would cut it in half to make it manageable — six people and one host.

Naturally, there are differences. The members of the TDS have never, in real life, attempted to solve mysteries, and none of them is as idiosyncratic as the members of the Black Widowers. In fact, the members of the TDS are, one and all, lovable people, and there is a mutual affection that is touching to see. Therefore, please be assured that the characters and events in the stories in this book are my own invention and are not to be equated with anyone or anything in the TDS, except insofar as they may seem intelligent or lovable.

In particular, Henry, the waiter, is my own invention and has no analogue, however remote, in the TDS.

Most of the Black Widowers stories appeared in Ellery Queen's Mystery Magazine (EQMM) *and a few in* F & SF. *Three of the stories in each book, however, did not see prior publication, and I will choose one of them to include here, complete, as a sampling of the group. It is "Earthset and Evening Star."*

"Earthset and Evening Star" (1976)

Emmanuel Rubin, whose latest mystery novel was clearly proceeding smoothly, lifted his drink with satisfaction and let his eyes gleam genially through his thick-lensed glasses.

"The mystery story," he pontificated, "has its rules, which, when broken, make it an artistic failure, whatever success it may have in the marketplace."

Mario Gonzalo, whose hair had been recently cut to allow a glimpse of the back of his neck, said, as though to no one, "It always amuses me to hear a writer describe something he scrawls on paper as 'art.' " He looked with some complacency at the cartoon he was making of the guest for that month's banquet session of the Black Widowers.

"If what you do is the definition of art," said Rubin, "I withdraw the term in connection with the writer's craft. One thing to avoid, for instance, is the idiot plot."

"In that case," said Thomas Trumbull, helping himself to another roll and buttering it lavishly, "aren't you at a disadvantage?"

Rubin said loftily, "By 'an idiot plot,' I mean one in which the solution would come at once if an idiot investigator would but ask a logical question, or if an idiot witness would but tell something he knows and has no reason to hide."

Geoffrey Avalon, who had left a neatly cleaned bone on his plate as the only evidence of the slab of roast beef that had once rested there, said, "But no skilled practitioner would do that, Manny. What you do is set up some reason to prevent the asking or telling of the obvious."

"Exactly," said Rubin. "For instance, what I've been writing is essentially a short story, if one moves in a straight line. The trouble is the line is so straight, the reader will see its end before I'm halfway. So I have to hide one crucial piece of evidence, and do it in such a way that I don't make an idiot plot out of it. So I invent a reason to hide that piece, and in order to make the reason plausible I have to build a supporting structure around it — and I end with a novel, and a damn good one." His sparse beard quivered with self-satisfaction.

Henry, the perennial waiter at the Black Widowers' banquets, removed the plate from in front of Rubin with his usual dexterity. Rubin, without turning, said, "Am I right, Henry?"

Henry said softly, "As a mystery reader, Mr. Rubin, I find it more satisfying to have the piece of information delivered to me and to find that I have been insufficiently clever and did not notice."

"I just read a mystery," said James Drake in his softly hoarse smoker's voice, "in which the whole point rested on character one being really character two, because the *real* character one was dead. I was put on to it at once because, in the list of characters at the start, character one was not listed. Ruined the story for me."

"Yes," said Rubin, "but that wasn't the author's fault. Some flunky did that. I once wrote a story that was accompanied by one illustration that no one thought to show me in advance. It happened to give away the point."

The guest had been listening quietly to all this. His hair was just light enough to be considered blond, and it had a careful wave in it that looked, somehow, as though it belonged there. He turned his rather narrow but clearly good-humored face to Roger Halsted, his neighbor, and said, "Pardon me, but since Manny Rubin is my friend, I know he is a mystery writer. Is this true of the rest of you as well? Is this a mystery writers' organization?"

Halsted, who had been looking with somber approval at the generous slab of Black Forest torte that had been placed before him as dessert, withdrew his attention with some difficulty and said, "Not at all. Rubin is the only mystery writer here. I'm a mathematics teacher myself; Drake is a chemist; Avalon is a lawyer; Gonzalo is an artist; and Trumbull is a code expert with the government.

"On the other hand," he went on, "we do have an interest in this sort of thing. Our guests often have problems they bring up for discussion, some sort of mystery, and we've been rather lucky —"

The guest leaned back with a small laugh. "Nothing of the sort here, alas. Of the mystery, the murder, the fearful hand clutching from behind the curtain, there is nothing in my life. It is all very straightforward, alas; very dull. I am not even married." He laughed again.

The guest had been introduced as Jean Servais, and Halsted, who had attacked the torte with vigor and, in consequence, felt a friendly glow filling him, said, "Does it matter to you if I call you John?"

"I would not strike you, sir, if you did, but I pray you not to. It is not my name. Jean, please."

Halsted nodded. "I'll try. I can manage that *zh* sound, but getting it properly nasal is another thing. Zhohng," he said.

"But that is excellent. Most formidable."

"You speak English very well," said Halsted, returning the politeness.

"Europeans require linguistic talent," said Servais. "Besides, I have lived in the United States for nearly ten years now. You are all Americans, I suppose. Mr. Avalon looks British somehow."

"Yes, I think he likes to look British," said Halsted. And with a certain hidden pleasure he said, "And it's Avalon. Accent on the first syllable and nothing nasal at the end."

But Servais only laughed. "Ah yes, I will try. When I first knew Manny, I called him 'Roo-bang,' with the accent on the last syllable and a strong nasalization. He corrected me very vigorously and at great length. He is full of pepper, that one."

The conversation had grown rather heated by this time over a general dispute concerning the relative merits of Agatha Christie and Raymond Chandler, with Rubin maintaining a rather lofty silence, as though he knew someone who was better than either but would not mention the name out of modesty.

Rubin seemed almost relieved when, with the coffee well in progress and Henry ready to supply the postprandial brandy, the time came for him to tap the water glass with his spoon and say, "Cool it, cool it, gentlemen. We are coming now to the time when our guest, Jean Servais, is to pay for his dinner. Tom, it's all yours."

Tom scowled and said, "If you don't mind, Mr. Servais," giving the final *s* just enough of a hiss to make his point, "I'm not going to try to display my French accent and make the kind of jackass of myself that my friend Manny Rubin does. Tell me, sir, how do you justify your existence?"

"Why, easily," said Servais pleasantly. "Did I not exist, you would be without a guest today."

"Please leave us out of it. Answer in more general terms."

"In general, then, I build dreams. I design things that cannot be built, things I will never see, things that may never be."

"All right," said Trumbull, looking glum, "you're a science fiction writer like Manny's pal what's-his-name — uh — Asimov."

"No friend of mine," said Rubin swiftly. "I just help him out now and then when he's stuck on some elementary scientific point."

Gonzalo said, "Is he the one you once said carried *The Columbia Encyclopedia* around with him because he was listed there?"

"It's worse now," said Rubin. "He's bribed someone at the Britannica to put him into the new, fifteenth edition, and these days he drags the whole set with him wherever he goes."

"The new, fifteenth edition —," began Avalon.

"For God's sake," said Trumbull, "will you let our guest speak?"

"No, Mr. Trumbull," said Servais, as though there had been no interruption at all, "I am no science fiction writer, though I read it sometimes. I read Ray Bradbury, for instance, and Harlan Ellison." (He nasalized both names.) "I don't think I have ever read Asimov."

"I'll tell him that," muttered Rubin. "He'll love it."

"But," continued Servais, "I suppose you might call me a science fiction engineer."

"What does that mean?" asked Trumbull.

"I do not write of lunar colonies. I design them."

"You *design* them!"

"Oh yes, and not lunar colonies only, though that is our major task right now. We work in every field of imaginative design for private industry, Hollywood, even NASA."

Gonzalo said, "Do you really think people can live on the Moon?"

"Why not? It depends on what mankind is willing to do, how large an initial investment it is ready to make. The environment on the Moon can be engineered to the precise equivalent of Earth's, over restricted underground areas, except for gravity. We must be content with a lunar gravity that is one sixth our own. Except for that, we need only allow for original supplies from

Earth and for clever engineering — and that is where we come in, my partner and I."

"You're a two-man firm?"

"Essentially. While my partner remains my partner, of course."

"Are you breaking up?"

"No, no. But we quarrel over small points. It is not surprising. It is a bad time for him. But no, we will not break up. I have made up my mind to give in to him, perhaps. Of course, I am entirely in the right and it is a pity to lose what I would have."

Trumbull leaned back in his chair, folded his arms, and said, "Will you tell us what the argument is all about? We can then state our own preferences, whether for you or for your partner."

"It would not be a hard choice, Mr. Trumbull, for the sane," said Servais. "I swear it . . . This is the way it is. We are designing a full lunar colony, in complete detail. It is for a motion picture company and it is for a good fee. They will make use of some of it in a grand science fiction spectacle they are planning. We naturally supply far more than they can use, but the idea is that if they have an overall picture of what may be — and for a wonder they want it as scientifically accurate as possible — they can choose what they wish to use of it."

"I'll bet they bollix it up," said Drake pessimistically, "no matter how careful you are. They'll give the Moon an atmosphere."

"Oh, no," said Servais, "not after six lunar landings. That error we need not fear. Yet I have no doubt they will make mistakes. They will find it impossible to handle low-gravity effects properly throughout, and the exigencies of the plot will force some infelicities.

"Still that cannot be helped and our job is merely to supply them with the most imaginative material possible. This is my point, as you will see in a moment . . . We plan a city, a small city, and it will be against the inner lip of a crater. This is unavoidable because the plot of the movie demands it. However, we have our choice as to the identity and location of the crater, and my partner, perhaps because he is an American, goes for the obvious with an American directness. He wishes to use the crater Copernicus.

"He says that it is a name that is familiar; so if the city is called Camp Copernicus, that alone will breathe the Moon, exotic adventure, and so on. Everyone knows, he says, the name of the astronomer who first placed the Sun at the center of the planetary system, and moreover it is a name that sounds impressive.

"I, on the other hand, am not impressed with this. As seen from Copernicus, the Earth is high in the sky and stays there. As you all know, only one side of the Moon always faces the Earth, so that from any spot on that side of the Moon's surface the Earth is always more or less in the same spot in the sky."

Gonzalo said suddenly, "If you want the lunar city to be on the other side of the Moon so that the Earth *isn't* in the sky, you're crazy. The audience will absolutely want the Earth there."

Servais held up his hand in agreement. "Absolutely! I agree. But if it is always there, it is almost as though it is *not* there. One gets too used to it. No, I choose a more subtle approach. I wish the city to be in a crater that is on the boundary of the visible side. From there, of course, you will see the Earth at the horizon.

"Consider what this introduces. The Moon does not keep the same side to the Earth exactly. It swings back and forth by a very small amount. For fourteen days it swings one way and then for fourteen days it swings back. This is called 'libration.'" He paused here as though to make sure he was pronouncing it correctly in English. "And it comes about because the Moon does not move in a perfect circle about the Earth.

"Now, you see, if we establish Camp Bahyee in the crater of that name, the Earth is not only at the horizon but it moves up and down in a twenty-eight-day cycle. Properly located, the lunar colonists will see the Earth rise and set, slowly, of course. This lends itself to imaginative exploitation. The characters can arrange for some important action at Earthset, and the different positions of the Earth can indicate the passage of time and raise the suspense. Some terrific special effects are possible, too. If Venus is near the Earth and Earth is in a fat crescent stage, Venus will then be at its brightest; and when Earth sets, we can show Venus, in the airless sky of the Moon, to be a very tiny crescent itself."

"Earthset and evening star, and one clear call for me," muttered Avalon.

Gonzalo said, "Is there really a crater called Bahyee?"

"Absolutely," said Servais. "It is, in fact, the largest crater that can be seen from the Earth's surface. It is 290 kilometers across — 180 miles."

"It sounds like a Chinese name," said Gonzalo.

"French!" said Servais solemnly. "A French astronomer of that name was mayor of Paris in 1789 at the time of the Revolution."

"That wasn't a good time to be mayor," said Gonzalo.

"So he discovered," said Servais. "He was guillotined in 1793."

Avalon said, "I am rather on your side, Mr. Servais. Your proposal lends scope. What was your partner's objection?"

Servais shrugged in a gesture that was more Gallic than anything he had yet said or done. "Foolish ones. He says that it will be too complicated for the movie people. They will confuse things, he says. He also points out that the Earth moves too slowly in the Moon's sky. It would take days for the Earth to lift its entire globe above the horizon, and days for it to lower entirely below the horizon."

"Is that right?" asked Gonzalo.

"It's right, but what of that? It will still be interesting."

Halsted said, "They can fudge that. Make the Earth move a little faster. So what?"

Servais looked discontented. "That's no good. My partner says this is precisely what the movie people will do and this alteration of astronomical fact will be disgraceful. He is very violent about it, finding fault with everything, even with the name of the crater, which he says is ridiculous and laughable so that he will not endure it in our report. We have never had arguments like this. He is like a madman."

"Remember," said Avalon, "you said you would give in."

"Well, I will have to," said Servais, "but I am not pleased. Of course, it is a bad time for him."

Rubin said, "You've said that twice now, Jean. I've never met your partner, so I can't judge the personalities involved. Why is it a bad time?"

Servais shook his head. "A month ago, or a little more, his wife killed herself. She took sleeping pills. My partner was a devoted husband, most uxorious. Naturally, it is terrible for him and, just as naturally, he is not himself."

Drake coughed gently. "Should he be working?"

"I would not dare suggest he not work. The work is keeping him sane."

Halsted said, "Why did she kill herself?"

Servais didn't answer in words but gestured with his eyebrows in a fashion that might be interpreted in almost any way.

Halsted persisted. "Was she incurably ill?"

"Who can say?" said Servais, sighing. "For a while, poor Howard —" He paused in embarrassment. "It was not my intention to mention his name."

Trumbull said, "You can say anything here. Whatever is mentioned in this room is completely confidential. Our waiter, too, before you ask, is completely trustworthy."

"Well," said Servais, "his name doesn't matter in any case. It is Howard Kaufman. In a way, work has been very good for him. Except at work, he is almost dead himself. Nothing is any longer important to him."

"Yes," said Trumbull, "but now something *is* important to him. He wants his crater, not your crater."

"True," said Servais. "I have thought of that. I have told myself it is a good sign. He throws himself into something. It is a beginning. And perhaps all the more reason, then, that I should give in. Yes, I will. It's settled, I will. There's no reason for you gentlemen to try to decide between us. The decision is made, and in his favor."

Avalon was frowning. "I suppose we should go on to question you further on the work you do and I suppose, moreover, that we should not intrude on a private misfortune. Here at the Black Widowers, however, no questions are barred, and there is no Fifth Amendment to plead. I am dissatisfied, sir, with your remarks concerning the unfortunate woman who committed suicide. As a happily married man, I am puzzled at the combination of love and suicide. You said she wasn't ill?"

"Actually, I didn't," said Servais, "and I am uncomfortable at discussing the matter."

Rubin struck the empty glass before him with his spoon. "Host's privilege," he said vigorously. There was silence.

"Jean," he said, "you are my guest and my friend. We can't force you to answer questions, but I made it clear that the price of accepting our hospitality was the grilling. If you have been guilty of a criminal act and don't wish to discuss it, leave now and we will say nothing. If you will talk, then, whatever you say, we will still say nothing."

"Though if it is indeed a criminal act," said Avalon, "we would certainly strongly advise confession."

Servais laughed rather shakily. He said, "For one minute there, for one frightened minute, I thought I had found myself in a Kafka novel and would be tried and condemned for some crime you would drag out of me against my will. Gentlemen, I have committed no crime of importance. A speeding ticket, a bit of creative imagination on my tax return — all that is, so I hear it said, as American as apple pie. But if you're thinking I killed that woman and made it look like suicide — please put it out of your heads at once. It *was* suicide. The police did not question it."

Halsted said, "Was she ill?"

"All right, then, I will answer. She was not ill as far as I know. But after all, I am not a doctor and I did not examine her."

Halsted said, "Did she have children?"

"No. No children. Ah, Mr. Halsted, I suddenly remember that you spoke earlier that your guests had problems that they brought up for discussion, and I said I had none. I see you have found one anyway."

Trumbull said, "If you're so sure it was suicide, I suppose she left a note."

"Yes," said Servais, "she left one."

"What did it say?"

"I couldn't quote it exactly. I did not myself see it. According to Howard, she merely apologized for causing unhappiness but said that she could not go on. It was quite banal and I assure you it satisfied the police."

Avalon said, "But if it was a happy marriage, and there was no illness and no complications with children, then — Or were there complications with children? Did she want children badly and did her husband refuse —"

Gonzalo interposed. "People don't kill themselves because they don't have kids."

"People kill themselves for the stupidest reasons," said Rubin.

"I remember —"

Trumbull cried out with stentorian rage, "Damn it, you guys, Jeff has the floor."

Avalon said, "Was the lack of children a disturbing influence?"

"Not as far as I know," said Servais. "Look, Mr. Avalon, I am careful in what I say, and I did *not* say it was a happy marriage."

"You said your partner was devoted to his wife," said Avalon gravely, "and you used that fine old word 'uxorious' to describe him."

"Love," said Servais, "is insufficient for happiness if it flows but one way. I did not say that *she* loved *him*."

Drake lit another cigarette. "Ah," he said, "the plot thickens."

Avalon said, "Then it is your opinion that that had something to do with the suicide."

Servais looked harassed. "It is more than my opinion, sir. I *know* it had something to do with the suicide."

"Would you tell us the details?" asked Avalon, unbending just slightly from his usual stiff posture as though to convert his question into a courtly invitation.

Servais hesitated, then said, "I remind you that you have promised me all is confidential. Mary — Madame Kaufman and my partner were married for seven years and it seemed a comfortable marriage, but who can tell in affairs of this sort?

"There was another man. He is older than Howard and to my eyes not as good-looking — but again, who can tell in affairs of this sort? What she found in him is not likely to be there on the surface, for all to see."

Halsted said, "How did your partner take *that?*"

Servais looked up and flushed distinctly. "He never knew. Surely, you are not of the opinion that I told him this? I am not the type, I assure you. It is not for me to interfere between husband and wife. And frankly, if I had told Howard, he would not have believed me. It is more likely he would have attempted to strike me. And then what was I to do? Present proof? Was I to arrange matters so as to have them caught under conditions that could not be mistaken? No, I said nothing."

"And he really didn't know?" asked Avalon, clearly embarrassed.

"He did not. It had not been going on long. The pair were excessively cautious. The husband was blindly devoted. What can I say?"

"The husband is always the last to know," said Gonzalo sententiously.

Drake said, "If the affair was so well hidden, how did you find out, Mr. Servais?"

"Purest accident, I assure you," said Servais. "An incredible stroke of misfortune for her, in a way. I had a date for the evening. I did not know the girl well and it did not, after all, work out. I was anxious to be rid of her, but first — what would you have, it would not be gentlemanly to abandon her — I took her home in an odd corner of the city. And, having said good-by in a most perfunctory manner, I went into a nearby diner to have a cup of coffee and recover somewhat. And there I saw Mary Kaufman and a man.

"Alas, it jumped to the eye. It was late; her husband, I remembered at once, was out of town, her attitude toward the man — Accept my assurances that there is a way a woman has of looking at a man that is completely unmistakable, and I saw it then. And if I were at all unsure, the expression on her face, when she looked up and saw me frozen in surprise, gave it all away.

"I left at once, of course, with no greeting of any kind, but the damage was done. She called me the next day, in agony of mind, the fool, fearful that I would carry stories to her husband, and gave me a totally unconvincing explanation. I assured her that it was a matter in which I did not interest myself in the least, that it was something so unimportant that I had already forgotten it. I am glad, however, I did not have to face the man. Him, I would have knocked down."

Drake said, "Did you know the man?"

"Slightly," said Servais. "He moved in our circles in a very distant way. I knew his name; I could recognize him. It didn't matter, for I never saw him after that. He was wise to stay away."

Avalon said, "But why did she commit suicide? Was she afraid her husband would find out?"

"Is one ever afraid of that in such a case?" demanded Servais, with a slight lifting of his lip. "And if she were, surely she would end the affair. No, no, it was something far more common than that. Something inevitable. In such an affair, gentlemen, there are strains and risks which are great and which actually add an element of romance. I am not entirely unaware of such things, I assure you.

"But the romance does not continue forever, whatever the story books may say, and it is bound to fade for one faster than for the other. Well then, it faded for the man in this case before it did for the woman, and the man took the kind of action one sometimes does in such affairs. He left — went — disappeared. And so the lady killed herself."

Trumbull drew himself up and frowned ferociously. "For what reason?"

"I assume for that reason, sir. It has been known to happen. I did not know of the man's disappearance, you understand, till afterward. After the suicide I went in search of him, feeling he was in some way responsible, and rather promising myself to relieve my feelings by bloodying his nose — I have a strong affection for my partner, you understand, and I felt his sufferings — but I discovered the fine lover had left two weeks before and left no forwarding address. He had no family and it was easy for him to leave, that blackguard. I could have tracked him down, I suppose, but my feelings were not strong enough to push me that far. And yet, I feel the guilt —"

"What guilt?" asked Avalon.

"It occurred to me that when I surprised them — quite unintentionally, of course — the element of risk to the man became unacceptably high. He knew I knew him. He may have felt that sooner or later it would come out and he did not wish to await results. If I had not stumbled into that diner they might still be together, she might still be alive, who knows?"

Rubin said, "That is far-fetched, Jean. You can't deal rationally with the ifs of history. But I have a thought —"

"Yes, Manny?"

"After the suicide your partner was very quiet, nothing was important to him. I think you said that. But now he's quarreling with you violently, though he has never done that before, I gather. Something may have happened in addition to the suicide. Perhaps *now* he has discovered his wife's infidelity and the thought drives him mad."

Servais shook his head. "No, no. If you think I have told him, you are quite wrong. I admit I think of telling him now and then. It is difficult to see him, my dear friend, wasting away over a woman who, after all, was not worthy of him. It is not proper to pine away for one who was not faithful to him in life. Ought I not tell him this? Frequently, it seems to me that I should and even must. He will face the truth and begin life anew. But then I think and even *know* that he will not believe me, that our friendship will be broken, and he will be worse off than before."

Rubin said, "You don't understand me. Might it not be that someone *else* has told him? How do you know you were the only one who knew?"

Servais seemed a bit startled. He considered it and said, "No. He would, in that case, certainly have told me the news. And I assure you, he would have told it to me with the highest degree of indignation and informed me that he at once attempted to strike the villain who would so malign his dead angel."

"Not," said Rubin, "if he had been told that *you* were his wife's lover. Even if he refused to believe it, even if he beat the informant to the ground, could he tell *you* the tale under such circumstances? And could he be entirely certain? Would he not find it impossible to avoid picking fights with you in such a case?"

Servais seemed still more startled. He said slowly, "It was, of course, not I. No one could possibly have thought so. Howard's wife did not in the least appeal to me, you understand." He looked up and said fiercely, "You must accept the fact that I am telling you the truth about this. It was *not* I, and I will *not* be suspected. If anyone had said it was I, it could only be out of deliberate malice."

"Maybe it was," said Rubin. "Might it not be the real lover who would make the accusation — out of fear you would give him away? By getting in his story first —"

"Why should he do this? He is away. No one suspects him. No one pursues him."

"He might not know that," said Rubin.

"Pardon me." Henry's voice sounded softly from the direction of the sideboard. "May I ask a question?"

"Certainly," said Rubin, and the odd silence fell that always did when the quiet waiter, whose presence rarely obtruded on the festivities, made himself heard.

Servais looked startled, but his politeness held. He said, "Can I do anything for you, waiter?"

Henry said, "I'm not sure, sir, that I quite understand the nature of the quarrel between yourself and your partner. Surely there must have been decisions of enormous complexity to make as far as the technical details of the colony were concerned."

"You don't know even a small part of it," said Servais indulgently.

"Did your partner and you quarrel over all those details, sir?"

"N-no," said Servais. "We did not quarrel. There were discussions, of course. It is useless to believe that two men, each with a strong will and pronounced opinions, will agree everywhere, or even anywhere, but it all worked out reasonably. We discussed, and eventually we came to some conclusion. Sometimes I had the better of it, sometimes he, sometimes neither or both."

"But then," said Henry, "there was this one argument over the actual location of the colony, over the crater, and there it was all different. He attacked even the name of the crater fiercely and, in this one case, left no room for the slightest compromise."

"No room at all. And you are right. Only in this one case."

Henry said, "Then I am to understand that at this time, when Mr. Rubin suspects that your partner is being irritated by suspicion of you, he was completely reasonable and civilized over every delicate point of lunar engineering and was wildly and unbearably stubborn only over the single matter of the site — over whether Copernicus or the other crater was to be the place where the colony was to be built?"

"Yes," said Servais with satisfaction. "That is precisely how it was and I see the point you are making, waiter. It is quite unbelievable to suppose that he would quarrel with me over the site out of ill humor over suspicion that I have placed horns on him, when he does not quarrel with me on any other point. Assuredly, he does not suspect me of ill dealing. I thank you, waiter."

Henry said, "May I go a little further, sir?"

"By all means," said Servais.

"Earlier in the evening," said Henry, "Mr. Rubin was kind

enough to ask my opinion over the techniques of his profession. There was the question of deliberate omission of details by witnesses."

"Yes," said Servais, "I remember the discussion. But I did not deliberately omit any details."

"You did not mention the name of Mrs. Kaufman's lover."

Servais frowned. "I suppose I didn't, but it wasn't deliberate. It is entirely irrelevant."

"Perhaps it is," said Henry, "unless his name happens to be Bailey."

Servais froze in his chair. Then he said anxiously, "I don't recall mentioning it. Sacred — I see your point again, waiter. If it slips out now without my remembering it, it is possible to suppose that, without quite realizing it, I may have said something that led Howard to suspect —"

Gonzalo said, "Hey, Henry, I don't recall Jean giving us any name."

"Nor I," said Henry. "You did not give the name, sir."

Servais relaxed slowly and then said, frowning, "Then how did you know? Do you know these people?"

Henry shook his head. "No, sir, it was just a notion of mine that arose out of the story you told. From your reaction, I take it his name *is* Bailey?"

"Martin Bailey," said Servais. "How did you know?"

"The name of the crater in which you wished to place the site is Bahyee; the name of the city would be Camp Bahyee."

"Yes."

"But that is the French pronunciation of the name of a French astronomer. How is it spelled?"

Servais said, "B-a-i-l-l-y. Great God, *Bailly!*"

Henry said, "In English pronunciation, pronounced like the not uncommon surname Bailey. I am quite certain American astronomers use the English pronunciation, and that Mr. Kaufman does too. You hid that piece of information from us, Mr. Servais, because you never thought of the crater in any other way than Bahyee. Even looking at it, you would hear the French sound in your mind and make no connection with Bailey, the American surname."

Servais said, "But I still don't understand."

"Would your partner wish to publicize the name, and place the site of a lunar colony in Bailly? Would he want to have the colony called Camp Bailly, after what a Bailey has done to him?"

"But he didn't *know* what Bailey had done to him," said Servais.

"How do you know that? Because there's an old saw that says the husband is always the last to know? How else can you explain his utterly irrational opposition to this one point, even his insistence that the name itself is horrible? It is too much to expect of coincidence."

"But if he knew — if he knew — he didn't tell me. Why fight over it? Why not explain?"

"I assume," said Henry, "he didn't know you knew. Would he shame his dead wife by telling you?"

Servais clutched at his hair. "I never thought — Not for a moment."

"There is more to think," said Henry sadly.

"What?"

"One might wonder how Bailey came to disappear, if your partner knew the tale. One might wonder if Bailey is alive. Is it not conceivable that Mr. Kaufman, placing all the blame on the other man, confronted his wife to tell her he had driven her lover away, even killed him, perhaps, and asked her to come back to him — and the response was suicide?"

"No," said Servais. "That is impossible."

"It would be best, then, to find Mr. Bailey and make sure he is alive. It is the one way of proving your partner's innocence. It may be a task for the police."

Servais had turned very pale. "I can't go to the police with a story like that."

"If you do not," said Henry, "it may be that your partner, brooding over what he has done — if indeed he has done it — will eventually take justice into his own hands."

"You mean kill himself?" whispered Servais. "Is that the choice you are facing me with: accuse him to the police or wait for him to kill himself?"

"Or both," said Henry. "Life is cruel."

I have also been writing mystery stories for the junior high school age level at the instigation, originally, of an editor at Boys' Life.

*Naturally, I made a junior high school boy the detective, and
when I had written five of them, I put them together as a collection entitled* The Key Word and Other Mysteries (*Book 190*). *It
was published by Walker and Company in 1977.*

The story I choose for inclusion here was rejected by Boys' Life
but was snapped up at once by EQMM. *I can't explain these
things.*

"The Thirteenth Day of Christmas" (1977)

This was one year we were *glad* when Christmas Day was over.

It had been a grim Christmas Eve and I had stayed awake as
long as I could, half listening for bombs. And Mom and I stayed
up until midnight on Christmas *Day*, too. Then Dad called and
said, "Okay, it's over. Nothing's happened. I'll be home as soon
as I can."

Mom and I danced around as if Santa Claus had just come
and then, after about an hour, Dad came home and I went to bed
and slept fine.

You see, it's special in our house. Dad's a detective on the force
and these days, with terrorists and bombings, it can get pretty
hairy. So, when on December 20, warnings reached headquarters
that there would be a Christmas Day bombing at the Soviet
offices in the United Nations, it had to be taken seriously.

The entire force was put on the alert and the FBI came in, too.
The Soviets had their own security, I guess, but none of it satisfied Dad.

The day before Christmas was the worst.

"If someone is crazy enough to want to plant a bomb and if
he's not too worried about getting caught afterward, he's likely
to be able to do it no matter what precautions we take." Dad's
voice had a grimness we rarely heard.

"I suppose there's no way of knowing who it is," Mom said.

Dad shook his head. "Letters from newspapers pasted on
paper; no fingerprints; only smudges. Common stuff we can't
trace and a threat that it would be the only warning we'd get.
What can we do?"

"Well, it must be someone who doesn't like the Russians, I guess," Mom said.

Dad said, "That doesn't narrow it much. Of course, the Soviets say it's a Zionist threat, and we've got to keep an eye on the Jewish Defense League."

"Gee, Dad," I said. "That doesn't make much sense. The Jewish people wouldn't pick Christmas to do it, would they? It doesn't mean anything to them; and it doesn't mean anything to the Soviet Union, either. They're officially atheistic."

"You can't reason that out with the Russians," Dad said. "Now why don't you turn in, because tomorrow may be a bad day all round, Christmas or not."

Then he left. He was out all Christmas, and it was pretty rotten. We didn't even open any presents — just sat listening to the radio, which was tuned to the news station.

Then at midnight when Dad called and nothing had happened, we could breathe again, but I still forgot to open my presents.

That didn't come till the morning of the twenty-sixth. We made *that* day Christmas. Dad had a day off and Mom baked the turkey a day late. It wasn't till after dinner that we talked about it at all.

Mom said, "I suppose the person, whoever it was, couldn't find any way of planting the bomb once the Department drew the security strings tight."

Dad smiled, as if he appreciated Mom's loyalty. "I don't think you can make security that tight," he said, "but what's the difference? There was no bomb. Maybe it was a bluff. After all, it did disrupt the city a bit and it gave the Soviet people at the United Nations some sleepless nights, I'll bet. That might have been almost as good for the bomber as letting the bomb go off."

"If he couldn't do it on Christmas," I said, "maybe he'll do it another time. Maybe he just said Christmas to get everyone keyed up and then, after they relax, he'll . . ."

Dad gave me one of his little pushes on the side of my head. "You're a cheerful one, Larry . . . No, I don't think so. Real bombers value the sense of power. When they say something is going up at a certain time, it's got to be that time or it's no fun for them."

I was still suspicious, but the days passed and there was no bombing and the Department gradually went back to normal. The FBI left and even the Soviet people seemed to forget about it, according to Dad.

On January 2, the Christmas–New Year's vacation was over and I went back to school. We started rehearsing our Christmas pageant. We didn't call it that, of course, because we're not supposed to have religious celebrations at school, what with the separation of church and state. We just made an elaborate show out of the song "The Twelve Days of Christmas," which doesn't have any religion to it — just presents.

There were twelve of us kids, each one singing a particular line every time it came up and then coming in all together on the partridge in a pear tree. I was number five, singing "five gold rings" because I was still a boy soprano and I could hit that high note pretty nicely, if I do say so myself.

Some kids didn't know why Christmas had twelve days, but I explained that if we count Christmas Day as one, the twelfth day after is January 6, when the Three Wise Men arrived with gifts for the Christ child. Naturally, it was on January 6 that we put on the show in the auditorium, with as many parents there as wanted to come.

Dad got a few hours off and was sitting in the audience with Mom. I could see him getting set to hear his son's high note for the last time because by next year my voice would have changed.

Did you ever get an idea in the middle of a stage show and have to continue, no matter what?

We were only on the second day with its "two turtle-doves" when I thought, "Oh my, it's the *thirteenth* day of Christmas." The whole world was shaking about me and I couldn't do a thing but stay on the stage and sing about five gold rings.

I didn't think they'd ever get to those stupid "twelve drummers drumming." It was like having itching powder on instead of underwear. I couldn't stand still. Then, when the last note was out, while they were still applauding, I broke away, went jumping down the steps from the platform and up the aisle calling, "Dad!"

He looked startled, but I grabbed him, and I think I was babbling so fast, he could hardly understand.

I said, "Dad, Christmas isn't the same day everywhere. It

could be one of the Soviet's own people. They're officially atheist, but maybe one of them is religious and he wants to place the bomb for that reason. Only he would be a member of the Russian Orthodox Church. They don't go by our calendar."

"What?" said Dad, looking as if he didn't understand a word I was saying.

"It's *so,* Dad. I read about it. The Russian Orthodox Church is still on the Julian calendar, which the West gave up for the Gregorian calendar centuries ago. The Julian calendar is thirteen days behind ours. The Orthodox Christmas is on *their* December 25, which is *our* January 7. It's *tomorrow.*"

He didn't believe me just like that. He looked it up in the almanac; then he called up someone in the Department who was Russian Orthodox.

He was able to get the Department moving again. They talked to the Soviets, and once the Soviets stopped talking about Zionists and looked at themselves, they got the man. I don't know what they did with him, but there was no bombing on the thirteenth day of Christmas, either.

The Department wanted to give me a new bicycle for Christmas after that, but I turned it down. I was just doing my duty.

Which brings me to my favorite book of all two hundred I have written so far.

In April 1975, Larry Ashmead, then at Doubleday, suggested I attend the seventy-fifth annual meeting of the American Book-sellers Association (ABA), which was to be held in New York over the Memorial Day weekend. I said I had to be there in any case since I had agreed to autograph books there for Fawcett Books.

Larry said he wanted me to attend all *the sessions so that I might gather background information for a mystery he wanted me to write that was to be entitled* Murder at the ABA.

I attended, and when it was over, Larry asked me if I could write the book. I said, yes, I already had a plot in mind.

"Good," said Larry. "We need it by next year's convention."

"You'll have the manuscript by then," I said.

"Not the manuscript," he said. "The finished book."

I said, horrified, "Then when do you want the manuscript?"

"By August."

"But it's June 1 already."

"By early August, if possible."

Fortunately, the book went with incredible ease and rapidity and I finished it on August 3. It was published in 1976 as Book 172.

One of the reasons I loved the book was this: Though it was told in the first person by my character Darius Just (based distantly on my good friend Harlan Ellison), I introduced myself as a character in the third person, describing myself quite accurately, I think, through the not entirely sympathetic eyes of Darius (pronounced "duh-RY-us").

Here is how I enter the story:

from MURDER AT THE ABA (1976)

I found myself a table that had not yet collected anyone at any of its four chairs and sat down with a little sigh. If I were left alone, if I were allowed to eat in peace, I might yet brush away all the implacably humiliating events of the day. Some people dissolve their woes in wine; I'm quite likely to assuage my sadness in spiced sausage.

It wasn't to be. Nothing broke right that Sunday. I hadn't completed my first mouthful when a cheerful voice boomed out, "Good old Darius Dust. Mind if I join you?"

I've got to explain about the name Darius. It was wished upon me by a self-educated father. You can't trust self-education — it goes too far, gets too bloated, knows no moderation. My father's name was Alexander and he knew that Alexander the Great had defeated Darius III of Persia, and that was it. Perhaps he had the feeling that even though he would see to it I had a thorough education (he did) I would never be able to surpass *him*. Since he was five feet ten, I guess I never did.

My mother, a very little woman whose genes, in that respect, I inherited, went along with it. She had no choice. No one ever had a choice within hearing distance of my father.

To be the smallest kid in class is not exactly a passport to happiness. To be any kid named Darius, surrounded by Jims, Toms, and Bills, produces little joy. To be the smallest kid in class and named Darius, too, is something like sitting under a neon sign that flashes on and off with the message, "Kick me!"

It wasn't until I was in college that my name stopped serving as an insult to everyone my age I ever met, an insult to be personally avenged at once.

I hated that name at first, but held on to it with a wretched obstinacy. No one was going to force me out of it. By the time I acquired a coterie of friends old enough and sophisticated enough to be able to pronounce it and feel at home with it, I began to like it.

Correct pronunciation helps. Even among relatively sophisticated adults, it isn't a familiar name. Outside Herodotus, one is only likely to come across it in an old chestnut of a poem called "Darius Green and His Flying Machine," by John Townsend Trowbridge, written a little over a hundred years ago. I hated that poem. Naturally the only Darius in popular literature was served up as comic relief.

I'm not sure what proportion of the general population knows how to pronounce the name, but even in the rarefied circles within which I have my being (God help me), I hear it more often mispronounced than pronounced. The first impulse is to pronounce the name so as to rhyme it with "various," but that's not right. The accent is on the second syllable, with a long i, so that it rhymes with "pious" and "bias."

That has its disadvantages, too, for once you learn to say Darius properly, you are bound to notice that it sounds something like "dry as." Then, if you have a particularly feeble mind, it occurs to you that if you change Just to Dust, the name becomes "Dry as Dust," which is not exactly ideal for a writer.

Actually, only one person I know has the kind of perverted sense of humor that thinks this is funny. When I heard someone say "Good old Dry as Dust. Mind if I join you?" I knew, without looking up, that it was Isaac Asimov. Word play is his idea of the empyrean heights of wisdom.

I didn't let it bother me. I just said, "Hello, Ikey. Of course I mind having you join me, but sit down anyway."

As it happens, there's nothing that Asimov can possibly call me that I would hate as much as he hates being called Ikey. So one of these times, when it finally dawns on him that every "Dry as

Dust" will elicit an "Ikey" without fail, he will quit. Anyone else would quit after two tries. I give Asimov twenty years.

Since this book is rather in the nature of a collaboration, with his name on it as sole author, however, I had better be particular about describing him.

He's five feet nine inches tall, rather fat, and more than rather grinning. He wears his hair long, and it's clear he does it out of laziness rather than out of any desire for a splendid leonine effect (which is how I've heard him describe it), because it never seems more than sketchily combed. The hair is somewhat gray and the sideburns, which run down to the angle of his jaw and which have been aptly described as looking like Brillo, are nearly white. He's got a bulbous nose, blue eyes, a bolo tic, and glasses with black frames. He has to remove his glasses to read or eat because he won't admit his age long enough to get bifocals.

He's like me in some respects. He doesn't smoke or drink any more than I do. Like me, he also likes to eat, but I don't get fat on it and he does. He thinks the difference is metabolism, which is funny for a guy who claims to be a biochemist. I know the difference is exercise. I work out in a gym nearly every day — but once Asimov has managed to lift himself out of bed in the morning, that is his exercise for the day. Except for typing, of course. His fingers are in good shape.

He had his plate heaped much higher than mine, but he couldn't stop himself from glancing anxiously at what I had retrieved, as though I might perhaps have found a goodie he had overlooked.

"What's the score now, Isaac?" No use calling him Ikey except under provocation.

He knew what I meant. "A hundred sixty-three at the moment," he said with his mouth full, "but who's counting?"

"You are," I said.

He swallowed and said in an aggrieved tone, "I *have* to. That's my shtick. Everyone wants to know how many books I've published, and if I don't tell them they're disappointed. What's more, if they ask me the question in two successive months and the figure doesn't go up by at least one, they feel cheated. Look, there's no need for you to be resentful. You've had a movie made out of one of your books. I haven't."

I winced. The matter had been profitable, but it was easily the worst movie ever made by the worst set of idiots you could find even in Hollywood. I kept hoping no one would see it.

A hundred sixty-three books is no record, of course, but I never met anyone for whom writing is as painless as it is for Asimov. And he's aware of it, and his pleasure over it can be rather disgusting to see.

Once he crossed the room at a book-and-author luncheon, and someone muttered in my ear, "There goes Asimov pushing his self-assurance ahead of him like a wheelbarrow." (The same might be said of his abdomen, of course.) Someone else once said that Asimov walked as though he expected the air to part in front of him.

Actually, my own theory is that he lives so much of the time inside his own head that he is unaware of the outside world. So when he seems to be utterly self-possessed, it's just that he's unaware that there's anything to be disturbed about.

I said to him, "What are you doing here, Isaac? Why aren't you home writing a book?"

He groaned. "In a way that's what I'm doing here. Doubleday wants me to write a mystery novel entitled *Murder at the ABA*. I don't know what I was thinking of when I signed up."

"Why did you sign?"

"What did you expect me to do? I've signed so many contracts, it's a reflex action with me. And they want a completed manuscript by August. I've got three months at the outside."

"That's all right. It will only take you a weekend, won't it?"

Asimov made himself a cold-cut sandwich on a giant scale and demolished half of it at a bite. With most of the bite gone, he said, "The worst of all my literary troubles is the fact that I'm not allowed to have any literary troubles. If you said you had to do a book faster than you could do it, everyone would soak your jacket with sympathetic tears. When I say it, I get cheap jokes. The same cheap joke every time, I might add."

This from a man who thinks Darius Dust is epigrammatic wit.

I didn't break down in tears. "Just the same you'll do it. You've done mysteries before, haven't you?"

It was a pretty safe assumption. The man has written on every subject imaginable and if ever anyone didn't look it, it's Asimov. He looks stupid at first sight. And when you hear him tell endless jokes, hug every girl in reach, and never by any chance say anything thoughtful, you're convinced of it. It takes considerable time before you find out that the man is so secure in his intelligence that he never troubles to display it.

Which annoys the hell out of me, actually.

"Of course I've done mysteries before," he said indignantly. "I've written straight mysteries and science fiction mysteries; novels and short stories; for adults, for teenagers, and for grade-schoolers."

"Then what's the trouble?"

"I've got to give this local color. I've got to hang around here for four days and see what's happening."

"You're doing it, aren't you?"

"But I *can't* see what's happening. In my whole life, I've never seen anything that goes on around me."

"Then how have you written a hundred sixty-three books."

"*Published,*" he said. "I have eleven in press . . . Because my books are without description. I have an unornamented style."

"In that case, get someone to help you."

It was odd that I should say that, for at that moment I couldn't possibly have supposed that matters would end up in such a way that *I* would help him.

After all, he *did* manage to do the book in time. You're reading it — *Murder at the ABA*, by Isaac Asimov.

It's just that it's *my* story and *I* am first-person while he is third-person. And since I've left the writing entirely in his hands and don't entirely trust him, the agreement is that I am to be allowed to add any comments of my own (within reason) in the form of footnotes where I consider him too far off base.*

* For instance, I can point out that while Asimov is sticking to the outline, he's dramatizing me into total distortion. I am five feet five and not five feet two. The subtle (or not so subtle) saturation of the story with my supposed pygmy complex is just designed to make him shine by contrast. — *D. J.*

Just is five feet five if you count his platform shoes! I'm not supposed to be literal here anyway. This is a work of fiction and I will take any liberties I choose with the facts. And as for making myself shine, I ask anyone who knows me to read these last few pages, in which I figure, and testify that I am sticking to Just's ridiculous attitudes vis-à-vis myself at some considerable cost to my self-respect. — *I. A.*

He had finished his platter, and by that time the room was considerably more crowded than it had been when we had entered. It was quite hopeless to expect to see Giles in that mess. The noise level had become uncomfortable and the filth of cigarette smoke hung in the air. There was still time to leave, and then Asimov would have had to make up his own story — but I didn't budge because I hadn't had my coffee yet. There was always something to prevent the evasion of fate.

I said, "Do you want some coffee, Isaac?"

"Sure, but let me go get it. I need the exercise."

That wasn't it at all, of course. He came back with coffee for both of us and five assorted cookies for himself. At least he didn't offer me any of them.

He dipped the chocolate-covered one in the coffee, transferred it expertly to his mouth without losing a drop, and said, "And what are you doing here, Darius? You don't look particularly ecstatic."

"I've no reason to look ecstatic," I said. "I've had a hell of a day and I don't intend to go into details."

"Considering that you have no family responsibilities at all and write only one book every three years, what can possibly give you a hell of a day?"

I could almost believe he was serious in that question, but I ignored it anyway and said, "You haven't by any chance seen Giles Devore at the convention?"

"Yes, I have."

I was astonished. I was not expecting that answer. "In here?"

"No, at the registration booth. He's autographing books tomorrow morning. At the same time as I, in fact."

"I know he's autographing books," I said. I swear I said it in the flattest possible way, without any hint of hidden meanings. In fact, I was cooling down and — who knows? — everything might have come to nothing, when Asimov stirred up my resentment against Giles for no reason I could see except to amuse himself, and laid *his* flagstone.

His blue eyes glittered and his eyebrows lifted and fell rapidly. (For someone who claims to see nothing of the world outside himself, he can have an unerring touch for the sore spot on the soul.)

He said, "I'm glad he's your protégé and not mine. I don't know about you, but I would find it sickening to have a protégé zoom past me."

"He's not my protégé," I said.

"Listen, that first book of his was written out of your vest pocket. Everyone knows it — and the more fool, you."

"Why? For helping?"

"No, of course not. For expecting gratitude."

I shrugged but, inside, where he couldn't see, I burned. Damn it, I *had* expected gratitude, and whether that made me a fool or not, the lack of it made me furious.

I said, lying through my teeth, "I never expected anything."

But Asimov's eyes were no longer on me. They were straining across the room and I didn't have to follow them to know he was looking at a girl. I forgot to say that despite his general inability to see anything in the outside world, he has an odd capacity to see every girl within two hundred feet.

PART 15

AUTOBIOGRAPHY

*THE LONGER I kept writing books, and the more books I
published, the more the publishers were willing to let me do as
I pleased, even when what I pleased was unorthodox.*

*It has always pleased me to talk about myself, and little by
little I let that creep into my books — and my publishers permitted it.*

*To begin with, my F & SF essays grew more and more highly
personal, and eventually I took to beginning each with an autobiographical essay. Then I began to be highly personal in my
introductions to stories in the anthologies I edited, then in the
collections of my own stories.*

*Inevitably, I thought of doing a collection of my early stories
against an autobiographical background of my life in those years.
Doubleday published it as* The Early Asimov *(Book 125) in 1972.*

*When that did well, I was simply confirmed in this tendency
of mine and had Doubleday publish* Before the Golden Age
*(Book 151) in 1974. This was a long book of nearly half a million
words in which I anthologized my favorite stories from the 1930s
against an autobiographical background of my life before I became a writer.*

*And, just to show you that this tendency toward autobiog-
raphy is no recent phenomenon, let me quote a passage from*
Before the Golden Age, *in which I managed to find and reprint
my* first *published literary production — and it was autobiographical.*

from BEFORE THE GOLDEN AGE (1974)

In February 1934, I entered "sixth term" at Boys' High. As a
startling innovation, the school offered a special course in creative
writing for those who chose to take it, and I jumped at the chance.
I had been writing, on and off, ever since I had worked on the

Greenville Chums. I don't remember any of the details at all, except that I remember being occasionally driven to attempt to write poetry.

Now there seemed a chance for me to demonstrate my literary prowess. (Somehow I saw the class only as a chance to shine. It never occurred to me that I might learn something. I felt I already *knew* how to write.)

The result was a fiasco. Surely few young men have had so marvelous a chance to make fools of themselves and then took advantage of the chance as liberally as I did. Everything I wrote was laughable, and it was all laughed at thoroughly, both by the teacher and by the other students.

I mentioned this in *The Early Asimov* and mentioned further that the one useful result of the course was that I wrote a humorous essay entitled "Little Brothers," which was published in the Boys' High School literary semiannual.

Until I mentioned the essay, I had never thought of it particularly, but once *The Early Asimov* appeared, I began to wonder if I ought to try to get a copy. In February 1973, I gave a talk to a group of librarians from the New York metropolitan area, and attending was the present librarian of Boys' High School. When she introduced herself, I asked at once if there was any chance she might perhaps locate a copy of the literary semiannual in some of the dusty storage bins of the school.

In June 1973, she succeeded, and sent me a copy. This book had already been put together but was still in an early stage of production, so I could make the necessary revision.

When the magazine came — its name was *Boys' High Recorder*, incidentally, and the issue was spring 1934 — I turned to "Little Brothers" at once and read it eagerly. I was sure I would find in it the clear signs of writing talent.

Alas, I didn't. It sounds exactly as any essay would that was written by a precocious fourteen-year-old. How disappointing! And yet, in order to keep the record complete and to prevent myself from receiving a horde of letters demanding to see it (presumably in order that all my readers have the same chance to laugh at me as the members of the damnable writing class did), here it is:

Little Brothers

My mission in life right now is to express the venomous feelings that we "big" brothers have for the bane of our lives, the "little" brothers.

When I first received the news that I had a little brother, on July 25, 1929, I felt slightly uncomfortable. As for myself, I knew nothing about brothers, but many of my friends had related at great length the inconveniences (to say the least) of attending babies.

On August 3, my little brother came home. All I could see was a little bundle of pink flesh, with apparently no ability to do the slightest mischief.

That night, I suddenly sprang out of bed with goose flesh all over me and my hair on end. I had heard a shriek apparently made by no earthly being. In response to my frenzied questions, my mother informed me in a commonplace manner that it was just the baby. Just the baby! I was almost knocked unconscious. A puny, nine-pound baby, ten days old, to make such a scream! Why, I was convinced that no less than three men together could have strained their vocal cords to such an extent.

But this was only the beginning. When he began teething, the real torture came. I did not sleep a wink for two months. I only existed by sleeping with my eyes open in school.

And still it wasn't all. Easter was coming, and I was feeling joyous at the prospect of a trip to Rhode Island, when that kid brother of mine got the measles and everything went up in smoke.

Soon he reached the age when his teeth had cut, and I hoped to obtain a little peace, but no, that could not be. I had yet to learn that when a child learns to walk, and talk baby-language, he is rather more of an inconvenience than a cyclone, with a hurricane thrown in for good measure.

His favorite recreation was that of falling down the stairs, hitting each step with a resounding bump. This occurred on the average of once every other minute and always brought on a scolding from my mother (not for him, but for me for not taking care of him).

This "taking care" of him is not as easy as it sounds. The baby usually shows his devotion by grabbing generous fistfuls of hair and pulling with a strength that you would never have thought possible in a one-year-old. When, after a few minutes of excruciating torture, you persuade him to let go, he seeks diversion in hitting your shins with a heavy piece of iron, preferably a sharp or pointed one.

Not only is a baby a pest when awake; it is doubly so when taking its daily nap.

This is a typical scene. I am sitting in a chair next to the carriage, deeply immersed in *The Three Musketeers*, and my little brother is apparently sleeping peacefully; but he really isn't. With an uncanny instinct, in spite of his closed eyes and inability to read, he knows exactly when I reach an exciting point and with a malicious grin selects that very moment to awake. With a groan I leave my book and rock him till my arms feel as if they will fall off any minute. By the time he does go back to sleep, I have lost interest in the famous trio and my day is ruined.

Now my little brother is four and a half years old and most of these aggravating habits have disappeared, but I feel in my bones that there is more to come. I shudder to think of the day when he'll enter school and place a new burden upon my shoulders. I feel absolutely sure that not only will I be afflicted with the homework that my hardhearted teachers will give me, but I will also be responsible for my little brother's.

I wish I were dead!

Needless to say, this essay is completely fictional except that the dates of my little brother's birth and his arrival home are correct. Actually, my brother Stan was a model child, who gave me very little trouble. I did wheel him about in his carriage an awful lot, but that was always with a book open on the handlebar, so it didn't matter to me. I also sat by the carriage when he was sleeping, but again I invariably read — and he rarely disturbed me. What's more, he always did his own homework when it came time for that.

One final comment concerning this tendency of mine.
As the time approached for my two hundredth book to appear,

Doubleday let me know they would like to do it. I explained that this was impossible since Houghton Mifflin, having done Opus 100, was sure to feel condemned to do Opus 200 as well.

Doubleday, which understands the warmth of my feeling for Houghton Mifflin (as Houghton Mifflin understands the warmth of my feeling for Doubleday), argued no further but cast about for some other project to mark this milestone.

We agreed that I would write an autobiography, a formal auto-biography of all aspects of my life and not only of my literary productions. I pointed out that nothing much had ever happened to me, but they said they didn't care.

So I sat down, and between March 9 and December 31, 1977, I turned out 640,000 words of autobiography. Poor Cathleen Jordan, who is now my editor at Doubleday, turned pale when I brought in the manuscript and muttered something about how much I might have written if something ever had happened to me. The only conclusion possible was to put it out in two volumes.

The first volume is coming out simultaneously with this book. I wouldn't dream of putting pressure on any of my gentle readers, but if you would like to buy my autobiography and read it, you have my permission to do so.

Indeed, if this book has so fascinated you with its samplings that you feel the urge to go out and buy all two hundred books — do so with my blessings.

APPENDIX

MY SECOND HUNDRED BOOKS